A Kindness in Their Hearts

The Journey

By Jim Weafer

ISBN: 978-1-7345520-1-0
Library of Congress Control Number 2020901682

Any references to historical events, real persons, or real places are used fictitiously. Names, characters and places are products of the author's imagination.

Book cover design by Creative Publishing Book Design
Published by Jim Weafer DBA The Writer's Friend
First printing edition 2020

https://jimweafer.com

F
WEA

A special thanks to the following:

My wife, Dixie

Bill Kitchens

Lola Perkett

Linda Palmer

Leah Frisch

Jefferson

My daughters, Candice and Robin

Table of Contents

Chapter I

2019

The Goose

"Can you believe the governor, our two senators, and three congressmen of the state of Kentucky, along with numerous other politicians and celebrities, are in the other room partying with our friends and we are in here sitting by ourselves by choice?" Elbie asked almost to himself as the clamor of the party escalated in Colby's large family and entertainment rooms.

Colby's grand, elegant home and beautiful grounds, situated just outside Seattle in the Sammamish area, was a far cry from the simple homesteads in Western Kentucky where he'd grown up.

Elbie, Anna Lee, and I quietly escaped for a few moments of respite to reflect on how we had arrived at this moment. We sat alone in the ornate sitting room, next to the oversize windows overlooking the captivating views of a large but charming lake. A solitary goose entertained us as he floated silently on the water, gliding aimlessly in the middle of the lake, surrounded by woods on three sides. He had been there since we had arrived.

It was late summer in the year 2019. This wasn't the first time we had witnessed a lone goose like this in the middle of a lake, nor what we were about to see next.

"There's a large flock of geese circling above," I said casually as I glanced out the large window overlooking the placid lake.

The three of us gazed curiously, silently, as the flock of geese descended upon the calm water. They landed in unison, creating a scene of theatrical flair, and then began gliding across the lake, approaching the solitary goose.

They circled him several times, and then each goose took turns swimming up to him as if comforting an old, forlorn friend. Once each had shared their brief, private moment of solace with the lone goose, the entire flock began honking loudly, rose in unison, and took flight in a spectacular, breathtaking display. They resumed their journey, leaving the goose abandoned and alone again.

"Are you kidding me?! Are you really kidding me?!" Anna Lee cried.

***

We came from dirt-poor families, with parents who struggled for years to raise their children. Some may say that rising from where we came to where we are now required selfish greed and a lack of compassion, but they would be wrong.

Many said the four of us were an aberration, even an anomaly of nature. I'm not sure if that is true, but over sixty years, every detail, every laugh, every cry. and every moment of suffering became an incremental pebble in the foundation of this day in Colby's home. We didn't realize the importance of those events in our lives at the time, only that some brought joy and some wrought unbearable tears. We could have never reached this moment in our lives without any one of those seemingly unrelated events. However, as you will eventually see, the sum of the parts does make the whole.

But I think I'm putting the cart in front of the horse here. Let me go back to a time over sixty years ago, to when it all started. It has been said it was a time when things were different, much simpler. I don't know if that is true, but it was a time with less chaos than some other periods may have experienced. It was a time mostly free of the dangers and concerns we see today, but it was certainly not devoid of intrigue, perils, or anguish.

The year was 1958 when I realized for the first time that life was not always as simple for some as it was for me.

Chapter II

1958

The Silver Fox

When I was seven years old, my friends and I often took long walks along Free Silver Road. It was best when the weather was warm on a clear night around the time of a full moon. It seemed nature was more active at that time, but it might simply have been that we could see better with the moon casting a fluorescent glow across the fields, valley, and woods.

One night, Elbie, Donnie Joe, and I headed down the road about an hour after dark. The large, bright moon had just begun to rise, yet its light already overpowered the flickering of the thousands of fireflies. The crickets were in fine tune, loud enough that one could not hear another's whisper unless it emanated within an arm's reach. The light breeze, just forceful enough to keep the mosquitoes at bay, made it the perfect night for three seven-year-olds to take an adventurous stroll.

As we walked, we planned to trade tales of heroes, villains, ghosts, and mysteries. Elbie began with a story about a haunted house, and Donnie Joe followed with a suspenseful tale. His was a version of one we had heard before, about a mysterious stranger who came out only at night. The stranger's eyes glowed in the dark, and he spoke a strange language no human could understand. He also supposedly carried a double-headed ax as big as a toolbox, and he wielded it with a vengeance on anyone unfortunate enough to cross his path.

About the time Donnie Joe got to the good part of the story, Elbie stopped dead in his tracks. Startled, Donnie Joe and I spun around and stared curiously at him. The whites of his eyes glowed in the light of the plump rising moon as his gaze fixed on

4

something distant down the road. We slowly turned to see what it was.

There, on the old wooden bridge over Pup Creek just ahead, stood the silhouette of a vile creature waiting for us. With the moon to its back, we could not make out any features, but we could easily see it was slightly larger than us and of a very peculiar shape. Its upper-right side had a strange bulge, and there was a curious, somewhat larger bulge on its lower left side that extended from its waist down to its feet. It made no sounds and did not move, obviously preparing to attack. Cold chills raced down our necks, as they would have for any boy that age. We slowly began to back up one careful step at a time.

"It's the stranger!" Donnie Joe suddenly shouted, his voice rising high above the chatter of the crickets.

Elbie and I gasped, almost falling backward. We had heard many stories about him but were still skeptical of his existence. But here he was, only fifty yards in front of us. His stance indicated he was crouching, readying to lurch forward to inflict unspeakable torture upon us.

The stranger lowered his head as if he were looking at something, undoubtedly the bulge on his left side, where he surely carried his horrid ax.

"He's getting ready to get his ax!" Elbie cried aloud.

We turned to run as fast as we could when I heard a woman's soft voice.

"Will you help me?"

Elbie and Donnie Joe continued to run as fast as they could, stirring up small clouds of dust from the gravel road. They were already a hundred feet away, halfway to the Lanham's place.

I knew it was probably a trick; the stranger was changing his voice to entrap me, but I could not help but stop. I turned slowly, expecting the stranger to be staring in my face and holding his menacing ax high above my head. It was difficult to breathe, and my knees shook uncontrollably; I had never been so frightened in my life.

The stranger had not moved from the bridge, but the bulge on his left side suddenly shifted, moving away from him. I could not believe my eyes, but in the moonlight, it appeared to be a small girl. I suddenly realized he had captured a little girl and now was after me.

"Will you help us?"

The voice appeared to come from the stranger, and it perfectly imitated that of a woman. But every boy knew the stranger had magical powers, and for him, changing his voice would be an easy ploy to undertake.

Then I noticed the bulge on his other side, squirming in his arms. At first, I assumed it was an animal he carried for food, but then I heard the unmistakable whimper of a child. I thought, *If that is the stranger, he must be incredibly gruesome to capture a little girl and a baby, on the same night.* That would make him even more heinous than the stories told about him. Yet I could not shake the notion that it possibly could be a woman asking for help.

"Please help us."

"Are you hurt?" I nervously asked, still not sure if it was the stranger or a woman and her children on the bridge.

"I'm okay, but we are tired and thirsty. My babies are hungry," she answered in a soft, pleading voice.

"Are you from around here?" I cautiously took a few steps forward.

"No, not here," she replied patiently. "Please, my babies need help."

I turned to see if Elbie or Donnie Joe were within sight. They were long gone and probably halfway home to tell their parents of my capture by the mysterious stranger. I inched cautiously down the sloping road toward the bridge, to either my gruesome death or a woman in need.

6

I suddenly realized the seriousness of the situation I had put myself in, and I stopped. At this point, I had to make the most difficult decision I would ever make: should I trust my instincts or my heart? I chose my heart and committed myself to whatever consequences lay before me.

I inched forward again, ready to turn and run even though I knew that at this distance, the stranger could quickly overcome me. Drawing closer, I realized it was a woman, or at least, it appeared to be.

"Well," I answered, unsure what to do, "we can go to my house. Mom has some leftovers from dinner." I couldn't remember if there were any leftovers or not, but that was what I said; either way, creature or woman, I couldn't take it back now.

"Thank you so much. That would be wonderful. How far is it?" she replied in a soft, worried voice.

"About a mile," I said, pointing up the road. "Do you need any help?"

"You can take my daughter's hand for a few minutes," she replied.

I walked up to them slowly, still frightened, until I could clearly see it was a woman instead of the creature. I examined her as best I could without being too obvious. She appeared very dirty, her clothing torn and disheveled. With the moon's light filtering through her hair, I could see it was mussed and frazzled. Trembling, I reached out to take the little girl's hand. She was probably about four or five years old, and her hand was curiously cold for an August night.

The woman groaned as she shifted the baby to her other arm. I noticed that the arm she'd first held the baby with looked strangely odd from the elbow down to her wrist; it was grotesquely crooked as if broken.

We walked toward my house in silence. On the way, neither the woman nor the little girl spoke, but occasionally I could hear a muffled cry coming from the baby.

"You are such a miracle to us," the woman finally said to me as we approached my house. "You cannot know how much I appreciate your kindness. We could not have made it had you not appeared."

She introduced herself as Silvie and told me the babies' names as well: Lena Frances and Danny Dale.

When we got to my house, my surprised mother took the baby gently from Silvie's arms and offered her a kitchen chair. Then, with her free arm, she quickly put some vegetables, ham, and milk on the table, caring for Silvie and her babies' needs.

In the light of the kitchen, I noticed how pretty the young mother was despite the mass of bruises, dried blood, and dust from the gravel road completely covering her. I saw that her dirty, bare feet were bleeding, and her arm appeared severely broken. My father immediately called the doctor and explained the situation, urging him to come right away.

After Dr. Kalis arrived, he tended to her injuries and reset her broken arm. She reacted with a horrible scream that frightened her daughter and me, and I hoped I would never have to witness that again. He then made sure the babies were okay and told my mom Silvie should not travel for a while. As he left, he stopped at the door and spoke to my dad privately for a moment before leaving. We let Silvie and her children stay in my room that night, hoping they would get some rest.

They stayed with us for about three weeks. The little girl was younger than I, so I tried to help take care of her. It was not in my nature to befriend a strange adult, but I took a fond liking to Silvie, and I think she to me. During those three weeks, I spent more time with them than I did with my friends. Silvie and I would talk, laugh, and play games when she wasn't tending to her daughter and the baby or trying to help mom as best she could with one arm in a sling.

Although we never spoke about her injuries or how she got them, we became close, and she even said she hoped her baby boy would grow up to be like me. That filled me with immense pride, and I felt like I had two moms.

When the day came for my dad to take them to the bus station in town, I could not hold back the tears. Silvie walked over to me, bent down, and gave me a warm, emotional embrace.

"Don't cry, Razz. You saved my life and my children's, too. I will never forget the miracle fox that silently appeared that night and saved us. When I first saw you, the moon cast a silver glow on you. You are the Silver Fox in the night, and you will always be special to me."

I have always remembered those kind words and the pretty face that spoke them to me. I've often wondered why Silvie was walking alone with her children on a dark road that night and how she got hurt. It wasn't until I was older that I realized what had happened to her. That caused me to be very sad, and I wished I could tell her so. It must have been difficult for her to start over as a single mom, but that surely was the better alternative. I think she changed my life as much as I did hers, and I always tried to be a little more helpful to others after that.

As the story spread in the community, everyone started calling me the Silver Fox—for a while, anyway.

As the years passed, there were times when I saw faces in a crowd that I thought might be Silvie, but I could never be sure. I am confident, though, that she and her children lived a better life because of our encounter; I know I have. Many times, I've sat alone, remembering that pretty young mother in need, and I've always hoped that somewhere, far away, she, too, might be remembering the Silver Fox in the night.

Chapter III

1961

The Dispensation

The next few years went by uneventfully. But in 1961, Colby, Elbie, Anna Lee, and I began the journey toward our destiny. Over the next decade, we developed an inner sense that we were here for a higher purpose. It didn't quite feel like a religious purpose, but we had no idea what it was or when it would happen, only that it would happen.

At that time, Elbie and Colbie were my two best friends. No matter which one I was with, we always got into trouble or into an adventure that we would not forget for many years. Elbie and Colbie both said that since I was the common denominator in all those infractions, I must have been the errant member.

When my friends and I were ten years old, we carried a few superstitions and a few mistaken beliefs that made situations a lot more interesting than they needed to be. Elbie and I were starting fifth grade when we first noticed that girls might have some redeeming value. Until then, we had determined a girl's worth by the length of her ponytail and the proximity of it to our hand. The loudness of her screech from a quick yank might add a little more value, but not much; it also might merit a small snicker, but only if another boy saw it, too.

We were surprised at how some of the girls had magically changed during the summer. We noticed for the first time that many of the girls were beginning to look, well, pretty.

We speculated that they had eaten some different foods at some secret ritual during the summer that had excluded boys. We guessed it was possibly an elective ritual because some of the girls had still not changed at all. Just judging on appearance, most of the boys figured Anna Lee Frazier and Mary Jane Toler must have attended more of those rituals than the other girls. Regardless, we no longer pulled ponytails, not only because very few of them were wearing them anymore, but because we just felt an unspoken urge to be a little more cordial to them, or at least, less punitive.

I had never noticed Anna Lee Frazier before. I supposed she had been in my classes since first grade, but I could not be certain. I had no memories of her before the fifth grade, or any girl for that matter.

Anyway, we heard that Jeannie Marie was planning a birthday party at her house. It was her tenth birthday, and she asked all the girls to come over on Friday. There was no school that day because of a teacher's day or something like that. She didn't invite any of the boys, and that suited us just fine because we didn't have to worry about coming up with some excuse not to go.

Jeannie Marie's parents had a large, beautiful house sitting on a hill above their farm; at least, it was much bigger than the small, humble homes where most of us lived. There were some woods in the back of their house, and not too far into the woods was a large lake where their family often went fishing or swimming. Those woods backed up to Elbie's home as well, and he told me he had seen the lake several times while walking and exploring. Elbie said it was a really nice place and that they had even built a wooden dock so you could go fishing or jump off into the lake to swim and cool down a bit.

The morning of the party, Elbie and I walked down the road to see a bridge that had washed out over Pup Creek during a storm earlier in the week. On our way there, he quietly pulled a Baby Ruth candy bar from his pocket. I had never had one before, but I was sure any candy bar named after Babe Ruth had to be good, and I hoped he would share some with me. He made no effort to do so, and when I noticed he was already half-finished, I couldn't hold it in any longer. I knew it was about time for a little hint.

"Is that candy bar good?" I asked as a starter.

"No…but I'm not going to waste it," Elbie replied as he quickly stuffed the remainder of the bar into his mouth.

"Elbie! You rascal!" I said as I pushed him aside.

Elbie burst into a fit of laughter, desperately fighting to hold the candy bar in his mouth. It was a battle lost as he spewed the mostly chewed Baby Ruth bar all over the ground.

We shared a good laugh over that, and then I asked if he wanted to go fishing after lunch. He said he couldn't as he had things to do that afternoon.

After inspecting the mangled bridge, upended in the water of the creek, Elbie left for home, and I rode my bike over to Colbie's place to see what he was doing.

The next day, Saturday, I met with Elbie to get a plan for the afternoon, and I asked him what he'd done the day before.

"Oh, I had to hoe the garden," he said sheepishly.

"Elbie, that would take every bit of an hour. What did you do for the rest of the day?"

"Not much," he said a little hesitantly, which aroused some suspicions.

"What do you mean, not much?" I asked.

"Just not much."

Now, Elbie was a great friend, and smart, too. But he couldn't tell a fib without the words jumping out in big, bold red letters so everyone knew it was a fib right away.

"Elbie, you told me yesterday you had something to do. Now, what else did you do?"

"I don't know, probably nothing."

I stopped and grabbed his arm.

"Elbie, if you don't tell me, I'm going to tell your mom you have a secret," I threatened.

"Don't do that, Razz!" he quickly begged, looking at me with fear in his eyes. "Please, I might get in more trouble if you do that."

"What did you do, Elbie? You know you can trust me. Now, spit it out. What did you do?" I demanded and gave him a look that I knew would scare it out of him.

"Well...I might have accidentally been walking in the woods yesterday."

"What do you mean, accidentally?"

"Well, I was accidentally walking in the woods behind my house."

"Elbie!"

"Well, I might have accidentally seen something. It was an accident for sure!" he said, continuing to evade my questions.

"Elbie, what did you see?!"

"Well, I was walking in the woods, and I might have heard some girls laughing and playing."

"Elbie!"

"Well, I was just walking, and before you know it, I was looking out at Jeannie Marie's parents' lake. Accidentally, you know."

"And???"

"Well, I might have accidentally seen all the girls at her party swimming."

"So? There's nothing wrong with that, Elbie."

"Of course not. So, I didn't do anything wrong. Let's go over to Colby's." His attempt to change the subject aroused my suspicions even more.

"Elbie!!!" I warned. "You better tell me the rest of it."

He squirmed for a moment and then gathered his courage and answered.

"Well, they might have been in their skivvies."

"You mean, you saw all those girls swimming in their skivvies?" I asked with a slight tone of envy. I guess Elbie picked up on that, as he quickly changed his attitude as well.

"I did. That's a fact. But it was an accident for sure," he insisted, nodding to affirm.

"In their skivvies?"

"Yep."

"Elbie, did you turn your eyes away after you saw those girls swimming in their skivvies?"

"No, I didn't, Razz. It was sure something to see, alright. But I did cover one eye with my hand in case my other eye was blinded."

"How long did you look?"

"Razz, you know I wouldn't look at that any longer than I was supposed to."

"How long, Elbie?"

"Until they were done."

"Until they were done?!"

"Yes."

"Was Anna Lee Frazier there?"

"Yep. She sure was."

"In her skivvies?"

"Yep. And Mary Jane Toler, too."

"Mary Jane Toler, too?!!! Holy Moly, Elbie. You saw all that?"

"I did. I watched for thirty minutes or more, too," he said proudly.

"Oh, Lordy, Lordy, Elbie. We aren't supposed to be looking at things like that," I chastised. "There are repercussions. It's a good thing that you covered one eye, because, as sure as I'm standing here, you'll wake tomorrow morning and find the other one struck down as blind as a mole's eye. You know we can't look at those kinds of things without getting punished."

14

"Well, it's not blinded yet. I can see out of it just as good as my other eye," he answered smugly.

"Elbie, it doesn't work that way. You might go a day or two thinking you got away with it, but then, like a bolt of lightning, God will strike you blind for looking at all those girls in their skivvies, especially someone as pretty as Anna Lee Frazier or Mary Jane Toler."

"You think so?" Elbie sounded like he was beginning to worry.

"I know so, Elbie. They say that is why Tommy Lanham got blinded. They say he got caught looking at something he wasn't supposed to be looking at, and no amount of praying or apologizing could take it back."

"Well...well...what am I going to do, Razz?!" Elbie cried as he began rubbing his left eye, checking to see if his vision was disappearing. "I don't want to be blind in that eye. I can't unsee what I saw! What can I do to stop it?"

He blinked his eye several times.

"Razz, I think it's starting already. It's starting, Razz! My eye is going blind! What can I do?" he cried pitifully.

"You get your bike and go over to Father Till as fast as you can, Elbie. You confess your sin to him. He might be able to save some of your eyesight, but it may be too late already. You know we aren't supposed to look at those girls in their skivvies."

"It's not my fault, Razz. I didn't know they were in their skivvies. I just chanced upon them, and then the devil himself made me look. It wasn't my fault."

"But you kept lookin', and you knew enough to cover at least one good eye to protect it from being blinded; sounds like a clear-cut case of guilty to me, Elbie. Now, hurry up and run over to Father Till. Maybe he can intervene on your behalf some way and stop it from being blinded all the way."

Elbie turned and skedaddled out of there as if the devil himself was nipping at his heels, and I'm not so certain that he wasn't.

I took a more leisurely approach toward getting home, mulling over Elbie's indiscretion. It wasn't long before I noticed a sickening feeling deep within my stomach that I had never experienced before. I couldn't explain it, but the closest thing I had ever felt was when my brother, Vester, had taken my prized marbles to school to play with his friends. He'd won a bagful of marbles that day, and I resented him for that. I didn't mind that he'd won those marbles, but I was upset that he'd done it with my marbles. They were my favorite marbles, and they were mine! I got over it eventually, but I made certain Vester knew not to borrow them again.

This feeling was similar but a little different, and it kept gnawing at me like a dog on a bone. In the past few weeks, I had taken a keen liking to Anna Lee Frazier. I would never admit that to anyone, especially Anna Lee or any of my friends. But the more I thought about Elbie seeing Anna Lee in her skivvies, the worse that feeling got.

I didn't like this feeling one bit, and I didn't appreciate where it was going, so I decided to put those thoughts down and lay my mind upon better things. It didn't take long for that foul feeling to disappear, and I no longer carried any ill will toward my friend, Elbie. My nascent feelings about Anna Lee, however, began to grow. I knew Elbie would never harm anyone in any way, but I felt somehow that Anna Lee and the other girls had been aggrieved.

The next day, Elbie and I met up several hours after church. Back then, the Gospel was read in Latin by the priest and then reread in English by someone else, usually somebody important like a holy man or something. However, this Sunday, Elbie read it, much to the astonishment of all the parishioners. I

16

had never seen Elbie recite the Gospel before, or any kid for that matter, and wanted to be the first to compliment him on the fine job he'd done. But first things being first, I needed to know what Father Till had said.

"Can you see, Elbie?"

"For now."

"What do you mean? Didn't you see Father Till?"

"I did, but he wasn't pleased with me. He said I should be punished especially hard for this infraction. He gave me ten Our Fathers and ten Hail Marys to say."

"Ten!!! Are you kidding me? That's nothing! I got that many for fibbing about breaking my dad's mirror on his truck, and I didn't even get to see a single girl in her skivvies."

"Well, he also said this needed a special dispensation that was going to require some extra punishment. He said God would probably sit up there and think about it for a month or two before he decided whether to blind my eye or not, so I have to read the Gospel out loud at church every Sunday for a month. On top of that, he's making me stay after church for a whole month and wash his car, spick and span. And that's not all, Razz. Father Till said that since I was staying after church for a month, I needed to tell my parents to bring something they could fix for breakfast after Mass. He explained that he, my parents, my sister, and little brother would prepare breakfast at the rectory and eat it while I cleaned his car."

Elbie paused a moment, shaking his head.

"What am I going to do, Razz?!!! Everyone will know I did something terrible to get that much penance, and I can't tell them what I did. Everybody will think I did something awful."

"Wow, Elbie. I guess that's a worse sin than I thought. Looking at girls in their skivvies must rank right up there with murder or cursing, or maybe even as bad as cheating at marbles. What if you do all this penance and still get blinded in your eye?"

17

"I thought about that, and I asked Father Till the same question. He said if I do all this and don't cry about it, he might be able to pull in some of his connections to help me out. He said I might get a little blurriness in that eye for a while, just as a warning, but he doesn't think it would be permanent. Father Till said it all depends on how hard I cleaned and how good I read the Gospel on Sundays."

"Wow, that's terrible, Elbie."

"But it gets worse, Razz. The worse part was when I got home, my parents already knew about my penance, and they wanted to know what I did."

"You didn't tell them, did you, Elbie?"

"No way, Razz, not at first, anyway. My dad said he respected my right to nondisclosure but would assume the worst, and then he tanned my hide something awful. I could barely sit during Mass this morning. My mom kept trying to intervene on my behalf, and she even begged him to lessen the punishment since they didn't even know what I did.

"But Razz, then I made the worst mistake of my life. Since I thought my mom was on my side, I went ahead and fessed up and told them what I did."

"Elbie!!!" I screamed in horror.

"I did, Razz, but as soon as I spit out the last words of my sin, she lit into me with the fury and wrath of a mother bear protecting her cubs. I never saw her that mad, and neither did my dad because he backed off real quick, afraid he might be taken up in that storm and become a victim himself. I swear she looked like Beelzebub, or something had possessed her. My mom ranted and raged at me for ten minutes in some kind of foreign language I never heard. I'm telling the truth, Razz. There's not a soul in Purgatory that has suffered more than what I did.

"When she calmed down a bit, at least enough that I could understand what she was saying, she said I had to do my sister's chores for two weeks while my sister got to go out and play. No sin is worth that, Razz. None! No ten-year-old boy can survive that!"

"Wow! Elbie, that's worse than a life sentence in prison."

"I know! My sister will be laughing at me for two weeks, and I can't do anything about it. Also, my mother then said she was going to have to say ten rosaries for her penance for having a son that committed such a serious offense. She also said she was probably going to have to do a lot more penance than that 'cause God was going to blame her for being so deficient and not raising me proper. She said I probably would have to become a priest and teach other kids not to do what I did to get completely exonerated."

"Whoa! You think you might be a priest, Elbie?"

"I don't know, Razz. I'm just a kid. I didn't know all this was going to come about for something I did without thinking. I'm just a kid, you know!"

"Elbie, I guess they think that if you are old enough to do it, then you're old enough to take the punishment," I explained, shaking my head. "You know, if you did this when you were seven or eight, all you would have got was a spanking. But the older you get, the harder the punishments."

"Maybe, but I don't know any other kid that ever had to do this much penance."

"I don't know, Elbie. This predicament here is a real scourge. This might scar you for life. Do you think it was worth it?"

"No way!"

Then he lowered his head while looking up at me out of the corner of his eye and whispered, "Maybe, since Mary Jane Toler was there, it might be."

Elbie finished all his penance, and he survived just fine. I don't think he got scarred for life after all, but he learned a valuable lesson of respect, one that some other folks would have benefited from had they had been taught it. He must have done a respectable job of cleaning Father Till's car, too, because, several times, I noticed Father Till driving it and looking mighty proud of how clean and shiny it was. And I suppose God was pretty satisfied himself as he didn't blind Elbie's eye after all.

Over the years to come, we shared many laughs while reminiscing about his indiscretion and our misguided beliefs.

Elbie never did become a priest, and he eventually married Mary Jane Toler, always treating her with the respect and kindness that every woman deserves. Their four children recently threw them a forty-fifth wedding anniversary party. I had the chance to talk and share some laughs with Mary Jane at the party. I asked her if she knew about Elbie's indiscretion in the fifth grade. Oh, yes, she said. And when Elbie told her, she said she had given him the worst punishment of all. She wouldn't tell me what it was, so I set that aside, not wanting to pry, but I did ask her why she would punish him for something he had done so long ago.

"Razz," she said, "it's not the offense that defines us, but it's the punishment that will determine who we are."

Chapter IV

1961

A High Horse

Years ago, if you had enough help, you could build a barn from the ground up in a day. It was a community event with all the neighbors eagerly joining in. There was lots of food: fresh vegetables from the garden, fruit picked that morning long before the dew had dried, and country fried chicken that left even the pickiest of eaters begging for more. And of course, there was enough tea and lemonade to quench any thirst. Men and boys alike pitched in, setting the poles, putting up the roof, and then nailing the newly cut planks to the sides of the barn.

It was a festive affair, and with the smell of the freshly cut oak planks, everyone was in a pleasant mood. As soon as they completed the barn, the ladies brought out desserts to celebrate. There were fresh apple pies, hot cinnamon rolls, and enough cakes to satisfy every sweet tooth. Later the men gathered around to admire the new barn, with its clean white oak sides and shiny tin roof, while catching up on any local news of interest.

I remember the spring when Colby was ten years old, the same as me. His family first came to our community, about four miles down the road from us. They moved into a very small two-bedroom abandoned farmhouse with about ten acres of pasture, adjacent to a sprawling woodland in the bottoms.

The house was in sad disrepair, but Colby's dad was a handyman and said he would have it in livable condition before fall. They didn't have a lot of money at that time, but a few farmers graciously supplied some used materials to help them out. Not everyone participated in that endeavor, so I respected those who did. I noticed the first project Mr. Harris completed was a one-hole outhouse, and I was sure Mrs. Harris was pleased with that since they had no bathroom, or even plumbing, in the small home.

A one-hole outhouse could be a minor inconvenience for a family at times, especially when two unfortunate souls caught a nasty bug and had the trots at the same time. Under those circumstances, it was first come, first served. That didn't happen too often, but it was the only time when I thought a two-holer might be preferred. However, no one appreciated the shared closeness during that activity. And for those not familiar with why they called it the trots, it was so named after watching a family member suffering from an unwelcome bug perform a hurried, delicate trot to the outhouse over a hundred feet away. It was a humorous event, at least to younger boys, until we caught the bug ourselves and strained under the pressure while trying to reach an inconveniently located privy.

However, as putting up a barn was a standing community affair, most everyone shared in that event for those folks. But because of the Harris' finances, the barn was small compared to most, with only four stalls and little room for any other purpose.

The Harrises had two cows that seemed right proud of the newly built stalls in the barn, but most everyone noticed right off that there were still two stalls sitting empty.

"This is the only barn in the county without a horse in it," said Niner, sarcastically to no one in particular. Niner Peak, one year older than I, was somewhat of a loner and an outcast. He lived with his grandmother, but rumors were that his mother had left him, and his dad didn't want him around. Occasionally he stayed with his dad in Owensboro, but he always showed up bruised and cranky a few weeks later.

On several occasions, we tried to befriend him, but his short temper and odd behavior made that a difficult task. It seemed he would rather fight than get along, so we decided to make no further efforts to include him as a friend, a decision we would come to regret for many years of our lives. With his ill-tempered attitude, it was no surprise to anyone that he would make such a cynical remark. Still, unfortunately, he said it loud enough that all could hear, a terrible faux pas, leaving all family and friends aghast and speechless.

"Hush yourself!" Niner's grandmother scolded, but it was too late. Colby and his entire family suffered the public embarrassment of the apparent lack of a proper horse to reside in their barn.

After a short, awkward moment of silence, Colby's dad spoke up.

"Well," he said, scratching his head, trying to regain some dignity in this awkward situation, "I had intentions of finding us a good horse. Guess now that we have a barn, I suppose it is time to get one."

Colby's eyes widened with excitement.

"Really?"

"Yes. We'll start tomorrow."

With that, all the neighbors nodded in approval, gratifying Colby's dad and resolving this embarrassing situation for everyone.

I didn't know it at the time, but I realized many years later that Mr. Harris carried no concerns about social appearances. He was confident enough of his character not to be bothered that a horseless barn might be considered a peculiar oddity to others of higher financial standing. But he had planned on getting a horse next year anyway, and with Colby being ten at the time and his younger brother six and sister four, he hoped to give his children a boost in making new friends by avoiding any unnecessary stigma, real or perceived. What Mr. Harris didn't realize at that time was that Colby had already developed friendships that would last a lifetime. That day was the first time Elbie and I met Colby, and it was if we had been friends since the day we were born.

The next day, Colby and his dad asked around to see if anyone might have a horse to sell. It turned out an older man named Basil, who lived on the other side of the bottoms, had a young, commendable horse he needed to sell.

When Colby first laid eyes on that stallion, he knew it was the horse he wanted. He was a majestic horse, as tall as any other in the county, with a reddish-brown coat and a white diamond-shaped spot on his forehead. His sturdy, muscular legs proved him worthy of any job on the farm, and his soft, silky mane was a perfect adornment. He held his head high, in a seemingly haughty pose, as if he expected everyone's admiration. It cost Colby's dad a little more than he probably could afford right then, but there was no turning back now.

They brought him home and led him ceremoniously into his stall. With his head held high, he was a respectable addition to the barn.

"He'll do," Colby's dad said contentedly.

"We'll call him Regal," Colby announced proudly.

His dad nodded in approval, fastened the latch to the stall, and went to the house, with Colby following close by his side.

The next morning, Colby rushed excitedly out to the barn, only to find the door to Regal's stall open and the horse missing. Horrified at the thought of losing his prized stallion, he desperately searched the barn and surrounding area. Failing to find Regal, Colby panicked and rushed to the house, but then he stopped quickly. He had noticed something off in the distance, next to the woods, near the bottom of the hill. He turned to see Regal prancing around as if he owned the land.

Colby grabbed a rope and ran down the hillside as fast as he could. Regal watched him curiously, if not contemptuously. As Colby approached Regal, he tried to lasso his horse, but as soon as he raised his hand, Regal snorted, shook his head, and stepped defiantly backward, away from Colby. After several more unsuccessful attempts, Regal raised his head as if laughing at Colby, turned, and headed to the barn. Colby followed, uncertain whether to throw the lasso around this strange horse's neck or quietly follow him.

When Regal reached the barn, still holding his head high, he stepped pretentiously into his stall. He turned, staring at Colby, almost as if he were mocking him. Colby closed the stall door and fastened it tightly, checking it twice.

When he told his dad what had happened, neither could figure out how the horse had opened the stall door in a brand-new barn. They both agreed, however, that it probably wouldn't happen again.

The following morning, when Colby entered the barn, again the stall was empty, and the door open. More perplexed this morning than filled with the horror that he'd felt yesterday, Colby refused to panic and looked through the open barn door to see if his proud stallion was near the woods. Just as before, Regal strutted contentedly across the field next to the woods as if he owned the land.

Colby grabbed the rope and walked determinedly down the hill to get his horse. Again, just as he'd done yesterday, as soon as Colby approached, Regal laughed defiantly at him several times and then stubbornly strode at his own pace and with what could be called an equine swagger back up the hill, taunting Colby every step of the way to the barn.

"That horse is contrary enough to run away whenever he wants," Colby's dad said upon hearing this. "He thinks he owns the barn and the farm."

Each morning, no matter how tightly they fastened the stall door, Regal could be found at the bottom of the hill, doing as he pleased, displaying nary an ounce of shame. He defiantly forced Colby to walk the entire way down the hillside, and then he would prance proudly back to the top, with Colby following obediently behind. Strangely, Colby began to look forward to Regal mocking him with this nomadic adventure each morning. Colby began to brag to Elbie and me about how smart his horse was, but no one could figure out how Regal opened the stall door each morning.

As spring moved into May, Colby noticed that Regal had become even more stubborn in his refusal to head back to the barn. His blatant resistance had slowly changed into a cruel taunt, and when he finally gave in, he would trot up the hill as if it were his idea in the first place. With his royal demeanor, his swagger now carried a distinct aversion to leaving the area and an increasing contempt for Colby.

By mid-May, it was becoming increasingly difficult for Colby to get Regal to return to the barn each morning. His dad started having second thoughts about a horse he couldn't keep in his stall, even if it was a fine-looking one.

One late-May morning, Colby fastened the latch to Regal's stall after finally getting him to agree to head back to the barn. Colby wasn't sure why he even bothered to secure the lock anymore since Regal would soon have it undone. When he turned to leave, he briefly noticed a brown animal stepping into the woods where Regal had just paraded. Colby only caught a quick glimpse, but enough to know it was a large animal. He could not imagine what kind of animal it could be, but he decided to go down there to see. He picked up a pitchfork just in case and started down the hill.

Nearing the edge of the woods, he cautiously probed the leaves with the pitchfork, nervously testing to see if the animal was hiding there. He prepared to run if necessary since there had been some sightings of a large bobcat in the area. Bears had disappeared from that part of the state long ago, but that didn't mean that a rogue bear wouldn't venture back for a visit. He pulled back a branch with the pitchfork and suddenly heard a snort. It frightened him so that he fell backward, landing squarely on his bottom.

"That was a horse," he said as he regained his composure.

He rose to his feet and set the pitchfork down on the ground. More astonished than frightened, he pulled the branch back again and found himself staring straight at a healthy mare. She was a beautiful horse, not as tall as Regal, but a fine-looking horse.

"Come on, girl," he said as he motioned the horse toward him.

She snorted and took a step backward.

"What's wrong, girl?" he asked in a softer tone. Then he noticed something move behind her. He slowly inched closer, trying to see it without startling the mare.

He peered around her and gasped upon seeing a beautiful young foal. The colt's clean chestnut hair appeared as fine as silk. He stood straight, with his head held up high, and did not seem to be the least bit afraid of Colby. And there, right in the middle of his forehead, was a brilliant white diamond spot just like Regal's.

"So that is why Regal comes down here every morning."

Colby spent an hour trying to get the mare and her timid colt comfortable with him. Once he had their confidence, he coaxed them out of the woods. With a little more encouragement and patience, he finally persuaded them to follow him to the barn. They walked quietly in a single file with the colt closely following his mother up the small, worn path that the cows used each day back to the barn, the same one that Regal had strutted down contemptuously only an hour or so before.

As they entered the barn, Regal became very excited, letting out a loud whinny and stomping his foot repeatedly on the ground. Colby opened the empty stall next to Regal's and stepped aside. The mare looked at Colby and then at Regal. She nodded and stepped into the stall with her precocious colt close behind.

Colby latched the door and watched as Regal, the mare, and their prodigy enjoyed their reunion.

The next morning, Colby rushed excitedly to the barn and found the mare and her colt still in their stall. Right next to them stood Regal, in his stall for the first time. He let them out to run and play, and that, they did. All three pranced and jumped, enjoying their festive reunion with the frisky colt, who never frolicked too far away from his mother. Regal and the mare doted over the youngster, encouraging him to run and jump.

While Colby watched his new equine family, his dad returned from an overnight trip to Breckenridge County. A neighbor, Mr. Nash, had asked Mr. Harris to build an addition to the home of his brother, who lived in Breckenridge County. Since the Harrises did not own an automobile, Mr. Nash was kind enough to drive him home. Stepping out of Mr. Nash's truck, he said goodbye and turned to go into the house.

Colby's screams startled Mr. Harris as he walked to the house. Uncertain if they were of delight or something direr, he rushed to see the cause of the commotion.

"Well, I'll be," he said with a broad smile. "So, that's why Regal is so proud."

That afternoon, Mr. Harris checked with Basil to see if the mare and the colt were his. Basil assured him they weren't and said he would let him know if he found out who had lost them.

Colby continued to let the three cavort and play as they pleased, leaving their stall doors open for when they were ready to return. When he ran to the barn every following morning, Regal, the mare, and the growing colt greeted him from inside their stalls. It wasn't long before he could see the flourishing foal peering just over the top of the stall door. He eventually grew to be just as tall and proud as his father.

Colby and his dad continued to ask every neighbor if anyone had lost a mare, but they could never figure out where she'd come from or how she'd gotten on their farm. They also never figured out how Regal could open the stall door, but both agreed that Regal and his family were the best part of their new barn.

Chapter V

1961

The Deed

In October of that year, I had the fortunate occasion to go on a school bus trip to New York to see a Yankee's baseball game with my class, including two friends, Antz and Elbie. Antz was a jovial fellow, full of jokes and pranks. Sometimes he could be a little preoccupied with himself, but we usually enjoyed being around him. Elbie was a little quieter, sometimes a little apprehensive, but he was more thoughtful than most others his age, and I was proud to call him my friend. Elbie and I had mown a lot of lawns, cleaned barns, and begged for any job that summer to help pay for the trip. Colby, unfortunately, had not had that opportunity, nor was he allowed to go since he attended another school.

It was the last game of the season, and the Yankees were playing their archrivals, the Boston Red Sox. With Roger Maris having just tied Babe Ruth's home run record of sixty in one season, the game could not have been any more exciting for a ten-year-old boy. Kids our age, from that part of Kentucky, seldom got to see a live professional baseball game in New York, so this was a once-in-a-lifetime opportunity. I have always heard that a life-changing event can be almost sinister, if not duplicitous; it can bestow immense pleasure to one and, at the same time, abject misery to another. But the chance to see someone hit their sixty-first home run was every American boy's dream, even if it meant breaking Babe Ruth's record.

The school officials had planned our trip over a year ago, long before the season had begun, so purchasing the tickets in advance proved a very fortunate decision. The long and arduous bus drive wore on all of us, but it was well worth it. We left at six o'clock the night before, driving through the night, but few of us slept.

We couldn't wait to see the vivid green grass in the outfield, manicured with those special mowers in crisscross patterns, or the enormous scoreboard and those lofty flags flying proudly in the wind just above the top of Yankee Stadium. And of course, the roar of tens of thousands of fans cheering on the home team was something we had never experienced.

The bus trip to New York was more than I could have ever dreamed. The constant chatter of excited young boys was music to my ears, and there wasn't a seat bold enough to hold a ten-year-old boy down for long. We'd each packed a breakfast and lunch for the day, but the excitement and anticipation of the afternoon game suppressed any hunger, and besides, who would want to eat now and ruin a perfectly good hot dog at the game?

Right-handers and left-handers alike held their gloves tightly, knowing they would be the one to catch that record-breaking home run. Some of the boys rubbed oil religiously into the pocket of their glove to soften it up so the ball wouldn't bounce out. Others wrapped their glove tightly around a ball, trying to form a perfect fit for that elusive home run trophy. Bets were bandied about on which one of us would catch that record-breaking home run. It was of no consequence that none of us had any financial means to pay any debt.

We arrived at the stadium on October 1, two hours before the game started. It was a perfect day, in the mid-seventies and with the bluest sky that New York had probably ever produced. All the other kids, teachers, and coaches headed straight to the stadium to catch the team's batting practice, but Elbie thought otherwise.

"Let's look around before we go in," he suggested, pointing to all the fans tailgating and reveling in the festive atmosphere in the parking lot. We had never seen anything like this before, and it was way more exciting than the annual church carnival back home.

"Yeah, let's walk around a bit before we go in," said Antz. "We'll still have time to see batting practice."

"Guys, I don't want to miss anything," I argued.

"Come on, Razz. I promise we won't miss anything. Just fifteen minutes, and then we will head in."

"Alright, fifteen minutes."

Awestruck, we circled the lot, listening to music, laughs, chants, and cheers from both Yankees and Red Sox fans. To my surprise, it was an exhilarating experience, and I was glad I'd agreed to go along.

"Okay, guys," Elbie finally said, motioning us toward the stadium entrance. "Are you ready?"

"Sure," said Antz.

Though I was a little reluctant about missing the fun in the parking lot, I knew there was an even better piece of heaven inside. I followed them to the entrance but noticed a small girl, about six years old, across the street, hurrying with a big brown paper bag full of groceries. She seemed overly distressed, running determinedly, holding tightly to the bag. Suddenly she tripped over the uneven sidewalk, sending her groceries flying irretrievably forward onto the walk and ground. When it hit, the paper bag burst, and her groceries scattered in every direction like salt spilled from a shaker. The little girl began crying while frantically trying to stuff her scattered, evasive groceries into the remaining fragments of the paper bag. As soon as she tried to place an item in the bag, it quickly escaped from the torn remnants, much like a restive child slipping from the gentle clutches of its admonishing mother. She eventually sat down, covered her face with her hands, and sobbed hopelessly.

"Wait a minute, guys," I yelled to Antz and Elbie, who were already far ahead of me. I trotted over to help the little girl.

"Razz, are you crazy? Come on!" shouted Antz, shocked at my priorities.

"Razz, let's go," pleaded Elbie. "We're going to miss practice."

"It's okay," I shouted back. "This will only take a minute."

I ran as quickly as I could across the street to the little girl.

She looked up at me with hopeless, tearful eyes, which seemed a little excessive for the situation. Her plain dress, stained and worn, was likely a second, or even a third, hand-me-down. Her long, clean hair, mussed from her fall, looked much like that of a feral cat, and she made no attempt to right it.

"Let me help you," I offered.

With tears still creeping down her cheeks, she looked up at me with a vestige of hope, yet despair remained the more prominent of her emotions. We attempted to gather her groceries, but the bag, torn beyond repair, was of no help, and there were too many groceries to carry in her arms.

"Do you have far to go?" I asked.

"Yes, my house is fifteen minutes from here," she answered, her voice shaking, and she made no effort to hold back the tears.

"Okay," I said to her. "Hold on."

I took off my backpack and placed it on the ground. I quickly opened it, took out my glove and our three bottles of soda, and set them on the sidewalk. Then I motioned for her to help me fill the backpack with the groceries, and she did so eagerly and without a word. We hurriedly finished, and then I helped her put the pack over her shoulders.

"You better hurry," I said with a smile.

She burst into tears again and covered her mouth with her hands, the hopeless despair in her eyes replaced with gratitude. Without a word, she rose swiftly and turned, and then she ran as fast as she could down the sidewalk. She never looked back, but I

33

heard her yelling as she ran down the street, "Thank you, thank you, thank you!" until she disappeared around the corner.

I hurried back to Antz and Elbie, who were both furious with me.

When we reached the gate, the line stretched seventy feet or more.

"Here's your Sunkist. Let's go watch the game," I said as I handed them their bottles of soda.

"If we miss Maris's batting practice, Razz, I will never forgive you," Antz growled. "We could have already been inside by now if it weren't for you."

"Hand me my ticket, Razz," Elbie requested, holding out his hand. Though he didn't say so, I could tell he, too, was upset with me.

"Yeah, mine, too," Antz demanded impatiently.

I reached into my pocket and froze.

"That's not funny, Razz," Antz said anxiously.

I couldn't speak.

"Razz?" Elbie asked, becoming more concerned, his eyes widening.

"They are in my backpack," I said, almost bursting into tears myself.

"You better be joking, Razz!" Antz screamed angrily.

"Let's try to find her," I said in desperation as I turned and ran to where the little girl had spilled her groceries.

We raced up and down so many streets while hunting for her that we almost got lost. With the streets filled with Yankee fans streaming toward the stadium, it was impossible to see a small girl who already had a head start running away. It wasn't long before we began to realize our tickets were gone and we were going to miss the game.

We walked back to the stadium entrance, silent except for an occasional ballistic rant from Antz. We sat down off to the side

34

of the gates and waited for three horrible, long hours. Elbie never said a word to me, but Antz could not contain himself, jumping up every so often, frantically ranting about how stupid I was and that he would never speak to me again. I had always heard adults speaking of life-changing events; now I understood what that meant.

Waiting for the game to end seemed to take an eternity, but I calculated it must be time for the fourth or fifth inning. I wished desperately for the game to end soon so I could get home and hide for the rest of my life. It was bad enough that I'd missed the game, but I'd caused my friends to miss it, too, all because I'd decided to help some strange little girl pick up some stupid groceries. What a dork she was, anyway. Who would cry over a few dumb groceries, and why would anyone be in that big of a hurry to get home? How could I have been so inconsiderate, and how could I have been so stupid?

Suddenly a thunderous roar came from inside the stadium. The cheering of thousands of fans shook the walls of the stadium behind our backs. Even the sidewalk seemed to tremble as the roar continued for several minutes. All three of us knew Maris had just hit his sixty-first home run. Antz screamed angrily, jumping up and running wildly in circles, throwing his arms in a maniacal frenzy while ranting incoherently. Elbie just turned and looked at me sadly, which hurt far more than Antz's chaotic screaming. The hurt felt like a jagged dagger thrust into my stomach. That was the only time in my life that I wished I were dead.

As depressed as any ten-year-old could be, I sat alone on the long bus ride home, feeling as if I had been abandoned on a small, isolated island while the world celebrated without me. Elbie and Antz, sitting in seats far from me, would not speak to me. The other boys, full of euphoria, kept repeating the exciting story of Maris's towering home run, and they could not believe how fortunate they were to have seen this once-in-a-lifetime event.

Antz never did talk to me again. He joined another group of friends and never had anything to do with me at school. Elbie soon got over it, and we were best friends all through school and beyond that. However, I never forgave myself for causing him to miss that game. It was a thorn that never went away, agitating, nagging, and creating a constant, horrible discomfort inside.

After high school, Elbie, Anna Lee, Colby, and I went our separate ways to college, but we remained close friends. At Christmas break in our freshmen year of college, Elbie and I went to Evansville, Indiana, to pick up something at the Sears store for his dad. We decided to stop at a diner before returning home to get a milkshake and a sandwich. Not long after we sat down in our booth, we both noticed Antz walk in with that familiar swagger of his. He attended the University of Evansville, a mid-sized university near the diner. When he glanced at me, I hung my head as that old, familiar anguish settled in my stomach again. Strangely, he walked over and sat down beside Elbie.

"How's it going, guys?" he asked cheerfully.

I looked at him briefly, unable to speak. The knot in my throat kept me from saying anything, not even a feeble "I'm sorry."

"That was a long time ago, Razz," Antz said with a smile. "You didn't mean to lose those tickets. It really wasn't the end of the world."

I don't think I ever heard words more appreciated than those from Antz that night. Finally, that oppressive burden lifted from my shoulders. We talked for a long time, just as we had years ago, and it was good to be with Antz again.

Suddenly Antz sat up stiffly, staring at something behind me.

"Who is that?" he asked as if in a daze, nodding over at the rear of the diner.

I turned to see a beautiful, enchanting young waitress tending a table, preparing it for the next customers. She wore a slightly worn ball cap that covered little of her beautiful brown hair, which bounced softly off her shoulders when she walked. Her smile was the prettiest I had ever seen, and she was as tall as most boys. She walked with a confidence that enhanced her cheerful presence, while her welcoming smile and the lively twinkle in her eyes would put even the most irritable patron at ease.

"I don't know," I answered, staring, unable to take my eyes off her.

"I'm going to get a date with her," Antz brashly assured us. "Just watch me."

She finished taking an order from another table, and with a pencil and pad, she walked gracefully toward our table.

"Hello, beautiful. What time do you get off?" Antz said with the same arrogance he carried in high school.

She ignored him and, smiling, turned to Elbie.

"What can I get you boys?" she asked with her pencil and pad in hand.

"How about a movie later?" Antz interjected with his sophomoric confidence.

Again, she ignored him and motioned to Elbie. He ordered a dressed burger and fries. Antz ordered a cheeseburger, fries, and two milkshakes; one for him and one for her, he said. Still ignoring him, she wrote down his order, minus one milkshake.

"I'll just have a grilled chicken sandwich," I said quietly.

"Do you want any fries with that?" she asked, raising her head to look at me.

"No thank you."

She tilted her head and stared at me briefly, curiously, with squinted eyes.

"What is your name?" she asked, easing into a simple smile that warmed my heart.

"Razz."

"Razz," she repeated, nodding.

"Do I know you?" I asked sheepishly.

"No, probably not," she answered, "but I remember you now. I noticed you as you first walked in the door. You seemed very familiar to me, but I couldn't figure out who you were.

"My mother passed away when I was born. I lived with my dad, but my Grammy was always a mother to me, and I loved her dearly. One summer, she was going to Europe to visit some relatives when I was six years old. I was hurrying home from the grocery the day she was leaving. The trip to the grocery had taken longer than I thought, and I only had a few minutes to spare before she would have to go. I desperately wanted to say goodbye to her before she left because I would miss her so much, but I tripped and spilled the groceries all over the sidewalk. I realized that I wouldn't make it home in time to see her off. Then you appeared from nowhere, like an angel from heaven, and gave me your backpack to put the groceries in. I hurried back home just in time to give Grammy a big hug and kiss goodbye."

She paused, still staring at me. We sat motionless, too shocked to speak. Then she continued.

"Grammy got sick in Europe and died before they could get her back home. Shortly after her death, my father's employer transferred him to the pharmaceutical plant here in Evansville, and of course, I moved with him. It was very hard on me, moving to a new city and losing my Grammy at the same time. I don't know if I could have forgiven myself if I hadn't had the chance to say goodbye to her. Because of you, I can always remember hugging her and saying goodbye. Every night since we moved here, I have prayed to Grammy to have God bless the boy who made it possible for me to say goodbye to her one last time. Now, when I say my prayers at night, I can ask her to have God bless Razz."

"I'm sorry. I didn't know," I muttered.

"No, you didn't, but you helped me anyway. You will never know how much you changed my life with that simple act of kindness."

"I, I didn't know," I repeated feebly.

She paused for a moment.

"Well, I'm going to keep your backpack," she smiled. "I would give you the tickets back for the ball game, but I don't think they are any good to you now."

I laughed sheepishly and looked at Antz and Elbie, who were both speechless and wide-eyed.

I couldn't take my eyes off her for the rest of the night. When we were leaving, Antz was the first out the door. I shuffled my feet, trying to watch her as long as possible without being too obvious. Finally, Elbie tapped me on the shoulder.

"Hey, Dufus," he said, laughing, "we will wait outside until you get the nerve to ask her for her name."

I stood there for a minute, finally gathering enough courage to walk over to her.

"I, uh, I mean, I..." I stuttered foolishly like an idiot, and then I turned to walk away.

She gently tugged at my shoulder, and with the most beautiful smile I had ever seen, she reached into her pocket. Without a word, she handed me a folded green food ticket. I opened it and noticed there was only the name Angie and a telephone number on it. I looked at her quizzically, not entirely certain of her intent. Giving me a mischievous smile, she nodded and turned to wait on another table.

I did call Angie for that date, but that was the last time I saw Antz. Elbie and I, though, as I have said before, remained friends for the rest of our lives. Although the lesson was costly at the time, I learned that even the smallest act of kindness rewards the giver, the receiver, and all those who may follow.

Chapter VI

1961

The Chicken Coop

Colby lived several miles down the gravel road from our house. It was a pleasant hour-long walk to get there, less than that on a bike, but not so pleasant when the weather was disagreeable. I didn't mind. Colby and his family were special. His dad, a respected handyman, could handle almost any task by himself. There was little he couldn't do, and if he did it, he did it well. Because of his talents, Mr. Harris could have made a respectable living had he chosen another place to live. But in our rural area, most folks had little expendable income and had learned to do most things themselves, so there weren't too many jobs for him. He managed to get by without the conveniences other folks enjoyed because he was determined to raise his children on a farm away from some of the temptations a city might harbor.

Everyone came to know he was a man of his word who treated each person fairly. He always had a kind word to say about others, and when he laughed, it bellowed across the valley, enticing everyone to join in. To those of us who knew Mr. Harris personally, he was a perceptive man whose wisdom and common sense evoked the admiration of all. I admired him as much as any, and a genial smile from him warmed my heart.

Colby's mom was a large woman with a heart and a laugh just as big. Her jovial demeanor and comical facial expressions often sent me into fits of laughter without a word being spoken. When I visited them, they usually invited me to stay for dinner. That was always a special treat for me since she was one of the best cooks I'd ever known, and the conversations at their meals, filled with gaiety, stories, and laughter, entertained us all. I often had no idea what I was eating, but I always eagerly wiped my plate clean with the last remnant of bread.

Colby went to a different school than I. It was some kind of separated or segregated school; I didn't know which. I never did understand all that as he was in our school district and the bus drove right by his house. It didn't keep us from being best friends, though. We enjoyed each other's company and spent a lot of time together. Of course, there were times we often got into trouble over some mischievous endeavor, just as any boys our age would. After an escapade of that nature, if required, Colby's dad would sit us down for a well-deserved reproach. Strangely, I think I looked forward to his reprimands. With his deep voice and calculated speech, I listened intently with the feeling that he knew more about the good and the bad in life than anyone. I learned a lot from him and envied Colby for that.

One hot August morning, I started on a journey to Colby's house. By the time I got there, the temperature was racing to the mid-nineties, and the humidity wasn't far behind. Colby, waiting impatiently, eagerly encouraged me upon my arrival to follow him to explore an old barn he'd recently discovered on a neighbor's property. He said it was just a couple of miles or so down the road and looked to be two hundred years old or more. We took off immediately in search of it, and forty minutes later, we reached the area where it should be. We pushed vines and saplings aside for another ten minutes, but there was no sign of a barn.

"I saw it here last week, Razz," Colby said, a bit perturbed at his inability to find it.

"Well," I said jokingly, "it must have gotten up and walked off, 'cause there's no barn here."

"Just you hold on," he answered, a little offended at my slight, as he turned to search in another direction. "We'll find it."

The tangled thickets of briars and brush made it difficult to move, and even more challenging to keep our bearings. The heat continued to rise, and with no wind, the humidity became increasingly unbearable.

"Colby, I'd rather find a cool spring to quench my thirst than that barn of yours. Are you sure it wasn't on the other side of the woods?" I asked, hoping he would give up the search.

"No, sir," Colby answered. "It's right here somewhere." I continued looking but had lost interest in searching for his barn.

"How could you lose a barn, Colby?" I finally joked.

He didn't answer. I wasn't sure if his silence was a result of embarrassment or if I had hurt his feelings, but either way, he remained silent for a while.

Because of my lack of enthusiasm and increasing disinterest, I found myself immersed in a blackberry bush that was two feet taller than I. I kicked at it contemptuously, peeved that the hundreds of thorns on the briars were getting the best of me. After a bitter brawl, I finally dispatched the bush with one last indignant kick. I picked at the briars embedded in my sweat-drenched clothing for a few minutes and then noticed a thick, tall mound of green just ahead.

"Is that it?" I asked, pointing to what appeared to be a structure covered with vines and brush.

"That's it," Colby said with a renewed excitement as he dashed through the briars, oblivious to the thorns tearing at his pant legs.

I followed but at a bit more cautious pace. I wasn't too keen about getting another leg full of thorns. Besides, I had seen many barns before and wasn't sure why Colby was so worked up about this one.

The barely visible barn, covered from top to bottom with weeds, briars, and vines taller than any grown man, probably hadn't seen the full sun for a century or more. We ripped just enough of the vines and brush from the door to squeeze inside the shaded structure. Inside, the barn was unlike any we had ever seen, with massive, aged logs, some as long as twenty feet. Despite the wear from the elements, you could still see the undeniable evidence of long-ago hand-hewn shaping and ax-chiseled notches for perfect fittings. The log frame remained intact, but the roof had long since disappeared. Above, the long, thick vines stretched from one end to the other, blocking most of the sun.

The barn contained four stalls, probably for a couple of cows and a team of horses. In one corner, a large bin now sat empty; it had likely been used as a storage room for corn or hay for feed in the winter and most certainly had been home to a few serendipitous field mice over the years as well. A few sickly weeds struggled for life on the dirt floor, trying their best to appear respectable, but the lack of sun had stunted any efforts they could make in that direction. In one of the stalls, the dirt floor was much lower than the others, at least a foot deeper.

"Might have been a pig wallowing around in here," Colby suggested.

"Probably," I answered. "This is a cool find, Colby. I have never seen a barn this old."

Colby's eyes widened with pride.

"I bet they built this when Daniel Boone was alive," he speculated, admiring his newly found barn.

That was important because, if it had been around when Daniel Boone had explored the forests, that would make this barn even more impressive.

"Could have been, Colby," I suggested. "Maybe Daniel Boone himself built this."

The mere suggestion of Daniel Boone excited both of us. We searched fervently for signs of Indian arrowheads, tools, or even a rusty musket that might have belonged to Daniel himself.

We searched, kicked, and explored the barn for another twenty minutes without any results. As the excitement of finding the barn wore off, I realized how lightheaded I had become from the irrepressible heat. It wasn't as hot in the barn as outside, but the stale, stuffy air increased my unbearable thirst and parched lips.

"Colby, let's find some water before I die of thirst."

"Yeah," Colby agreed. "We can come back here another day."

We both knew there was no water between the barn and Colby's house, so we decided to walk further onto the neighbor's property, hoping to find a creek, a cold spring, or, even better, an old, deserted well. There was nothing better to quench a debilitating thirst than dipping a metal cup down into a shaded well and bringing up the purest, coldest water a thirsty man could put to his lips.

It wasn't long before we reached a clearing containing a large, cultivated patch, but we could not determine right away what grew there. The ground crop covered at least ten acres, and as we drew closer, we realized it was a watermelon patch, undeniably the grandest patch of sumptuous, juicy watermelons we had ever seen. The creeping melon vines covered the ground as far as we could see, with thousands of plump watermelons as big as basketballs peeking proudly above them.

"There must be millions of watermelons in there," I said to Colby, amazed at the sight.

Now, let me tell you something about watermelons. We waited impatiently all winter and spring, dreaming of mid-August, when the sweet melons ripened. Nothing tasted better than a cold watermelon on a hot August day. Even if you picked it straight from the vine, at least before late afternoon, it would still be cool on the inside. We would normally stick a knife into it and run it down the middle, lengthwise, to reveal the fresh, juicy, deep-red fruit that every earth-born boy and girl craved. We didn't have a knife with us, but we could burst it open easily on the hard, dry ground.

However, there were two problems with that. First, bursting a watermelon on the ground was okay in a pinch, but you wouldn't do that unless in a dire emergency because it was a reminder of the egregious Saturday night raiders. Nearly every year, as an unspoken annual ritual, two or three miscreant boys, with mischievous intent, would sneak onto a random farm and quietly bust open every watermelon in that poor farmer's patch. Word would circulate quickly, and by dawn, every boy would be pulled from a deep slumber and given a censured quizzing by his parents to see if he'd done it or knew who had.

Every family in the county would take a detour on their way to church to drive by the poor, aggrieved farmer's land to see the plunder of the ravaged watermelon patch. No one could be certain who the culprits were yet, but there it was, right in front of them, the pillage of hundreds of burst watermelons lying irreparably despoiled on Mother Earth's land. It was a sad, dolorous sight for all. Seeing the carnage evoked indignation in some, total umbrage in a few, and anguished tears in others.

"What a shame," parents would say. "Now, what kind of boy would do that?"

Everyone would stare hopelessly at the appalling destruction, trying to imagine which evildoers had committed that heinous crime and what excruciating punishment they would surely endure once caught.

The concerned parishioners would arrive at church to an unusually overflowing parking lot. When Father Till solemnly began his sermon, it would be apparent to all the subject of the day's lecture. For fifteen minutes, he would stare intently at two or three chosen boys, apparently the culprits, and rage passionately about the evil of destroying another man's property, especially a crop that the farmer planned to sell at the market to support his poor, struggling family. The boys would hang their heads in shame as the entire congregation glared contemptuously at them. The boy's embarrassed parents would look away as they slowly and discretely inched further down the pew, distancing themselves as if they were not related to the misfit boys. I never could figure out how Father Till knew who committed the crime every year, but he always did.

The second problem with bursting them open was that eating someone else's watermelon wasn't proper.

"He has millions of them," insisted Colby.

"He would never miss it," I rationalized.

"It probably would rot before he could harvest it."

"And I don't think he would mind, 'cause we probably would die of thirst without it."

With that, I grabbed the closest one and headed straight to a shade tree. It was an unusually large watermelon, too heavy for me to carry with one hand. Once in the shade, we broke it open it on the cool green grass and eagerly ate every bite of that succulent fruit. It was undeniably the most delicious watermelon we had ever tasted. It quenched our thirst and filled our bellies to only one bite short of exploding. Of course, there were enough seeds to get in some good spitting practice, too. When we finished, we hid the rinds under a bush, hoping to conceal our transgression, and headed to Colby's home.

As we walked up to Colby's house, his dad stood on the porch, waiting patiently for us. He was leaning against the post with his muscular arms folded across his broad chest, a portentous stance we both recognized.

"Boys," he said slowly in his deep voice, "put yourselves down here on this porch."

Genuinely ashamed by his tone of voice, we immediately hung our heads, but we were utterly clueless as to how he could have found out so quickly.

"Don't want to know whose idea it was to steal another man's property, and I don't want to know why you did it. But the fact is, you did," he admonished as we sat silently, lowering our heads even further with increasing shame while he towered above us.

I raised my head and blurted out a desperate plea, "But Mr. Harris, we were dying of thirst."

"Don't matter, Razz; it wasn't yours to take."

I have never forgotten those words: "It wasn't yours to take."

For the next thirty minutes, he marched us in silence over to the farmer's door. He knocked politely, and soon a gruff older man with frazzled gray hair and wearing dirty denim overalls and no shirt came to the screen door. His overalls, unfastened on both sides, revealed the elastic of his white underwear. I recognized him as Pious Porter, a grumpy old codger. His darkly tanned, freckled arms and face were a noticeable contrast to his rotund, lily-white chest, shoulders, and belly, which burst out around the overall straps. His enormous, protruding belly was the largest I had ever seen. I felt confident that if he were to enter a room full of people, his belly would have time to introduce itself and already engage in a conversation before the rest of him made it through the door.

We stood behind Mr. Harris as he complimented Mr. Porter on his fine daylilies still blooming in August. I thought that a strange compliment as there was only one lone, scraggly flower barely hanging on to its wilted stem. Mr. Porter smiled proudly, proclaiming that he'd planted them himself just last year.

Then Colby's dad proceeded to explain how ashamed he was of Colby and me for taking one of the farmer's mighty fine watermelons. Mr. Porter's smile quickly disappeared, replaced with a growing scowl that puckered his tightened lips, now jutting nearly two inches from his red face.

"How many watermelons did they take?" he asked gruffly, folding his arms across his hairless chest.

"Just one, sir," Colby's dad answered. "Now, how much could you get at the market for a watermelon this year?"

"Fifty cents!" Mr. Porter growled quickly, looking down over his raised nose and pulling back his pursed lips. I think he did that as a necessity; he could see over his raised nose, but not his salient, puckered lips.

We knew that in a good year, he might get thirty-five cents, but in a year like this, with everyone having a good crop of watermelons, twenty-five cents each would be a stretch. So, it surprised us when Colby's dad answered submissively.

"Well, sir, I will pay you those fifty cents as compensation for the loss of your watermelon. Or, if you prefer, if you have some chores that need tending to, I'll make certain they take care of it or clean it to your satisfaction instead."

Mr. Porter thought for a moment with two fingers pressed to his now-retracted lips and then raised his head. "My chicken coop needs a good cleaning; haven't cleaned it for quite a while. Can they take care of that?"

"Yes, sir. I'll see that they get right to it."

"But Dad," Colby tried to object.

"Quiet, son," his dad said softly. "You left your integrity on the ground with those watermelon rinds. Now you have to work to get it back."

A chicken coop is a small wooden shed usually about five feet by three feet; some are even smaller than that depending on the number of chickens that need a place to roost. Near the back wall, three or four, tiered tree branches stretched from one side to the other for the chickens to fly upon at night to roost. Usually, several wooden shelves would be attached to each of the two sides for the cantankerous mother hens to nest and lay their eggs.

If you have never seen a chicken coop, it is a filthy, foul shed, filled with stray feathers, dirty straw, and chicken droppings piled several inches thick. Our job was to clean out the dirty feathers, straw, and chicken droppings. It is one of, if not the worst job on a farm. Everyone knows you only clean it early in the morning before the heat of the sun starts cooking the chicken droppings. In the middle of a hot, humid August day, the stench is suffocating. But clean it, we did.

I will never forget that pungent odor, nor the strong stench that permeated my sinuses. It felt as if the fetid air were stinging my entire body and burning the insides of my nose. Both of those senses far exceeded the nauseous feeling that accompanied them. With shovels, rakes, rags, and brooms, we cleaned that chicken coop as well as any could be.

On the way home, Colby's dad made us walk a reasonable distance behind him. I'm sure it was to avoid the reek of our tired bodies. He did allow us to stop at a creek to rinse off and clean up a bit. That helped make the trip home less nauseous for both Colby and me, and Mr. Harris as well.

Although I didn't think much about it at the time, I never forgot that day and the lesson Colby and I learned from Mr. Harris. It was, however, a long time before I could enjoy a good piece of fried chicken.

Chapter VII

1962

The Visitor in the Forest

By this time, Anna Lee was an integral part of our group. Colby, Elbie, and I accepted her completely, and we developed an equal friendship for each other regardless of gender. She and Colby would lock horns now and then, but it never altered their friendship. I soon realized they enjoyed their competitive spats, and both looked forward to annoying each other. Elbie, at times, could irritate her, but she was unwavering in her respect for him as well. Anna Lee and I also became much closer, sharing a comfortableness that allowed us to confide with complete trust in the other.

When Anna Lee celebrated her eleventh birthday, it wasn't the usual birthday; with her mom recovering from hip surgery in the hospital and her dad working out of town, she felt alone. Her parents tried to remedy that by having her stay with her papaw for a couple of days in his small farmhouse far from town. Anna Lee loved her papaw, but he couldn't erase the sadness she felt that her mom and dad could not be with her. She was eleven years old now, and that is an important birthday for anyone.

Her mamaw had passed away when she was three years old, and her aging papaw lived by himself in the old house, nestled in between the narrow gravel road and a vast, 1,400-acre forest. Papaw was always fun to be around, but he was eighty-four years old now. He needed his cane when he walked and often grew tired quickly. Anna Lee noticed how difficult it was for him to get out of his chair, an arduous task that took him quite some time to complete. The sounds of his bones creaking and popping each time he struggled to climb out of the chair caused her to wonder how they kept from breaking.

With no one else there but papaw, to pass the time, she found some old photo albums and thumbed through them.

"Papaw how come there are no pictures here of you and Mamaw?" she asked.

"Well," he said slowly without looking up from his book, "we didn't have a lot of money back when we were young, and we didn't buy a camera until we were both up in age. We do have that picture over there of our wedding day, if that interests you. There were a few others that mamaw had. She kept them in a manila envelope, but I don't know what happened to them."

"That's sad," Anna Lee said. "I don't remember what mamaw looked like when I was little."

"I suppose not," he answered. "You were three years old when she passed away. But she sure loved you, just as much as she loved your mom."

Anna Lee walked over to the window overlooking the vast forest just behind his house. She loved to explore and take hikes there, but she was also aware of the dangers lurking in a forest that size. Today, however, was especially inviting, with the autumn colors at their peak. The evening sun danced effortlessly across the foliage, making it appear to change colors as the light softly brushed each leaf.

"Is it okay for me to take a short walk in the forest?" she asked, gazing out the window.

Papaw looked up from his book, over the rim of his glasses. He turned his head and studied her for a minute from his comfortable rocking chair, with only a well-worn cushion between him and the hard, wooden seat.

"It's getting late, sweetheart," he said as he turned back to his book.

"Please, Papaw. I promise I won't take long. I need some fresh air and a little outside time."

He turned again toward his granddaughter as she stared out the window. He held a special pride for her and the independent spirit that she possessed.

"You'll need a jacket. It'll be getting chilly soon. Stay on the path, and be back before dark," he insisted. "It's getting dark earlier this time of year, and since you are a grown-up eleven-year-old, you know what 'before dark' means."

"Yes, it means before dark, Papaw," she replied quickly, grabbing her jacket and putting it on as she raced towards the door. "Thank you, Papaw!" she yelled back, already outside and heading toward the forest.

It was a pleasant fall evening, with a temperature in the mid-sixties and a gentle wind from the south that made the air seem much fresher than back home. The colors in the forest were more vibrant and more prevalent in these woods than on Free Silver Road. She picked up a stick that she thought would make a perfect hiking stick. Needing only a couple of small branches to snap off, she did so, and then away she went. She remained mindful of Papaw's warning to stay on the path. One could quickly get disoriented and lost if you didn't.

With the gentle breeze to her back, she tightened her jacket slightly and watched as the sun began to drift down from the top of the trees. She could not take her eyes off the foliage above as it changed from one color to another, and she did not want to miss the last few minutes of the sun illuminating the crimson, yellow, and orange leaves. As the western sun slowly began its descent to set for the night, she figured there was more than enough time to get back to papaw's house, but she might as well turn and start her retreat just in case.

Lowering her eyes as she turned around, she realized she was not on the path. She searched quickly for any sign of the trail through the thick branches and dense brush, but it was not visible from any direction. Preoccupied with the bright foliage, she had ventured astray, and she had no idea when she'd left the path or from what direction she'd come.

Anna Lee was not one to panic. She possessed a dangerous amount of courage; at least, that was what her papaw said. However, she began to worry, remembering papaw's warning to stay focused. She, too, knew how difficult it could be to find your way out of the forest without the path to guide you. If she could not locate it before darkness, she would not be able to determine the way out of the woods until morning. She tried her best to figure where east and west were, but with the sun gone and tall trees surrounding her, she had little hope of that. She decided to walk in the direction that she felt she had just come from and hope for a fortunate glimpse of the path.

She plodded anxiously for several minutes through the trees and underbrush with no sign of the trail home. The darkening shadows and fading light caused some anxiety and increasing concern. She picked up her speed and hurried frantically through the brush. There was no way to tell how long she had been walking or where she was, but without a moon, the forest would soon be in total darkness.

Worried about wolves or coyotes, she struggled to remain calm, but now realized how hopelessly lost she was. Frustrated and concerned that she might be walking further away from papaw's house, she sat down on a rotting, moss-covered log and became perturbed over her carelessness. She could not turn away her fears of being alone in the dark, nor of facing the dangers of the massive forest, both known and unknown. But despite her efforts, the emerging noises of the night made her restive and tense. Pressing her arms tightly to her body, she lowered her head and tried to block out the unfamiliar sounds. There was no relief, as she could still hear the unsettling noises, but she did not care to see the source. If it were a pack of coyotes or something even more dangerous, seeing them would not help. Suddenly, above the many sounds, one stood out from the others, seizing her attention. It sounded like footsteps or something similar stirring the leaves on the ground behind her.

Her only thought was of a wolf, and she stood, ready to run, but found herself frozen in fear. She forced herself to turn to look behind her, knowing she would be helpless to fend off any predator. Through the darkening forest, she could barely make out a figure working its way toward her. In the distance, with the minimal light left, it appeared to be human. As it drew nearer, Anna Lee realized it was a woman, and from the way she walked, an older woman.

Anna Lee, still filled with fear, wasn't sure that this was real, nor that she was no longer in danger. It was not likely that a friendly woman would just appear in the middle of the forest.

"Are you lost, little lady?" the woman asked in a friendly, welcoming voice.

"Yes!" Anna Lee shouted, relieved but still shaken. "Will you please help me?"

The lady finally worked her way through the maze of trees and brush and approached Anna Lee's side. She wore a blue flowered dress with a waist-length black sweater. With a full head of soft white hair, a warm smile, and kind eyes that twinkled even in the fading light, she swept Anna Lee's fears away.

"What on earth are you doing out in the forest this time of night?" the lady asked, surprised.

"Somehow I got off the path, and I can't find my way back to papaw's house," Anna Lee explained, still shaken by her harrowing experience.

"Well, you are a long way from anywhere, young lady. Where does your papaw live?"

"I don't know which direction it is," Anna Lee explained, frustrated. "But it is a small house on a gravel road; Ridge Road, I think. The one that you turn on after a church. Papaw has a big barn, and there is a clothesline in the back with an iron bell hanging from one of the posts."

The lady's smile widened as she tilted her head sideways.

"Oh, I know that house well." She giggled. "But that is in the other direction. Come on. We need to hurry. It's a long way from here. We need to get you back before your papaw worries too much."

With that, she reached for Anna Lee's hand and led the way. She walked briskly for an older woman, and Anna Lee had to hurry to keep up with her.

"What are you doing in the forest this time of night?" Anna Lee asked.

"Oh, I'm just a visitor here," the elderly lady replied.

"Are there any wolves in these woods?" asked Anna Lee, slightly out of breath, while nervously scanning the forest.

"There aren't any wolves, but there were a few bears when I was a girl your age. They are all gone now. You only need to worry about a pack of coyotes, but they shouldn't bother you with me here. What is your name, young lady?"

"Anna Lee Frazier."

The lady said nothing but seemed to pick up the pace a little more. Suddenly they stepped onto the barely visible path, and Anna Lee breathed a sigh of relief.

"It will be completely dark soon and much colder," the lady said, picking up her pace. "We need to keep moving."

The nocturnal sounds in the forest grew louder with each passing moment. The noises of the night were very different than those of the daytime. Most were of unknown origin, some soothing, some eerie, and some frightening, and she was glad the lady was with her. Anna Lee's legs grew weary from the long, hurried trip back, but she tried her best to keep up.

Suddenly the lady stopped. Anna Lee looked up to see the kitchen light in her papaw's house. Relieved to be back home, she no longer felt the soreness in her legs.

The lady let go of her hand and turned to Anna Lee. "Now, you go on in and mind your papaw next time. Okay?"

"I promise I will. Thank you!" Anna Lee almost shouted as she threw herself upon the smiling lady and gave her a tight hug. "You saved my life," she said, and with that, she turned and ran into the house.

Her papaw was on the telephone as she burst through the door.

"Here she is," he said to whomever he was talking to on the telephone. "I'll call you right back."

He scolded her for worrying him so but hugged her tightly when she ran to him.

After she told him about how an old lady in the forest had saved her, he grew silent and listened.

"Where did she go?" he asked curiously.

Anna Lee suddenly felt remorse for not asking the lady to come in from the dark.

"I don't know," she replied. "Maybe she is still out there." She grabbed a flashlight and stepped out the back door, searching the edge of the forest for her lady friend. She repeatedly called for her, but there was no sign of her.

When her parents picked her up and took her home the next day, they also scolded her for being so careless and not listening to her papaw. Anna Lee apologized, promising never to do it again. She began to think of her papaw and felt sad at the thought of him sitting all alone at his house.

They arrived at their home on Free Silver Road, and she followed close behind her parents into the kitchen. Her father headed to his office to work, and her mother began washing the dirty dishes they'd left before her surgery.

"Mom, should you be doing that this soon after surgery?" Anna Lee asked, almost scolding her mother.

"The doctors said I could do anything I felt like doing. I just need to limit my time walking."

"Mom," Anna Lee said, changing the subject, "do we have any pictures of Mamaw?"

"I'm not sure…a few, maybe. Why?"

"I don't know," Anna Lee answered quietly.

"Well, if we do, they would be in the chest upstairs."

Anna Lee turned and quickly hurried upstairs to the storage room. It really was just a small third bedroom in the house, but they used it for storing small household items and other boxed things that they either no longer needed or just had never opened when they'd moved from their former house.

The wooden chest, about three feet long and two and a half feet high, sat alone in a corner. Old, rusty hinges still hung tightly to the top, and a dried-leather strap with a small, flat, keyed lock fastened to the bottom had secured it at one time. The lock no longer worked, so to open it, you only needed to pull up the wooden top by the leather strap.

Anna Lee began sorting through the albums containing pictures of her as a baby and little girl, and her parents as well. There were four photo albums, but none of her papaw or mamaw.

She noticed another older album with a red velvet cloth covering under a pile of newspapers. As she opened it, an old, faded manila envelope slipped out, falling to the bottom of the chest. She slowly picked it up, peered inside, and took out the handful of pictures resting within. Most were aged black and white pictures of people Anna Lee did not know. Near the bottom was a photo with an inscription penciled with beautiful penmanship unlike any Anna Lee had seen. The faded writing on the backside

57

appeared water-damaged, making it difficult to read, but she finally made out the words: "Mamaw with Anna Lee, three years old."

She turned it over slowly. The picture was faded as well, but Anna Lee could now see the water lines that had damaged the image. It was the only color picture in the envelope, and on the left was an older white-haired lady with a small child in her arms. The lady had a broad smile on her face and wore a white and blue flowered dress with a dark sweater across her shoulders. On the right was a clothesline post with a bell hanging from the top. Anna Lee knew at once she was the visitor in the forest.

Clutching her newly discovered photo, she raced downstairs to the kitchen and her mom, who was still cleaning dishes.

"Mom was this Mamaw?" she asked, holding up the photo.

Her mother turned from the sink, holding a damp towel.

"Yes, that is her holding you when you were a small child."

"This is the woman in the forest who helped me find my way out. Same sweater, same dress, and it looks exactly like her."

"Anna Lee, that wasn't Mamaw in the forest. She died eight years ago."

"But this is her! It looks just like her, and she said she knew Papaw's house."

"Anna Lee!"

"Mom, it is!"

"Anna Lee, it can't be. Mamaw is dead. It was eight years ago when she died. Maybe there were some similarities, but it wasn't Mamaw."

"I'm sure of it, Mom. I know it was."

"Think about it, Anna Lee. Mamaw is gone. Maybe you were hallucinating, or maybe you imagined it was her. Papaw said it was completely dark when you got back. Where did the lady go?

It was too dark in the forest for anyone to find their way back. We are not even sure there was a lady."

"You think I made this up!" Anna Lee shouted angrily.

"No, Anna Lee," her mom said, softening her voice with a little more compassion. "I don't know what happened. But think about it. It couldn't be Mamaw, and if it was a woman in the forest who helped you, how did she get home? Why would an older lady be wearing a dress in the middle of the forest in the dark? Where did she come from, and how did she just appear? She wouldn't be living in the forest by herself, wearing nice clothes like a sweater and a dress. It just doesn't sound logical." Her mother turned back to washing her dishes.

Anna Lee looked at the picture again and began to doubt herself. "I don't know. Maybe you are right. Maybe I did have a hallucination or something. Why would someone be in the middle of the forest at that time of night? I know she didn't live there because she said she was just a visitor."

Anna Lee's mom dropped the silverware she was drying, creating a loud clatter, and turned quickly to Anna Lee.

"What did you say?" she asked Anna Lee in disbelief.

"I said, maybe you were right."

"No, about her not living there."

"I asked her if she lived there, and she said no, she was just a visitor."

Her mother set down her towel, stepped slowly over to Anna Lee, and took the photo from her hands. She stared at the picture in her trembling fingers for a moment and then looked at Anna Lee with tears in her eyes. She wiped them away and then sat down on the chair beside Anna Lee, still holding the photo.

"My mother and I used to take long walks in the forest. It was a place where she could share her joys, her fears, her comforts, and her insecurities with me and where I could share mine with her. It was a special time for both of us, and we

59

treasured it so. I will always miss our time together and our walks in that forest more than anything. She once told me that we were only visitors in the forest, but that it would always reward us in some way for visiting. After that, we always used a code word when one of us needed a walk in the forest. We simply asked, 'Would you like to take a visit?'

"When my mom was dying, she told me how much she loved me, and she promised that she would always watch over me. Maybe that was Mamaw who helped you out of the forest. Maybe she is watching over you, too."

She rose, leaned over to Anna Lee, and hugged her tightly. They both cried softly, filled with emotions. Then Anna Lee pulled away, still holding her mother's hand, and looked up at her.

"Mom, would you like to take a visit tomorrow?"

Chapter VIII

1962

The Cemetery

In the latter part of the sixth grade, to put it politely, Niner Peak had become more a part of our lives than we were comfortable with. To put it more accurately, he had become the bane of our life.

We passed many stories between us about his dad's belligerent demeanor, and we soon found out Niner was an apple from the same tree. He had short blonde hair that, with a generous helping of wax, stood straight up. His smile wasn't a smile at all; it was more of a nefarious smirk. He was a year older than us, a seventh grader, and his size dwarfed Elbie's and mine. He wasn't in our class, so we did not have to deal with him all day, but at lunch and after school, he tormented us mercilessly.

Elbie, who was a little shorter and smaller than I, was the unfortunate recipient of most of his wrath. Niner took great pleasure in eating whatever he chose from our plates at lunch and taunting us in other ways as well. Some of his inflictions were of a nature that I would prefer not to disclose here.

Elbie quickly learned to bring two cookies each day, one for him and one for Niner, hoping to appease his vile nemesis, but it wasn't unusual for Niner to take both. After school each day, Niner continued to inflict pain upon us until he was pleased with his efforts. Occasionally, he found another victim to inflict his punishments upon, but most often, it was Elbie and me who were the recipients of his unspeakable torture. I don't know why he picked us out from the others, but maybe it was because of Elbie's size, and I was victimized simply by association.

Anyway, we welcomed summer for many reasons but mostly because we were free of Niner Peak. In the summers, his grandmother sent him to Owensboro to live with his dad, far from us, so we would not see him until school started in the fall. Until then, we could relax without fear and enjoy being kids again. We spent most of our free time playing baseball or exploring the woods, barns, and cemeteries.

A cemetery is the one place where the rich and the poor, the educated and uneducated, and the good and the bad all rest side by side, most within arm's reach. One should certainly expect it to be a little unnerving at times.

We frequented an old cemetery that lay hidden deep into the woods about a mile from where we lived. Often, if we had nothing else pressing to do, Elbie and I traipsed through the Free Silver Woods to that hidden cemetery for an afternoon. We were both around eleven years old at that time, and a graveyard was as good a place to explore as any. Of course, neither of us dared to venture that far back into the woods at night, and certainly not to the cemetery

I don't know if the cemetery had a real name, but everyone we knew called it the Alder Ridge Cemetery. Most folks around there pronounced it "cemetry", but that is beside the point. I suppose it received its name from the many red alder trees in the area. Alder wood was favored for smoking fish and other foods, giving them a savory flavor. You could also use the bark to help soften the effects of poison oak, or even poison ivy. That was a useful tonic since both of those produced a powerful itch that would last for days if not treated.

As I said, any cemetery was an interesting visit unless you happened to know someone taking up residence there. But Alder Ridge was unique. It was a small cemetery, hidden from view for at least two hundred years. An old rusting wrought iron fence surrounded it. Its gate no longer protected the entrance, probably carried off by someone to replace a broken gate at home or for a stall door to keep a nomadic horse from wandering off. Large, aged trees, as thick as two or three barrels together, surrounded the cemetery. However, nothing grew inside it; no weeds nor briars, not even a single worthless blade of grass had managed to take hold. Crisp, dried, dead leaves and rotting twigs, cast with umbrage from the proud oak trees, covered the ground as if they, too, needed a final resting place.

When walking, the crunching of the crisp leaves resonated through the forest, breaking the silence and disturbing the serenity only as man can do. The remote cemetery was so far into the woods that aside from the crunch of your footsteps, the only sound was the gentle stirring of the leaves from a transitory wind or the dulcet song of a clandestine whippoorwill.

We counted many people buried there in the early seventeen hundreds, with the latest stones we found having a date of 1762. The markers, worn from age and the elements, were made from the indigenous limestone, each artistically stained from more than almost two centuries of acid rain. Most were covered with mildew and deep green moss, enriching the beauty of the scene. Some were difficult to read, but we could make out most of them. Many were merely small flat stones set in the ground and with the names and dates etched into them. We found some barely visible beneath the soil, and we wondered how many had disappeared completely long ago.

The same last names appeared on some of the stones, encouraging us to try and guess who was related to whom. Some provided other information that allowed us to piece together a part of the story of their lives, creating ample excitement and making the day's trip worth the effort.

The most interesting was a family of five who had died on the same day, with the date, August 14, 1762, inscribed on the tombstone. We speculated that a surprise attack by thieves, or ruffians after their gold and silver, had caused their demise. However, no one in this area had possessed anything worth taking back then: an ax for chopping wood, some garden tools, several tallow candles, and maybe a few parcels of food, but that would have been about all they possessed. We found no tombstones with a later date than that family, making them, at least to us, the most mysterious markers of all. We became tenacious in our search for other clues about that enigmatic family.

Elbie and I had visited that cemetery many times, but we never forgot our visit on August 14, 1962.

We both packed a sandwich and a mason jar of water and then headed to the cemetery, expecting nothing more than a routine visit. It was a hot, sunny day, yet in the shaded woods, a cool breeze kept us feeling spirited. We had in mind to discover a new marker or stone, especially one that had been covered by decaying leaves and dirt for decades. It wasn't often we could find a new stone, but the possibility of it always created a bit of excitement for us.

As we approached the cemetery, a ray of sunshine pierced the small opening of the canopy, illuminating it. With the surrounding trees dimly lit and the dark forest behind them, it was as if the entire forest embraced the now-glowing gravesite as its pride and joy. We stepped up our pace in excitement, knowing this was certain to be the day we discovered a new, mysterious stone, or at least one with some names that we could place as relatives of the others and possibly learn something about how they lived.

With the sun gleaming vibrantly upon the cemetery, we stepped through the opening in silence as if we were walking on sacred ground. The Alder Ridge Cemetery always instilled a bit of respect in us, but today seemed eerily different; the hair on our necks stiffened, and our hushed silence matched that of the muted serenity of the forest. We quietly moved the dirt and leaves aside with our shoes, hoping to find a long-hidden marker. Methodically searching from one end to the other, our hopes began to wane as no new grave markers appeared. Suddenly, Elbie's whisper broke the silence.

"Razz!" he whispered urgently.

I knew he had found an important marker. When I turned, I noticed he was not looking at the ground, but off into the distance.

"What is it?" I whispered.

He said nothing, remaining motionless.

"Elbie?"

He did not move. As I slowly stepped over to him, the strange look on his face startled me. Then I turned in the direction of his stare. When I saw what frightened him, I, too, was unable to speak. There before us, on top of the most prominent marker, the one marking the family of five, was a bright yellow rose as fresh as if it had been plucked from a graveside flower garden and set gently atop the stone by a bereaved loved one. Its foot-long stem sported reddish-brown thorns in between five green petals. Neither of us had noticed the flower before, and we felt confident it had not been there when we'd arrived. We stared for several minutes as if we expected it to get up and move on its own, or at least have the appropriate manners to explain how it had gotten there.

"Was that there when we got here?" Elbie quietly asked, even though he knew the answer.

"No. I always look at that marker first as soon as we get here. There wasn't a flower when we got here," I said with a slight quaver in my voice.

"I didn't see it either."

Neither Elbie nor I knew whether to run or stay put. I think staying put was our only option as neither of us could manage much of a run at that moment.

We slowly surveyed the quiet cemetery to make sure we were alone.

We heard a gentle breeze easing its way through the trees from a distance. It finally reached us and briefly ruffled the petals on the rose, followed by a stronger gush of wind that tossed a few leaves in front of the marker to the side. The wind quickly changed directions, and the temperature dropped slightly. With a final theatrical effort, the wind pushed the rose off the marker and onto the cleared ground where the leaves had once lain.

Now, both Elbie and I always tried to act braver than we were, but when that yellow rose fell to the ground, Elbie grabbed my arm tightly to keep me from running away. That was his only option as his shaking knees would not allow him that luxury. What he didn't know was that my knees were trembling more than his.

The wind disappeared quickly, leaving us standing like two stone statues guarding the cemetery. I looked down at the fresh, clean rose lying proudly on the dirt and with a small rock embedded in the ground under it. I tilted my head slightly, staring at it, and realized it wasn't a rock at all; it was a buried marker. I finally gathered enough nerve to speak.

"Elbie," I whispered. "I think there is a stone marker under that rose."

"Really?" he said, his voice rising slightly.

I loosened my arm from his tightened grip, walked over to the stone, and bent down on one knee before the rose.

"Careful, Razz," he warned.

"It's a rose, Elbie," I replied. "I don't think it is going to bite me."

I gently picked up the rose and replaced it atop the monument. Elbie and I both carefully, and respectfully, began to remove the remaining layers of dirt from the stone. We used our fingernails to clear the earth from the etchings on its face. It took some time and a few broken fingernails, but we finally cleared away years of dirt to expose the marker for the first time in possibly over a hundred years.

We read the inscription half aloud, sat back on our heels, and looked back up at the rose. I looked at Elbie, he looked at me, and then we lowered our heads to look at the inscription again. It read:

```
These five graves are empty; we moved out west.
We left these markers here to be with the rest.
Where and when our journey ends, no one knows,
But with the wind, we send a bright yellow rose.
```

"So, the family didn't die?" Elbie asked.

"Well, not here," I answered.

"Good...that makes me feel better."

"Me, too."

"But where did the rose come from?" he asked, turning toward me.

"Don't know."

"But where did it come from?!"

"I don't know, Elbie! But someone or something put it there for a reason, so we should respect that."

"Do you think it was a ghost that put it there?"

"Maybe. Probably not, though. Ghosts are just like little kids, Elbie; sometimes they just need a little attention. But I think that rose was there for us, not a ghost's ego."

"It doesn't bother you that it just appeared?"

"Nothing I can do about it. You can't explain everything, Elbie. It's just a mystery. Come on, let's go home."

"We need to take the rose with us so that everyone will believe our story," Elbie insisted.

"It's not ours to take, Elbie. Let's go home."

Elbie looked at the rose for a few seconds, acquiesced, and quietly followed me out of the cemetery. We were relieved that the family had moved on and, hopefully, had a happy life, but after that day, the cemetery had changed for us. With the mystery of the family explained, it just wasn't as exciting anymore. We did go back there once, hoping to see another yellow rose, but when we got there and saw none, we quietly turned and went back home.

One day, not long ago, Elbie and I talked about that cemetery. We never could figure out where the yellow rose came from, but both of us admitted that from that day on, the sight of a yellow rose brought memories of the mystery family that had moved from Kentucky to California on August 14, 1762.

We both speculated with our own stories of how their lives might have unfolded after they moved west, and eventually we realized how similar they were to each of us today. They went about their lives during their time here, living an existence relevant only to those of their time and place. But after the third or fourth generation, their lives, and even their names, began to fall silently into obscurity as if they'd never been, yet that could never diminish their existence, nor their importance.

Throughout their time here, they most likely touched many other lives, and no matter how significant or insignificant, they inadvertently helped to shape, by varying degrees, all those whose path they might have shared. It was with that almost imperceptible touch that they left a piece of themselves behind. Each of us today, at least to some degree, is the aggregate of all those who came before. In that way, they are still here with us, much like the yellow rose drifting softly in the wind for the rest of time.

Chapter IX

1963

Niner

Niner continued his torments with alacrity throughout the seventh grade. It may have been our imagination, but it seemed the methods he used worsened and the intensity of pain increased that year. We tried every trick to avoid him, but there seemed to be no place to hide from this unscrupulous ruffian. Elbie and I made every effort to conceal our bruises, but as one began to fade, another appeared.

I will never forget one day in the spring of that year. Niner cornered the two of us after school. With an excited eagerness, he grabbed our books and sent them sprawling across the grass. He then pushed Elbie down and jumped on top of him. He twisted Elbie's arm until he cried out horribly in pain. He continued to twist his arm further, and the louder Elbie screamed, the broader Niner's wicked smile became.

I could not take it any longer. Tossing aside any caution I might have carried, I jumped on Niner's back and grabbed his head with one arm, trying to get him off Elbie. With the other arm, I pummeled him as hard and as fast as I could. Although the effort to save my friend was commendable, the futility of it soon became apparent. Niner rose and threw me to the ground.

Usually when he tormented us, he wore a sinister smug and an appearance of complete satisfaction. This time, when he looked down upon me, I saw anger in his eyes, extreme, fearless anger. His dark eyes riveted on me, displaying a zealous ferocity much like a lion staring down a competing male just before engaging in a fierce battle.

I lay there, him over the top of me, and realized that this time, he would not quit until he had seriously hurt me. Elbie, writing in excruciating pain, lay helplessly on the ground. I saw Niner descend upon me with an unmatched fury I had never known. His first punch met my face so hard it felt like a brick. His fist rocked my jaw, and I heard a loud pop as the force dislodged it, followed by a flurry of stars in my eyes. I had always thought that was just an expression, but I can assure you, anyone hit as hard as Niner's fist hit me that day will see those stars as well.

My mind went blank briefly, and then the second blow hit. This was followed by the third and fourth, and then I lost count. He continued the barrage unimpeded. I felt myself passing out when the hitting suddenly stopped.

I opened my eyes, and through the blood, I saw someone holding Niner by the collar and then flooring him with one punch. He lay on the ground beside Elbie, crumpled and not moving. I wiped away the blood streaming freely into my eyes.

"Are you okay?" someone asked as he helped me up.

It was Bobby Day. He was an eighth grader, as big as and stronger than Niner.

I had only talked to Bobby once before, when I was in the third grade and he the fourth. He'd sat down beside me on the bench at lunch. At first, I had been intimidated by him, but his gentle demeanor and the kindness in his eyes had soon put me at ease. We'd talked for a while, and I'd felt privileged that this big fourth grader had not only sat by me but had also spoken to me. That was the last time I'd talked to him until now. It wasn't a slight; it was just that he had his friends in his class and I was just a kid.

"Are you okay??" he asked again.

"I think so," I said, although my head pounded with pain.

"Stay here," he said and turned to Niner.

He grabbed Niner by the collar and pulled him from the ground. Niner was still dazed, but he came to his senses when Bobby thrust his face inches from Niner's.

"If I ever see you go near these two kids again, I will make sure it will be the last time," Bobby threatened in a voice that even intimidated me. "Understand!?"

Niner mumbled something.

"Understand!!?" Bobby shouted.

"Yes," Niner said, meekly hanging his head.

"Get out of here!" Bobby ordered as he shoved Niner away.

Niner hurried out of sight without looking back.

Bobby helped Elbie up and then looked at my swollen face. "If he bothers either of you again, you let me know, okay?"

"Thank you," I said, and Elbie repeated it.

With that, Bobby turned and walked away. We heard him mumbling something to himself about Niner, but we could not make it out.

Two weeks went by without seeing hide nor hair of Niner. The world was once again at peace, for the time being, anyway.

About three weeks later, Elbie and I were on the sidewalk after school when we noticed Niner charging toward us, as enraged as any man could be. We froze, unable to run at the sight of this terrifying monster barreling toward us with his uncontrollable and unrelenting anger, petrifying us. We knew he was about to hurt us like never before.

"Peak!!!"

We heard the shout from across the street. It was Bobby Day.

Peak stopped dead in his tracks, looked across the street, turned, and ran as fast as he could as Bobby chased him. When Peak rounded the corner out of sight, Bobby stopped. He turned toward us, nodded with a kindly smile of satisfaction on his face, and slowly walked away as if nothing had happened.

I looked at Elbie, still shaking in fear. He turned his head toward me and smiled sheepishly. Peak never bothered us again.

71

The next year, we were in the eighth grade, and Peak was in high school, allowing us a full year without seeing him. However, we worried that the following year, when we would be freshmen in high school, Peak might again be able to torment us. We could only hope Bobby Day was there as well.

Before school let out in our eighth-grade year, we heard that Niner Peak had been kicked out of school, and we assumed we would never see him again. Elbie and I, along with some other eighth-graders, celebrated with great relief as that dark cloud lifted from our lives.

However, it wasn't long before I began to feel sorry for Niner. I was a little perturbed that I held those feelings for the bane of our lives for two years, but I did. I could not help but wonder what kind of life he had at home, what types of torment his father might have inflicted upon him, and what kind of anguish he'd endured that had turned him into a person who could only experience joy by taking it from others.

Elbie and I never forgot the name of Bobby Day or the kindness he held in his heart. We vowed that if we ever were put into a position to help someone caught in the grips of another Niner Peak, we would do everything in our power to right it. We hoped that someday we could experience what it felt like to be Bobby Day.

Chapter X

1964

The Storm

Sandlot talk, often called by other names, sometimes can be disparaging, but a disparaging word, no matter where spoken, is still a disparaging word. Although this story is mostly about two brothers, Carmel and Harley, friends of ours, we learned a valuable lesson from their misfortunate transgression.

In 1964, we were thirteen years old, and summers, filled with new experiences, awaited us. Many of us also began to pick up small jobs here and there to earn a little money. However, one thing that never changed was our passion for baseball. Most summer days, there was at least one impromptu game at the sandlot behind the school, with enough boys to make two teams of six or more.

Anna Lee was a fixture at the sandlot and was always the first chosen to be on a team. Her skill and athleticism allowed her to play any position flawlessly, and she could hit a ball as far as any boy. Few could field as well as she, and only a handful could burn the first baseman's glove with throws so fast some jokingly claimed to see nothing but smoke. We envied her for her natural ability but could not understand how a girl could be that talented at sports.

Girls were not allowed on the school baseball teams at that time, but many of us secretly shared our disappointment that she could not play. A few of the boys schemed a plan to disguise her as a boy, but I finally said, "Guys, look at her. Do you honestly think anyone in the world could confuse Anna Lee Frazier for a boy? How can you disguise that?"

They leaned over, looked at her, shook their heads, and muttered, "Dang it!"

***

"Did you boys sleep through that storm last night?" Mr. Tierney asked Carmel and Harley from just inside the sixteen-foot wooden door to his barn. It could slide open wide enough to get his tractor inside while pulling an implement.

"It was a doozy, the wind was howling around my windows and doors like a pack of hungry wolves. There must have been four or five inches of rain. I'd bet that creek was overflowing and moving faster than a deer chased by a mom coyote."

It was early morning, and the June sun still lay low in the east. By midday, however, the sun and June humidity would turn the barn into a sauna, so the two brothers knew they needed to finish their work before that happened. They'd agreed to clean his barn for two dollars each. That was a lot of money for them at that time, even for four hours of work. Two dollars could buy a new baseball, or possibly even a used bat with Lou Gehrig's name on it.

"No, sir, Mr. Tierney," answered Harley, the older of the two Knott boys. "All that thundering, and lightning kept us up most of the night, too."

Mr. Tierney lowered his head and shook it from side to side. "Lost a new calf last night. Can't imagine a coyote out in that storm, but something surely got my calf."

He looked up at the boys again. "Keep your eyes open for my calf on your way home. If you find it, I'll pay you five dollars."

They both looked up excitedly.

"Five dollars?" Carmel, the younger brother, asked, wide-eyed.

"Five dollars," Mr. Tierney repeated.

"We'll find him, Mr. Tierney," Harley promised, picking up his pace.

74

The boys hurriedly cleaned the barn, intent on finding the calf and collecting the five dollars. Cleaning it wasn't a difficult chore; it just took a while to get it done. There were tools to clean and put away and large sheets of plastic, or tarp, used for ground cover, that needed to be washed and folded. Any horse or cattle droppings had to be shoveled and taken out, and since the barn housed tobacco in the fall, all the loose leaves and remnants needed to be picked up and put in the garden, along with the horse chips and cow manure, for nitrogen fertilizer.

Once finished and having collected their two dollars, they raced from the barn in search of the missing calf. Skipping lunch, they searched the entire farm and the surrounding area as well, but with no luck. Two hours in the hot, humid weather exhausted them and they decided to go home. They planned to come back in the evening, when the sun had cooled, hoping for a refreshing breeze.

They trudged slowly down the gravel lane from Mr. Tierney's farm to the main road, disappointed yet still holding hope. Mr. Tierney had not put any new gravel on the road since the spring thaw, so there was only a small amount in the middle and even less on the edges. There was nothing but muddy tracks where his car and tractor tires met the lane.

At the end of his farm, about twenty feet from the road, an old wooden bridge crossed over Pup Creek. Eight-inch-wide, seasoned white oak planks stretched across the two four-by-eight wooden braces supporting the bridge: the planks, about seven and a half feet long, some more, some less, allowed only enough room for a car to cross with a few inches to spare on each side. With no rails, there was little room for error when traveling across in any vehicle. The nails in most of the planks were long gone, resulting in a loud clatter when a car crossed.

As the boys tramped across the twelve-foot long bridge, they looked over at the still-fast-running creek and decided to sit and rest for a few minutes.

"I guess a coyote must have gotten Mr. Tierney's calf," Carmel said quietly.

Harley, sitting on the wooden bridge, his legs dangling only four feet above the creek, did not answer at first. Finally, he said, "It's hot."

"Yeah," said Carmel. "You want to walk in the creek for a while to cool off our feet?"

"I don't see why not. It's only a little over knee-deep, and as long as we get back home by dinner, we'll be fine."

"Let's go!" shouted Carmel, pulling off his shoes as they raced off the short bridge and then down the bank to the creek.

The refreshing water soothed their swollen feet, and the sandy bottom massaged their toes as it oozed between them. It wasn't more than knee-deep in most places, but the water collected in an occasional washout rose closer to their belt buckles. The sloping banks on both sides of the creek were thick with trees, briars, and brush. They could see the farmland through an occasional opening in the foliage, but the further they went, dense woods and brush replaced the cultivated crops.

The thicker foliage protected the creek from the hot June sun while darkening their way the farther they went. The only sound heard was the gentle splashing of their feet as they waded through the clear water, creating a peaceful trek with no desire to talk. They sensed a feeling of tranquility, much like that of sitting alone in a quiet, empty church on a late afternoon as the sun shines softly through the stained-glass windows. But the further they traveled, the more the atmosphere changed, becoming less familiar and more unwelcoming.

"How far do you think we have gone?" Carmel asked after thirty minutes of walking.

"Don't know. A couple of miles, probably," answered Harley. "We passed the Pence's place a long time ago, so we must be pretty deep into the woods."

"Do you think we should be heading back?" Carmel asked, a little worried.

"Wouldn't hurt," replied Harley, ready to give up himself.

They stopped for a few seconds, and they'd begun to turn around when Carmel noticed something just ahead.

"What is that?" he whispered, pointing straight ahead.

Harley turned to see what had startled Carmel. Just ahead, half-hidden in the brush, there appeared to be an animal, possibly a coyote or a bobcat.

"Let's back away slowly," Carmel advised in a hushed voice.

"Wait a minute," Harley whispered, staring at the motionless animal.

The boys waited and watched a moment, yet there was still no movement. It appeared lifeless, nestled in the brush, half out of the water.

"If that cat is alive and wakes up, we'll be dead ducks," Carmel whispered, motioning Harley to come on.

"I think it's dead," Harley said in a slightly louder voice.

Carmel peered apprehensively from behind Harley at the animal.

"Let's check it out," Harley said as he began creeping slowly toward the animal.

"No, Harley!" Carmel said in a loud whisper.

Harley continued toward the half-submerged animal. Carmel stayed behind, crouched and ready to run. Harley stopped and turned slightly toward Carmel.

"It's a calf," he said in a loud voice. "I think it's alive!"

He leaned over the limp calf. Its wet hair was matted and full of weeds, briars, and other debris. The twisted calf, caught in the thick brush, was barely hanging on for life.

"It's alive!" shouted Harley. "Come and help me get him out."

Harley and Carmel worked for ten minutes, trying to free the injured calf. The thorns on the briers bloodied their hands and arms, but they eventually worked the calf loose from the tangled brush. He was breathing but possessed little energy, certainly not enough to walk on his own.

"Hurry, we need to get him out of here," Harley said urgently.

"Harley," said Carmel, looking at the calf, "I think this is Mr. Tierney's calf."

"Must be. Let's go."

Carrying a forty-pound calf through the creek made for a difficult trip back to the bridge, even with each boy taking turns. Carmel was smaller than Harley and could not carry the heavy calf as far as his brother. Both boys often slipped, falling into the shallow creek with the calf tumbling on top of them. It took the two of them to lift the calf from the slippery bottom. When they finally made it back to the bridge, they grabbed their shoes, put them on, and rushed up the gravel lane, carrying the lost calf to Mr. Tierney. They were as excited about finding it as they were about the five-dollar reward.

Mr. Tierney was busy tossing hay from his wagon for his cows when he realized the shouting boys were carrying a calf. He threw down his pitchfork and ran excitedly toward them. As Mr. Tierney approached, his pace slowed dramatically. Then he stopped and stared at the weak calf. He walked over to Harley, took the calf, and set it down to inspect it for broken bones, massaging it to help perk it up.

"Boys, I hate to tell you this, but this is not my calf," he said dejectedly, looking up at the boys.

"Sure it is," Harley countered. "Look at him."

"Harley, this is a Holstein calf. My cows are all Herefords."

"I don't understand," Carmel said. "You lost a calf, and we found it."

"I wish it were that simple, Carmel," Mr. Tierney replied. "I raise Hereford cows. They are beef cattle; this is a Holstein breed of cattle, usually used for milking. It's probably Karly Clemens's calf; he has the only dairy farm around here."

"But…" Carmel started to say, but then Harley grabbed his arm and shook his head.

"Do you think Mr. Clemens would pay us for finding his calf?" Harley asked.

"Don't know. I can't speak for Karly," Mr. Tierney answered.

"So, we don't get a reward for bringing that calf back here," Carmel said disappointedly.

Mr. Tierney rose and put his hand in his back pocket.

"I'll tell you what I will do," he said, seeing the disappointment in the boys' faces. "I'm going to pay you one dollar each for trying to find my calf. I'll take the calf to Karly Clemens this evening on my way to the farm store. I promise to put in a few good words for you boys and see if he will pay you something for finding his calf. Just remember, I can't promise Karly will pay you anything."

He pulled out two dollars from his wallet and gave each of them one with a smile on his face.

"Thank you, Mr. Tierney," Harley said, and then he poked Carmel in the ribs after a moment of silence.

"Thank you, Mr. Tierney," Carmel said grudgingly.

"I'm sorry, boys. I appreciate you spending all the time and hard work you put into trying to find my calf. I wish it were my calf that you found."

"Thanks, Mr. Tierney," Harley replied, pulling Carmel by the arm.

They walked in silence down Mr. Tierney's lane. When they reached the bridge close to the road, Carmel said, "Harley, do you believe him?"

"No, I don't, Carmel."

"I'm not sure about his story, either," Carmel added.

"Yeah. How come Mr. Tierney didn't tell us what kind of calf he lost before agreeing to pay us?"

"How many calves get lost in a creek, Harley?"

"You saw how happy he was at first. He knew it was his," Harley said with a tinge of anger.

"That's his calf, alright, Harley. He's just trying to cheat us out of our money."

"I think you're right, Carmel. Did you notice his smile when he gave us that dollar?"

"I did. It was like he was gloating that he cheated us!"

"I bet he never had any intention of paying us five dollars in the first place. That's the last time I clean his barn!"

"We ought to sneak back up there and mess it up," Carmel suggested angrily.

"Naw, we can't do that, Carmel. But we can tell everyone else what he did."

"I certainly will. Everybody needs to know what a cheat Mr. Tierney is."

"Yeah, we need to tell everyone else so that they won't get cheated, too."

The two brothers fumed all the way home, vilifying Mr. Tierney with every step.

By mid-July, the boys' anger with Mr. Tierney continued to fester. They had not heard from Mr. Tierney after his "supposed" meeting with Karly Clemens. They now felt certain they had been duped.

Saturday morning, late July, the two brothers were playing baseball in a pick-up game on the sandlot with several other boys, including me, Colby, Elbie, and Anna Lee. Our team was at bat, and Harley and Carmel were sitting on the bench next to me and my three amigos when they told us the story about searching for Mr. Tierney's calf.

"Razz, Mr. Tierney's a crook," Harley said after finishing the story.

"Don't any of you guys do anything for him because he will cheat you out of every penny that he owes you," Carmel insisted. "A crook is too kind of a word for him."

"The worst part of it was he gloated right there in front of us when he cheated us, knowing all along he could get away with it," Harley continued.

"They should put a crook like that in jail," Carmel added.

"Wow, I always thought Mr. Tierney was a nice man," Elbie said, shaking his head.

"Well, he's not!" Harley responded.

"That's strange," Anna Lee said. "I helped him once, and he paid me just as he promised. Are you sure it was his calf?"

"Without a doubt," Carmel said. "I wouldn't have believed it either if it didn't happen to us, but it did."

"Was the calf black and white?" I asked Harley.

"Yeah, but what difference does that make?"

"Well, a Holstein is the only breed around here that is black and white. Mr. Tierney doesn't have a dairy farm, but I suppose that doesn't mean he couldn't own some Holsteins. I would want to be certain about it first, though."

"It was his calf, alright," Carmel insisted. "You should have seen how he ran to it when we carried it up the lane. Then he checked it out real good and petted it like it was his kid."

"Razz, I'd bet a hundred dollars if we went out there right now, we would see that calf romping about with its mother," Harley added.

"Maybe," I said, "but it would be interesting to know for certain if he had any Holsteins in his pasture. Maybe you should go back out there to see if that calf is on his farm."

"Well, you can go out there if you want," Carmel said gruffly. "Just be prepared for him to cheat you out of something when you go."

One dark, late-October evening, about five thirty, a persistent cold rain breached all proper etiquette by overstaying its welcome long before lunchtime. The light rain started just before dawn that morning and continued throughout the day, varying only in its intensity. It didn't matter; heavy or light, a cold October rain chills to the bone, causing one to wonder if a wintry snow might be the better of the two insufferable evils.

Just before dinnertime, someone knocked on Harley and Carmel's front door. Their mom, sitting at the kitchen table, put down the shirt she was mending and answered it.

"Well, Karly, what are you doing way out here?" she asked, surprised.

"Just taking care of some business. How are you doing, Dorothy?"

"Oh, I'm fine. I wish we could have gotten some of this rain back in August."

"You and me both. My pasture dried up by the middle of August. It seems we got all our rain in June and then it quit raining until now," he answered, turning back to look at the pouring rain.

"What can I do for you, Karly?"

"Are your boys here?"

"They're in the back room. Come in, and I'll get them. Do you want some coffee?"

"No, I'm fine. Thanks."

She walked from the kitchen to the back room and told the boys that someone was there to see them. Harley and Carmel walked in, wondering which one of their friends was foolish enough to come over on a night like this.

"Hello, boys," Karly Clemens greeted as the brothers came into the kitchen.

"Hi, Mr. Clemens," they responded, completely surprised.

"This is for you." Karly said, then handed each of them fifteen dollars.

"Joe Tierney brought me a lost calf of mine back in June. He said you boys spent a lot of time and hard work finding it and said he knew you would appreciate a reward if I could afford it. I told him I was tight on money right then but, when I sold the calf in the fall, I would give you boys half of what I got for selling it. I know that pleased Joe a lot as he thinks highly of you two boys. He really bragged about what a fine job you did cleaning his barn. Anyway, I sold my calf at the market this afternoon for sixty dollars. That's your share."

They thanked him generously, trying to hide the shame from their faces. After he left, they both stood there, dumbfounded for a moment, staring at their money.

"Sit down, boys," their mother instructed sternly. "I've been studying your faces since the day you were born. You might have fooled Karly Clemens, but you can't fool me. That's more money than I have. Normally, your eyes would pop right out of your head, and you would be celebrating until tomorrow if someone gave you that much money. But you two are as guilty about something as Cain was with Abel. So, you sit down right here and tell me what is going on."

They both squirmed in their chairs for a minute. Finally, Carmel said, "Well...we..."

"Be quiet. You are getting ready to tell me a fib, and I just saved you a terrible punishment. Harley, you have one chance to tell the truth, or I am going to take that money away from you and buy me a couple of nice dresses, a pretty hat, and some shiny high-heeled shoes. Now, what is going on?"

Harley took a deep breath and told her the entire story as she sat motionless, not saying a word. After he finished, they lowered their heads, expecting the worst. Their mother sat quietly with her hands folded in her lap for several minutes.

"How many people did you tell that Mr. Tierney was a crook?"

"I don't know, maybe ten?" Harley guessed.

Their mom rose, walked to the cabinet drawer, and returned with two pieces of paper and two pencils.

"Give me your fifteen dollars."

They handed the money over to her, knowing that was the last they would ever see of it.

"Now, all three of us know that ten is the wrong answer. If you don't want to see me walking around here tomorrow with a new dress and fancy shoes, you better give me the names of every person you spoke disparagingly to about Mr. Tierney."

It took the boys fifteen minutes to recollect everyone they'd told their story about Mr. Tierney. They wrote down each name and then put down their pencils. Their mother finally spoke after a long, excruciating silence, and both boys winced, knowing their punishment would be severe. However, she did so in a calm, quiet voice, but with an unmistakable sternness that captivated the attention of the two contrite brothers.

"When you speak, the words spoken reflect who you are, and once spoken, you can never take them back. If you disparage someone, you are telling everyone you are a person who

84

disparages others. If you speak falsely, you are telling people you are a person who speaks falsely.

"You did two things wrong here; first, you assumed something without checking to see if it was true. Then you spoke as if it were a proven fact.

"Second, you disparaged another person, damaging his name and character. Whether it is assumed or factual doesn't matter; you should never, ever, disparage another, at any time, for any reason, period! If you do, you are telling others that you are a person who likes to disparage others and damage their name. Is that what you want others to think of you? Is that what you want to think of yourself? I am going to tape these lists of names on the wall. Every day, when you come home, I want each of you to put your initials by the name of anyone you apologized to for speaking untruths and told what a good man Mr. Tierney really is. Do you understand that?"

"Yes," they both replied submissively.
"When you both have initialed every name on this list, I will give you your fifteen dollars back. But if I find out that you put your initials by a name on the list and didn't give that person a sincere apology or reaffirm the kindness of Mr. Tierney's character, I will personally march you over to Mr. Tierney's house, and you will tell him what you did. Got it?"

In the first week of November, Harley and Carmel pulled me off to the side and apologized to me, explaining the truth about what Mr. Tierney had done for them. I could see it hurt them to do that, so I tried to pick them up a bit.

"Guys, it means a lot that you think enough of me to tell me the truth. I don't know if I would have enough courage to do it, so I respect you for that."

"Thanks, Razz. It's been tough telling everyone. Not everybody has been as nice about it as you," Harley said.

"You guys have a great mom. You guys are great, too, just like she is."

They smiled sheepishly, and we all headed to the lunchroom.

I guess they whittled that list down and eventually told everyone the true story, that Mr. Tierney and Mr. Clemens had given each of them a total of sixteen dollars for finding that calf. As a matter of fact, they tried to tell some of us two or three times.

Now, I don't want to assume anything, because I don't know this for a fact, but I think those two boys gave some of their money back to their mom. I noticed one Sunday in church that their mom was wearing a brand-new, pretty dress and acting mighty proud of her two sons.

Chapter XI

1964

Tywhoppity Bottoms

We loved mystery stories about people or places that weren't completely understood or possessed even the slightest differences from our ordinary, simple life. But the stories of Tywhoppity Bottoms, a large bottomland area sitting on both sides of Panther Creek, were as colorful as they were captivating. The mere mention of Tywhoppity Bottoms aroused fear and intrigue in every one of us; young and old alike.

Most people said Panther Creek was just a gallon of water short of being a river. The annual spring rains always proved too much for its deficient banks, resulting in extensive flooding of the entire bottomland. Back then, the bottoms were mostly wooded, full of deer, rabbits, coyotes, and even a lone black panther, most likely the last survivor of the many who had once inhabited the area. There were a small number of homes in the bottoms, or more specifically, shacks built on stilts high above the ground to avoid the spring floods. The few people who lived in Tywhoppity Bottoms had small john boats tied to their homes to help navigate the deep, cold water when the creek rose.

There were many stories, most of them ill-natured and unfounded, maligning the peculiar people who lived in the bottoms. Some people were even afraid to go down there. They said you didn't go down to Tywhoppity Bottoms unless you lived there or knew someone who did. I could not vouch for the accuracy of those stories as I had never been there, but this is a true story that happened to me.

There was a man named Cleevie who lived in Tywhoppity Bottoms. He was a tall drink of water, as everyone described him.

87

Folks said he was over seven feet tall, but no one knew for sure because he wouldn't let anyone measure him. His bushy beard of mingled red, brown, and gray hair and his large feet gave him the appearance of a giant. Some said he was of Saskatchewan descent, and others said he was half-man, half-Bigfoot. Other stories described him as a witch or sorcerer, and some even claimed he was a cannibal, an unproven conjecture as anyone who entered his property supposedly never came out alive. For reasons unknown, he lived alone, far from the other Tywhoppity denizens. He most likely survived by hunting game, catching fish, and eating off the land, as no one ever recollected him coming to town for anything. It didn't matter whether any of the stories were true; boys my age were enthralled with each account of him, and of course, we were too afraid of him to get close enough to find out any different.

I remember the day some friends and I were walking along the ridge above Tywhoppity Bottoms. It was an unusually warm, sunny February day, and after a bitterly cold January, it was refreshing to be outdoors, especially in the woods. When we were younger, we pretended to be explorers, like Davy Crockett or Jim Bowie, but at thirteen, a hike through the woods was a good time to swap stories or just be boys. Either way, it was easy to forget about time or where you were, so it was no surprise that we got caught up in it, not realizing how far we were from home.

We stopped and briefly enjoyed a conversation of whether to turn back or not when Elbie interrupted in a hushed tone, "Look! Over there!"

He pointed to an area off to the east, far down the ridge. We turned to see a beautiful albino deer, standing as stately as a thoroughbred and staring at us as a king would at a trespassing pauper. We counted at least eighteen points on his majestic rack. None of us had ever seen an albino deer before, and his clean white appearance contrasted with the browns and greens of the forest, creating a surreal picture of mythical eloquence. With its pure white hair and not even the tiniest speck of dirt blemishing its coat, it was the prettiest animal any of us had ever seen. The minutes seemed to stand still, just us staring at him and him at us. It reminded me of a group of tourists standing silently in awe before a revered painting inside a famous museum. Then, as if he'd suddenly grown tired of us, he turned his head in a brief show of arrogance. Without a sound, he leaped, almost in slow motion, silently disappearing into the mystical woods before touching the ground again.

"Wow! That's beautiful," Colby whispered

Without thinking, I urged in a soft voice, "Let's follow him," and off we went.

The deer toyed with us, staying close enough to encourage the chase but never letting us draw closer, either. We could see this beautiful white creature gliding effortlessly through the forest, adeptly navigating his way through the trees and branches. After a few moments, he sped up a little faster as if he were testing our stamina. Occasionally he would stop and turn his head smugly toward us as if he were mocking us. I picked up speed, trying to keep up with him, fighting the weariness growing within my legs, but the excitement of the chase kept me going.

Several minutes later, this magnificent deer took it up a notch, running even faster, displaying the confidence of his superiority. I ran with all the speed and energy I had, trying to keep up. But it was to no avail as the deer knew I was no match for him and quickly lost interest in me. He drifted off into the thickness of the forest, and I gladly gave up the chase, desperately gasping for air.

I turned to look at my friends to clamor over the excitement, but I was alone. I had no idea when or where we had become separated, and to make matters worse, I didn't even know where I was. None of the surroundings were familiar, and I felt an eerie sense that I should not be there. I was no longer on the ridge but resting on flat ground. The trees were mostly sycamore and cedar, with a few large black oaks towering magnificently above all else. The area was littered with massive limestone boulders as if they had been picked up from a faraway place and scattered randomly for no other reason than a momentary whim. I could see the high-water marks halfway up the boulders, about shoulder high for me, from the most recent flooding. The crisp, dry leaves on the ground, coated with dried mud from the receding waters, bore no resemblance to their former proud state, swaying high in the trees with each gentle breeze. An owl woke from his afternoon nap with a lazy hoot, a waste of effort that served no purpose other than to ineffectually break the silence.

Oh no, I thought. *I'm in Tywhoppity Bottoms.*

My heart raced, filled with fear, and I had no idea which direction to go. If I went the wrong way, I could end up meeting some stranger who might not appreciate my being there and have me hung for trespassing. I decided to head back in a westerly direction, running as fast as my weary legs would carry me. Already exhausted from the chase, I tired quickly with each step and began gasping for air again. I felt my right foot hit a root or a vine concealed beneath the crusty leaves, and I fell headfirst into a limestone rock the size of a bushel basket. That is the last thing I remember.

I felt something tugging at me. I awoke lying on the side of the familiar road to my house. Mr. Higdon, a neighbor, was leaning over me, helping me up off the ground. As he helped me into the back seat of his blue '57 Chevy, I could tell it was early morning. He closed the door, and I glanced back at the woods, over two hundred yards away, and noticed we were alone.

"Where have you been, boy?" he asked. "We've been searching the woods for twenty-four hours."

"I don't remember," I replied.

"Well, I don't know who fixed you up, but that is a nasty gash on your head. I have never seen bandages like that before. It looks like a conglomeration of weeds and some kind of homemade ointment. It seems to be healing up okay, though. You go to a witch doctor to fix that up?" he joked.

"I…I don't remember."

Mr. Higdon turned his head over to the back seat and stared at me with a puzzled look on his face. "Your friends were sure worried about you. They thought you were dead." He turned his eyes back to the road. "Everyone has been searching the woods for you."

I looked out the window and began to recall a dream I'd had after hitting my head on the rock. I'd dreamed I was lying on a strange bed, very narrow, but almost long enough to hold two men. There was no headboard or footboard, and it was supported by a wooden box or something similar, with just a few blankets laid on top as a mattress. An exceptionally tall man with a full, long beard appeared and came over to my side to look at a cut on my head. He was very gentle and had a warm smile that made me feel safe. He rolled something in his hands and then rubbed it gently on my head without a word passed between us. He looked at me with a kindness that helped me relax and fall asleep.

There was a very brief period after that when I awoke alone in the small room. I turned to see where I was only to find myself in a one-room structure with just a tiny, wood-fed iron stove and a small, four-foot-tall, rusted refrigerator next to a table with one chair. A large metal bowl rested on top of an old, faded three-drawer chest. One of the drawers was slightly ajar, with a dishtowel hanging from it to dry. A two-and-a-half-gallon galvanized pail, partially full of water, sat on the floor beside the chest. Several knives, a fork, and other utensils had been placed neatly in a row next to the metal bowl on top.

I noticed in a corner some books stacked on the floor beside a thick, nearly three-foot-tall log standing on its end with a worn, flat pillow resting on top. It was a relatively clean room with little else on the wooden floors and walls other than several hooks placed high on one wall by the wooden door. Two long, ragged jeans, a shirt, and a jacket hung from the hooks beside a very stained and frayed straw hat on the last hook. A small stepping rug lay on the floor next to the windowless door. I remember nothing else until Mr. Higdon woke me.

When I returned to school, everyone wanted to hear my story. Everyone said I was lucky to be alive and that it was a miracle that none of those people from Tywhoppity Bottoms had found me, because they would have surely left me for dead, or worse.

I've always thought, though, that maybe it was a miracle that one of those people from Tywhoppity Bottoms did find me and that is why I am alive today.

Over forty years later, I decided to go down to that part of Tywhoppity Bottoms. No one lived there anymore. I'd heard that the March flood of '64 had submerged even the tallest of the homes in Tywhoppity Bottoms and that the inhabitants, having lost everything, had never returned. The few remaining stilt shacks sat empty and rotting, while others had given up and tumbled to the ground, half-covered with mud and leaves. The years of flooding and falling leaves had erased most signs that life had ever existed there. I supposed that everything not bolted down had been carried away by the creek currents or sunk deep into the soft ground.

I left the area and headed back to the road several miles away. About a third of the way back, I noticed far off in the distance one wooden shack atop four large wooden poles about eight feet off the ground. I walked over to it, wondering why it was so far away from the others. When I reached the deserted shanty, I climbed up, wary of it crumbling beneath me, and peered into the decaying one-room house. Part of the old, rotting roof had fallen onto the floor, and I doubted that anyone could explain how the other half of the roof remained in place. A couple of rusting pans lay in a far corner, and a few books covered with mildew, or what had once been books, sat scattered in the opposite corner, next to the rusted remnants of some metal food cans. There were bits and pieces of other items, mostly indiscernible, littered on the floor among the leaves and dust.

Over in another corner, against the wall, was a once-sturdy wooden platform made with short, four-inch-diameter log posts and several two-by-six braces, each ten feet long. It had suffered dearly from the elements, barely able to support the moss and mildew covering it. It appeared to have once been a bed, but the ten-foot length was puzzling. The years of rain and weather had left it barely able to stand on its own, and it patiently waited for the next breath of wind to send it toppling over. I somehow sensed that this had been a peaceful home at one time, filled with kindness and gentleness. I softly rubbed the remnants of the scar on my forehead and whispered, "Thank you."

I climbed down the rickety ladder, unsure if it would disintegrate before I reached the ground. Despite some uncertain moments, I safely reached the ground, and as I turned to leave, something caught my eye. There, a hundred feet away, stood a beautiful albino deer staring fearlessly at me. He nodded his majestic head and shook his huge rack as if he were saying goodbye, and then he quickly disappeared like a magical spirit into the forest.

I no longer listen to postulated stories of people I have never met. Most of those stories are tainted with other people's opinions that I've often found bear no resemblance to fact. I also regret never getting to know any of the people of Tywhoppity Bottoms. I will never have that opportunity now.

93

One at a time, they all silently disappeared into the forest, taking with them all they owned and all they knew, just like the albino deer.

Chapter XII

1964

The Entrepreneurs

In 1964, it seemed someone, or something, had lit a fire under Colby's feet. He curiously developed a burning desire to be successful and was always scheming to start a business or endeavor of some type. He devoured any book he could get his hands on, especially those on finance, engineering, and aviation. When I asked why he was reading all those books, he simply replied, "One cannot have too much knowledge." I did not have the fire in my belly that he did, but his contagious and endless passion often aroused my interests as well.

One day, a couple of years after Colby and I had our first encounter with cleaning a chicken coop, we had nothing to do but pass the time by sitting on a large oak log that had fallen across Pup Creek. It had been an unusually warm spring; the redbuds and dogwoods had already lost their blooms several weeks ago, and the maples and oaks were flush with leaves nearly a month earlier than in a typical year. It was mid-April, with a slight southerly breeze and a balmy seventy-eight degrees instead of the cold dogwood winter we usually experienced that time of year.

Among other subjects, we began to reminisce about the chicken coop episode. Colby suddenly got the idea that since we were now experts at cleaning chicken coops, we should start a business raising chickens. He said if we wanted to be wealthy, we needed to be entrepreneurs. Before long, he had me fired up and ready to get started.

"Razz, what we need to do is raise the chicks for about twenty weeks. By July, we could have at least a couple of dozen adult chickens to sell," he said excitedly. "We would keep a few to hatch more chicks, so our investment would just keep on paying off."

"You don't want to sell the eggs?" I asked curiously.

"No, no. Eggs are about fifteen cents a dozen. But we could sell a grown hen for about two dollars and a rooster for three."

"Colby, two dozen chickens at two dollars each would be forty-eight dollars! We will be rich!"

And with that, we were off to Colby's house to tell his dad. We knew he would be proud of our idea to help us all get rich, and we hurried as fast as we could back to his house.

"Ma!" Colby yelled out to his mother, who was turning over the soft soil in the garden with her shovel. "Where's Dad?"

"He'll be home soon. He had a job helping Mr. Mattingly put up a fence," she replied. "What are you so stirred up about, Colby?"

"Nothing, Ma."

Colby wasn't one to waste any time once he got fired up about something, and he knew his mom would want to hear all the details. Knowing he could explain them to her later, he motioned for me to follow as he bolted down the road, hoping to meet his dad as he returned home from Mr. Mattingly's. We met him about a mile from Colby's house, carrying his wooden toolbox in one hand and holding a post hole digger with the other, balancing it across his shoulder.

We walked alongside him the rest of the way home, explaining our idea to be entrepreneurs. Of course, as usual, Colby's dad was a bit more pragmatic, but he didn't want to discourage our spirit.

"Boys, are you willing to put in the work necessary to own a business? It will take most of your time. No more time for playing."

"Yes, sir," we both replied enthusiastically.

"How are you going to raise these chickens, and where?"

We hadn't thought of that.

"You will need a coop and a fenced area for them to forage. Who is going to pay for that? Who will pay for their feed, the fence, and wood and nails for the coop?"

He could see our hopes deflating.

"Don't give up, boys, but you first need to plan for all these things, so you will know the expenses that are going to offset your profits."

"I can see if my dad will loan us the money to get started," I suggested.

"Well, if Razz's dad will spot us the money, maybe you can show us how to build the fence and coop," Colby added.

"That might work if you can manage all that," his dad replied. "However, anyone can raise a few ordinary chickens. You can't make any money doing that. But now, if you had a rare breed of chickens, one that is favorable to two inexperienced boys raising them, you might make a go of it." He thought for a moment and then added, "What you need is some EOs to get started. Not many of that breed around here, though."

"EOs?" we asked. We just thought chickens were chickens.

"Euskar Oiloa. They are a Spanish breed of Basque hens. They are friendly little fellas and very curious, especially with shiny objects. They're confident, very nosy, and easy to tame. Pretty intelligent, too, for a chicken, anyway."

"What do they look like?" I asked.

"Oh, they are a striking breed," he explained. "The cocks have a large bright red comb, and the hens have light cream and light brown speckled feathers with a few light black speckled feathers mixed in with the others. Their long tail is full of light gray and light black feathers, giving them a regal appearance. They are an easy breed to care for if you will commit to it, and

97

since there are very few of them in these parts, you might find a profitable market for them."

"Yeah, that's what we want. Where can we get some?" I asked.

"The only man around here that might have a few to sell is Shae."

Now, he could have said any other name, and that would have been fine with us. But Shae was not a man you would want to see or meet. Everyone called him Shae, but that was assumed to be his last name. No one knew for sure, and none of us possessed the courage to ask. He lived like a hermit down on the banks of the Ohio River. There was talk about his place, but very few people went down there; had no reason to and most certainly didn't want to. He was a contrary older man, probably in his fifties, but it was hard to tell as he had a full beard as long as a fox's tail and a head of hair that received a combing maybe once a month when he bathed, if that often. He came to town occasionally, but the stench he carried kept all but the bravest of souls at bay. The few fools who asked any questions of him would only commit that error once after incurring his low, animal-like growl and a stare from those dark brown eyes that instilled an immense fear in any man and certainly would forever stunt the growth of a young boy.

A couple of hunters once drifted onto his property accidentally and suddenly found themselves hunted by an angry Shae brandishing his loaded shotgun. He was eager to unleash a flurry of pellets on those poor souls, who either were oblivious to the "No Trespassing!!!" signs or had foolishly disregarded them. But those hunters, who'd miraculously escaped their imminent death from the hands of a violated Shae, were able to give scant insight into his homestead. They'd never gotten close to his home as Shae had found them well before in the darkened canopy consisting of scraggly sycamore, pine, and hemlock trees. In many areas there, wild grapevines crept to the top of the trees, blocking out the sun completely. Although they'd still been far from his homestead when he'd found them, they said they'd heard a cacophony of animal noises from creatures that were most likely caged up by Shae. Some suggested there might even be some people caged up there, too.

"Pa," Colby objected fearfully, "Shae would surely kill us before we got halfway down his road."

"Mister Harris," was all I could get out, horrified at the mere thought of us going to see Shae.

"Now, boys, I wouldn't send you down there if I thought there was any danger. I know Shae. You tell him I'm your dad, and he won't hurt you. If you boys are going to go into business, there will be a lot of things you will have to do that you don't want. You better start getting used to it. But first, you go over Ed Mattingly's place and see if he has any chicken fencing left. He owes me a debt, so see what he has. After that, Razz, talk to your dad to see if he could lend you seven dollars. You will need that to buy two hens and a rooster from Shae. There probably won't be enough daylight to go to Shae's place today and be back here before dark, so plan on heading out early in the morning. You will have to get there before eleven, or you will have to wait until late afternoon when he gets back from trapping."

Neither of us had ever experienced a more contrasting mix of emotions than what we carried after talking to Mister Harris. We were excited, both of us brimming with enthusiasm over starting a business, but the mere thought of going to Shae's place alone sent shivers of fear from head to toe.

First, we went to Ed Mattingly's place. It was a couple of miles down the road and took just a little over twenty minutes to get there. We walked up to the front yard from the gravel road. It was a beautiful, immaculate yard with the flower beds sprouting peonies and roses, each with several nascent buds making an early appearance. The Easter lilies and hyacinths had completed their display back in March and were now showing their first signs of dormancy. The lawn was dissected precisely in the middle by a narrow concrete walkway to the porch, and the recently mowed grass possessed only a very few weeds disturbing the deep green fescue. We had never seen a lawn so manicured, nor grass mowed in April, as most people in the country didn't have time to mow the lawn until mid-May, after planting season. Colby was too excited to pay attention to any of that and started walking across the plush, green grass on his way to the porch.

"Colby!" I scolded quietly. "These folks may not like you walking on their grass."

"What?" he responded incredulously. "Whoever heard of such a thing?"

"I'm just saying that folks who would take this much care of their yard and put in a sidewalk probably prefer to keep people off the grass."

Colby looked curiously down at his feet on the green grass.

"Razz, that's about the dumbest thing I ever heard you say."

"Don't you worry about that, son." It was Mrs. Mattingly, standing inside the screen door. "It's alright, Colby. What do you boys want?"

Before we could reply, a tiny dog, not much bigger than a man's boot, ran to her side, yapping so fast I thought he might start convulsing. We always called them city dogs because there wasn't much use for them in the country. They couldn't chase a rabbit or outrun an opossum, and they were so small a bobcat or coyote would be licking their chops for a delightful snack if they ever got close to one. But there he was, and inside the house at that. Back then, folks would shoo, stomp, and grab a broom handle to chase any dog that possessed enough audacity to slide his nose in the crack of the door, if even for just a sniff.

"Will that little fella bite, ma'am?" Colby asked, stepping back a bit.

100

"Oh, no." She laughed. "Precious wouldn't hurt a flea. He has never bitten anyone."

By now, the little imp was jumping at the screen door, frantically trying to get out at us. If he hadn't been so tiny, the constant yapping would have almost sounded menacing.

"Are you sure he won't bite, Mrs. Mattingly?" I asked.

"Oh, I promise." She giggled. "You boys don't have to worry about little Precious."

With that, she opened the door to step outside, but before she even had one foot on the porch, that dog had my pants leg in a death grip between his teeth, pulling with all his might to topple me.

"I thought you said he wouldn't bite?" I said, slightly irritated.

"He's not biting, son; he's just playing."

"Well, Mrs. Mattingly, would you mind telling him I don't want to play?" I pleaded, trying to break free of the tenacious little critter.

"Precious," she scolded, "get back in the house."

With that, the little dog let loose of my pants leg and scurried obediently back into the house.

"Now, what is it you boys want?"

"We need some chicken fencing and hoped Mr. Mattingly had some to spare," Colby replied.

"Well, he is in the back in the garden. Go on around. I'm sure if he has some to spare, he will give it to you."

Mr. Mattingly did have some chicken wire and was happy to give it to Colby. We took it back to Colby's house and then headed off to see my dad. After explaining our plan to make money, he thought for a bit and then agreed to lend us ten dollars and some scrap wood for the coop. The ten dollars should be enough to buy two hens and a rooster, with enough left to pay for the feed until we sold the matured chicks.

However, we did have to entertain his lecture on being businessmen. My dad made us sign a note to pay back the ten dollars. I couldn't figure that one out, as we both knew he would make me pay back the ten dollars one way or another if our venture failed. He finally explained that even family should keep best practices when doing business. I think it was just his usual way of trying to teach another lesson.

He drove us back to Colby's place with the wood in the back of his truck.

When we arrived, there were about four hours of daylight left. Colby, his dad, my dad, and I all pitched in and built the finest chicken coop you ever saw. It sat proudly in the middle of a twenty-by-twenty-foot pen made from Mr. Mattingly's fencing. Colby and I were feeling pretty good right then, being big entrepreneurs and all, and had forgotten about the next part: a trip to Shae's alone. I heard my dad ask Mister Harris if he were sure we would be okay going to Shae's. Mr. Harris quietly said something to him that I couldn't make out, but my dad nodded and shook his hand. It was too late to start now, so we scheduled the trip for an early-morning departure.

Neither of us slept much that night. I tossed and turned so many times my head spun like a dime on a glass table. The few times I did drift asleep, I awoke quickly in a panic, sweating from a nightmare involving Shae in one frightening trial or another. Aside from that, we had heavy rain and strong winds that woke me several times.

The next morning, I rose early for a quick breakfast as the sun began its ascent, barely peeping over the trees at six thirty. I gathered my things and headed off on my bike to Colby's place a few minutes before seven. It is not easy to ride a bike on a gravel road, especially in the spring. Most of the gravel on county roads sinks into the ground over winter where the tire tracks are, making for a reasonably smooth ride. But in the places where the gravel is thick, it's just best to get off and walk. Small bike tires are no match for loose gravel and will abruptly slip out from under you, sending you and the bike skidding across the rough road.

I made it to Colby's about a quarter to eight, and he stood in the yard with his bike, anxiously waiting for me. We took a deep breath, got on our bikes, and headed off to Shae's place, certain this was not going to go well. The journey was long as we had to leave Daviess County and go all the way through Hancock County and part of Breckenridge County.

After finally reaching Breckenridge County, we were eager to find the road to Shae's. The trip seemed to be taking longer than we thought, and we wondered if we hadn't already passed it up. We noticed a car approaching us from the east and decided to flag it down for directions. We stopped and waited for it to reach us. As it drew near, we could tell it was an old, faded green 1951 Ford truck, half-covered with mud. With the mud almost completely covering the whitewall tires, one could barely tell they were whitewall tires at all. The driver's arm rested on his open window, with the elbow and most of his arm outside, taking advantage of the wind. We flagged him down, and he came to a slow stop. He looked at us curiously, without a greeting.

"Hi," I said, "are you from around here."

"Who wants to know?" he asked suspiciously, his eyes examining our bikes.

"My friend Colby and I are trying to find Shae's place. Do you know if we are going in the right direction?"

"Shae!!!" he shouted, taken aback, his eyes widening. "What business do you boys have with Shae?"

"We need to buy some chickens," I responded.

"Boys, you don't know what you are doing," he warned. "You don't go to Shae's for anything."

"We are from Daviess County, sir," I explained. "Shae has a certain breed of chicken we need."

He looked at us as if we were fools, rolled his eyes, and laughed in disbelief.

"Okay… you keep following this road a little ways down yonder," he said, pointing his left thumb back from where he'd come. "When you get to the bottom of a long, steep hill, you keep going on a bit more past Addison and then turn left on the gravel road. Keep going down the hill on that road until you reach the bottoms. You'll see a sign on the left beside a dirt road. Now, you listen to me. You heed the words on that sign. Don't you boys be goin' down that road to Shae's. You hear me? No chicken is worth what you will find down there." He began to sound angry. "You best turn your bikes now and go back home to Daviess County."

With that, he put his truck in gear, continued down the road, and never looked back. I looked at Colby, gathered some courage, and silently took off toward Shae's, and Colby reluctantly followed me.

When we got to Old River Road, the gravel road the man in the truck had mentioned, we slowed our pace. Old River Road might have been a graveled road at one time, but there was little gravel left. The County Road Department didn't gravel any roads in this part of the county until July, long after they had tended to all the others. Most of the gravel from last year had sunk into the ground with the freezing and thawing during the winter, turning it into little more than a dirt road covered with lime dust. The rain last night had changed the dust into a layer of white mud, making it slippery to navigate on bikes, while our fenderless tires tossed splatters of white muck onto our backs and legs.

The road was full of sharp curves outlined with trees and woods just a few feet away and with no shoulder. On a bike, we could not get up much speed while navigating the narrow passage. Every hundred feet or so, we came across a dead opossum in the road.

"Where did all these dead possums come from, Razz?" Colby asked after passing the first seven or eight.

"Probably hit by a car, Colby."

"A car would have to move mighty slow on this road, Razz. Even a lazy possum would have plenty of time to get out of the way."

"I don't know." I shrugged, turning silent as we passed several more.

The thick canopy prevented even the slightest trace of sunlight from reaching the road. The steepening hills on our right indicated we were getting close to the river. The Ohio River in this area was almost a mile wide or more, with moderate currents allowing one to swim close to shore, but it was too dangerous to try to swim across to the Indiana side. The nearest bridge across was over forty miles away, at Owensboro. The next was nearly a hundred miles to the East, in Louisville. So, to us, looking across the river here was almost like staring into a foreign country.

We entered an opening in the canopy to see a beautiful but small meadow. The sunlight thrust its rays downward, filling the area with brilliant light. Closer to the river was a wetland full of wildlife such as deer, possums, raccoons, coyotes, and rabbits, not to mention the snakes and other little critters. We saw an enormous bald eagle, with its incredibly long wingspan, floating effortlessly high in the sky, scanning the river for fish. That momentarily took our minds off Shae, as bald eagles were rare back home, and we sat in awe of how beautiful and large it was. The river glistened under the midday sun, appearing to be alive with its millions of tiny silver ripples. We lived only a little less than forty miles from Shae's place, but this was a world we had never seen.

We continued, reentering the forest and the thick canopy. From that point, we felt we were entering a lost continent, or at least a haunted forest. The forest seemed much darker, and the

105

road narrowed without a trace of gravel. Wild grape vines and other vegetation found the bare road alluring and stretched their tentacles, hoping to reclaim the lost ground. The trees, however, struggled for life, and there wasn't a respectable one among the lot.

Directly ahead, on the left side of the road, we noticed a side road or possibly a lane to a homestead. As we approached, we saw a small sign made of an unevenly cut, eight-inch-wide wood plank shoved into the ground for all to see. Two simple words had been hastily painted on the rotting, weathered wood many years ago:

KEEP OUT!

"Razz, let's go home," Colby whispered fearfully as he began to turn his bike around.

"No," I said, grabbing his bike handle. "We have to do this."

Both of us took a deep breath and stared at the dangerously narrow road, which was barely wide enough for a truck to pass, though not without brushing the tree branches that extended, unimpeded, across the lane. We tightened our grips on our handlebars and then started our descent into the abyss. The dirt road, filled with thousands of annoying tree roots that jutted freely above the ground, made for a jarring, teeth-rattling adventure. Vines and eager saplings, hoping to find a home on this narrow stretch of what they felt was free ground, only added to the difficulty.

To our inconvenience, the previous night's storm had littered the road with many small, fallen branches, none of which were broken, indicating that no one else had yet traveled the road this morning. That quickly dashed any hope that Shae would not be home, but at least the abundance of tree roots had eagerly sucked away most of the moisture, leaving only a few isolated mud holes here and there to avoid.

None of the trees deserved more than a furtive glance from even the most incompetent of botanists. Their gnarled limbs and knotted trunks, none thicker than a man's leg, created a scraggly and infirm appearance that would have caused considerable embarrassment to any of the sturdy and proud oaks back home. Poison ivy had become the most prominent vegetation demonstrating any signs of vigorous growth, and we tried to avoid it despite its defiant encroachment onto the road. Just like at home, this noxious plant displayed a relentless and vile effort to brush even the smallest patch of unprotected skin.

Half a mile down the road, maybe a little more, we came across a large ravine, at least fifteen feet deep. It appeared hurriedly washed out as if nature had grown impatient or simply given up trying to create anything of beauty in this barren place. The sandy red soil was no match for even the slightest of cloudbursts and offered no resistance to the cascading flood of water searching for the river on its way downhill. The ravine weaved aimlessly this way and that, creating an awkward spectacle unworthy of nature's other majestic efforts.

At its narrowest point, where the ravine intersected the road, a bridge, or more appropriately put, a facsimile of a bridge, was the only way to cross. Two old tree trunks stretched across, with rotting wooden planks placed across them, forming, at best, a treacherous and worrisome crossing. A few of the wooden planks were missing, leaving eight-inch gaps, making it impossible to ride a bike across. We could not fathom how Shae could safely cross this decaying bridge in his truck, but regardless of any success he might have, it was undoubtedly intimidating for us to even walk across with our bikes.

We tried to calm our nerves and decided to walk our bikes across one at a time. Colby offered to go first, possibly a false sign of courage as I genuinely think he held hopes that the bridge would crack beneath him, sending him tumbling down into the ravine, breaking a leg, and discharging him of this travail. As he stepped onto the bridge, I whispered to him to stop.

Off to the side of the road was another wooden sign, this one seemingly even older than the first, and with its post rotted away, it lay helplessly on the ground, just out of sight. I reached over to pull back the vines and undergrowth and then immediately stepped back, looking at Colby with wide eyes. He backed up to take a look. In the same crude writing, the sign read:

This means you!

We both were ready to turn around at this point, but then I remembered what Colby's dad had said.

"It's okay, Colby. When we get to Shae's, just remember to tell him who your dad is. I trust Mr. Harris."

"What if he is crazy and can't remember my dad?"

"I heard he is crazy, Colby. But if your dad said it would be alright, then it will."

"Oh boy," Colby mumbled nervously. "I hope these chickens are worth it."

With that, he crept slowly across the precarious bridge with his bike in tow. Each step was followed by the creaking and cracking of the rotting wooden planks. He couldn't see it, but with each step, dust and small fragments of wood fell precipitously to the bottom of the ravine. I suspect he heard something below him hitting the bottom, because he looked over the side.

"Don't look down, Colby!" I shouted. "You'll lose your balance."

He froze in place, turning his head back over his shoulder, toward the bridge. He hesitated for a moment and then turned back to look over into the ravine again.

"Colby!" I fussed, trying to get him to focus.

"Razz, you need to come here and look at this," he answered in a shaking but hushed voice, still not moving.

"What?"

"You need to come here."

"What is it, Colby?" I asked, not wanting to step onto the bridge with him still there.

"Razz, I ain't moving till you come here and look at this."

I sensed his fear and knew he wasn't about to move until I joined him. I took a moment to gather my courage, and then I walked beside my bike toward him. With each step, I heard the wooden planks cracking, and I was confident they were about to crumble beneath me. I also heard small pieces of the wooden planks hitting the bottom of the ravine. I lowered my head and continued until I saw his feet in front of me. I stopped and noticed he was still staring over into the ravine, silent and motionless.

I looked over the bridge, into the gorge below, and gasped. A huge boulder lay in the bend of the ravine. A large tree trunk, over two feet in diameter and at least twenty feet in length, had fallen on top of the boulder. The tree balanced itself across the massive stone, with the root end planted firmly in the narrow bottom of the ravine, constructing a small dam. There was very little water built up behind it, but the dam had created a holding place for thousands of bones and skulls stacked up in a massive pile. We recognized many of them: there were the bones of cows, dogs, deer, large bobcats, and many hundreds, if not thousands, of smaller critters, all gathered together as if it were an open burial ground. They seemed to have been thrust with a vengeance into a tangled heap in the ravine.

"Where did all these bones come from?" I asked.

"I don't know," Colby replied. "I don't even know what some of those animals are. I see a bobcat's skull over there. How did bones of wildcats end up in the same place as all these other animals and critters?"

We stared silently for a moment.

"Do you think there are human bones in there, Razz?"

"I don't recognize any," I answered, "but that doesn't mean anything."

A brief gust of wind rustled through the trees and ravine, unannounced, rattling some of the loose planks on the bridge. The noise startled me, and I bolted to the other side of the ravine with Colby right beside me. As we reached solid ground, we let go of our bikes and dropped to our knees, both of us unnerved and visibly trembling. We had crossed and were still alive and intact, but unfortunately, we were now on the other side.

"What do we do now, Colby?" I asked, realizing where we were.

"I don't know, but I'm not getting on that bridge again," Colby answered.

I turned slowly, looking down the dark road to Shae's house.

"There is only one way to go, Colby."

"Oh, Lordy me," he mumbled under his breath as he turned his head toward Shae's place.

We rose, picking up our bikes, brushed off our pants' legs, and began the descent to Shae's.

We carefully crept as quietly down the road as we could, assuming a gruesome death was imminent. Trash of every kind littered the path. We noticed other strange signs of life, such as mangled webs of rusted barbed wire, some old, rusting Burma Shave road signs nailed to a select few trees, and a dilapidated 1931 Ford truck. The truck sat fifty yards off the road, into the woods, with little metal left to hold it together. No glass remained, and only one sagging door barely held on for no apparent reason, least of which was appearance. Off in the distance, the remnants of an old abandoned liquor still sat amidst the trees and brush.

We heard the distant crowing of a rooster and the eerie cry of a male peacock. For the next ten minutes, we said nothing, walking slowly beside our bikes, submitting our fates to whatever trial or suffering lay before us. We rounded a slight bend in the road and then noticed another wooden sign nailed to a tree at the bottom of a small hill. The sounds of animals seemed much closer now, most likely just over the next crest. The paint on the sign indicated it wasn't as old as the others, but the wood was aged and weathered the same. We could make out a human skull with crossbones painted on it. As we neared the sign, we made out the words just above the skull and crossbones:

Cain't read?

We stopped for a moment, staring at the message, both of us uncertain what to do.

"Razz, you think he'll kill us?" Colby asked in a voice of resignation.

"I don't know, Colby," I answered, filled with as much fear as he carried. "Maybe something worse than death."

As we crested the hill, a scene appeared, one more bizarre than anything we had ever seen. It was a mostly cleared area, with only a few scattered trees providing a limited amount of shade. The garbage and litter scattered everywhere indicated this was Shae's place. Weathered lumber of all different sizes and cuts lay strewn about the entire area, begging for a proper stacking. Cages of different sizes held a variety of animals: dogs, a fox, rabbits, coons, a fawn barely two or three weeks old, pigs, chickens of all different colors, and a single sullen mule.

The cages and pens appeared to have been made from whatever had been handy at the time. Some were made of old metal roofing sheets and wooden planks. Others resembled a haphazard construction of rusted car hoods, sheets of rotting plywood, tree branches, fence gates, house doors with nary a speck of paint left, old car doors, rope, and anything else the river might have washed up that could restrain an unfortunate mammal. A few animals, tethered with ropes or string, lacked for a roof of any type.

The dogs were like no other we knew. Their tight-knit fur was completely black, except for the one in the back, who was all brown. They were short dogs, reaching only two or three feet in height, but were the sturdiest of any dog we had ever seen. Their muscular legs, shoulders, and neck gave them a fierce, warrior-like appearance. Neither Colby nor I could have put up much of a fight against any one of them if they chose to engage us in a fray. The preoccupied dogs were viciously devouring the indeterminable remnants of skinned animals, gnawing them down to a few bare bones for a later snack. As we passed by them, well out of reach, none bothered to bark, but each snarled menacingly, displaying their large canine teeth, not necessarily an act of intimidation, but a notice leaving no doubt they were not willing to share their meal.

There were about thirty wooden whiskey barrels cut in half, with the cut side face down on the ground and a one-foot square opening above the ground. A seven- or eight-foot string, secured to a nail on top of the barrel at one end and tied to a cock's foot on the other end kept the cocks from wandering too far. Each barrel housed a single cock, with the barrels spaced far enough apart that the cocks could not reach each other. It was illegal to fight cocks, so we weren't quite sure why he had so many.

There were hides of many different animals strung from trees throughout the area. We noticed a half-finished house with little more than the exposed framing and bare rafters. Construction had likely been stopped many years ago, leaving all the lumber and framing weathered from years of exposure to the elements.

One side, partially finished with wooden planks, was covered with coonskins stretched to dry, explaining why any effort at all had been made to nail those few planks onto the skeletal frame.

Close by, three wooden peach bushel baskets sat in a row, each filled not with peaches, but with coons that appeared to have been freshly skinned this morning, already attracting a hoard of flies.

Not far from the cages and pens sat an old beat-up blue pick-up truck with no tailgate. As we drew closer, we could see the entire bottom of the truck's bed was covered with dead opossums. We assumed that a hasty drive home in his pick-up truck, with no tailgate on the bumpy road, explained the dead opossums that had surely bounced helplessly out onto the road. Not far from his truck sat a camper about fifteen feet long and seven feet wide, just big enough for two small rooms, perhaps a bedroom, and a kitchen/living area. The exterior, clothed only with rust and mildew, had not seen the underside of a paintbrush in three or more decades. On the side facing us, three small windows still survived, yet only one possessed the dignity of having any glass. However, it was so yellowed and dirty you could not be certain of that dignity. The other two windows were even less fortunate, suffering a complete covering of worn, fraying duct tape. There were no other suitable living structures, so we assumed that it was Shae's home.

There was no sign of Shae as we moved cautiously toward the camper. All the animals grew quiet as we passed, except for some nervous hens clucking softly. Even the dogs were strangely silent. As we neared the front door, we stopped, not from fear, but from the stench reeking from the camper. I motioned for Colby to knock on the door. He reluctantly climbed the two rickety wooden steps to Shae's door, steadying himself as there were no handrails.

He closed his eyes and knocked lightly on the door.

"Colby," I whispered. "Knock louder."

"What do you boys want?!!!" growled Shae.

I jumped, and turning, I saw him standing a few feet behind me with his loaded twelve-gauge shotgun firmly in his hands. I sank to my knees, confident I would be the first one to be shot. Colby was not so lucky. He fell from the wobbly steps and landed face first in a brown puddle that, unfortunately, had not been muddied by rainwater. He slowly rolled over and looked up at Shae, whose shotgun was not far from his face.

There he was, the infamous Shae. He stood about six feet tall, but his long, wiry gray hair made him appear taller. His full beard, stretching down to his chest, was gray as well, but it was stained an odd yellowish-brown color around his mouth. Visible gray hairs grew from the inside of his ears and nose, and there was nothing about him that gave the appearance of being contaminated with a bar of soap. His bloodstained hands and arms, suffused with oil, made it appear as if he had recently murdered someone. However, it was most likely brain oil, customarily used for tanning hides, indicating we had interrupted his tanning process. His strong, sturdy body was as intimidating as his shotgun. His menacing scowl, only slightly obscured by his beard, made it evident that we were unwelcome miscreants to be reckoned with by whatever laws, if any, survived in this horrid place.

"What are you doing on my land?" he demanded, his angry voice rising.

I could not speak. The fear grabbed hold of me, strangled me, barely allowing me an occasional breath but not the luxury of uttering a single word. I looked at Colby, hoping he could tell Shae who he was, but he, too, was shaken beyond his senses.

"I, I, I…my dad is my dad!" was the best he could do.

Shae was not impressed and looked at him menacingly and then at me.

"Boys, you move an inch, and I'll stuff you in one of those peach baskets dead as the coons. This here is my property, and you are violating my rights! Who sent you here?! You better tell me why you are here, or your bones will end up in that ravine with all the other carcasses."

"My dad, my dad, my dad sent us." Colby stammered, still unable to make much sense.

Shae looked curiously at him for a moment. I was confident he was going to shoot this mumbling thirteen-year-old kid just as he would any of his animals that dared to annoy him.

"You Mose Harris's boy?" Shae snarled.

Colby nodded furiously.

"He send you here?" Shae's voice softened slightly.

Again, Colby nodded furiously.

"Get up. The two of you," Shae said in a calmer voice, lowering his gun. "Mose is a good man. Can't say that about most other people around here."

He turned and looked at me as if I were a hopeless, mangy dog in desperate need of liberation from its misery.

"You friends of Mose Harris?" he asked suspiciously.

"Yes, sir," I answered, my voice trembling.

"Boy, don't you be calling me sir!" he shot back angrily, glaring at me with a menacing scowl. Then he turned back to Colby.

"What did Mose send you here for?" he asked in a firm but softer tone.

"We are going to be entrepreneurs," Colby answered, gathering some courage. "We want to raise chickens and sell them so we can get rich."

"Why do you want to get rich? I've never met a rich man or woman that was happy. They all get greedy and forget how to be happy. There ain't never enough money, and they end up losing everything trying to get more."

"We are just trying to learn, Mr. Shae," Colby pleaded. "We want to be independent someday."

"Well, I ain't selling you boys no chickens; they'd be dead in a week. You don't know nothing about raisin' fowl. Why would I want to do that to my chickens?"

"We've been reading and learning all about raising chickens. We'll take good care of them," Colby explained.

"Reading, huh? What are you going to do when the chicks start losing weight and get diarrhea?"

"Well…" Colby replied hesitantly, "they probably got worms, so we could put a little garlic and cucumber seeds in their feed and maybe some apple cider vinegar in their water."

I was real proud of Colby right then, and I think Shae was a little surprised, too.

"Hmph," Shae mumbled from his throat, studying Colby with his piercing brown eyes, which were nearly hidden beneath his overgrown brows. "What if they got lice?"

"Um…" Shae had stumped Colby with this one.

"We could try putting some wormwood cuttings in their coop. That might help," I interjected, and I was pretty proud of myself, too. But Shae wasn't.

"I'm not talking to you, boy!" he said sharply, glowering at me, sending me back in retreat and making me regret my audacious response.

"What kind of chickens does Mose want you to buy?" he asked, turning to Colby.

"Razz and I decided on EOs. They seem to be best suited, and no one else around is raising them."

"I'm raising them, ain't I?" Shae said, raising his voice, perturbed with Colby's slack.

"Yes, but we would like to give it a try, too," Colby said, trying to make amends for his offense.

Shae studied him for a moment longer.

"EOs, huh? If Mose said that, then I'd sell you two EO hens and a rooster. Those hens will start hatching a couple of

116

dozen chicks in a few weeks. If I hear you let them chicks die, I'm comin' after you boys. The hens are two dollars apiece, and the rooster is three dollars."

"We only have ten dollars, Mister Shae, and we'll need five for feed. Can we pay you three now and another two dollars when we start selling the young hens?" Colby asked with a renewed hint of confidence.

I could have choked Colby for trying to bargain with Shae and could not figure out where he'd picked up the audacity to do so, but I said nothing. I knew Shae was going to send him to his maker, and my only chance of survival was to remain silent.

"I'll take four now and two more when you start selling the hens. That's it. Take it or leave it," Shae bargained, daring Colby to counter.

"It's a deal," Colby said confidently, reaching his hand out to Shae.

Shae shook it and turned to me.

"You part of this deal, boy?" he growled.

"Yes," I said, meekly holding out my shaking hand. Shae's strong, leather-like hand grasped mine, nearly crunching the bones. I tried my best to keep from wincing from the pain, but he knew I was hurting, and I think it pleased him some.

"Alright, then, step aside," he quickly said as he plodded up the steps to his camper.

When he opened the door, the full force of the foul stench nearly suffocated us. There were so many odors coming from inside that it was difficult to determine what they were, but there was no doubt they were all offensive.

He left the door open as he turned to his right and out of our view. The cluttered camper provided little but a small, narrow path for him to get by. Everything in it was filthy as far as we could see. Dried mud covered most of the floor in the narrow pathway. Straight ahead was a tattered bookshelf blocking the only window on the opposite side. He had hammered a nail into the side of the bookshelf to hang a pouch full of shredded tobacco and a small bag of rolling paper. A stained cloth chair with sagging cushions sat beside it, and a bare lamp with no shade rested nearby on the floor. On the top shelf sat many old, worn hardbacks containing the works of Shakespeare, Keats, Hugo, Homer, and others. The second shelf held math and physics books by Poincaré, Newton, Gauss, and Einstein. The bottom shelf contained books on aerodynamics and of political nature, by Bradley Jones, the US Army, Tocqueville, Plato, Marx, Paine, Hamilton, and Locke. At the end of that shelf sat two newer books that seemed oddly out of place from the other aged hardcovers, one written by George Orwell and the other by Mark Twain.

We heard Shae rummaging in the back room, and then his lumbering footsteps shook the entire camper. He appeared at the door, quickly descended the wooden steps with ease, and walked briskly between us with a quick, gruff instruction: "This way."

As he passed between us, I could see the hair on the back of his head was matted down where his hat had once rested. The top clearly showed the imprint of the absent cap, with the rest of his unkempt hair spread out below. The crown of his head displayed a perfectly round lily-white bald spot that seemed out of place compared to his tanned arms and face. Tucked under his arm was a box made of thin, fragile wooden slats, barely an eighth of an inch thick and with thin wiring holding them together. The wooden box was about twenty-four inches long and twelve inches in height and width, with each piece of wood separated by half an inch to allow air to flow through. The top was loosely fit, with no latch, but it wasn't going anywhere under Shae's strong arms.

He led us past the cocks as they clucked with fear and hastily retreated into or on top of their barrels. Behind them were several pens, each holding numerous chickens and chicks, all separated by their various species. The baby chicks were small enough that they could easily squeeze through the wire fence, but they hastily retreated once they found themselves distanced from their mom. There were varieties with flaming red combs, some with beautiful feathers as long as the distance from a man's elbow to the nails of his fingers. Some were short, with feathers tucked close to the body, and others were of all different shapes and colors. Then there were the EOs. The hens, with their beautiful feathers of light tan, grays, and blacks, and the stately roosters, with their strikingly large combs, made a fine species. Both mine and Colby's eyes lit up at such a creature, even if it was a chicken.

I expected Shae to go into the pen, grab three chickens by the feet, and throw them at us, demanding we get off his property or suffer a shot from his gun. But that is not how it happened.

"You boys pick out two hens and one rooster for your bizness," he said calmly to Colby, in his still gruff voice as he gently handed him the box.

We opened the gate, closed it, and stepped slowly through the pen, trying to determine which three were the perfect ones to start our enterprise. The EOs were surprisingly calm, and when we chose one and picked it up, it made little fuss, allowing us to place it into the box. When we had the two hens and the statuesque rooster safely tucked into the container, we left the pen, about as excited as any entrepreneur ever was.

I nervously gave Shae his four dollars. He counted the money twice and then reached into his pocket, pulling out the largest roll of cash I had ever seen. It was nearly as thick as a baseball and held tightly together with a thick rubber band wrapped around it. He took off the rubber band and opened the wad of cash. Mine and Colby's eyes bulged as he separated so many hundreds and fifties that we could not count them. It was the first time we had seen a hundred-dollar bill, or even a fifty-dollar bill for that matter. He put our four dollars on the bottom of the pile with the other ones in his roll, carefully placing them all right-side up and facing the same direction. Taking his rubber band from between his fingers, he wound it around the wad of cash and stuffed it back into his pocket, shoving it twice to make sure it remained safely in its home. Reaching into his other pocket, he pulled out a long piece of twine.

"Hold the box out," he instructed Colby. He tied one end of the twine to the wire support, wrapped the string around the box three times, and then tied it tightly to another support wire.

"You boys go on now and take care of those chickens. Don't you or any of your friends ever come back here. You understand?"

"We won't, Mr. Shae. Thank you," Colby answered.

We picked up our bikes, fastened the box, full of our new pride and joy, with a strap to Colby's handlebars, and walked to the hill to head home. Just as we topped the crest, I heard Shae's familiar, gruff voice.

"Hey, boy!"

I turned submissively, expecting him to chastise me again.

"You live on Free Silver Road?"

"Yes, sir," I replied, screwing up again.

"You're a long way from home. You Dominic's boy?"

"Yes, sir."

He looked at me silently for a few seconds.

"He's a good man, too, carries a kindness in his heart. You carry that, too?"

"I…I don't know."

"Figures. Most people that do never know it. That's what makes them so special," he said almost to himself. His persistent frown faded slightly, coming as close to a smile as Shae would ever get.

He turned around and tended to his animals as if we were already long gone.

I wanted to thank him, but I didn't feel he would appreciate it. Regardless, those kind words meant a lot to me and were just the medicine I needed for my bruised ego.

On our way back, we were content with ourselves, and just a few hundred feet from the main road, we began to relax from our encounter with Shae. Colby's excitement had left him a little careless, resulting in an unexpected bump into an overhanging branch. Luckily, he quickly caught his bike and kept our prized chickens from falling. He then righted his bike and shoved the kickstand with his foot so he could go back and pick up his cap.

"Don't move, Colby! It's a hornet's nest. Don't look back," I shouted to him as I saw the swarm of hornets leaving the nest he had just disturbed.

He took off running and immediately looked back to see if they were following him. They weren't until he looked back, and then a thick swarm of angry hornets began the chase, closing in on him after just a few steps. They descended upon him, inflicting a punishment no boy deserves.

A handful of vengeful hornets will get your attention in a hurry; a swarm of them, you will never forget. Their sting is like a fiery-hot nail driven into your skin with a hammer, hard enough to embed it into your bone. That is just one sting. Twenty or more can bring a grown man down. The worst part is the hurt doesn't diminish in strength for about half a day or more. The sight of poor Colby running through the trees and brush with arms desperately flailing, trying to swat the enraged hornets from his body, would have been comical to anyone who had never suffered the sting of a hornet. But I had, and I pitied him so.

After the hornets calmed down, I walked our bikes up close to the main road, making sure not to look back at the nest. I stopped just before reaching it and waited for Colby. He arrived about ten minutes later, picking out the last few hornets still stuck in his clothing. Welts of varying sizes already covered his entire body.

"Razz, I hurt," he mumbled pathetically.

"Those little fellas pack a powerful punch, Colby. I told you not to look back."

"What did that have to do with it?" he asked, annoyed.

"They're vengeful, Colby, but not smart. They didn't know who or what hit their nest until they saw you look back. If you hadn't looked back, they would have just swarmed around a bit and then calmed down. You just told them right off that you did it."

"Why didn't you help me?" he grumbled.

"Half of them stayed here to protect the nest, and if I'd taken off after you, the rest of the hornets would have hit me. The other half had already committed to you."

"This hurts something awful, Razz. I feel sick."

"Come on. We need to keep moving, or the hurt will get worse. If you want your cap, you will have to go back after it."

"Shae can have it. I'm never going back there again," Colby said defiantly.

About halfway back to Colby's house, we reached Vern Payne's place, He wasn't home, but his wife was, along with their seven kids. We stopped, hoping to get Colby some relief. Mrs. Payne told Colby to go into the other room and wash his stings with a cold rag, and she handed him some apple cider vinegar to put on his welts. After he finished washing, she made a paste from baking soda and water and applied it to the stings. That helped ease the pain some for Colby and gave me a respite from listening to his moans and groans. I had to make a concerted effort to keep from snickering as he looked like a polka-dot clown with all the little dots of white baking soda covering the welts, a stark contrast to the rest of his dark skin. Still, the seven kids were unable to restrain themselves, and they burst into a fit of uncontrollable laughter.

"Quit laughing, kids," Mrs. Payne scolded. Then she turned to Colby.

"That washing and paste would have helped more if you had gotten here sooner. Are you boys going back to your place or Razz's?" she asked, a little concerned about the time.

"We're going to my house, ma'am," Colby answered. "We told his parents that if it got too late, he could spend the night with us."

"Well, you better get going. We don't want your mom getting worried. It will be getting dark around five, and you are still over an hour away by bike."

She reached into the small fridge, pulled out a couple of sandwiches, and handed them to us.

"That was dinner, but I can fix more," she said, opening the door for us to leave.

We thanked her for the sandwiches and for nursing Colby's still swollen welts, and then we headed to Colby's.

It was almost five when we reached his house, already nearly dark. The light bulb on the porch cast a pale yellowish glow across the front yard, and we noticed a thin layer of leaves covering the grass. That was unusual for spring, but the two large white oak trees in the yard, which had been so determined the entire winter to hang on to their dead brown leaves, had finally tired of the effort and let them go in the heavy rain and wind of last night's storm.

We parked our bikes, and Colby unfastened the box with the chickens from his bike and then headed to the porch. I followed closely, but I stopped when I saw a snake slithering through the brown oak leaves, following Colby.

"Colby!" I shouted. "There's a snake after you!"

He turned to look, and by the dim lighting of the porch light, he saw the ominous telltale sign of a snake weaving its way through the leaves close behind him. He switched directions and picked up his pace a little. The snake did not falter, changing course as well and continuing its pursuit of Colby. He began to zigzag quickly, trying to confuse the snake, but to no avail. I could not imagine what kind of snake was so determined to get Colby, or why, but no matter what he did, he could not lose the snake.

"Faster, Colby!" I shouted. "He's right behind you!"

Colby, being petrified of snakes, let out a terrible scream and ran as fast as he could in every direction, yet the snake kept pace right behind him with every step.

"Jump up on the porch, Colby!" I shouted. "Snakes can't jump!"

Colby darted to the porch, with the snake rustling the leaves right behind him. When he was six feet away, he leaped high into the air, landing square in the middle of the porch. He glanced back over at the leaves on the ground and let out a sigh of relief after noticing no movement, assuming the snake was gone. Then I began to laugh hysterically.

"What are you laughing at, Razz? That wasn't funny."

"Look at the box, Colby," I said between laughs. "It was the string. Somehow the string tied to the box became unraveled. You have been running away from the string wiggling behind you in the leaves."

Colby looked down at the string that had once fastened the top of the box. The full length of it, about eight feet, had become untied at one end, but it still held tightly to the box at the other. As Colby had walked, the string had trailed behind, meandering ominously beneath the leaves.

"Did you know it was the string all the time?" Colby demanded suspiciously.

"No, Colby. It was too dark to tell it was the string. I promise I thought it was a snake that was after you."

Colby looked down at the string, then at me, and burst into a fit of laughter himself.

"I hope we make some money off these chickens, Razz, because I sure have earned it already."

"You sure have, Colby. Let's put the chickens in their pen and get something to eat."

After washing, we sat down with Colby's family to eat. Colby and I repeatedly shared our exciting adventures of the day, regaling them into the night with laughter and amusement.

We cared for those EO chickens and their chicks through spring and summer. Both of us learned a lot with that endeavor. At times, it tested our friendship, but I think we came out of it closer than we ever had been before. It was hard work for Colby and me, but we did it. By August, we had twenty-three hens and eleven roosters to sell, not including the original three we'd bought from Shae.

We decided to sell the entire enterprise to Mrs. Barker, who lived down the road. She was a nice lady who had lost her husband a few years back. We knew she would take care of them, and Shae would have approved. We could have gotten more selling them to someone else, but we were ready to get out of the business, and she needed help in finances. We'd spent four dollars on feed and paid Shae four dollars to start. We sold the entire lot to her for fifty dollars, netting forty-two dollars minus the two we still owed Shae, so it turned out that our expenses met the ten dollars we'd borrowed from my dad. We didn't get rich, but twenty dollars profit each was a lot of money to us back then.

Fortunately, or unfortunately, we never saw Shae again. We heard during the summer that he tried to run for the local county commissioner's office, but after spending a good sum of money on political signs, they would not allow him to run for some technical reason that we didn't quite understand. I can imagine that didn't sit too well with him. Anyway, after selling the chicken business, we headed off to his place one Saturday in late August to pay him his two dollars and satisfy the debt. The trip there was uneventful, with Colby making certain to keep plenty of distance between himself and the hornets' nest. The road looked unusually overgrown, and when we crested the small hill to his place, the homestead appeared abandoned.

There were no animals or any signs of life. His old camper was no longer there, and only a few weeds emerged from where it had once rested. Most everything else was still there except for the barrels that had once been the homes of the cocks and his old blue pick-up truck. Weeds had taken over the entire area, evincing a desertion some time ago.

In front of the spot where his camper had once sat, right about where we'd first met Shae, was a mound of dirt about six feet long and three feet wide. At one end was a hastily placed wooden cross, sitting noticeably awry, with something painted on the cross board. We drew closer and were able to read it:

SHAE 1964

On the top of the sign rested a weathered cap, and we both recognized it right off. It was the cap Colby had lost when the hornets had decided to teach him a lesson about leaving their home alone.

We looked at each other, and then Colby reached over to pick up his cap. He pulled out his dollar and placed it neatly into the hat, and then he turned to me. I pulled my dollar out of my pocket and put it on top of his. We both knelt and began pulling back some of the soft dirt with our hands. When it was a few inches deep, Colby placed the cap into the shallow hole, and we respectfully covered it up.

When we returned to Colby's house, we informed his dad about Shae's death and what we had done, he burst into laughter.

"Boys, Shae isn't buried there just yet. He moved off to someplace in Montana or Wyoming last month. Shae said he didn't know where he would end up but that he would find a quiet place to settle in the wilderness there. I think he was having a little fun with you, but at least you have settled your debt."

Just before Thanksgiving, Colby's dad received a letter from Shae. The envelope contained two one-hundred-dollar bills, the signed deed to his property, and a brief note to Mr. Harris to keep the two hundred dollars in return for selling his property. Shae instructed him to give the rest of the money from the sale of the property to the school that Colby attended. I know his school greatly appreciated that, as their budget was much smaller than the other schools in the county.

It's funny how someone who can pass so briefly through your life can leave a lasting memory so different than your first impression. As frightened of him as we were, our meeting with Shae had a positive influence on us for many years to come. The difference between Shae and the two of us was as much as night considers itself to day. At the time, I could only see a gruff, ornery old man. I resented his show of respect for Colby and his flagrant disdain for me, even though he did pick me up some at the end.

I had never experienced that disdain before, but Colby had, and for the first time, I began to understand how it hurt my friend. I see now that Shae knew what he was doing all along. He propped up Colby by giving him the gift of confidence and softened me by offering me the gift of empathy, both virtues that we sorely needed and without which we would have never succeeded in our accomplishments. Had I attempted even the slightest of effort, I would have seen the kindness that Shae carried in his heart and the salient fact that he didn't even know it.

Chapter XIII

1964

The Concert

They say things happen for a reason. I don't know about that, but, at least sometimes, we're just happy that they did.

When Anna Lee was in the eighth grade, she lived with her mom and dad in their sparsely furnished, five-room home, which was not too far past Elbie's house. Most older folks called her a spitfire because she was as feisty as a squirrel and had no qualms about saying what she thought.

Anna Lee was an only child, but she was far from spoiled. She had to help her parents with duties on the farm and the house, as her mom was too preoccupied with two small jobs in Hancock County to help make ends meet. When the thirteen-year-old did have some free time and wasn't with us, she listened to the few records she possessed of her favorite rock star, Chris Crae. Anna Lee could listen to his sweet voice for hours, playing the same songs over and over again, oblivious to her mother's admonishments.

Hardly a day passed that she didn't dream of seeing him in concert; however, she knew it was only a dream. With the large mortgage on the farm and her mom's medical bills, neither she nor her parents would ever be able to afford the tickets. Besides, the closest his tour had come to Daviess County had been the year before when he'd played in Indianapolis. Even if they could pay for the admission, it was on a school night, and the three-and-a-half-hour drive prevented that. This year, though, his Christmas concert included Freedom Hall in Louisville, on a Saturday. The trip to Louisville was only a two-and-a-half-hour drive, but the tickets were twenty dollars for the cheapest seats. She knew her mother could not afford that, so listening to his albums would have to do.

It was a cold Thursday evening, early December, and the dark gray skies began to cast a few tiny snowflakes. While Anna Lee cleaned her dinner dishes, she occasionally glanced out the window at the very light snowfall. By the time she'd wiped the last spoon dry, however, the light flurry had increased to a heavier snow, boosting her hopes that they might close school the next day. Going to the concert was out of the question, but if they did cancel school, she could listen to Chris Crae's songs all day. Her glances out the window became more frequent as the snow began to accumulate, but at this pace, it needed to snow all night to close classes. When Anna Lee saw her mom's car coming down the road from work, she noticed the tire tracks in the snow; that was promising.

"Mom, are they calling for more snow tonight?" she asked as soon as her mother opened the door.

"Welcome home to you, too, dear," her mother teased as she hung up her heavy black winter coat.

"Hi, Mom. Are they calling for more snow tonight?" Anna Lee repeated.

"Hoping school will close?" Her mother laughed.

"Oh, yeah. Anna Lee is ready for a day off."

With her usual limp, her mom walked over to her and kissed her on the cheek. She had been born with one leg almost an inch shorter than the other. Limping for thirty-four years had eventually weakened her hip joint, creating a deep, constant pain when she walked, but it didn't stop her from working two jobs. The money she earned helped support the family and reduce some of the medical bills. Jobs were scarce, and that was the best she could do in a small rural town. Anna Lee's dad's employment at the factory in Owensboro helped, but still, there was nothing left for niceties. However, they were happy with their life and never considered themselves any other way. Last month, her mom had taken a temporary third part-time job, so this was the first time in a while that she arrived home this time of day.

"How was your day?" she asked Anna Lee.

"Fine. Do you think they will call off school tomorrow?" Anna Lee stubbornly asked again.

"I have something for you," her mom said, smiling as she handed Anna Lee an envelope.

"What is this?" Anna Lee looked curiously at the envelope.

"Open it."

"But what about—"

"Open it," her mother insisted with a smile.

Anna Lee opened the envelope, hesitated, and then slowly peeked inside. Trying to read the contents, she stared intently at two small pieces of paper resembling a long business card. She screeched, jumping backward, staring at the two tickets to Chris Crae's concert nestled inside the envelope. She screamed again, pressing the envelope tightly to her chest. With the tickets firmly guarded, she looked at her mother.

"Are these real?"

"Yes."

"Are they ours?' she asked, her voice rising.

"Yes."

"But we can't afford these."

"That is why I took a temporary job at the convenience store, Anna Lee."

Anna Lee screamed again and danced about the room, unable to stand still. She jumped onto a kitchen chair and then stomped her feet on the seat excitedly.

"It's all I want!" she shouted as she embraced her mother with a tight hug. "It's all I want!"

Anna Lee tossed and turned in bed that night, finally getting into a wrestling match with the blankets. Excited over the concert, she kept glancing out the window to see if it was still snowing. Unlike earlier, she now hoped it would stop; it didn't. The heavy snow continued relentlessly throughout the night. In good weather, it was a two-and-a-half-hour drive to Louisville, but if it kept snowing, it would take much longer, or worse, make the trip impossible.

When the snow finally stopped in the morning, eight inches of fresh white snow covered the ground. School, of course, was canceled, but Anna Lee was more concerned about the forecast of the dropping temperatures. It was expected to remain in the single digits through next week. She worried all day how they would get to Louisville now with the roads covered with snow and ice.

When her mom returned from work that evening, Anna Lee immediately began asking if they would be able to make the concert.

"I promise we will get there," her mother patiently repeated each time.

On Saturday morning, Anna Lee was dressed and ready to go before breakfast. She kept insisting all morning that they should go now in case the snow-packed roads caused some delays.

"The concert isn't until seven o'clock tonight, Anna Lee," her mother replied. "There is plenty of time."

Finally, tired of Anna Lee's incessant begging, she agreed to leave at three. Since Anna Lee's dad worked the night shift this weekend, she had no other recourse.

At two thirty, Anna Lee sat in the car, waiting impatiently with the two cherished tickets firmly in hand. Her tardy mother finally got into the car ten minutes after three o'clock.

"We have four hours to get there, Anna Lee," her mom reminded her. "I don't know what we will do with all that time."

"We can wait in our seats," Anna Lee insisted quickly. "I will die if I miss a single second of it."

Her mom grinned and settled into the driver's seat. Taking off her gloves, she started the twelve-year-old car, and they were on their way. The roads, much worse than either of them had anticipated, were scarcely traveled, with only a few tracks in the eight-inch-deep snow. Holding firmly to the steering wheel, her mother drove very slowly, increasing Anna Lee's worry that they would not get to the concert on time. It was challenging to keep the car on the road, and even at the slower speeds, the car occasionally began to slide sideways before her mother could regain control.

Fretting the entire trip, Anna Lee began to do the math around five o'clock. She realized the increasing possibility that they might not make it on time. The thought of an accident was merely an afterthought for Anna Lee. Her main concern was arriving at the concert on time, and now, there was the possibility that they might not get there at all.

"Hopefully, the roads will clear up a little when we reach Highway 60. I promise we will get there on time, Anna Lee," her mother assured her. But with the treacherous two-lane roads, her mother seldom reached speeds of thirty miles an hour.

"I hope so," was all Anna Lee could say.

With several minor accidents that caused some delays and no improvement in the road conditions, they finally reached the halfway point two and a half hours after leaving the house. Anna Lee tried to be quiet, not wanting to distract her mother from being careful, but she continued to check the clock every few minutes from the corner of her eye.

At six thirty, they finally reached Fort Knox, usually only forty-five minutes away. But Anna Lee now realized that at these slow speeds, they would not make it in time. She hung her head and wiped away the tears, hoping her mother wouldn't notice.

"I'm sorry, Anna Lee. These roads are much worse than I thought," her mother apologized, realizing Anna Lee had been right.

The next hour and a half were the worst. Anna Lee's dream, which had been so close this morning, was now gone. At best, they might make it to Freedom Hall to catch part of the second half of the concert, if there was one.

It was almost eight o'clock when they finally parked the car at Freedom Hall. There were no sounds of music, yet the parking lot was still full. Anna Lee hurried across the treacherous ice, but she hesitated and stopped to wait for her mother, who could not keep up.

"Go on, Anna Lee. I'll be there as soon as I can," her mother encouraged.

"We are going together, Mom," Anna Lee answered. "I wouldn't have gotten to go at all if it weren't for you."

After what seemed like an eternity to Anna Lee, they reached the doors, expecting them to be locked. Surprisingly, they weren't, and they walked in. There was an empty table inside the doors, but no one was there to take their tickets. Anna Lee and her mother could hear the murmur of the crowd, but no music.

"Maybe it is still intermission," her mother said hopefully.

The lump in her throat prevented Anna Lee from answering. They reached the stairs, and Anna Lee could not refrain from racing to the top. Again, she tried to control her impatience, and waited patiently for her mother to climb the steps to the third level, the location of their top-row seats. When her mother finally reached the top of the stairs, they passed the empty concession area and headed to the entrance of the arena. Suddenly the crowd roared as a single continuous note resonated from the enormous speakers. She wasn't sure, but it sounded like an organ key emanating from the darkened stage, igniting a vestige of hope for Anna Lee. It started low and slowly began increasing in volume. Anna Lee hurried to the entrance tunnel leading from the concession area into the arena, but then she stopped abruptly. In front of her was a group of about ten men, all wearing the same t-shirts and blue jeans. They appeared to be mechanics or maintenance workers, and they were blocking the entrance.

"Hurry, Mom!" she shouted to her mother, who was still struggling to catch up. "It's starting."

Her mother finally reached her and tried to peer over the taller men.

"Excuse me, please," Anna Lee said, trying to squeeze her way through the muscular men.

"I'm sorry, miss," one of the workers said. "You will have to go to the next entrance."

"But he's getting ready to come out," Anna Lee pleaded. "We already missed the first half; I don't want to miss any more of it."

"I'm sorry, " he insisted politely as he signaled toward the other entrance.

Anna Lee held back the tears at yet another setback. She grabbed her mother's hand and began to turn.

"Billy, send them up here," someone toward the front instructed.

Anna Lee turned back upon hearing the shuffling of feet as the men parted, allowing her and her mom to walk to the front. Just as they neared the arena, another man held out his arms, stopping them from going any further.

"I need you to wait right here for a minute," he said politely.

"But he is getting ready to come out. We have been driving for five hours, and I don't want to miss it," Anna Lee pleaded.

"How come you missed the first half?" asked another man to her left. He was taller than most of the others and had his back turned to her, but she noticed him adjusting the Santa Claus suit he wore. Anna Lee had previously read that Chris had had a Santa come out into the crowd while he sang at some of his other concerts on this Christmas tour. Finally, this was an encouraging sign that Chris would come back out for more songs.

"It was my fault," Anna Lee's mom apologized. "I didn't know the roads were as bad as they are."

"It's okay, Mom," Anna Lee assured her.

"What is your name, young lady?" the Santa asked, his back still facing her.

"Anna Lee."

"That's a pretty name."

"Thank you," Anna Lee snapped impatiently. "Would you tell him to let us through? He's getting ready to come out."

The noise from the audience began to rise as the single note continued to grow much louder, increasing the excitement. Suddenly a single booming strike of the drum brought the roaring crowd to their feet.

Anna Lee strained her head to see the still-darkened stage.

"Well, Anna Lee, everything happens for a reason; sometimes it just takes a while to figure out why." the Santa said calmly, though loud enough for her to hear over the crowd. "The second half is always better than the first. There are over twenty thousand people out there, and I promise that if you are patient, not one of those people out there will see him before you do. Is that a deal?"

"Okay," she said reluctantly, still straining to see past the men in front of her as the drummer now struck his drums two times in rhythm. The dimly lit stage made it difficult for her to see, but she could feel the electricity of the crowd. She had seen enough concerts on TV to know the star was about to burst onto the stage.

The Santa turned to face her, preoccupied with an instrument in his hands. Anna Lee noticed his full white beard and the keyboard guitar strapped over his shoulders. He played a few notes on the keys, but no sound came from the board.

"Hmm…it doesn't work," he said, still looking down with curiosity at the keys.

The crescendo of the single note on stage continued rising as the drummer rhythmically struck his drums four times, driving the crowd wild in anticipation.

"Anna Lee, would you mind flipping that switch?" Santa asked, still focusing on the keys.

Anna Lee forced herself to turn away from the stage.

"What?" she said, agitated at his interruption.

"That switch there," he said, pointing with his pinkie to the bottom of the keyboard. "Flip that switch."

She reached over to the keyboard guitar and flipped the switch down.

"Now, let's see what it will do," Santa said as he placed his fingers on the keys.

He pressed down several keys, and the speakers on stage burst out the notes, which resonated loudly throughout the building. The crowd screamed, but not as loudly as Anna Lee and her mother did from fright as they jumped back against the concrete wall.

Santa raised his head and stared straight at Anna Lee.

"Merry Christmas, Anna Lee!" he said. It was Chris.

She jumped up and down with both feet and covered her mouth as she screamed again.

Chris moved in rhythm with the music, playfully staring at Anna Lee as he played the notes again, this time singing, "T'is the season to be jolly," with a huge smile beneath his white beard.

The entire band joined in filling the arena with music, and then someone near Chris shouted, "Go!"

Chris smiled at Anna Lee and said, "Gotta go," and then he turned and rushed into the arena, his muscular bodyguards following closely behind. He stopped at the end of the tunnel, and the bodyguards squatted in a circle around him, protecting him in every direction from overly excited fans. Just as several blinding spotlights shone upon Chris, he played the notes again to "T'is the season to be jolly."

The deafening roar of the excited crowd shook the building. There was Chris, dressed as Santa, in the rear of the building, playing his keyboard guitar just a few feet from the worst seats in the arena.

After a moment of playing in the rear of the building, he nodded to Anna Lee, and then he turned and walked through the entire arena, playing the song on the keyboard to those in the upper seats before finally ending up on the stage.

Anna Lee and her mom gathered their composure enough to find their seats, but neither could sit down.

After two more songs, Chris took off the keyboard guitar and sat down at the piano.

"I met a wonderful young lady and her mom in the back just a few minutes ago," he said, leaning over to the microphone and looking at the back of the arena. "They missed the first half of the show, so Anna Lee, this song is for you."

Placing his hands gently on the piano keys, he began playing a beautiful version of Johann Pachelbel's Canon D while his backup singers sang a new Christmas song of his to the melody. Anna Lee and her mom hugged each other, both unable to hold back the tears.

The evening, the most magical ever for Anna Lee and her mom, left them exhausted but euphoric. After the concert ended, they both remained motionless and in awe in their seats. Thoroughly mesmerized, they watched the boisterous crowd disappear while the workers began clearing the stage. It seemed they were now in a different place, and they noticed how strangely silent it was in the arena except for the occasional clamor of the cleanup crew echoing toward them.

They were in no hurry to leave and were contentedly absorbing the night in the nearly empty arena when a man dressed in a tieless black suit stepped out onto the stage. He checked on the progress of the cleanup crew and scanned the stadium seats. Anna Lee thought he stopped to look at them, but she realized they were probably too far back for him to see them in the darkened upper deck. He turned and disappeared backstage. A short moment later, the suited man came out again, descended the side steps of the stage, and headed to the rear of the arena. Anna Lee and her mom watched him curiously as he started up the stairs toward them. Approaching them, he looked up and stopped.

"Would you mind coming with me?" he asked.

"Oh, I'm sorry," Anna Lee's mom apologized. "We will leave." They both rose, picked up their belongings, and readied to leave.

"No, no," he objected, putting up his hand. "I want you to follow me. There is someone who needs to see you."

Anna Lee realized it was the man who had stopped them in the tunnel next to "Santa." They followed him downstairs, curious as to who would want to meet them.

"Probably security guys wondering what fools would still be sitting there twenty minutes after the show," Anna Lee whispered to her mom with a muffled laugh.

Reaching the main floor, he turned with little emotion to see if they were still behind him and motioned with his hand to follow. He led them onto the stage area, stopping to help Anna Lee's mother up the steps. The stage was much larger than it had appeared from the rear of the arena. They both gazed in amazement at the mostly empty scene, knowing Chris had just been there, putting on his show. The man led them through the curtains to the backstage area and continued further to a door, which he opened for them.

As they entered the room, Anna Lee quickly grew excited as she noticed several of the backup singers.

"They wanted to meet you," the man said, and then he introduced the awestruck mom and daughter to each singer.

When he introduced her to a tall, slender man, Anna Lee smiled, shook his hand, and said, mimicking his deep baritone voice, "You are the one with the deep, deep, deep voice."

Everyone laughed and nodded.

When the man introduced her to a beautiful young lady, Anna Lee smiled excitedly.

"You are Marina, the one who sings like an angel."

"I just love her," Marina said to the other performers and bursting into a smile. She turned to Anna Lee, hugged her, and said, "I wish you could be my sister."

Anna Lee hugged her affectionately and whispered into her ear, "I would love to have a sister."

After being introduced to the last singer, Anna Lee and her mom thanked them profusely. As they turned to leave, Marina grabbed Anna Lee's hand.

"There's one more," she said, stepping off to the side.

Sitting in a chair behind her was Chris.

Anna Lee screamed and stomped her feet excitedly several times. Chris rose from his seat while Anna Lee screamed again, covering her mouth with her hands, her eyes filling with emotions. He walked over to her and gently hugged her, and she squeezed him back tightly. Chris seemed taller and more muscular than in the pictures she treasured at home. He smelled of soap, and his hair was still damp, most likely from an after-show shower. His warm embrace caused her legs to shake uncontrollably beneath her, and a dizzying lightheaded sensation raced through her head. Not only was Chris Crae hugging her, but he was also keeping her

140

from falling. Once he was able to calm her down, they all sat down and talked for twenty minutes. Anna Lee had never been so happy. She never moved from the edge of her seat and never took her eyes off Chris.

All too soon for Anna Lee, the man in the dark suit whispered to Chris that it was time to go. Chris asked him to get Anna Lee and her mom a limo and a hotel room. He was worried about them driving back home in the snow, especially at night. Despite their polite refusal of his kindness, they spent the night in a luxury hotel, the kind they had only seen on TV.

The room, adorned with marble floors, crystal chandeliers, and a huge walk-in shower big enough that you could stretch your arms as far as they would reach and not touch a wall, was like none they had ever seen. The beautiful plush bed, three times the size of hers, with more pillows than she could count, was too tempting for the two of them, and they both bounced on it repeatedly, screeching with joy as if they were two six-year-old kids. They lived like two queens for the night, realizing some dreams do come true. Anna Lee told her mother that being late for the show was the best thing that had ever happened to her.

The school remained closed Tuesday, so Anna Lee was home when the UPS driver knocked on the door. It was an overnight package addressed to her, and she was already opening the small box before the driver pulled out of her driveway. It was from Chris. A note, with Chris's signature and thanking her for coming to the concert, rested atop the contents of the package. Inside were pictures of Anna Lee and her mom meeting all the singers, and Chris, too, even though Anna Lee had never noticed anyone taking pictures that night. There was also a note from Marina wishing the best for her new sister, including her address so Anna Lee could write to her.

As soon as her mother returned from work that night, Anna Lee gave her the biggest hug yet.

"I'll never forget this, Mom, and I'll always have these pictures to remember."

Her mom smiled and wiped a tear from her eye. It was the best Christmas ever, indeed.

Chapter XIV

1965

The Road to The Mansion

It was June 20, 1965, the day before the summer solstice, when Elbie and I planned to meet up with Colby for the afternoon. We weren't sure what he had in mind, but Colby said he had something exciting to discuss. We walked briskly as Colby's house was a little over an hour's walk away. As we passed Anna Lee's home, we noticed her running excitedly toward us down the lane from her house to the road.

"Hey, guys, wait up!" she shouted.

I glanced at Elbie as he hung his head briefly.

"Are you alright, Elbie?" I asked, fully aware of his reservations.

"I am, Razz. Really, I'm over it."

"Are you sure?" I wanted to make certain before Anna Lee caught up with us.

"Yeah, it's all good."

I hoped he was over it. Both Anna Lee and Elbie were my friends, and I had worked hard to help them make amends. I knew the two of them regretted that the fracas had ever happened and wanted to put it past them, but that was easier said than done.

It had all started last May at school. Anna Lee was different than most thirteen-year-old girls. She was more comfortable with plowing a field on her dad's tractor than socializing, and she could toss forty-pound bales of hay onto a wagon all afternoon, something many boys her age could not do. She fancied blue jeans and a t-shirt instead of dresses. For her, long, curly hair would never do. She kept hers cropped short, just a few inches in length, but her hair looked good in that fashion, and I could not imagine her looking better in any other appearance.

One might understandably have considered her a tomboy, but physically she was already an attractive young lady despite her efforts to diminish that. I honestly don't think she ever noticed, but when she walked down the hall at school, nearly every boy's head turned, including mine.

Anna Lee carried an air of confidence that caused a considerable amount of jealousy among a few of the other girls— and envy in some boys. Most times, she seemed more comfortable with boys than girls, but to her, that was as natural as being left-handed.

Anna Lee's smile and good-natured demeanor won her many friends, both boys and girls. But there were some days when she seemed oddly irritable, and we knew to tread lightly at those times. We were in the eighth grade, and everyone, even the boys, knew it was best not to tangle with her on those rare occasions. However, Elbie once made that mistake and dug a hole so deep some said they saw Tiananmen Square at the bottom of it.

Occasionally Elbie could test her patience. It was never intentional; Elbie just had a way of doing or saying things sometimes that didn't quite come out as he intended.

At lunch break one day, near the end of the year, a group of our friends sat in the quad, chatting. When Anna Lee joined the group, Elbie, unfortunately, lost control of his senses and blurted out how pretty she looked. Now, if he had just stopped after this first infraction, he might have made it out of this predicament with a simple frown from Anna Lee. But instead, he tried to cover it up and said, "For a girl, I mean."

I know he heard the very audible gasps from the other boys and girls in the group, but Anna Lee didn't; she turned as red as a beet, and I swear I think she snorted like an angry bull.

"What did you say?" she growled at Elbie, her fists clenched so tightly you couldn't have slipped a dime through her fingers.

I think Elbie had cemented his fate at this point, but again, if he had just remained silent, he might have been able to walk away, losing only his dignity. He didn't. He glanced around the group, and upon seeing the horror on everyone's faces, unfortunately, he mistook those expressions as genuine concern for his lost respect instead of looks of fear for his life. So, he tried to salvage what little he had of that instead of cutting his losses and moving on.

"Well, Anna Lee, I meant that as a compliment. I wouldn't call a guy pretty, but for a tomboy, you're not bad."

Oh, poor Elbie. I don't know what possessed him to say something so condescending to anyone, especially Anna Lee Frazier. Whatever it was, I hope I never become a victim of that possession, because it took him a long time to get over what happened next.

Anna Lee fumed so fiercely, that we all thought she might explode before saying anything. She took a deep breath and leaned over into Elbie's face, with barely an inch between their eyebrows and even less than that between the tips of their noses.

"Elbie Pierce, I am going to count to three. When I say three, I'm going to punch you so hard you will never forget how hard a PRETTY TOMBOY can hit!" she snarled, shouting the words "pretty tomboy" in a voice that scared the bejeebus out of me and everyone else within the quad.

"So," she continued, "I would advise you that when you hear the word 'three,' you better protect yourself."

With that, and as a stunned Elbie stared at her, she took one step back and lowered her fists to her hips.

"One, two, three!"

Her left hand moved so fast I never saw it hit Elbie. I only saw his head snap back and the blood trickling down from his nose.

One punch, that was it. Anna Lee folded her arms across her chest, glaring at Elbie, daring him to react in any way other than a punished, whimpering dog would.

Elbie grabbed his nose and fell to his knees. He looked up at Anna Lee, conquered, his pride hopelessly crushed like a felon banished from the homeland. Although he had walked himself back into that corner, I'd never felt so sorry for anyone in my life. I think Anna Lee suddenly realized what she had done to Elbie's ego and felt immense remorse.

"I'm sorry, Elbie. I'm sorry," she quickly apologized as she helped him to his feet. "I just lost my temper, and I shouldn't have done that."

And with that, just as Elbie had foolishly bumbled his apology, Anna Lee had unintentionally worsened the injury to his humiliated ego; and she knew it.

Trying to make amends somehow, she turned to Mary Jane Toler.

"Mary Jane, go get some paper napkins for him."

We all knew Anna Lee was in the right on this one and any of us might have reacted in a somewhat similar fashion had we been in her position, but Elbie's battered ego was hopelessly destroyed, and it would take more than an apology to repair it. Even though Anna Lee tried to make amends, and everyone hoped they could extricate themselves from this mess without more suffering, the damage was irreparable.

"It's okay, Anna Lee. I deserved it. It's not your fault," Elbie answered contritely.

"You're a good guy, Elbie," Anna Lee replied, still searching for a way to make amends. "I'm sure you didn't mean it the way it came out. That was totally wrong of me to blindside you. I am so, so sorry."

Mary Jane returned with a handful of napkins and nursed Elbie's nose until it stopped bleeding.

I could still see the regret and guilt in Anna Lee's entire body. She desperately wanted to make amends, but only time could do that now.

It took several weeks for Elbie's ego to mend, but he'd learned a good lesson, and Anna Lee had as well. Everyone, including Anna Lee and Elbie, accepted the truce and moved on.

When word got out about their brief fracas, some kids in the school teased Elbie mercilessly for letting a girl best him. Anytime Anna Lee saw this, she took the derelicts aside and privately threatened to do the same to him, or her, if they ever teased Elbie again. Even the boys didn't want to cross Anna Lee, so that worked, and as word got around, the teasing eventually stopped.

So, you can understand my concerns when Elbie hung his head. I'm sure seeing Anna Lee briefly brought back some painful memories of that day.

"Hi, Elbie!" Anna Lee greeted cheerfully with a sincere smile.

"Hey, Anna Lee," Elbie returned, reaching his hand out to her to shake.

She stood close to his side, engaging in a friendly conversation with him as if I were not there.

I was happy for the two of them, but I also felt a little left out. In the last few months, I'd developed a crush on Anna Lee. On the inside, I was begging for a "Hi, Razz" from her. Unfortunately, I could never let her suspect, as she would have nothing to do with me if she knew I harbored feelings for her other than as just one of the guys.

"What are you guys up to?" she asked Elbie.

"Colby said he has something exciting for us to discuss, so we are off to his place," Elbie explained.

"Cool. He called me, too. Mind if I walk with you?" she asked, finally looking at me for permission.

"Sure," I answered without any hesitation. "You and Colby are like ice cream and cake; by themselves, they are okay, but put them together, and you got one fine dessert."

"It's not like that, Razz. It's just that I like to get Colby's goat," she explained.

Elbie and I both laughed, having witnessed many of Anna Lee and Colby's verbal sparring matches. They were amiable adversaries, always trying to best the other. With Colby's intellect and Anna Lee's quick wit, it was a match of consummate contenders.

"Well, let's go, then," Anna Lee said as we all headed off to Colby's.

The rest of the trip went a lot faster with Anna Lee joking and Elbie's chattering. I, however, felt like the third wheel, but if that was what it took, I was happy for them.

When we arrived, Colby was excited to see us, especially Anna Lee. His younger brother and sister were playing in the yard, and his mother was hanging laundry on the clothesline.

"Hi, Mrs. Harris!" Anna Lee shouted.

"Well, Anna Lee Frazier, you are a sight for sore eyes. How are you?"

"Great, Mrs. Harris. Is Mr. Harris around?"

"No, he's doing some work for Karly Clemens. Won't be back until late. What are the four of you up to?"

"They're just visiting, Mom," Colby answered, shooing us away from his mom and steering us down the hill. We could tell he wanted to talk without any distractions.

He led us down the hill to their water well, which was conveniently situated between four large shade trees. The hand-dug well was about four feet in diameter and about fifteen feet deep, with the water level remaining at four or five feet from the top except for during the drought season of late summer and early fall. The round well, lined with bricks and mortar, provided a

148

comfortable place to sit while sipping a refreshing drink. Several planks, strategically placed across the top, kept out leaves, debris, and critters.

To get water out of the well, we used a nearby galvanized bucket. A tin cup with a twelve-inch handle remained within reach, hanging from a nail on one of the three trees. Drinking the fresh, clean water out of that metal cup was as pleasing as eating homemade ice cream on a hot August day. We could sit on the sides of the well in the shade for hours if the conversation was agreeable.

The well, fed by an underground spring, provided all the water for the Harrises. They needed to carry the bucket of water up to the top of the hill for cooking, washing, and laundry; that was Colby's job. The Harrises didn't have any plumbing, so the one-seater outhouse in the back took care of those needs. During times of drought, especially in August and September, the spring nearly dried up, resulting in some inconvenient rationing of the water until the fall rains replenished it. In severe periods of drought, they often needed to go to town or a neighbor for drinking water. Since Mr. Harris did not own a car, Colby or his brother would hitch a ride with a couple of buckets in hand.

"What's going on, Colby?" I asked after he motioned for us to sit on the well.

"Have any of you guys ever heard of the Marshal Mansion?"

We all shook our heads.

"Razz, remember that neat old house we passed on the way to Shae's place last year?" Colby asked me.

"Yeah. That was a cool old house. We said we would like to see the inside of it, but we had Shae on our mind then," I answered, remembering the old three-story home that looked like it was from the Civil War era.

"It is an antebellum home built by a man named Marshal. He was appointed judge by Abraham Lincoln. It was part of the Underground Railroad in the pre-Civil War period."

"What railroad?" Anna Lee asked.

"The Underground Railroad," Colby repeated. "Before the Civil War, there was a secret organization of people who helped slaves cross the river to reach the Northern states, where slavery was prohibited. They helped thousands of slaves and their families escape to freedom. That organization was called the Underground Railroad because it was illegal at that time to help slaves to freedom in this area. They had to do that secretively to avoid being lynched or hung if caught."

"Wow. That's cool, Colby," Elbie said excitedly. "But what's an antebellum home?"

"I don't know." Colby shrugged.

"It means built before the Civil War. If you don't know what it means, how did you know how to use it." Anna Lee laughed.

"That's what my dad called it," Colby answered defensively.

"Why didn't you ask your dad what it meant? He was right there!"

"I don't know, Anna Lee. I just didn't," Colby replied, irritated at her sarcasm and her satisfied smile.

"So, all that happened right here in this area?" I asked.

"Yeah. The slaves slipped out at night and found their way to the Marshal Mansion. The Marshals and their friends hid them in the basement, fed them, nursed them back to health if needed, and helped them cross the river at night into Indiana. From there, the slaves traveled on up north. Some of them made it, but some didn't."

"How did you find all this out, Colby?" Anna Lee asked.

"I happened to mention that house to my dad the other day. Once he realized what house I was talking about, he told me the whole story about it."

"Wow. I never knew about all that, Colby. Now I really want to see the inside of it," I said.

"Me, too," Anna Lee insisted excitedly.

"Count me in," Elbie agreed.

"Well, that is why I wanted to talk to you guys. I want to see it, too. They say it's haunted with more ghosts than you can count!" Colby said, unable to conceal his excitement.

"That's a great find, Colby." I was getting excited myself. "When do you want to go?"

"I thought about taking some snacks and camping inside the house tomorrow night. It would be awesome if we all went together. Anna Lee, you think your parents would let you go with us?"

"No. But if you are inviting me, I'm going. I'll tell my parents I'm spending the night with Mary Jane. She'll cover for me."

"Wait a minute, guys," Elbie cautioned. "Do you think it's safe to spend the night in a haunted house? Maybe we could just go for an afternoon."

"Come on, Elbie, toughen up," Colby chastised.

"There will be the four of us together, Elbie," I encouraged.

I noticed Anna Lee didn't join in on this one, and I gave her credit for that. I was sure she didn't want to embarrass Elbie in any way.

"I don't know," Elbie answered cautiously. "Maybe if we left before dark. Who knows whether those ghosts are angry or not? I've heard—"

"Elbie!" I scolded. "All four of us will be together the whole time. If there is such a thing as ghosts, they don't hurt people."

"Razz, I've heard stories of haunted houses, and some ghosts are angry and mean."

"I swear, Elbie, you must lie awake in bed at night, trying to think of things to worry about," Colby fussed.

"Those are just stories, Elbie," I said. "There's no proof."

"Come on, Elbie, it'll be fun," added Colby. "Besides, tomorrow is the summer solstice; it will be the shortest night of the year."

"It will be more fun with you there, Elbie," Anna Lee finally said.

"Alright, alright," Elbie replied. "But how are we going to get our parents to let us spend the night there?"

Colby and I looked at Elbie in disbelief and then at Anna Lee, who remained tight-lipped, saying nothing.

"Elbie, we do what Anna Lee said," I explained.

"My parents wouldn't let me spend the night at Mary Jane's house, Razz. No way," Elbie answered in disbelief.

Colby burst into a fit of laughter and spent little effort trying to hide it. Anna Lee, on the other hand, lowered her head and pretended to scratch an itch so Elbie couldn't see her face.

"Elbie, you and Colby tell your parents you are spending the night at my house. I will tell mine I'm spending the night at Colby's," I explained, trying not to sound condescending.

"Razz, now, why would you spend the night at Colby's when we are at your house? That's crazy," Elbie said, not grasping our plot.

Colby lost it, falling to his knees in laughter. Poor Anna Lee nearly developed a hernia trying not to laugh, but finally she succumbed and let loose. Once she relieved herself of that internal pressure, she quickly tried to stifle any further outbursts. I, like Colby, couldn't hold it in either.

"It's a ruse, Elbie. That's the only way we can get to spend the night in that house," I explained.

Elbie stood there blankly for a few seconds. I could tell he was trying to comprehend the situation, and then it finally came to him. He closed his eyes and tried to stifle a burst of embarrassed laughter, covering his face with his hands. The four of us, including Anna Lee, enjoyed a long moment of laughter.

"I can't believe I did that," he finally said, shaking his head and closing his eyes. He grimaced with embarrassment, but at the same time, he was also satisfied that he'd authored our moment of laughter.

We developed our plan and made sure everyone knew their part. Colby and Elbie were to tell their parents they were spending the night at my house. I would tell mine I was staying over at Colby's house, and Anna Lee would tell hers she was staying at Mary Jane Toler's home.

We were all to meet tomorrow at two o'clock behind the church at Knottsville and then head out on our bikes on Highway 144. It was over thirty miles to the Marshal Mansion, straight down 144; more than an hour and a half trip by bike with all the steep hills to climb. That should give us plenty of daylight time to explore the house and then prepare a place to sleep for the night. However, straight is not usually a word used when describing the incredibly curving Highway 144.

We each planned to pack a blanket, a jar of water, a flashlight, and a sandwich. Colby suggested each of us take a club just in case it was needed to fight off a ghost. Anna Lee held up her clenched fist and said that would be all she needed. Elbie rubbed his nose and nodded in agreement.

We excitedly ran back up the hill and said goodbye to Colby. The trip back home was full of excited chatter and stories about ghosts.

The next afternoon, all went as planned. We met behind the church, making sure no one saw us gather together. Elbie and Colby unknowingly arrived wearing similar red t-shirts. I looked at Anna Lee, and we both snickered.

"You look like the Bobbsey twins," Anna Lee said, and we burst out laughing.

"We do not," Colby quickly shot back. I wasn't sure if his resentment resulted from the comparison to the fictional child twins or that he looked like Elbie.

"What's up with the red shirts? The two of you look like brothers." I said jokingly.

"Uh, Razz, really?" Elbie answered, holding his hands out with an expression of dismay at my ignorance of the apparent differences.

"Great minds think alike, Razz," Colby retorted as he began to laugh as well.

"I can tell this is going to be an interesting trip already. Let's go," Elbie said, shaking his head.

We clustered together on our bikes, all hand-me-downs more than ten years old: no multiple gears, just a handlebar, chain, pedals, and two tires. Colby's bike and mine had no fenders to keep the mud from splattering on our backs or feet. Anna Lee's bike had fenders, but the carelessness and accidents of the previous owner had left them dented, cracked, and with more rust than paint. The previous owner had tried to fix the dents by hammering them out from the underside, but obviously, he was as inept at hammering as he was riding a bike. Elbie's bike was the only one with more paint than rust. Despite their appearance, the bikes allowed us the freedom of transport.

Colby left first, heading east on Highway 144. A few minutes later, Anna Lee followed him. Elbie was next, and I followed, each of us leaving several minutes apart to avoid anyone seeing us together.

We met up at an abandoned strip mine about three miles from town and wasted little time getting on our way. Highway 144 was as curvy as any road in the county. It possessed more curves than pi has numbers, and most of them dangerously sharp. It was like a winding roller coaster than a road. Deep chasms separated many of the steep hills, most gorged by the plunging cataracts of summer thunderstorms. The wily farmers, adept at using even the most precipitous slopes, turned both the upside and downside of the land into pasture, effectively doubling the size of grazing land.

The woods framing the crops and pastures created a beautiful pastoral scene worthy of a gasp from even the most experienced of master artists. With the temperatures embracing the low eighties and without a hint of humidity, the weather was perfect for a ride through the countryside.

As the excitement subsided slightly, we enjoyed the sounds of the eight spinning wheels and the rubber rolling on the asphalt. We rode four abreast as there was little traffic in that area, merging into a single file only when a farmer with a truck full of hay or cattle passed us. They all stared curiously at four seemingly lazy kids riding bikes for no productive reason. We discussed various topics pertinent to soon-to-be freshmen in high school and then the one item the four of us had had on our minds since the last day of school in May.

The county still had many segregated primary schools at the time, but the high schools were not. Colby would be joining us as a freshman in the fall, and we were about as excited as a six-year-old on Christmas Eve.

"Colby, are you looking forward to school this fall?" I asked, glancing over at him.

"I guess," he answered pensively.

"What's wrong with you, Colby?" Anna Lee asked, surprised. "It's going to be so much fun with the four of us at the same school."

"Are you worried, Colby?" Elbie asked.

The question startled Anna Lee and me. The thought of him being worried had never entered our minds. We'd been so caught up in the excitement of it that we'd never gone any more in-depth than the surface of the occasion. Had we been more empathetic, we might have foreseen Colby's cause for anxiety.

"Yeah, a little," he answered quietly, just above the sounds of the wheels on the pavement. "I mean, I know it will be great. You guys will make sure of that. But going to any new place is always a cause for caution. I'm sure most of the kids will be great, but it seems like there is always one or two who want to stir up trouble."

"Don't worry about that, Colby," Anna Lee replied. "We will be there for you if some moron wants to be a jerkweed."

"Anna, you guys can't always be there. It's okay. It's something that I need to handle. I can take care of myself," Colby replied. "Trust me; I'm excited about the four of us in the same classes this fall."

"Well, at least Peak won't be there next year. I heard he got kicked out of school," Elbie added, reveling at the thought.

"Colby, I'm sorry we didn't think about any issues. We only see you as our friend," I said. "I think most kids at school are like us and will treat you no different, but it's our concern now as well."

"I'm good, Razz. It's not a problem that I can't handle. It will all work out."

"We are talking about you being a boorish pedantic, aren't we?" Anna Lee chimed in as Elbie and I burst into laughter.

"Yeah, that's it, Anna Lee." Colby smiled. "But I'm surprised you know what pedantic means. You must have stayed up all night looking for words that you could use on me."

Anna Lee snickered.

"Hey, wait a minute, guys," she said, slowing her bike to a stop.

"I've been here before," she continued. "Look over there across that field."

We looked across a narrow stretch of pasture with only a couple of cows grazing on it. The land sloped down to a gorge over a hundred feet below; then it was another hundred feet back up to the other side. The pasture was steep enough that the cows had worn paths winding up and down the slope. On the far side, several hundred feet away, was a barbed wire fence next to a road atop the ridge.

On each of the fence posts, rusted tin cans or pieces of rusted tin were nailed to the tops.

"Why did they nail tin cans on the posts?" Elbie asked.

"To keep the rain off the post to help prevent rotting," Colby replied.

"That's the stupidest thing I ever heard of, Colby," Anna Lee remarked skeptically.

"I didn't make that up, Anna Lee. I'm just telling you that is why the farmer did it."

"Well, either this farmer is a couple of eggs short of a dozen or he never built a fence before," Anna Lee replied. "Every farmer I know is smart enough to realize that those locust posts will rot at ground level years before the tops will."

"Well, if you are so smart, why don't you tell that farmer that he's an incompetent fence builder?" Colby challenged, knowing she would not do that.

"I will if I see him, but only if he's a snotty toad. I doubt that would be the case, though, as all the farmers I know are nice people. But if I do tell him he's dumb, you will have to admit I got one over on you." she rebutted, weaseling her way out of this one.

"Fat chance," Colby replied, laughing contentedly.

"Alright, guys," I interrupted. "Anna Lee, did you mean you have been to the pasture or to the road on the other side of it?"

"The road. That is Hwy 144."

"I thought we were on Hwy 144," Colby said, confused.

"We are. This road goes on a mile that way and then turns over a bridge and comes back to over there," Anna Lee replied. "We could cut out over two miles if we cut across this field."

"How are we going to get our bikes across there?" Elbie asked, looking nervously down the steep slope.

"We walk them. The bottom is dry, so we go down slowly and then hurry back up. It will be fun and save us some time."

"The cows can't even walk a straight line up or down that hill, and they have four legs," Elbie objected.

"Come on, help me get my bike over the fence," Colby said to Anna Lee with some excitement for the new adventure.

"But…" Elbie tried to dissent, but we were already passing our bikes over the barbed wire fence to Colby.

Elbie finally hoisted his bike over to Anna Lee and Colby, and then he slipped through the fence as Colby stepped on the bottom wire, and I raised the middle one to make room for him. We looked down the slope and decided to weave downward using the cow paths. Then we began pushing the bikes in a single file. Anna Lee went first, I followed, and Colby and Elbie brought up the rear.

The bikes made the footing more challenging as we walked below the path on the steep slope down. Elbie, being the shortest, had the easiest task on the way down, but going back up, we placed our bikes above the path. That positioned Elbie head-high to his handlebars, making for an awkward stance. Occasionally, one of us would lose our footing and narrowly avoid a treacherous, tumbling descent with a bike toppling close behind. We didn't realize Elbie had a fear of heights, but we noticed he said little, too frightened to take his eyes off the ground.

158

We finally made it to the bottom and enjoyed a brief respite as the air was much cooler there. We crossed the rocky bottom and began our ascent up the grassy slope. Surprisingly, for most of us, it was easier going uphill than downhill. We were nearing the halfway mark when Anna Lee suddenly turned to the rest of us and said in a low voice, "Don't turn around! Keep looking straight ahead and keep going slowly up the hill."

Well, she might as well have yelled for us to turn around and look because now we knew something was behind us. The three of us turned to see the biggest bull we had ever seen about thirty feet downhill. If there had been a fence between him and us, we would have enjoyed viewing the finest specimen of a bull in the county. His large head with two intimidating, curved horns quickly caught our attention. His massive shoulders, wide body, and enormous rump took up more space than the four of us put together. He stared at us intently for a moment with eyes as big as golf balls, and then he snorted loudly and stomped his left hoof upon the ground.

I wish I could have been a bystander walking along the road to witness the sight of four screaming kids scrambling up that steep hill with their bikes while this massive bull shook the earth as it rumbled up the hill after them. I swear we could feel the ground shake as that angry behemoth rushed to catch us. Anna Lee and I began to pull away from Colby and Elbie as they both began to lose their footing. We could hear the bull's heavy breathing above the screams and the hooves thundering on the ground as he closed in on them. Anna Lee and I turned to look at them and could see the bull would reach them shortly.

Anna Lee dropped her bike, turned, and ran past me and toward them. I was shocked to see her foolishly charging a bull almost twenty times her weight. She reached Colby and Elbie, screaming for them to keep running, and then dug her heels into the ground to stop. She waved her hands wildly into the air, stared

159

straight into the charging bull's angry eyes, and screamed, "Get out of here!!!"

The bull stopped no more than five feet from her.

"Get out of here! Go on! Get out of here!" she continued yelling while waving her arms above her head.

Colbie and Elbie finally reached me with their bikes and headed to the fence. I stood there, unable to move, watching Anna Lee stand face to face with an angry animal who dwarfed her in size and temperament. She continued yelling and waving as the bull stomped his hooves and snorted angrily. She took a few slow steps backward and then stopped to yell at the beast. With each step, the bull took one as well, never letting her get more than the five feet away. I was either mesmerized or too frightened to move and barely noticed Colby and Elbie at my side, taking mine and Anna Lee's bikes up the hill to lift them over the fence with theirs. Elbie stopped briefly and yelled for me to come with them, but I remained paralyzed, watching Anna Lee in her dangerous contest with the bellicose bull.

Finally, Anna Lee reached me and screamed for me to get over the fence. With the bull that close, she did not have to say it twice. I ran the last few steps up the hill to join Colby and Elbie, but I continued to watch over my shoulder for Anna Lee. She and the bull appeared as two oddly equal warriors, both sparring but both afraid to start the war. I suppose that with Anna Lee a little higher up on the slope, screaming and with her arms flailing wildly into the air, she appeared larger to the bull than she was. It was evident that the beast badly wanted to dispatch this annoying girl, and his hesitance to do so angered him even more.

When Anna Lee finally reached within ten feet of the fence, I yelled for her to jump over it. She turned, took three quick steps, and catapulted over the wire fence, barely an inch over the rusted barbs. Colby, Elbie, and I all fell backward onto the ground as the bull stopped mere inches from the barbed fence, snorting angrily. Smelling the stench of his awful breath and other body parts, we scrambled backward on the ground in retreat.

Anna Lee was on her hands and knees, trying to catch her breath. Finally, between gasps for air, she motioned to Elbie and Colbie to move on down the road. They had no idea why she wanted them to do that but had no intention of disobeying the girl who had just saved their lives. After a moment, still on her hands and knees, Anna Lee caught her breath and turned toward me.

"Their shirts," she said between breaths.

"What?"

"Red shirts."

"Oh, crap!" I said, realizing what she meant. "Come on, let's go." I helped her up.

We'd just reached Colby and Elbie, who had been waiting patiently for us, when a truck pulled up with its brakes screeching. The front dash of the black vehicle was piled high with cans, trash, tools, nuts and bolts, and things we could not make out. I wondered how the driver could see the road over the mound of garbage. The door flew open, and a farmer jumped out.

"What are you kids doing to my bull?" he screamed angrily.

"Nothing, sir. He was chasing us," I replied.

"What are you doing on my land?!"

"We were just trying to save some time by short-cutting over to 144," Elbie answered politely.

"You have no right to trespass over my land. Where are you kids from?"

"Daviess County, sir. Near Knottsville," I said. I noticed both Anna Lee and Colby were surprisingly silent.

"Daviess County?! What are you doing way over here in Hancock County?" he demanded, looking over at Anna Lee and Colby with suspicion.

"We are on our way to see some friends in Breckenridge County," I fibbed, hoping to get out of there without divulging any more than necessary.

"You kids can't fool me. You're up to no good. I'm not sure if you are trying to steal something or vandalize something, but I can see it in your eyes."

"No, sir, we aren't," Elbie said. "We're sorry we got your bull upset. We didn't do it on purpose. We didn't even see him until he started chasing us. I promise you we won't do it again."

"You better not!" he shot back, and then he turned his head toward Anna Lee again. "Girl, what is your name?" he asked gruffly, glaring at her.

"Anna Lee Frazier, sir," she answered meekly.

"You with these boys of your own volition?"

"Yes, sir. We are all friends."

"This is the queerest group I ever saw," he said, shaking his head as he examined the four of us. "You are the most peculiar mix of kids ever to trespass our fine county. You're up to no good; that's for sure. I'm calling Sheriff Prater to tell him to keep an eye out for you. Then I'm calling Sheriff Minton in Breckinridge County after that. I'm not letting a bunch of ragtag kids from Daviess County come over here to do their miscreant deeds. Now, get out of here and don't ever come back," he growled, waving his hand.

"Sir," Anna Lee finally said in a polite tone, almost dripping with honey and with her most charming smile, "I wanted to tell you that putting those tin cans on top of the fence posts is the most doltish thing I ever saw. How did you come up with an idea like that?"

I looked at Colby with fear in my eyes. His widening, dismayed eyes met mine, and I could tell that he, too, was holding his breath. When she'd spoken the word "doltish," she'd made it sound as if it were something to give one a sense of immense pride. But if Colby and I could detect the derogatory intent, I was certain the farmer could, too. However, her bewitching smile and charming voice delighted him, as it would any of us, so I don't think he even heard the word. Either that or he thought this charming young lady simply did not realize the error in her vocabulary.

"Well, thank you, young lady," he answered, his entire body flushed with a pompous flair. "I thought of that all by myself."

"I'm sure you did," she answered as his demeanor became even more pretentious.

"You go on and be careful now," he politely urged as the four of us quickly mounted our bikes and pedaled away as fast as we could.

I looked back to see the farmer inspecting his animal from the fence, and then he disappeared from sight as we rounded a curve. Our encounter with the bovine beast and the farmer had left us emotionally shaken, but I held no grudge against either of them. The bull had only been doing what bulls do, and the farmer was concerned for his livestock and land. Regardless, we would not cross his property again. Anna Lee's audacity, however, begged for some clarity.

"Anna Lee," Colby said, "didn't you mean ingenious instead of doltish?"

"Nope," she replied smugly, her confident smile widening.

Colby did not answer.

"Colby!" I chastised.

"No way!" he objected. "Technically, she didn't say he was incompetent."

"Colby," I said, laughing, "that's exactly what she told him, and you know it."

"I have a feeling she got another one over on you, Colby," Elbie teased.

Colby sped up, pedaling down the road as fast as he could, with Anna Lee close behind, finally catching up with him as they rounded a turn. At first, they stayed ahead of us, and we were unable to hear their conversation. They soon slowed their pace to a more reasonable speed, allowing Elbie and me to catch up. I could tell Colby was beside himself, but Anna Lee, quite the opposite, was brimming with satisfaction over her sneaky insult.

We continued our trek toward Breckenridge County for about five minutes or so without speaking. As we began to settle down, Elbie thanked Anna Lee for rescuing us. Colby, setting aside his wounded pride, expressed his gratitude as well, but a little more tersely. She was very humble about her bravery, but I wasn't about to let it go.

"Anna Lee, that was the bravest and the craziest thing I ever saw. That two-thousand-pound bull could have run right over you. Whatever possessed you to do that?" I asked incredulously.

"Crazy, I guess. You're my friends, Razz, I just did it," she answered matter-of-factly, without looking at us. She quickly picked up her pace, increasing the distance between her and us.

"You were unusually quiet back there, Colby," I said as the three of us tried to catch up with her.

"The farmer was angry, Razz. If I had spoken up, it might have riled him even more. I knew you all could handle it."

He needn't say any more; I understood what he meant. I couldn't help thinking about that, though, for the next few moments. No matter how hard one may try, no matter how satisfied one feels that he is aware of another's plight in life, you can never completely grasp the feelings or trials of another unless you walk the proverbial mile. I sometimes thought I completely understood Colby's walk, but it seemed that every day, a new perspective appeared, and I regretted that I could not fully comprehend it, as I could not walk that mile.

We finally caught up with Anna Lee and resumed our ride with a more relaxed conversation. Eventually we began to laugh at our encounter and entertained ourselves by trying to estimate the actual weight of the bull.

Just before leaving Hancock County, we came upon a large lake with a solitary goose drifting aimlessly in the center. That seemed unusual, at least to us, to see a single goose alone in a lake.

"Look at all those geese!" Anna Lee shouted, pointing to a flock of twenty or more geese above the lake.

"Holy smokes!' Elbie exclaimed, seeing the large flock circling the lake.

We stopped our bikes to watch as the flock of geese descended upon the lake in a spectacular show, with each agile goose landing softly, making the smallest of splashes upon hitting the water, and then gliding gracefully in a theatrical appearance.

"Wow!" Elbie said, amazed at the sight.

"I have never seen anything like that," I added.

We watched quietly as the geese circled the lone goose, inching closer to him. Then it seemed that as each goose approached the lone goose, they greeted him, or at least accepted him.

The geese's interaction continued until each goose had taken his turn approaching the lone goose. There was no animosity or bullying. It was as if he were a long, lost old friend or possibly that he was only friendless and deserving of some consolation for his sad state; we weren't sure which.

Suddenly all the geese began clamoring, honking loudly, still circling the lone goose. Then, as if on cue, they took flight in another spectacular display and headed off into the skies, still honking loudly. They left the lone goose behind, who again possessed nothing but his loneliness.

"What was that?" Anna Lee asked, confused at what we'd just witnessed.

"That was amazing," I answered.

"Yeah, but why did they leave that one behind?" Elbie asked.

"My dad and I saw something similar once at Kingfisher Lake," Colby replied excitedly. "He explained that when a goose loses its mate, it will mourn and never mate with another for the rest of his life. He said the other geese were probably consoling him and had a small party for his lost mate."

"Colby, you can come up with some of the dumbest things," Anna Lee said, snickering condescendingly.

"Well, that's what my dad said," Colby retorted defensively.

"If I heard your dad say that, I would believe it. But coming from you, I'm not so sure. Grieving geese? That's a tall tale if I ever heard one, and having a party when someone dies? Whoever heard of that?"

"Well, Miss Smarty Pants, that's what he said," Colby replied testily. "As a matter of fact, he said that's what he wanted us to do when he passed. He said he didn't want us crying for him; we should have a big, happy party because he was going to a better place."

"I've heard that, too, Anna Lee," I said, defending Colby on this one, "that ducks and some geese never mate again after losing their mate. I'm not sure about geese throwing a party for a mourning widower, but who's to say that's not what they were doing?"

"Razz, I think you've gone nuts, too. You're just saying that because you don't want to embarrass Colby," Anna Lee argued.

"I think all three of you are nuts." Elbie shook his head, laughing, and pedaled off. "Come on before you try to tell me dogs have weddings. Let's get going," he urged over his shoulder.

We followed Elbie, with Anna Lee and Colby bantering for several minutes. I enjoyed staying within earshot of them, listening to their good-natured bickering. A stranger happening upon their bantering might have thought they were fighting. The truth is, as equal competitors, they shared a mutual respect, but neither could tolerate losing to the other.

Colby eventually tired of arguing with her and cut her short.

"Anna Lee, one day, I will prove it to you beyond any doubt, and you will be completely powerless to argue with me anymore."

"Fat chance," Anna Lee replied with a laugh.

We rode in silence for a few minutes as we ascended a steep hill that required all our energy and breath. When we entered Breckenridge County, we began our descent into the bottoms near the Ohio River. That was a pleasant break as coasting downhill allowed a brief respite for our aching legs.

We coasted several miles down the scenic road, in awe of the beautiful views of the immense river. Sometimes, through the trees, we enjoyed a dazzling display of the sparkling water below us. Other times, we feasted on a perfect view of several miles of the river, both east and west, from atop the cliffs as the road wound its way down just a few feet from the edge. I wondered if anyone could ever appreciate the natural beauty as much as the four of us. As we passed an occasional home nestled among the trees overlooking the river, I tried to imagine waking up each morning to see the sun rising over the valley and the majestic river as it crept around one of its many bends.

"We don't have to go past the Hobo Woods, do we?" Elbie asked nervously.

The Hobo Woods rested just south of the town of Addison. At one time, in the late 1800s and the early 1900s, a train stopped at Addison to refuel and allow guests to spend a day or two at the lone hotel. Many years ago, the train quit stopping at the Addison station, and now it passed through without the slightest of courtesies as one would a spurned former friend. The hotel was eventually torn down, and the hustle and bustle disappeared with it.

But in the days that the train was a regular visitor, hobos often jumped off it and congregated in the nearby woods. They camped in the woods for a few days to rest and eat and then jumped back on the next train in one of the cargo or cattle cars and headed off to another place.

We'd heard that there were still a few hobos living in the woods. A lot of rumors survived that the hobos stole or caught distracted kids and sold them or their body parts for money to buy liquor and cigarettes. We didn't know if that was true or not, but we did not want to find out. So, avoiding the Hobo Woods was a priority.

"No, Elbie. We are not going all the way to Addison. The Marshal Mansion is about a mile before," Colby replied, easing Elbie's worries.

When we reached the bottoms, the view of the river disappeared even though it was only a few hundred feet away on our left. With the corn now waist-high and the water level of the river about fifteen feet below us, we had a clear view of the cliffs on the Indiana side, but we could no longer see the river. At times, we could see the edge of the riverbanks but not the flowing water.

"There it is!" Colby shouted.

Chapter XV

1965

The Marshal Mansion

We looked ahead to see the beautiful home called the Marshal Mansion. Elbie and Anna Lee had never seen it before, and I relished watching their faces as they gazed upon it for the first time.

We pulled up to the open iron gate with its four-foot-tall, ornate iron posts, each capped with a simple, but elegant cap. We entered the front yard and stopped our bikes, four abreast, to admire the magnificent home. We stood silently for several minutes, straddling our bikes, moving our eyes up and down, and from one end to the other. It wasn't long before Elbie noticed a small family cemetery about a hundred and fifty feet right of the home. We decided that the gravesite deserved a closer examination later, but the house was first.

Two large oak trees, one on each side, framed the aged red brick-and-mortar home. It was an impressive three stories tall, with five full-size windows illuminating an attic. A long, florid iron rail guarded the second-floor balcony, which rested atop the porch roof and stretched the entire length of the original building. A door from one of the second-floor bedrooms gave access to the balcony for a view of the countryside. A sizeable addition to the home, built in later years, complemented the original and increased its size by more than a third. Despite its neglected state, the first impression of the stately home engendered a sense of importance and dignity. Without any prior knowledge of the home, one could readily see that it carried a persona of nobility. It may sound odd, but I can only compare it to when a charismatic

169

dignitary enters a room, without even a breath of introduction, and immediately electrifies the air inside, causing every head to turn to see what, or who, has changed the milieu.

The long, narrow windows on the first floor were adorned with flat cast-iron lintels. The arched second-floor windows, and the third-floor windows as well, profited from even more elaborate amenities. The mysterious attic dormers gave the home a visual flare while serving to illuminate the inside during daylight hours, but they certainly would create many eerie shadows at night. I was confident that if there were ghosts, that area possessed more of them than the rest of the home.

We stepped off our bikes and decided to park them in the back, out of view from the road. As we walked around the side, we were surprised that the depth of the home appeared much shorter, about forty-five feet, including the fourteen-inch-thick brick walls. Typical of many stately homes from that era, the length was about twice the depth. We quickly noticed the broad, unobstructed river as we came around to the rear.

The backside, to our disappointment, wasn't as stellar as the front, but it still possessed some charm. However, a small wooden addition that appeared oddly out of place detracted slightly from the stately home. Not a single flake of paint had survived on the aging gray addition. That smaller addition had obviously been built in later years, and most likely by an austere carpenter concerned more with functionality than aesthetics. We assumed its purpose was to store a few culinary needs or other items, but we later determined it was an enlargement of the kitchen and dining area.

We ran excitedly around the house to the front door and entered as would any duly invited guest, stepping cautiously inside the silent house. Though badly deteriorated, its stature still impressed. The fourteen-foot tall ceilings on the first floor rendered a spacious feeling inside the rooms, and we stood in awe of the ten-foot doors. Nearly every room had suffered equally, with wallpaper peeling helplessly from every angle, much of it having succumbed to gravity long ago and resting lifelessly on the floor. Except for the entrance and parlor, all other rooms were nearly square, about twenty feet wide and a little more than that in length. Each room possessed a fireplace to break the chill on a winter's evening. We found two stairways, one on the east side and one on the west, both extending up to the third floor. Both stairwells suffered from disrepair as well, but that could not suppress the beauty of the skilled craftsmanship and aesthetics of the once grandiose masterpieces.

A twelve-foot-wide hallway led to each of the three bedrooms on the first floor, and another twelve-foot-wide hall led to the three bedrooms on the second floor. The ceilings in the bedrooms on the second floor, not quite as elaborate as the first-floor bedrooms, were twelve feet tall, still an enormous height to us.

Most of the tall, narrow windows still held the original glass, but a few of the upper ones had no glass at all and were boarded up to keep out the opportunistic bats and determined elements. Looking out the windows from the inside, we could still see through the years of film. Most of the glass appeared slightly wavy, creating a warped view of the outside, but this did not inhibit the windows' primary duty of allowing ample light the inside rooms.

We explored the entire house, inspecting nearly every nook and cranny. Once comfortable that we had surveyed all that was necessary, we chose the parlor as our sleeping area. That decision was based on the proximity of the front door if a hasty exit was needed. We found no evidence of ghosts, but we had not expected to in the daylight. Tonight, however, would be different.

Having completed our self-guided tour of the home, the four of us sprinted to the gravesite. It was a small cemetery with close to thirty stones marking the graves. Some of the gravestones were very large and of different shapes. There was a tall one shaped like a church steeple, another an obelisk. A few were square or rectangular, while others were rounded at the top like a window frame. Most of the inscriptions included dates in the 1800s. Many had the last name of Marshal, but others listed different last names; most likely, those were relatives or friends. Then there was Judge John Marshal's massive stone, taller than any man, with a life-size copper eagle resting atop it with its expansive wings spread, ready to take flight. The green color of the aged copper enriched the beauty of the impeccably detailed bird.

A rusted wrought iron fence, still as sturdy as the day it had been built over 150 years ago, enclosed the gravesite. The overgrown grass inside the burial site was about a foot high, but few weeds had taken up residence there.

We remained, leaning over the fence silently for a moment, surveying the markers. But Colbie and Elbie quickly grew bored with the small cemetery and became eager to explore the Ohio.

"Come on, Elbie," Colbie urged. "Let's go look at the river."

And with that, they were off to the banks of the Ohio. Anna Lee and I remained, quietly taking in the aura of the historic cemetery.

"Razz," she finally said, breaking our silence while gazing at the cemetery, "do you think I'm overbearing?"

I turned to her, surprised at this hint of a lack of confidence and her sudden change of conversation.

"No, not at all, Anna Lee," I answered cautiously. "But you are confident in yourself, and sometimes that may intimidate others who aren't so blessed."

She said nothing for a moment, still staring at the cemetery.

"Everyone thinks I'm confident, but sometimes, when I'm alone, I'm crying inside," she replied without emotion. "Do you think I'm…different?"

It shocked me to see this side of Anna Lee, and I was uncertain how to answer.

"What do you mean by different, Anna Lee?"

"I don't know. Sometimes I don't know who I am, and it eats at me until I get sick to my stomach. I know I'm different than all the other girls."

"Do they tease you?"

"Some do, but that doesn't bother me. It's just that sometimes I have feelings and thoughts inside that I don't understand. It scares me so, and there are times I just lie in bed, crying. I don't know how to deal with them." Her stare remained fixed on the gravesites.

I could sense how deeply those fears affected her, whatever they were, and I was awed at how her public persona was so completely different. At that time, I did not comprehend what she was trying to say, but her trust in sharing that with me made me feel closer to her than I ever felt to anyone before. I thought a moment before replying.

"We all have fears inside, some more than others, but we all have them. You are different, Anna Lee, and I don't always understand that. But that is who you are. That is how you were born, just the same as you and I were born left-handed. It may be an inconvenience sometimes, but we can't change that, so we deal with it."

I stopped for a few seconds to see her reaction to my answer. She remained motionless, staring at the cemetery. I took a deep breath and continued.

"Anna Lee, you are different, but I like who you are, whoever you are, and I hope you never change. I wouldn't want you any other way, and I'm glad you are my friend."

She turned to look at me with moistened eyes and a soft smile.

"Thanks, Razz," she said as she lowered her head and wiped her eyes.

We both stared silently at the cemetery for a few moments. The tears in her eyes had filled me with intense emotions. I was just about to put my arm around her shoulders when I heard her sniffle as she composed herself. She abruptly changed her composure, standing stiffly and displaying that familiar confidence once again.

"We better check on those other two before they get themselves into trouble," she said with a laugh.

We turned and walked toward the riverbank, quiet for a moment.

"Razz, I don't have a sister or anyone else my age I can talk to about these things. You are the only one I have. You won't say anything to anybody about our talk, will you?" she asked in an unusually timorous tone as she stared at the ground.

"No way, Anna Lee. I saw what you did to Elbie's nose," I replied, and we both broke out in a fit of laughter.

We reached Colby and Elbie, who were sitting on the bank just a few inches from the swiftly moving water. We sat down beside them in awe of the currents and the immense river. It was like nothing we had seen before and could not be compared, in any way, to the creeks back home other than that it was composed of the same element: water.

A large tugboat sounded its horn as it came around the bend, ever so slowly heading east, upriver. It pushed eight empty barges, two abreast in a line of four, against the currents on its way, most likely to Pennsylvania. Another blast of a tugboat's horn came from our right, heading downriver. We had not noticed this one, even though it was closer to us, and the blast of its horn startled the four of us.

174

The tugboat headed downstream, pushing six full barges overflowing with black coal, was most likely on its way to New Orleans. It moved much faster than the one heading upstream, even with its six full barges. We'd never realized how much the currents would affect their speed. We noticed how the barges full of coal were only a few feet from being submerged, while the empty barges going east sat high in the water, at least fifteen feet or more. Both barges were nearly silent, with only a slight humming of the tugboat engines. The waves generated by the large barges slowly slapped against the banks, creating a calming sound. We quickly climbed several feet back up the bank as the incoming waves rose well beyond our previous resting place.

As the two tugboats passed each other, we were amazed at how large they were, especially the one going upstream. It dwarfed the one full of coal and completely obscured our view of it momentarily. As they began to disappear around the bends, the waning waves continued to splash ashore for several minutes, completely mesmerizing us as we watched in silence.

Watching the tugboats, we hadn't noticed that the sun had begun its descent. Its glow reflected off the surface of the water, making the entire river appear as if it were an immense flow of liquid gold. At one time, the golden hue was so brilliant it nearly blinded us. As the sun began to set below the horizon, the river of gold began a slow conversion back to its natural gray. I suggested we get ready for darkness and return to the house.

We unpacked our blankets, shared our food, and settled down in the darkening parlor. Our emotions vacillated from excitement to fear as the reality of spending the night now became a reality, not just a frivolous game.

As the temperature cooled outside, the house cooled as well, but not quietly. The pops and creaks throughout the house, as well as other unexplained noises, demanded our attention.

"It might be a long night," Elbie said nervously.

"Hopefully, it will quieten down later," Colby added cautiously.

"Don't count on it," Anna Lee advised.

We began to talk to take our minds off the cranky house and its persistent, ominous sounds. Laughing helped to distract us from our fears, and we did so often, with little provocation. However, as night overcame dusk and the house darkened completely, our nervous laughter subsided as we became overwhelmed with apprehension. We turned on our flashlights, oblivious to any conservation of the batteries. Had we taken turns, turning on only one light at a time, the night might have turned out differently. But we didn't, and we paid dearly for that error.

There was no light within miles except for our flashlights. At one time, we turned off all the flashlights, experiencing complete, utter darkness. A finger placed an inch away from our eyes was no more visible than a blind man's. Unfortunately, when we turned off the flashlights, that opened a door for the ghosts and every other diabolical and malevolent creature to surface in a cacophony of unexplained noises. Although we turned the flashlights back on within seconds, it was too late as the door had opened, and the sounds continued unabated.

We remained huddled together in the parlor, trying to divert our attention to more agreeable thoughts, but we remained wary of every sound. Elbie suggested we leave the front door cracked open in case a hasty exit was needed, and everyone quickly agreed. Unfortunately, the old home had developed many drafts over the last 150 years, causing the door to slam shut shortly after opening it. The sudden noise frightened each of us, inducing unashamed screams from everyone. Finally, Colby placed his empty mason jar in between the door and the frame to prop it open.

We began to get used to the eerie sounds, and with four of us together, it helped us gather some courage. It seemed that it had been dark for hours, but without a watch to tell time, we could not be sure. However, one by one, our flashlights began to dim and then finally go dark. Colby's was the last one to falter. In the total darkness, unless we spoke, it seemed we each were utterly alone, with no friends to help ease our fears.

Colby suggested we continue talking to drown out the increasingly loud noises. That worked for a while, but the constant loud sounds coming from upstairs unnerved all of us. Elbie suggested we sleep on the porch so we could have easy access to run. However, we nixed that idea as that would not count as spending the night in the house.

After what seemed like several more hours, we tried to lie down, hoping to fall asleep. None of us expected that to happen with all the noises circling about us, but it was worth making the effort. Pulling our blankets over us and using our jackets for pillows, we lay side by side, Colby and me on the outside and Elbie and Anna Lee on the inside, with Anna Lee next to me. Colby and I had devised that order to keep Elbie from running off in the middle of the night. It didn't matter, though, as the curious pops, creaks, and outright bangs in the house prevented sleep of any duration.

After a few moments in the darkness, I felt Anna Lee's hand brush mine softly. Then she rested it aside mine, our hands touching each other's for a few seconds until she moved it away. I took a deep breath as a sudden rush overcame me. I sensed she was attempting to hold my hand. Trying not to push her, I chose not to move mine, and I lay there motionless, hoping she would do it again. All the eerie sounds in the house seemed to disappear for me as I closed my eyes, hoping that she finally might carry the same feelings for me as I did for her.

Suddenly Colby's jar rolled across the floor as if kicked, and the door slammed shut. Startled, we jumped and tried to determine what had caused it. We foolishly looked around the room, but with no light, that was as futile as trying to hold water in a sieve. We sat up and huddled together, Colby and Elbie sitting with their backs together and Anna Lee pressing her back to mine.

"Guys, I think we need to get out of here," Elbie pleaded.

"Be still, Elbie," Colby insisted. "I think someone is in here."

We heard the back-door slam and then steps running up the east stairs. We couldn't tell how many, but it sounded like more than one set of feet. A loud crash came from the upstairs as if someone, or something, had fallen to the floor, followed by several audible groans. Then more steps walked up and down the hallway on the second floor.

The four of us, frightened beyond clear thoughts, tightened our huddle as close as we could, disregarding any sense of privacy of one's space. Had we been of clear mind, we could have calmly gotten up and left; had we done so, we might have prevented what was to come.

"There's someone in here," Colby insisted again.

He was not one to exaggerate. His logical demeanor and rational, analytical nature were something we all admired. So, when he said that, we did not doubt him.

"Where, Colby?" I asked.

"I don't know, but there is someone definitely in this room."

I could hear Elbie breathing rapidly. I worried he was on the verge of hyperventilating, but I was more concerned about who was in the room with us.

"Calm down, Elbie," Anna Lee said, trying to ease his nerves.

However, as soon as she said that, we heard a horrible growl coming from the corner of the room. I screamed, as did the other three. Then we heard someone running down the stairs, accompanied by more growling. This was followed by determined steps in the parlor, and we jumped up into the darkness and ran wildly in every direction, trying to find the door. I heard Elbie trip over some blankets; then Anna Lee crashed into a wall, knocking her back to the floor. I bumped into a ghost or someone much taller than I and screamed as loudly as I could.

We spent the next minute bumping into walls or each other while tripping over everything we had brought into the room. Suddenly I heard Colby from across the room.

"Over here, guys. I think I found the do—"

Before he could finish, we heard the door burst open, and Colby slammed against the wall. I heard someone running behind me and then up the east stairs. Suddenly the brightest light I ever saw in my life shone right into my eyes.

Chapter XVI

1965

The Reckoning

"They're in here, Piper. I got them. Don't anybody move," a voice behind the flashlight ordered. He scanned the room with his light, finding the four of us sprawled out in every corner in every imaginable way. Elbie was crouching down with his hands over his head. I lay flat on my back after tripping, and Anna Lee hid on the floor under a blanket. Poor Colby sat against the wall behind the door, dazed.

Someone else entered with another bright flashlight. With the lights shining brightly into our eyes, we could not tell who they were. The two of them ordered us to get up and gather in the middle of the room, and then they placed handcuffs on us.

"Check the upstairs, Piper. Make sure we got them all."

We assumed he was the sheriff or one of his deputies. We pleaded our innocence but were met with a stiff reprimand to be quiet. He marched the four of us to a car, and when he opened a door, we could see the sheriff's emblem on the vehicle.

"Get in, all of you," he ordered in a gruff tone, and we scurried into the backseat as fast as we could. He then slammed the door shut, locking us inside the car. Squeezed tightly in the back seat, we were in total darkness again. We saw his flashlight heading toward the house, and then he disappeared inside.

"What are we going to do, Razz?" Elbie fretted.

"I don't know, Elbie. I don't know," I replied in the darkness.

"This is all my fault, guys," Colby apologized. "I'm sorry I got you into this."

"Colby, we all are in this together," Anna Lee said quietly. "It is all our fault, not yours, not Razz's, but all of us. We got ourselves in this mess together, and we will get out of it together. Together, got it?"

We became silent, waiting for our fate. None of us had ever been in a sheriff's car before or even ran afoul of the law in any way. Unaccustomed to any of this, we feared the worst. My gut, wrenching in terrible knots, made me feel nauseous. All we could do now was wait silently.

Suddenly the driver's door opened, and the ceiling light, as dim as it was, blinded me. The sheriff—or deputy, we didn't know which—got into the car and closed the door. He asked each of us our names and wrote them down. He started the engine, put the car in gear, ordered us to remain silent, and drove off. As he pulled away, I noticed another sheriff's car still parked in front of the house and a flashlight moving upstairs.

It was almost a twenty-minute drive before we pulled up to the jail in Hardinsburg. He marched us into the stone building in a single file. When we entered, the officer turned slightly, enough that I could see his deputy badge and a nametag with "Tom" on it. I was unable to see his last name as he directed us to keep moving. We passed an empty desk and then walked down a short hall to a metal door with a sign painted on it that read, "Holding Room."

We heard the jingle of keys, followed by a loud clang as the latch released, and then he opened the door. We entered a small room with two wooden folding chairs leaning against one wall. There was nothing else except for a single light bulb hanging from the ceiling.

"Stand over there," the deputy demanded, motioning us to the far wall.

We immediately formed a single line. He walked over to me and removed my cuffs and then the others' in silence. He placed the handcuffs on his belt, stepped across the room, and stared at us menacingly without a word.

We fidgeted in line as the silence wore on us and the anxiety began to build.

"Be still," he ordered tersely.

After about ten excruciating minutes, we heard keys outside the door and the loud clang of the latch, and then the door opened. Another deputy stood aside, holding the door as a tall man barreled down the hall and burst into the room.

"Are these the Marshal vandals?" he asked in a forceful, angry voice as he entered the holding room and surveyed the four of us with a stern scowl on his face.

He was a figure of stature, mature yet agile, and dressed impeccably for that time of night. He was a little over six feet tall, of medium weight, and stood as straight as an arrow. His gray hair was thick and wavy. He wore neatly pressed blue jeans and a starched, white shirt with the top two buttons unfastened, and his demeanor exuded a presence of authority. His brown house shoes evinced the fact that a leisurely evening at home had been abruptly disturbed, and his glower confirmed it. We cowered in his presence, knowing that this agitated man held our fate.

"We caught all four of them red-handed, Sheriff Minton," Deputy Tom replied smugly. "Piper and I found them camping in the front room. It looked like they planned on spending the night, with blankets, food, and water strewn all over the floor as if they owned the place. They ransacked the place, but we won't be able to assess any damage until morning."

"We didn't do anything!" Elbie cried. "We were just going to see if there were any—"

"I'm not talking to you," Sheriff Minton growled, and the four of us immediately lowered our heads in an involuntary response of deference. "I'm going to throw the book at you vandals, and I can assure you that if you leave here, dead or alive, you'll never come back again. I'm going to see to that. That house may not seem like much to you, but it is a source of pride for our county."

He reached for some papers that Deputy Tom held and glanced over them quickly. Then, rolling them up and holding them in his left hand, he stared at Anna Lee.

"Which one of you is Anna Lee Frazier?" he asked grumpily. We could not tell whether he meant that as a slight to Anna Lee or us. Either way, it was a slight that went unchallenged.

"I am, sir," Anna Lee replied submissively, her voice shaking.

"Cuff these three scoundrels and take them to the cell so they can get used to it," Sheriff Minton barked to the deputy, pointing to Elbie, Colby, and me. "If you lose the key, it won't matter. I'm going to see to it that they'll be here a long time. Then bring the girl to my office."

He turned briskly and disappeared behind the hall door, followed by Deputy Piper.

Our hearts sank. Our lives were about to change drastically over what we'd thought would be an innocent, harmless night of fun. Not once had we thought the night would end up with criminal records, jail time, juries, and judges in Breckenridge County and with unknown atrocities for Anna Lee. I think, at that moment, the three of us were more worried about her than ourselves. That was about to quickly change in a few minutes once we considered how our parents were going to react upon hearing we were in jail.

Deputy Tom put cuffs on the three of us and then grabbed Anna Lee's arm and briskly led her out of the room, locking the heavy door behind them. The clang of the lock on the metal door sealed our fate, and we began to realize the severity of our predicament.

Before disappearing quietly behind the hall door, Anna Lee glanced back at Colby and me and then at Elbie. I will never forget the look on her face; it was a mixture of fear and a complete realization that she had no control over her destiny. I think that lack of control weighed more on her than fear or any fate that lay before her. I cried inside for her, knowing I could not help her.

Elbie sniffed quietly, while Colby hung his head and stared at the floor. I realized that Colby had not said a word in the presence of the deputies, nor the sheriff.

"You okay, Colby?" I asked, almost in a whisper.

He did not answer.

"What is going to become of us, Razz?" Elbie asked, looking up at me with reddened eyes.

Before I could answer, we heard the clang of the hall door lock again, and the grim Deputy Tom returned, staring indignantly at us. He walked past us without a word and unlocked a door behind us with that now-familiar clang.

"Let's go," he ordered, motioning for us to exit through the door.

Closing the door behind us, he led us down a dimly lit hall with several other heavy, windowless doors. When we reached the end of the hallway, he unlocked a metal door. The sharp clang of the latch felt like a dagger thrust into my gut. We entered a very dim, small, windowless room with metal benches along the side walls and an open toilet with no tissue sitting alone near the wall opposite the door; there as nothing else except the smell of urine in the dark, dank room. He closed the door without a word, and the loud clang of the lock crushed any remaining spirit we might have harbored.

Colby and Elbie sat on one bench; I sat alone on the other.

"I'm sorry, guys," Colby said again, filled with remorse.

"It's not your fault, Colby," I replied.

We said no more, sitting in silence.

184

"Sit down," the sheriff said, and Anna Lee quietly complied.

Sheriff Minton put on his glasses, unfurled the papers, and read over them. After a moment, he laid the papers upon his desk, took his glasses off, set them softly on his desk, and looked at Anna Lee.

"Miss Frazier, what is a young lady like you doing two counties away from home, spending the night with three boys? What would your parents say if they knew that?"

"It's not like that, Sheriff."

"What do you mean, it's not like that? It sure looks like that!"

"They are just friends, Sheriff Minton."

"Right. And I'm still fifty years old. Boys are boys. Don't you know that?"

"Sheriff, they would not hurt me in any way, no more than I would them. We are friends."

"Maybe, but it still looks like that. Do you know what people will say when they find out you spent the night with three teenage boys? Don't you care about what people will think?"

"Sheriff Minton..." Anna Lee paused and took a deep breath. "I have no control over what other people may think. I have found that people see what they want to see, even if the facts are jumping up and down, screaming right in front of them. As a matter of fact, I think the more effort the facts put into showing them the truth, the more stubborn people will be in believing what suits them. So, no, I don't care what others may think. As long as I am comfortable with myself and hurting no one else, they can think whatever they want."

"What about your parents?"

Anna Lee hung her head and covered her eyes, pressing her fingers lightly to her forehead. Then looked at Sheriff Minton and

185

said softly, "My parents know Razz, Colby, and Elbie. My being with them would not bother them, no matter what the talk. But I have hurt them, Sheriff Minton." Tears began to swell in her eyes. "I have hurt them. I lied to them about where I was going. You can lock me up for as long as you want, but that won't come close to the hurt I will feel when they find out I lied. Losing their trust in me…" She stopped.

The sheriff leaned back into his chair, took a deep breath, and sighed.

Anna Lee looked up at him, and for the first time, she saw kindness in his eyes and an avuncular smile on his face.

"I like you, Anna Lee. You are a good person. You remind me of my daughter when she was your age. What are you going to do with yourself?"

Anna Lee wiped her eyes with the back of her wrists and stared at the sheriff. "What do you mean?" she asked, somewhat confused.

"After high school, are you going to college?"

Anna Lee paused, disconcerted with the change of subject.

"Well… I want to go to school in New York, but my parents could never afford that. I'll go to school somewhere, hopefully away from here."

"Why not here?"

"I want more than this. I don't mean that in a bad way, but I don't fit here. It's just not me."

"There are a lot of advantages to growing up in a smaller community, you know," the sheriff said patiently.

"Oh, I wouldn't want to grow up anywhere else, Sheriff. It's just that when it is my time to go, I want more. Do you know what I mean?"

"Yes, I do. We are all different. Not everyone fits in the same box." He paused for a few seconds.

"Anna Lee, I have a problem. You see, not only did the four of you trespass on private property, but there were also three hobos upstairs trying to get out of the cold. We officially don't allow them in there, but we tend to ignore them unless there is a disturbance. That is where the four of you come in. When my deputies searched the house, they found them as well and had to arrest them."

"They could have kidnapped us or killed us!" Anna Lee exclaimed, shocked that they hadn't.

"They said they were only trying to scare the four of you into leaving, Anna Lee. Despite the stories you have heard, those hobos are not evil. They are people just like you and me; they have simply had a run of bad luck that has spiraled them into a hole so deep that it is difficult for them to climb out. Most of them are trying to find work so they can send money back home to their families. But once they have an arrest record, it is almost impossible for them to get work again. They may never find work now. That is why they were trying to scare you away. They were afraid you would attract attention, and someone might call us; they did not want a record."

"That's awful. Can't you just let them go?"

"No. If word got out that we did that, the Marshal Mansion would become a hotel for all of them. And if the four of you get off with impunity, then every kid in five counties will be making a pilgrimage to the house. That's my problem. I don't want to punish some good kids who just got a little mischievous, but I have to let everyone know that house is off-limits. That is why my deputies and I tried to scare the four of you with threats of jail time."

Anna Lee hung her head, realizing what they had done.

"If you will make a deal with me, we might have a way out of this with minimal pain for everyone."

Anna Lee stared at him uncomfortably, worried at what he was proposing.

"What do you want?" she asked nervously.

"I want you to promise me two things. First, I want you to promise you will go to college somewhere and get that degree; you need to make your mark in life and help others, like the hobos, who are not so fortunate. Second, I want you to play along with me when we get back in the room with those boys and promise me you will never tell anyone about this conversation. Is it a deal?"

"Yes."

"So, tell me about those boys out there; are they all good kids?"

We heard the clang of the lock again. As the door opened, we squinted our eyes as the light in the hallway filtered into the cell.

"Follow me!" Deputy Tom ordered sternly.

He led us back into the holding room where they'd first cuffed us. Anna Lee stood against the wall, still handcuffed, hanging her head and staring at the floor. I wanted to ask if she was okay, but I was certain that a swift reprimand, at the least, would follow.

Deputy Tom lined the three of us against the wall next to Anna Lee and then walked to the other side and stood near the door with his feet spread, arms folded, and a grim stare fixed upon his face. The three of us joined Anna Lee in staring at the floor. That was less painful than seeing the deputy's glare.

Again, the sharp clang of the door startled us, followed by the sheriff entering briskly with Deputy Piper. He stared contemptuously at the four of us and then turned to the deputy.

"Piper, do we still have those thirty-pound weights in the workout room?"

"Yes, sir," the deputy answered without emotion.

"Go get four of them."

We waited silently for the deputy to return. I had no idea what was waiting for us with the weights, but the fear and agony in my gut made me feel faint. I could only imagine how the others felt.

Deputy Piper soon returned with the four thirty-pound barbells and stood by the sheriff. I was impressed he could carry two in each hand with little effort.

"Tom, take off their cuffs," he said, motioning toward us.

After Deputy Tom removed all our handcuffs, the sheriff nodded to Deputy Piper, who then marched over to us and handed each of us a barbell. I could throw a forty-pound bale of hay without too much trouble, but the thirty-pound barbell's weight was more concentrated and seemed heavier.

"Hold it with both hands and raise it over your heads," the sheriff ordered brusquely.

We complied without protest.

"You came over here to vandalize our heritage. What you didn't know is we do things differently here in Breckenridge County," the sheriff said in a stern, methodical voice. "Tom wanted to lock you up until your court hearing. Piper wanted to take you out back and teach each of you a lesson you would never forget. We could say the hobos roughed you up, and you would never tell anyone different; that is, if you knew what was good for you. Personally, I like something that will last a little longer and that you will never forget."

The weight was surprisingly heavy, even with two hands. I felt an aching in my shoulders and my arms. I could see Elbie's arms trembling slightly, his face grimacing. Colby and Anna Lee seemed to be struggling as well.

"So, here is what we are going to do. The first one of you that drops the barbell or lowers it, I will let him or her go home without any more punishment. But I'll lock the rest of you up and keep you locked up for as long as the courts will let me; it might be four or five days or a month. I'm hoping for a month."

The sheriff began to chastise us severely. We did not know it at the time, but it was the same talk he'd given Anna Lee about the house and the hobos, but more contentious.

We felt remorse for our actions, but the weights were becoming unbearably heavy. None of us wanted to be the one to betray our friends, so we struggled mightily to hold them above our heads. My legs began to shake, and the pain in my shoulders stiffened. I noticed Elbie was breathing rapidly and struggling painfully with the weight. Anna Lee was struggling as well, but I saw her glancing at Elbie as he struggled terribly to keep the weight above his head.

"Sheriff Minton, please, can we make this right some other way?" she asked in a halting voice. The weight of the barbell affected her breath.

"What do you have in mind, young lady? You do realize the seriousness of this offense, I hope," he growled.

"Yes, sir, I do. We want to make it right. Please, can we put the weights down, and we'll take whatever punishment you feel appropriate."

He looked sternly at Anna Lee as one would an impertinent child begging for forgiveness after sneaking cookies from the kitchen jar for the third time.

"Are you boys in agreement here?" he asked the three of us.

"Yes, sir," all of us replied quickly. That was the first word I'd heard from Colby.

The sheriff thought for a moment and then said, "Alright, then. Put the weights down gently, and you better not drop them!"

We complied, but Elbie put his barbell down considerably less gently than the rest of us.

"What do you suggest, Miss Frazier?" The sheriff asked, folding his arms across his chest.

"What if we come over here and clean up the cemetery, the grounds, and the house? The four of us can spend next Saturday and Sunday working on it," Anna Lee offered. We nodded fervently.

"Alright, but it will be two weekends, not one. I will have someone from the Marshal Preservation Committee stay with you to supervise. If I find out you didn't do everything she asked or to her satisfaction, I'll lock every one of you up and throw away the key."

There were four quick responses of "I will" and four responses of "Thank you, Sheriff Minton."

"But I'm not letting you go home," he added as our brief moment of relief quickly disappeared. "I'm going to take each one of you to your front door and wake up your parents. I'm looking forward to telling them the seriousness of this offense and letting them administer whatever punishment they deem proper."

I did not think my heart had any room to sink lower than it already had, but it did. We would have given a year of weekends in exchange for the sheriff not knocking on our parents' doors at one in the morning.

The four of us filed into the sheriff's cruiser in silence and remained in silence through all of Breckenridge County, Hancock County, and Daviess County. We sat with our hands in our laps, either with heads down or staring blankly out the window. Not a single car met us on the road, and the car's headlights shining on the black asphalt was all we could see; none of us could bear to look at the others.

We reached Colby's home first. The sheriff led him to the porch and knocked on the front door as the three of us in the car watched, knowing that would be our fate soon.

We heard the sheriff apologize for the late-night visit and then explain the reason for waking them. He pointed to the rest of us still in the car, explaining that all four were equal culprits. Colby's dad looked around the sheriff at us. In the dim light of the porch, I saw him drop his shoulders and exhale deeply. The look of disappointment from Mr. Harris was an unbearable dagger in our hearts. I heard Anna Lee let out a quiet cry, which she quickly stifled by covering her mouth with her hands. Elbie looked away, also unable to withstand the hurt in Mr. Harris's demeanor. Tears welled up in my eyes as well.

We heard Mrs. Harris ask Colby in an angry voice how he could desecrate the house that had given freedom to so many people. Colby could do nothing but hang his head. They thanked the sheriff for his kindness and led Colby into the house. Before closing the door, Mrs. Harris turned to look at the three of us in the car and shook her head, her hands firmly on her hips. That was only the second time I'd ever seen Anna Lee cry, both in the same night. I might have cried as well, but the knot in my throat prevented that, though not the flow of tears.

We later found out Colby's punishment was to help his dad at work for two weeks. That sounds like a light punishment, but Colby had never realized how hard his dad had to work to support his family. He also learned how honest and kind Mr. Harris was, and he could now understand why everyone respected him so. Colby emulated what he learned from his dad for the rest of his life.

Anna Lee's house was next. Her dad's disappointment equaled Mr. Harris's as he listened to the sheriff explain our transgression. Anna Lee stood with her head down while her mother covered her mouth in disbelief. The three of them remained silently on the porch as the sheriff walked back to the car. Mrs. Frazier looked at us and shook her head slightly as if to say, "I can't believe you did this." Elbie, again, looked out the other window, and I mouthed the words "I'm sorry" to Mr. and Mrs. Frazier, but I'm confident they could not see it in the darkness.

Anna Lee never shared her punishment with us, and it was a long time before she could talk openly about that night.

Elbie followed the script as well, hanging his head while the sheriff explained to his parents our poor discretion. When the sheriff finished, Elbie's mom said she would take care of his punishment, grabbed him by the collar, and jerked him into the house. We heard her yell something at him but could not make it out. Elbie's dad talked to the sheriff for a few minutes, thanked him, and waited until the sheriff had left before entering the house, which was now full of wide-eyed kids wondering what their big brother had done this time.

Elbie told me his father's reprimands had been many, but he did not tell me what they were except one: he had to self-impose a punishment as if it were his kid who had lied to his parents. Again, he would not reveal what he'd chosen, but he did say, "No way would I make my kid do his sister's chores."

I was last. Punishments are different when you reach fourteen: no spankings, no slaps on the wrists, no standing in corners, and no taking away toys or playtime. At fourteen, the disappointed looks hurt more, and the subtle reminders that parents can no longer trust you may go on for several months. Other punishments, such as doing volunteer work, are more of an inconvenience, but the most painful is that at fourteen, you begin to realize you are now nearing adulthood. Once treated as an adult, you begin to enjoy those amenities. Unfortunately, acts such as what we did that night are cause for immediate demotion back to childhood status, and we lost our parents' fleeting regard for us as an adult. The time it takes to earn it back again is excruciatingly long for a fourteen-year-old. I, too, prefer not to say what my punishment was, but one can readily understand that I tried my best never again to lose my parents' confidence or respect in me.

We had always been close, but we grew even more so after that night at the Marshal Mansion. When the four of us finally got back together, we noticed each of us seemed more mature. We didn't see it in ourselves, but we did in our friends. We'd matured more in those two weeks than in any of the previous fourteen years. When school started in the fall, many of our classmates now seemed immature in many ways.

Anna Lee did break her promise to Sheriff Minton and eventually revealed her cooperation with him on our punishment. However, it was many years later and only after Sheriff Minton had passed. She explained Sheriff Minton's concerns and his request that she ask for a lesser punishment when one of us appeared unable to hold up the weight. I now realize how wise the sheriff was and wish more were like him. He could have handled the affair in many ways, but he was astute enough to accomplish a result with minimal repercussions.

We learned several valuable lessons that night and never trespassed again. The hobos quit using the house, and the Marshal Mansion looked much better after we completed our cleaning duties. Sheriff Minton accomplished all that while evading as many legal records as possible. I don't know it to be a fact, but I would not be surprised if he also found a way to release the hobos without any records of arrest.

Sheriff Minton is long gone now, having passed in the early 1990s, but the Marshal Mansion still stands as proud and beautiful as it always was. The small community struggles to preserve the house, but many volunteers keep it alive, and their annual open house attracts many from all over the country.

I have been back to visit several times during the open house, and I still marvel at the home, its history, and its beauty. Each time I return, I remember the night, the four of us became inseparable friends for life and matured as young adults. But most of all, I will never forget the time Anna Lee and I shared at the cemetery and the night that she almost held my hand, or at least, that is how I wish to remember it.

Chapter XVII

1968

The Dress

After that night, and while we were in high school, the four of us spent as much time together as we could, and it was nice to have Colby attending our school. Most everyone soon took to him, and he quickly made a lot of friends. Unfortunately, there were some occasions when a few uneducated students gave him a difficult time, but that never stopped Colby. He had his goals and remained steadfast in his confidence to achieve them. We all knew he would make it and was destined to become someone of great importance.

Elbie matured into a respectable young man by his senior year, and he, too, was about to make his mark.

Anna Lee, as usual, acquired a lot of friends. We knew her confidence would take her a long way in life, but like me, she struggled in some ways with maturity at this age. Sometimes I thought she felt she had something to settle before she could truly fly. I did not know what that was, but I slowly began to realize that she would never share the same feelings that I had for her. I began to accept it but still had not completely let go of that dream. However, I was happy to have her as a friend in whatever capacity she was comfortable with; and she remained a true friend always.

In the fall of our junior year, the four of us stood outside the school after classes. It was a Monday, and we began discussing the Sadie Hawkins dance while waiting for the bus to take us home. The dance, less than two weeks away, was the only time it was acceptable for girls at school to ask a boy for a date. We discussed who we hoped would ask us to the dance. Elbie, of course, hoped Mary Jane Toler would ask him, but he held little hope of that. The last time he'd tried to ask her out, he'd looked like a bumbling fool in front of one of the most popular girls in school.

Colby said he would be happy just to be asked but, if he had his choice, he hoped Carrie Aud would ask. Carrie, a new girl to our school this year, had quickly made many friends with her outgoing nature and charming looks. She was also in two of Colby's classes: trigonometry and calculus.

I could not say who I hoped would ask me, so I replied that I was not sure if I would be going. Colby and Elbie both knew that was a lie, but Anna Lee didn't.

"Don't you have any girl in mind that you would like to ask?" she asked incredulously.

"Who are you going to ask, Anna Lee?" Colby jumped in, saving me from embarrassment.

"I'm not asking a boy to take me to any dance," she replied indignantly. "I'd rather not go."

"You are so vain."

"Why don't you ask Razz," Elbie said as I tried to hide my sudden enthusiasm. "That way, we all could go and have a great time."

"That's perfect," Colby chimed in.

"That's crazy. Razz would never go with me on a date," she answered.

I could not determine if she sincerely thought that I didn't want to go with her or if she was trying to find a way out of going with me. Either way, I was dying inside.

"Sure, he would, Anna Lee," Colby insisted. "It's not like it would be a real date. You guys could go just as friends so we could all be together. You'd do that, wouldn't you, Razz?"

"I would never turn Anna Lee down," I replied, hoping to hide my excitement.

"It's settled, then," Elbie said quickly.

"Wait a minute, guys," Anna Lee objected. "I haven't asked yet, and you two simpletons don't even have a date yet."

Colby and Elbie realized she was right and could say nothing.

"I'll tell you what I will do," she said smugly as she turned to me. "Razz, I will ask you to the Sadie Hawkins dance only after these two hopeless characters are asked to go. But to be honest with you, I think you and I are safe. No one in their right mind is going to ask them to the dance."

"If they get a date and you ask me to go, I will say yes," I agreed, but I, too, held little hope that would happen.

Elbie and Colby glanced at each other as disappointment spread across their faces. They realized their chances of both getting a date were slim. Then Colby became distracted as he noticed me staring across the street.

"What are you looking at, Razz?" he asked. "You look like you've seen a ghost."

"Niner," I replied as I turned my head toward Colby briefly.

"What!!!" Elbie screamed.

"He was right over there," I said, pointing to a group of students walking home. However, I did not see him in the crowd anymore.

"Where?" Anna Lee asked as all four of us scanned the crowd for our nemesis. "I don't see him."

"He was there a minute ago," I replied, puzzled at his disappearance.

"Razz, you must be dreaming," Colby said. "He is not there."

"He was!" I answered confidently. "It was Peak. Right over there. He was staring at us with that horrible anger in his face. It was him!"

"I thought he was gone," Elbie said with dread in his voice.

"It was him, and he was staring at us," I said again. "I don't know how or why he found us, but it was him."

"Alright, guys," Anna Lee interjected, "there are four of us now. We can take care of him if we have to."

"Anna Lee's right, Razz," Colby added. "If he was over there watching us, he knows there are four of us. He could handle two of us, maybe, but not four."

"I hope so," Elbie replied. I don't want to ever see that creature again."

Our bus arrived, and we boarded for the ride home. Colby and Anna Lee chatted, but Elbie and I remained preoccupied. We had forgotten about Niner and the hold he'd had on us. That old, unwelcome sick feeling in the pits of our stomach was back.

The next week was better. We had forgotten about Niner and become more preoccupied with the dance. Neither Colby nor Elbie received an invitation, and Anna Lee seemed to revel in their disappointment. I was disappointed as well, but I tried to hide it from Anna Lee.

On the Wednesday before the dance, the four of us were sitting together at a table during lunch when both Mary Jane Toler and Carrie Aud walked over. I thought that a little odd; the two of them were friends, but it wasn't often that I saw them together.

With a casual smile, Mary Jane approached Elbie and asked him to the Sadie Hawkins dance. It took a minute for Elbie to clear his throat, but then he gathered his senses and nodded affirmatively, finally getting a weak yes out. Carrie followed with a request for Colby to attend as her guest. Colby was a bit more composed and polite with his affirmative reply, but both Elbie and Colbie could barely contain themselves. Anna Lee watched with little emotion, but I nearly burst while waiting for her to ask me. Finally, she turned to me with a smile that exceeded Mary Jane's and Carrie's in both warmth and sincerity.

"Razz, would you honor me by being my guest at the Sadie Hawkins dance?"

"I would like that more than you will ever know," I replied truthfully, but trying to conceal my euphoria.

Mary Jane and Carrie sat down at the table, and we chatted excitedly until it was time to go back to class. As the bell rang and we rose to gather our books, I noticed Mary Jane slyly offer a quick wink to Anna Lee, who immediately lowered her head as if she didn't see it. No one else noticed, and I pretended not to as well.

Filled with so many emotions, I could not concentrate on classes that afternoon. The euphoria of going to the dance with Anna Lee sent me sailing as if I were floating on air. But the perplexing wink from Mary Jane worried me.

It became apparent to me that Anna Lee had had a hand in her two friends asking Elbie and Colby to the dance. But why? Had she done it because she wanted to go to the dance with me? It didn't seem logical that she would have a sudden reversal in her feelings for me. However, it also was not logical that she would ask her friends for a favor if she did not want to go with me. Regardless, I was going to the dance with Anna Lee Frazier, and nothing was going to ruin that.

After school, the four of us had a lively discussion while waiting for the bus. A smile widened across Colby's face then he snickered and turned to Anna Lee.

"My, my, my, Miss Anna Lee Frazier. It is going to be interesting to see what dress you will wear to the dance."

"I will not wear a dress!" Anna Lee exclaimed in horror.

"Oh, yes, you will," Colby added smugly. "It is required."

"I don't own a dress, and I can't afford to buy one."

"You have already asked Razz to the dance. You can't go back on that now. You better find one."

"What am I going to do? Make one?!"

200

"Anna Lee," I said, hoping to rescue her, "why don't you and I go to Patty's Resale tomorrow after school. She has tons of dresses that look like new, and they are very affordable."

"But what am I going to do? I've never worn a dress in my life."

"It will be okay, Anna Lee. We will pick out one that you are comfortable with, and it will be only for one night. I'll wear a tie, so we will both look deranged."

"Oh, God, help me," she cried, putting her head in her hands.

"This is going to be so much fun," Elbie added, filled with delight while rubbing his hands together.

"One word," Anna Lee said, pointing her finger in Elbie's face, "just one more word from you, and you will regret it for a long time."

Elbie quickly wiped the smile from his face, but it reappeared as quickly as it had disappeared, and with a little snicker added to it. Anna Lee succumbed to her demise with a small huff of a laugh, and then she buried her head into her hands.

That night, I asked my father if he could pick up Anna Lee and me at school on Thursday on his way home from work. I explained that I planned on taking Anna Lee to shop for a dress after school and we would need a ride home.

Thursday after school, Anna Lee and I waved goodbye to Colby and Elbie as they stepped on the bus home, both grinning in ecstasy. On our four-block walk to Patty's Resale, I was almost bursting with joy, but Anna Lee was unusually nervous and preoccupied; of course, I understood why. After a few moments, I tried to encourage her.

"We'll find the right dress, Anna Lee," I said. "If not, we will figure something out."

"I doubt it," she replied, shaking her head. "I cannot imagine a dress that doesn't make me look like a little girlie kid."

We continued, silently walking on Walnut Street toward Patty's.

"Let's go down this alley," she said with a quick wave of her hand. "It's shorter."

"Have you been here before?" I asked, surprised.

She looked at me, a little annoyed. "Not to buy a dress," she answered curtly. "Mom buys most of our clothes here."

It was apparent that Anna Lee had no enthusiasm for this and that the sooner it was over, the better for her.

We turned from the alley into the parking lot behind Patty's store and then walked around the building to the front door. When we reached it, Anna Lee stopped briefly, took a deep breath, and then entered.

"Let's get this over with," she said quickly, with a noticeable disdain in her voice.

The bell on the door jingled, and we heard Patty's voice from another room.

"Make yourself at home. I'll be with you in a minute."

Anna Lee browsed the racks of dresses with me silently following her. The few that caught her eye, she moved slightly on the rack, and then she would huff in disgust like she'd found an unflushed toilet. The prettier the dresses, the more disgusted Anna Lee became. I, on the other hand, felt as if we were picking out a wedding dress and could not have been happier. When I noticed one that I liked and felt would satisfy her, I proudly held up the fluffy pink dress for her approval. She directed a "death wish" look toward me, frightening me so much that I hurriedly thrust the dress between two others, not bothering to fasten it on the rack, and then backed away quickly, only stopping when I was two aisles away.

Sensing the drama, Patty came over to rescue me.

"Is this for the dance tomorrow, Anna Lee?" she asked politely, almost in a motherly tone.

"Unfortunately, yes," Anna Lee replied tersely.

"Well, girlfriend, you don't want any of these. They are not you. Follow me."

Patty turned and walked to another room, and Anna Lee and I followed, me a respectable distance behind.

"You look like a size four. Is that right?"

"I don't know. I've never worn a dress before."

"Try this," Patty said as she held out a tan lightweight dress with a darker brown belt.

Anna Lee held it up to her and noticed it fit a couple of inches above her knees.

"This is too short," she protested as she pushed it back to Patty.

"Trust me for a minute, Anna Lee. Try it on in the dressing room, put the belt on, and let me know when you are ready. Young man," she said, turning to me, "you step out the front door and wait outside until I call you."

***

Anna Lee tried on the dress and then turned to the mirror. The snug sleeves were cut just below the elbow, and the dress fit comfortably above the belt but looser below, allowing for a slight sway. She liked the dress, but she felt uncomfortable with the length. Returning to the other room, she called for Patty.

"It's too short," she insisted as Patty approached her.

"Slip this on under your dress," Patty instructed, handing Anna Lee a pair of thin shorts the same color as the dress.

Anna Lee quickly slipped the shorts on and was pleased when she saw in the mirror that they were not visible under the dress. That added layer helped, but she remained self-conscious with the length.

"Patty, don't you think the dress is still too short?"

"Now slip these on," Patty said with a smile as she handed Anna Lee a pair of tall brown snakeskin boots.

Anna Lee sat on a nearby chair and pulled the western-style footwear up over her feet. When she stood up and gazed into the mirror, she loved how the boots complemented her dress. She also appreciated how they reached upwards, covering her calves, making the dress appear the perfect length, or at least, less girlie for her tastes.

"I love it!" she exclaimed excitedly, turning to see how it looked from every side.

"Now let me go get your date," Patty said, smiling broadly.

***

Patty stepped outside the front door and motioned for me to follow her. When I walked into the back room and saw Anna Lee standing there in that beautiful dress and sharp boots, I was speechless. I tried to say something but could only stare at her with my jaw dropping lower each second.

The demure smile on Anna Lee's face disappeared, replaced with a growing scowl.

"Honey, that is a picture of a man who has seen the prettiest girl in the rodeo. When he catches his breath and can talk, I'm sure you will be pleased."

Anna Lee's scowl disappeared, and she waited patiently for me to say something.

"Anna Lee," I finally managed to say, "I've always been afraid to tell you how pretty I thought you were, but, but you're beautiful!"

I immediately regretted my honesty, but when Anna Lee flashed a broad, accepting smile and swung around to look at herself in the mirror again, I knew I had said the right words, even though they had blurted out on their own accord with little help from me.

"You really think so, Razz?" she asked, still unfamiliar with the girl in the mirror.

"Oh, Anna Lee. I really, really think so!"

Anna Lee's smile disappeared. "But how much does this cost?" she asked, turning to Patty.

"How much do you have?" Patty asked, not breaking her approving smile of the debutante.

"I only have two dollars," Anna Lee said dejectedly.

"Well, let me add it up," Patty replied as she closed her eyes, counting on her fingers. "Let's see. The dress, the belt, the boots, and the shorts come to two dollars. Does that work for you?"

The worry from Anna Lee's face quickly disappeared as she stepped over to hug Patty.

"Thank you," she said. "I hope I can make it up to you someday."

"You just go and have fun at the dance," Patty answered, smiling at Anna Lee. "Just promise me the two of you won't do anything you will regret. Okay?"

"I promise, Patty. I promise."

Patty put Anna Lee's attire in a bag, took her two dollars, and wished us well. As I left, I turned to Patty and quietly said, "Thank you."

I had never seen Anna Lee so happy. She was so excited she chatted about her outfit continuously to the rear of the building. But when we reached the parking lot, our lives quickly changed.

Chapter XVIII

1968

The Affray

As we turned the corner, there, standing before us, was Niner. He let out the most disgusting laugh I ever heard and then glared menacingly at the two of us.

"Well, what do we have here? Looks like Ken and Barbie," he snarled sarcastically.

Though Anna Lee said nothing, I could feel the heat of the anger emanating from her body.

"Well, Ken, I've missed you. We have some catching up to do," Niner growled, displaying his yellow teeth.

"Leave us alone, Niner," I demanded. "We are on our way home and have no business with you."

His snarl quickly turned to anger, and before I could move, he grabbed my shirt, threw me on the asphalt, and began stomping me as one would when trying to put out a grass fire. I tried to get up, knowing Anna Lee would not restrain herself, but I couldn't. And I was right; she didn't.

She dropped her bag, ran over to Niner, and punched him so hard his head jerked sideways, causing him to lose his balance. He turned to her with a repulsive look of pleasure on his face and stomped me one last time in the stomach with all his might. That stomp sucked every bubble of air from me, leaving me gasping helplessly and writhing in pain.

Anna Lee tried to swing at him again, but his powerful arm fended off her punch. He quickly grabbed her and squeezed so hard she could not breathe. He then began trying to touch her where he should not. Incensed, I gathered enough strength to get up and jumped onto his back, trying to free Anna Lee. With me still wrestling on his back, he pushed Anna Lee onto the asphalt.

Then he threw me onto the ground again. He quickly got into a position over me and kicked me with an immense force, one I had never experienced before, right in the tenderest part of the groin. I had never felt so much pain in my life.

As I writhed helplessly in pain on the hot asphalt, Niner laughed mercilessly at me. I noticed Anna Lee rising, and I tried to yell, "No!" but the words could not come out.

When Anna Lee charged him again, he was ready for her this time. His fist met her in motion, squarely on her nose. The sound of his massive fist ramming into her face sickened me. I will never forget the sight of her head snapping backward and her entire body going limp and falling onto the asphalt. That, now, was the worse pain I had ever felt.

Unable to move, I saw Niner walk over to Anna Lee's bag with her new outfit still inside. He reached inside, pulled out the boots, and said indifferently, "Wrong size." Then he threw them into the filthy dumpster nearby. He did the same with her belt and shorts.

When he pulled out her tan dress, he dropped the empty bag and stepped over to me.

"This yours?" he said derisively. "I think this is the wrong size, too; it's too big for you, wimp."

With that, he began to rip it to shreds. The sight of the remnants of the dress, the one that had made Anna Lee so happy, drifting softly onto my helpless body caused me a sense of deep, unbearable sadness, a feeling made worse by the realization that I had not been able to stop him.

I struggled with all my might to get up, but Niner gave me another swift kick in the side and said, "Not today, sissy." Then he turned and walked away, whistling as if he were leaving work for the day.

I felt sick, knowing I had not protected Anna Lee or her dress from Niner. I might not have been able to stop Niner today, but right then, lying helplessly on my side on the asphalt, I promised myself I would get even with him one day.

I crawled over to Anna Lee and noticed her nose was bleeding profusely. I gently rolled her over onto her back and wiped the blood with the remnants of her dress. Then I put two small pieces of the cloth into her nose. She began to stir, but I told her to remain still for a few moments until her nose stopped bleeding.

"Where is Niner?" she asked with a noticeable sinus twang.

"He's gone. Are you hurt anywhere else?" I asked.

"My head feels like it is going to explode. Other than some bruises and my throbbing nose, I'm okay. What about you?"

"Just a few scratches and bruises. But my left side hurts something awful. It hurt like the devil when I crawled over to help you. Anna Lee, I hate to tell you this, but I think you are going to have two mighty fine shiners by morning."

"Is it noticeable already?"

"Yes, a little. They're swollen and red right now, just like your nose. I think he broke your nose."

"I can't believe this. I will get even with Niner one day. I promise you that."

"Anna Lee," I said regretfully, putting my hand on her shoulder, "he tore your dress into small pieces."

She closed her eyes, and a weird sound came from her nose. I think she had started to cry, but her swollen nose prevented that.

"Your belt, boots, and shorts are in the dumpster. I will get them out for you in a few minutes. But the dress is gone. I don't guess we will need it now, anyway," I said, filled with sadness and resignation.

She grabbed my arm, gripping it so tightly it hurt my left side.

"We are going to the dance," she demanded angrily. "I will wear a dress even if I have to borrow a pink one from Mary Jane. That monster will never control my life! Nor yours!"

I smiled through the pain in my side. "And I will go with you. We'll have the best time ever."

"Can you get my things out of the dumpster?" she asked as she began to sit up.

"Keep your head tilted backward, Anna Lee," I urged. "You don't want it to start bleeding again, and it might help keep your nose from swelling."

I climbed into the dumpster to retrieve her belongings. It took me longer than usual as the excruciating pain in my side hindered any movement.

The boots and belt were in fair condition, but the shorts had stains in several places. I thought maybe Anna Lee's mom could fix that, but I could not be sure as I didn't know what kinds of stains they were.

Trying to hide my pain, I slowly climbed out of the dumpster and picked up the bag that had once held the source of her unbounded euphoria. I put what was left into the bag and tried to help Anna Lee up. I winced and grunted from the pain in my side, trying to keep her from falling.

"What's wrong, Razz?" she demanded. "What is hurting?"

"It's nothing, Anna Lee. Just a little pain where Niner kicked me in my side."

"Razz, no one grunts that deep from nothing."

"I'll be okay, Anna Lee," I replied, trying to fend her worries. "Let's get back to school. My dad will be there soon to pick us up."

She gave me a suspicious look but accepted my arm to help steady her. I had offered her my right arm as the left side was too painful. We walked gingerly down the alley and streets, back to school. We tried to take our minds off the pain and began to feel a little better, or at least, not as bad. However, even though Anna Lee kept her head tilted back the entire way, there was no dismissing that pain.

We were hoping to get inside the school to get a drink of water, but when we reached the building, the doors were locked. Fortunately, my dad arrived a few minutes later.

"What in God's name happened to you two?" he exclaimed, jumping out of the car.

He ran over to us and could quickly see Anna Lee had suffered the most damage.

He inspected her nose and face and then quickly checked to see if there were any other visible injuries.

"Anna Lee, what happened to you?" he asked worriedly.

"Niner Peak jumped us," she replied, hanging her head with shame.

He turned to me. "Son, are you hurt, too?"

"I'm okay, Dad, but I think Anna Lee's nose is broke."

"He's not okay, Mr. Ross," Anna Lee blurted. "His side is hurt."

"What happened, Razz?" my dad asked.

"Niner kicked me pretty hard in the side and hit Anna Lee even harder in the face."

"Get in," he instructed, helping Anna Lee into the car first. Once she was safely in the back seat, he started to close her door, but I grabbed it. I looked at him, and he nodded for me to climb in beside her. He sat in the driver's seat of his 1956 Ford Fairlane, put it in gear, and hurried to Dr. Kalis's office.

I had been there a couple of times before for measles and other minor illnesses. I always liked Dr. Kalis as he was kind but direct. His smile put a patient at ease, much like that of a kindly, old uncle. He could often take one quick look at you and immediately know what bothered you. He seldom needed to send a patient to the hospital for tests; he could determine what was

210

wrong in his office most of the time. If there was a home remedy, he knew what it was, and more often than not, that was how he cured most ailments.

When we arrived at the doctor's office, I helped Anna Lee out of the car and reminded her to keep her head tilted back. We entered Dr. Kalis's office and noticed the receptionist had already left for the day.

"Come on back here," Dr. Kalis instructed from the examination room. We could not see him at first, but finally we caught his eye as he sat behind his desk in his office.

"What in tarnation is this?" he asked as he quickly rose from his chair. "My Lord, Anna Lee, what happened to you?"

"They met up with a ruffian, Dr. Kalis," my dad replied.

"Peak's boy?" he asked, looking at my dad, even though he probably knew the answer.

"Afraid so."

"Humph." The doctor turned to look at Anna Lee's swollen face. "So, he's picking on girls now."

He tilted Anna Lee's head sideways for a different view.

"It's broke," he said. "Nothing serious. Looks like half his fist caught your nose and the other half caught your eyebrows. We will have to reset it, but I don't think we will have to put a splint in it as long as you promise not to bump into anything for a few weeks. We'll pack it, and you are going to keep ice on it for a few days. Are you hurt anywhere else?"

Anna Lee pulled up the leg of her shorts, revealing a massive bruise on her outer thigh. My dad and I promptly turned our heads out of respect. Dr. Kalis quickly stopped her and turned to us.

"Dominic, would you and Razz mind waiting in the other room for a few minutes? I'll check Razz after I'm through with Anna Lee."

"Of course," my dad replied, and we both scurried with heads down into the waiting room, closing the door behind us.

I sat down, and my dad walked over to the rotary telephone, which was sitting on a small table, and called Mr. Tierney. He explained the situation and asked him if he could pick up Anna Lee's mom and bring her to Dr. Kalis's office. He made certain Mr. Tierney would tell her that Anna Lee was okay, that it was just a broken nose. Then he called Sheriff Augie Welsh and requested he come over to the office as well. I tried to stop him, but he waved me off. I feared that would only anger Niner even more. Next, he called my mom. When he finished his phone calls, he sat down next to me.

"Razz, did you try to defend Anna Lee?" he continued.

"Yes," I answered quietly, hanging my head, immersed in humiliation.

"There is no shame in that, son," he replied. Then he said softly, "Razz, there will always be Niners in your life. Many times, it is simply best to move on and distance yourself from them as quickly as possible and then try to keep them from entering your life again. But with others, like this Niner, you will have to defeat them before they stop. You may never be able to defeat or overcome them in their court. You will have to do it in yours. In this case, you will have to outsmart him."

I turned to look at him, and for the first time in my life, I saw past his comforting smile; I saw the kindness in my father's eyes. I started to speak, but a scream from Dr. Kalis's office startled the two of us. We both knew he had reset Anna Lee's nose.

Minutes later, the front door of the office burst open as Anna Lee's mom rushed in. She moved quickly, in almost a one-legged hop, with her shorter leg barely touching the floor.

"Where is she, Dom?" she asked hurriedly.

"In there," he replied, pointing to the exam room. "Dr. Kalis reset her nose about ten minutes ago."

She disappeared into the examination room as quickly as she had arrived.

"Thank you for bringing her, Warren," my dad said to Mr. Tierney.

"No problem," he replied. "They going to be okay?"

"They'll be a little sore for a few weeks, but they will be okay," he answered. "Do you need to get back?"

"Well, I've got a few cows that busted through a fence. I need to get back before someone hits them with a car."

"You go on ahead, Warren. I'll take Helen and Anna Lee back to their house. Thank you for your help."

"Glad to oblige," Mr. Tierney said, and then he looked at me. "You take care of yourself, son. Stay away from that boy."

He turned and left as my dad put his arm around my shoulders. I needed that comforting since I had suddenly realized we would not be going to the dance.

A few minutes later, Dr. Kalis called us into the examination room. As we entered, we heard him tell Anna Lee and her mother to stay put.

Mrs. Frazier stayed by Anna Lee's side, now considerably less frazzled than when she had entered the office. Anna Lee, however, looked like a ghost. Her white, swollen face contrasted the pinkish reds and creepy blues surrounding her eyes and nose.

"What about you, Razz?" Dr. Kalis asked as he stepped over to me.

"I'm okay," I replied. "Just a few scratches and bruises."

"He is not!" Anna Lee insisted. "His left side hurts really bad."

Dr. Kalis pushed his finger gently into my left side.

"Ow!" I screamed.

Then he moved his finger up another inch and pushed.

213

"Ow!" I repeated, trying to move away.

He moved his finger up another inch and pushed. This time, it was less painful.

"That's not as bad," I said, hoping that would satisfy him.

"Cough," he instructed. I thought that weird as I hadn't said anything about a cold.

I coughed and screamed again.

"Got a couple of cracked ribs," he said. "Anything else?"

"No," I answered, still suffering from the pain in my side from when I'd coughed.

"Take some aspirin for the next couple of days for the pain. Don't play any sports for a couple of months and don't do anything that hurts that side. It will heal on its own."

Then he turned to Mrs. Frazier and my dad.

"Keep them home for a few days and let them rest. They will be okay. Call me if anything changes."

"No!" Anna Lee interrupted, her voice as firm as it was loud. "We are going to the dance tomorrow night."

"Anna Lee, neither you nor Razz, need to be dancing. I can't have you bumping that nose into anything."

"We are going!" Anna Lee insisted in her most adamant tone. "I'm not letting that bully rule my life."

Dr. Kalis took a deep breath and turned to me.

"I agree with Anna Lee," I quickly told him.

He shook his head in exasperation.

"I would rather you both stay at home, but if you promise me you won't do any dancing or any other strenuous activities, then I will leave that up to your parents. But Anna Lee, if that nose starts bleeding again, you call me right then and there. Understand?"

"Yes, Dr. Kalis. Thank you."

We walked out of the exam room, into the waiting room, and found Sheriff Welsh waiting for us.

"Hello, Augie," my dad greeted.

"Good afternoon, Mrs. Frazier. You, too, Dom. How are they?"

"Anna Lee has a broken nose and some terrible bruises, Sheriff Welsh," Mrs. Frazier answered.

"Razz has a couple of cracked ribs and bruises as well, Augie," my dad replied.

"You kids sit down in a chair there for a minute," Sheriff Welsh instructed. "I need to talk to you."

We both sat very cautiously, worried more about what he was going to request than the pain in our bodies. He watched us sympathetically.

"Who did this to you?" he asked.

We both remained silent.

"Augie," my father spoke up, "they are afraid that if they file a complaint, he will make it worse for them."

Sheriff Welsh turned back to us. "I already know who it was; I just need you to verify it for me."

"Sheriff," I finally said, "if he finds out we ratted on him, he'll kill us."

The sheriff pulled up a chair and sat in front of us.

"I understand what you are saying. But I need you to understand something. This incident is not the first time this has happened. This person has done this to others. So far, it has been a matter of one's word against another's. Although he has done some heinous things, never has it been on the scale of a criminal offense. This time is different. He has never hurt a female before, and there are some severe injuries here that qualify for a criminal offense.

"Anna Lee, this is a new feeling of power for him; now that he has tasted it, he will start hurting other girls. Please help me stop him."

215

"Niner Peak!" Anna Lee shouted, leaning forward with the ferocity of a lioness.

He looked at me for confirmation.

"Niner Peak," I said without the ferocity.

"Good. Let me explain what we are going to do and why. We are going to fill out a formal complaint. I need each of you to sign one. I will have a deputy arrest him and bring him to the county jail."

I tried to protest. "Sheriff Welsh—"

"Let me finish, Razz. I will explain to Niner that if I file these complaints, I will see to it that there will be an arraignment and he most likely will be charged by the judge. I will explain to him that he will then have a criminal record and could face years in jail. But I will also tell him that the two of you do not want that to happen to him. I will explain that against my advice to formally charge him, the two of you asked me to hold these complaints unless he bothers you again. I will tell him that my deputies will be watching him and if he so much as crosses the street in front of you, I will proceed with the arraignment.

"Now, Niner is a troubled kid. He is only doing to others what his dad did to him, but unfortunately, he has escalated the severity of violence. Niner is not stupid. He is now living on his own, away from his dad, and has a construction job. He knows if he has a criminal record, not only will he lose his job, but it will also be tough for him to find another one. I don't think he will want to risk that."

I looked at Anna Lee and then back at the sheriff.

"What if I am the only one to file the complaint," I asked.

"No way, Jose!" Anna Lee objected. "Where do I sign, Sheriff?"

Sheriff Welsh chuckled. "Razz, did you really think she would let you be the scapegoat?"

216

Everyone laughed with him, but the pain in my ribs cut mine short.

Anna Lee's mom picked up the bag from Patty's as we walked out the door. She wanted to sit next to Anna Lee despite Anna Lee's insistence that she wasn't a kid. I sat in front with my dad, and we headed to the Frazier home.

"What is this?" Mrs. Frazier asked after inspecting the boots, belt, and shorts.

I explained everything to her, including a description of the dress and how Niner had shredded it.

"That is about the evilest thing I ever heard," she said emphatically.

"I'm going to ask if Mary Jane has a dress I can borrow," Anna Lee said, trying to defuse the discussion.

"Even if she has one, Anna Lee," her mom continued, "it may not match the boots or belt."

"I don't care, Mom," Anna Lee said in her increasingly nasal twang.

"Razz," my father interjected, "what color did you say the dress was?"

"Tan," I replied.

"Gloria bought some nice tan-colored material last week for a kitchen curtain she planned to make," my dad said, glancing in the rear mirror. "Helen, if we gave that to you, would you have time to sew a dress by tomorrow night?"

I turned to see Anna Lee's eyes light up behind her darkening skin for the first time since Niner had hit her.

"I will make the time if Anna Lee will help me," she answered, turning to her daughter for approval.

"I will, and we will make it even better than the other," Anna Lee replied.

Chapter XIX

1968

The Dance

My dad let me borrow one of his ties, and I chose the only tan one in his closet. He showed me how to tie it but ended up tying it for me as I had never worn one before, and I made a mess of that effort. That aggravated me a bit as I could master any knot on a fishing line. With his help, I thought I looked decent in my white button-down shirt and black slacks, but I did not deserve my mother fawning all over me. I kept pushing her aside in embarrassment as my dad chuckled at my awkward plight.

He put the keys to his Ford Fairlane on the table and reminded me to drive carefully. My mother, however, was a bit more insistent in advising me how to treat Anna Lee. After hearing the word "gentleman" about five times, I rushed out the door as soon as I could break her grip from my arm, but then I suffered the horrible indignity of returning to retrieve the keys, which were still sitting on the kitchen table.

Elbie was to pick up Mary Jane, then Colby, and finally Carrie in his father's car. We all planned to meet up at the school gym and enter together.

When I arrived at Anna Lee's house, I noticed her trying to rush out the door, but then her mother grabbed her arm and pulled her back inside. I laughed to myself, knowing it was killing her to remain inside until her "suitor" knocked on the door, waiting patiently with flowers in hand. Oh crap! Crap!! I suddenly realized I had forgotten the flowers, which were still sitting on the kitchen chair. An apology would have to suffice.

Empty-handed, I knocked, and Anna Lee's mom opened the door and invited me in, remarking how handsome I was. I thanked her politely and apologized for leaving the flowers on the kitchen chair.

"Good!" Anna Lee shouted from the living room.

I walked into the living room, and despite her almost coal-black eyes and nose, she was as beautiful as she had been at Patty's. Her nose, still swollen and blackened, dominated her appearance even more than yesterday. The dress was only slightly different than the one from Patty's, but it looked perfect on her, and I could not contain myself.

"Anna Lee, that dress is almost as beautiful as you," I expressed sincerely. I was suddenly filled with worry that I had embarrassed her, but when she flashed that smile again, my worries disappeared. We both endured some more pictures, embarrassing Anna Lee mercilessly, and then we were on our way to the dance.

Elbie and Colby held hands with their dates as they entered the gym, where the music was already playing. Anna Lee gave no impression that she wished to hold hands, so I did not press it.

The six of us sat at a table together and quickly became submerged in laughter and fun. My injuries from Niner were not visible, so no one offered condolences to me. However, nearly everyone at the dance stopped at our table to offer their sympathies to Anna Lee. But that did not bother me, as I could see it pleased my date. Once everyone had their moment with her, the dancing began.

I remained at the table with Anna Lee since Dr. Kalis had forbidden us from dancing. We talked and laughed a long time, but eventually we settled for watching the others dance. I watched Colby and Elbie enviously as they danced with their partners. But when the DJ played "My Girl" by the Temptations, I could not resist any longer.

"Anna Lee," I asked above the music, "do you think we could dance to just this one?"

"Razz, you know what Dr. Kalis said. I don't want to take a chance on breaking my nose again."

"I don't blame you. I wouldn't want you breaking my ribs again, either." I laughed, a weak effort to mask my disappointment.

Everyone returned to the table after that song, and we laughed and talked for thirty minutes or more. Everyone agreed that tonight was special and the most fun we'd had all year. I think I was the only one who noticed that Anna Lee remained silent. I didn't know if her nose was hurting or that she was not enjoying the night. Eventually the other four returned to the dance floor while Anna Lee and I talked and laughed at the table. I think her pain might have subsided some as she finally began to let loose and we thoroughly enjoyed each other and our time together.

All too soon, the DJ announced it was time for the last song and the last dance, and then he began playing "Hey Jude" by the Beatles. As soon as the song began, everyone rushed to the dance floor. It was a magical last moment for the others, but I was dying inside. Then, Anna Lee reached over and touched my hand.

"Are you going to ask me to dance or not?" she asked, her reddened eyes sparkling from behind her blackened face.

"Anna Lee Frazier, would you like to dance with me?" I quickly requested in my most proper manner.

"Why, Mr. Ross, I would love to," she answered as she rose from her seat. "Just be careful not to bump into my nose," she pleaded in my ear.

"I promise I won't if you promise not to squeeze my ribs too hard," I answered jokingly.

We danced gingerly, at a much slower pace than even "Hey Jude" customarily required. Everyone on the floor glanced over their shoulders approvingly as the injured couple danced almost in slow motion. That pace suited me just fine as I treasured holding her, and I think she felt the same. Anna Lee held her nose away from any danger but kept the rest of her body close to mine. I gently pulled her a little tighter, and she did not resist, finally resting her head on my shoulder.

Fortunately for the two of us, the DJ played the long version of "Hey Jude," with neither of us showing any desire for it to end. When the last refrain faded, we stopped dancing but continued to hold each other. Finally, Anna Lee looked into my eyes with an intensity I had never seen her give me before.

I began to sense a feeling of electricity passing from her body to mine, and I was certain that she felt it, too. We continued staring into each other's eyes, both of us sensing a connection we had never experienced with each other before.

Suddenly Anna Lee pulled away and turned from me. It was if she had drifted off into la-la land and then been jerked back to normalcy, with no recollection of ever leaving.

All six of us readied to leave and said our goodbyes. Hugs for everyone were bandied about, free of any other previous relations, and everyone expressed an eager interest in getting together again. After we left our friends, Anna Lee was back to her usual self as if the dance never happened.

We did not say much on the way to her house. I had noticed her applying light pressure to the area around her nose.

"Is it bothering you?" I asked.

"Yeah, a little. I'll be okay," she answered. I knew she hurt much worse than she admitted.

We turned onto Free Silver Road off Highway 144, the last stretch to our homes, but instead of going straight, I immediately turned into the dark parking lot behind the church and stopped the car.

Anna Lee quickly turned to me with a look that was either threatening or fearful; with her blackened face and swollen nose, I could not tell which.

"What are you doing, Razz?" she asked in a firm voice.

"Relax, Anna Lee. I only want to talk for a minute before we get home."

"What about?" she said suspiciously.

"Why did you get Mary Jane and Carrie to ask Elbie and Colby to the dance?"

"What makes you think I did something that crazy?" she said, surprised at the question.

"Please, Anna Lee. I need to know."

She leaned back in the seat and stared out the front window. Finally, she answered reluctantly, "Colby asked me to do it for you. He said it would mean a great deal to you if we went to the dance together."

"So, it was for Colby," I said, trying to hide my disappointment.

"No, it wasn't," she replied, lowering her head. "At first, I refused, but Colby insisted he did not want any of his friends going through life regretting not ever having been on a date with the one they cared for the most. I told him he was crazy thinking that and that it would not bother you in the least. Then he said, 'Anna Lee, I wasn't talking about Razz; I was talking about you.'"

We were silent for a moment.

"Razz, he was right. I needed to know."

"Did you enjoy tonight?" I asked.

"Sure, I did. Didn't you?"

"Yes, it was the best night of my life." I paused. "But did you really enjoy tonight?"

"Razz, you are not asking me if I enjoyed the dance. You are asking me something else, aren't you?"

"Anna Lee, I would never want to lose you as a friend, but yes, I am asking something else."

She turned and stared out the window with her hands still on her lap. Then she turned toward me.

"Yes, I did. I really enjoyed our night together. It was a very special night for me, too, and I will never forget it."

She paused, and my heart sank, certain a "but" was coming.

"Razz, that moment when you first saw me wearing the dress at Patty's was the first time in my life I ever felt pretty. And when you told me I was beautiful, you made me feel like a princess. I felt like I was walking on air, and I don't know if I will ever be that happy again. At that moment, I was even happier than the time I met Chris Crae after his concert. But I do know I could never wear a dress all the time, and I may never wear one again.

"Tonight was the same way," she continued. "I felt just as happy with you tonight, but I'm not certain I could do this again. It would kill me if I hurt you, Razz, but I can't help how I feel. It's not you; it's me. I'm not normal; I don't know why I can't be excited and say, 'Let's do it again,' but I can't. I am so sorry, Razz. I wish it were different, but it isn't."

Those words devastated me, but at first, the fool inside me only heard the words "I'm not certain." *Maybe*, I thought, *she can change*.

"Anna Lee, you will never have to apologize to me. I understand, I think. I don't ever want to lose the friendship we have now. Just as I said at the Marshal Mansion, I like who you are and wouldn't want you any other way."

She reached over and gently hugged me, making sure her nose did not become a victim again. Then she scooted back across the seat and smiled at me.

"Razz, you are the most wonderful friend I have, and I wouldn't want you any other way, either."

I started the car and drove her home. When we reached her house, I started to open the car door to walk her to the house, but before I could get out, she silently reached for my hand. She stared into my eyes with the same intensity as she had after we'd danced to "Hey Jude," and the same electricity passed between us again. Completely mesmerized, I could not move. Without a word, she climbed out of the car, silently closed the door, and briefly pressed her open hand on the window. Then she ran to the house and quickly disappeared behind the front door.

I regained my composure, realizing that those last few moments we'd shared were probably as close to a kiss as I would ever get from Anna Lee. However, I wasn't consumed with disappointment this time, as I sensed that those few moments might have been even better. I did, however, finally begin to understand what Anna Lee had been trying to tell me.

Arriving home, I quietly slipped into my bedroom and crawled into bed. I don't know about Anna Lee, but I did not sleep that night.

Chapter XX

1969

The Scoundrels

As seniors in high school, college and Vietnam were most predominant in our minds. Also, at this point in our parents' lives, they needed us less on the farms but required each of us to find part-time jobs. We could play sports if we wished, but school and work came first. Elbie and Colby both played on the baseball team, and both held part-time positions. Anna Lee found a job filing papers and performing other minor office duties at an attorney's office, as well as some part-time work at school in the concession stands. Our school started a golf program for the girls, and Anna Lee quickly excelled at that sport. I worked at a grocery that was flexible with my hours, so I could still play sports.

Anna Lee and I began playing golf as freshmen. To my surprise, it didn't take long before I enjoyed golf as much as baseball, and by my junior year, I was the best player on our team. I don't know if that was much of an accomplishment, as few of us in school ever played golf until they added it as a sport in our freshman year. Somehow, I lettered in both baseball and golf in my junior year.

Our golf season was in the fall, allowing me to play both sports for three years. I eventually felt I had a better chance of receiving a golf scholarship and decided to give up baseball my senior year to increase my chances. There were a few tournaments in the spring that I hoped to compete in to get more experience. I had just received my varsity jacket, and I wore it every chance I got.

"Wow, that's awesome," Anna Lee said, admiring my two-tone blue and gold varsity jacket, slowly tracing the lettering with her fingers. "It even has your name embroidered on it!"

"Thanks," I replied sheepishly. I knew she was trying to make me feel good because she had received her varsity jacket, with her name on it, last year.

A brief period of unusually mild weather in February provided some opportunities to get out and play more. However, with the higher-than-average temperatures, I didn't get too many chances to wear my varsity jacket, and this was the first opportunity for Anna Lee to see it on me.

Anna Lee, still as pretty and tall as always, maintained a very high GPA. She was also the A player on the girl's golf team, with a handicap much better than mine, yet she never teased me about it. However, she never hesitated to admonish me to improve my grades. "You may get a golf scholarship either way," she would often gently remind me, "but a good golfer with good grades will have a lot more options."

"I'm going out Saturday to get some practice in," I told her. "Would you want to join me?"

"I can't. I have to work at school on the next four weekends," she replied. The part-time work helped her to repay her parents for the cost of her new golf clubs. "It's supposed to be cold Saturday, isn't it?"

"Not really, only in the morning. It's supposed to warm up into the fifties after one o'clock. I'm going out to the city course at twelve."

"You better take your jacket for the first three or four holes."

"I will."

"Have you done any more checking on the schools you are considering for next year?"

"Naw, I have plenty of time," I answered, trying to brush off her question.

"Razz, you only have about four more weeks to make a decision. You need to send out requests for scholarships now

226

before they are all gone. It takes time, and if you wait too long, they will have already given all of them away."

"I know, but I haven't decided where I want to go yet."

"Razz, I know this is stressing you out, but you can't put it off any longer. I will be at your house on Sunday night, and we are going to sit down and decide. You have everything ready for us to look at before I get there, okay?"

"I will."

"You promise?"

"I promise." I laughed. "Want to go out for a pizza when you get there?"

"We'll go after you have made a decision." She smiled and poked me in the ribs.

Saturday morning, I pulled my bag and clubs from a crowded, dusty corner in the cramped garage. I tossed a few well used Top Flights into its pocket, grabbed a towel, and put the bag along with my muddy shoes carefully into the trunk of my car. I'd purchased the old VW Bug with the money I'd earned working at the grocery. I took special care of it, keeping it clean and as shiny as a beat-up seven-year-old car can be. It was challenging for me to balance sports and a job, but I did it. Unfortunately, with little time to study, my grades suffered a bit.

Realizing I'd forgotten my jacket, I stepped quickly back into the house to get it. The forty-plus-degree temperature, accompanied by a brisk wind, was supposed to rise into the fifties by early afternoon. The jacket would help in between swings for the first hour or so.

"Are you going golfing in the cold?" my mother asked, surprised.

"It's supposed to warm up later," I replied.

"Razz, you do know you are running out of time to decide on a college, don't you? You can't keep putting this off," she reminded me for the third time this week.

"I've got it under control, Mom. You don't have to bug me about it every day," I grumpily answered as I closed the door behind me with my jacket in hand.

Just before noon, as I pulled into the course parking lot, I noticed it was mostly empty.

"It's going to be a bit nippy out there," the golf pro said, surprised to see me.

"I don't mind," I replied.

I signed in on the register, noticing only a few names on it, and headed to the tee box. To my delight, there was no one else there. I could focus more on my game if I didn't have to wait on slow golfers in front of me, or worse yet, meet up with a talkative golfer.

I took off my jacket and hit a decent first shot. I bogeyed the first hole, but in this weather, I didn't think that was too bad.

As I approached the second tee box, I noticed two old men standing there, each with a driver in hand. I thought that a little strange as there was no one in front of them to hold them up. They appeared to be in their sixties or seventies and bundled so tightly in coats, sock hats, and gloves that I wondered how they could even swing a club. Their bags appeared as old as they were, one an old, faded Wilson and the other in even worse condition and without the courtesy of a brand name on it. Both bags were frayed and ripped without constraint at virtually every seam. The men's fairway woods and drivers, made with real persimmon wood, had suffered numerous chips and scratches, and their irons were covered with so much rust it was difficult to make out the numbers on them.

"Great day for golf, isn't it?" the taller one proudly said as if he was the one responsible for the weather.

"Doesn't get any better than this, does it, my friend?" the shorter one said just as proudly.

"No, sir," I answered politely.

"Would you like to join us?"

"Well, I'm trying to work on my game," I replied, trying to find a way to avoid playing with them.

"Oh, well, we can help you with that," the taller one said. "Righty there played on the tour for three or four years, and I was on tour for more than that. We should be able to give you a few pointers. My name is Lefty."

"Okay, sure. I'm Razz," I said reluctantly, doubting they could give me any tips.

"Nice jacket. You get that at school?" Righty asked.

"Now, what kind of question is that, Righty? Where do you think he got it? Of course he got it at school. It's a school jacket." Lefty turned to look at me with a slight frown. "You did get it at school, didn't you?"

"Yeah." I laughed.

"Go ahead and hit, young man," Righty said, pointing to the tee box. "We'll watch your swing for you."

I put my jacket on my bag, pulled out my driver, and hit a drive close to three hundred yards.

"Nice swing," Righty said, watching my ball.

"Yeah, I think that swing will work," Lefty added. "Now, let me show you how a professional does it."

He stood and addressed the ball left-handed, fidgeting like a nervous cat, and readied himself to swing. He took the club back slowly and smoothly. His swing was more of a half swing followed by a herky-jerky stab at the ball. It took off straight down the fairway and then, abandoning all physics, turned abruptly to the left and headed straight for a house.

"Window!" yelled Righty just before the ball barely missed a window by less than a foot.

"Dagnabbit," Lefty said. "The wind must have got that."

"I think the wind is blowing in the opposite direction," Righty whispered to me with a barely suppressed smile. "Now, stand aside, and I'll show you the right way to do it," he said as he addressed the ball from the right side.

He wore golf gloves on both hands, each at least one size too large and nearly an inch longer than his fingers. He spent almost a minute repositioning his hand to keep the club from slipping. He swung quickly and took two steps mid-swing, causing him to hit the top of the ball, which dribbled lazily about twenty feet.

"Well, I was afraid of that," he said.

I quickly figured out the old, ragtag men probably had never been on tour, but I decided to continue playing with them anyway. I wasn't in a hurry, and I even found it a little fun to play with them.

On the sixth hole, while Righty performed his ritual to hit his shot, I noticed Lefty taking five balls and a handful of tees from Righty's bag and then discretely stuffed them into the pocket of his golf bag. When Lefty saw me watching him, he gave me a big wink and held one finger to his lips, silently mouthing, "Shh."

I lowered my head to hide the smile on my face. On the tenth hole, while Lefty was looking for his ball in the woods, I noticed Righty taking six balls and a golf towel from Lefty's bag and then placing them into his golf bag. He turned and smiled at me as if nothing had happened. It was only a few holes later that Lefty retrieved his ball from a muddy lake and reached for his towel.

"What happened to my towel?" he asked out loud to no one in particular.

"Well, looky here," Righty said, pointing to the empty hook that had once held the absconded towel. "You must have left your hook unfastened. There's no telling when it fell off. Some guy back there on the second hole is probably using your towel right now as we speak."

"Well, I hope he keeps it clean. That's an expensive towel," Lefty said as he grabbed his rusted two-wheeled pull cart.

"You got it at the Goodwill store," Righty argued. "You paid a quarter for it."

"Well, it was expensive when it was new. I heard it was pure silk, made in Egypt."

Righty shook his head and laughed as he reached for his equally rusted pull cart and walked alongside Lefty. Grinning, I picked up my bag, threw it over my shoulder, and followed the two bantering older men to the green.

I began to enjoy playing with them, but I knew I needed to focus on improving my game, and I realized I probably wasn't going to get any good advice from these two. My swing had been out of sync on my last three drives, so I was intent on straightening that out on number eleven. Despite my more determined concentration, I topped the ball on my next shot, sending it errantly into a ditch thirty yards away.

"What is going on?" I mumbled angrily to myself, putting my club into my bag with an extra push.

"See that bird flying up there?" Lefty asked, pointing to a bird flying overhead.

I looked at him and then at the bird.

I don't care about some stupid bird, I thought, quite agitated by now.

"Yeah, watch his wings," Righty said, his eyes following the bird.

"See how his wings go up and then down in a smooth, slow motion?" Lefty said, watching the bird.

I glanced up at the bird and followed it for a few seconds.

"The bird has the same relaxed, fluid motion when he moves his wing down as he did when he moved it up," Righty said, admiring the bird's flight.

"Almost effortless, isn't it?" Lefty added.

231

"Yeah," Righty agreed, "just an easy, natural motion."

"Well, now it's back to golf," Lefty said, changing the subject as he and Righty grabbed their pull carts.

"Wait," Righty said as he stopped and turned to me. "Maybe the boy would like to hit another one."

"My bad," Lefty said, and he and Righty stepped back out of the way, focusing on me.

I stood there for a moment, looking at them, not quite sure what to do. I reached into my pocket for another ball and placed it on a tee. I couldn't quite figure out these two men and their sudden fascination with a bird, but I recognized the expressions "a smooth fluid motion" and "a relaxed, natural swing," so I tried to slow my swing down a little to smooth it out. When I hit the ball, it was by far my longest drive of the day and straight down the middle. I watched in awe as it landed well over three hundred yards down the fairway. I looked over at Righty and Lefty, but they were gone, already walking down the fairway with their carts, seventy-five yards ahead of me.

I hurried to catch up with them, finally reaching them as they approached Righty's ball. They both turned to me and said in unison, "Nice swing," and then they preoccupied themselves with whether Righty could hit his next shot without the ball going into the lake positioned precariously on the left side of the fairway. When Righty hit the ball, it dove in a straight line into the lake, creating a small splash.

"Hallelujah!" Righty yelled, dropping another ball to hit.

This time, he hit it a little straighter, and it rolled down the fairway. Lefty shook his head and laughed.

When they finished putting on the seventeenth green, they both said their goodbyes to me, explaining they had to run. I thanked them for letting me play with them. They said I was welcome to join them anytime. I headed to the eighteenth tee box as Righty and Lefty turned with a wave of their hands and headed in the opposite direction.

In the parking lot, I put my bag in the trunk, and started my car. As I pulled out, I noticed there were only three other cars there. I wondered if one might belong to Righty and Lefty. I saw two shiny late-model cars and a rusty, beat-up old Ford Galaxy from the early 1960s not far from my vehicle. "That must be theirs." I laughed, got into my car, and turned the key.

On the way home, I stopped by Elbie's house. He and Colby were watching the Boston Celtics game, so I stayed for about an hour and watched it with them. Bill Russell and John Havlicek both had a great game, leading the Celtics to an easy win. When the game was over, I said my goodbyes and left. After climbing into my car, I waited a few minutes for it to warm up and then headed for home.

As I pulled into the drive, I noticed my sister, Kasch, practicing her basketball shots on the goal positioned at the end of the driveway. I had built the goal when I was in grade school. I'd found some old wooden boards, nailed them together for the backboard, fastened a rusty old basket to it, and attached it to a metal pole that swayed a little when the basketball hit it. It wasn't perfect, but it worked.

Kasch stepped patiently out of the way as I pulled carefully into the small garage. I took my clubs out of the trunk, located in the front of the old VW, and set them and my shoes back into the only empty corner of the garage. I walked around my mom and dad's car and stepped into the kitchen.

"What are you cooking, Mom? I'm starving."

"Chili," she replied, stirring the pot. "It will be ready in an hour."

"I'm starving. Anything here to snack on?" I asked, opening the pantry door.

"How was golf?"

"Fine."

"What did you shoot?"

"I don't know."

"Did you play with anybody?"

"Yeah."

"Well, who did you play with?"

"I don't know."

"You don't know who you played with?" she asked incredulously.

"Two old men."

"Did they have names?"

"I don't know...Lefty and Righty."

"Lefty and Righty?" she repeated, looking up at me. "Are you serious?"

"Yeah."

"Sounds like fake names to me."

"Well, that is what they said their names were."

"Tell me about them," my mom said as she put down her spoon, looking a little concerned.

"I don't know, just two old men. They kept stealing balls and golf towels out of each other's golf bags."

"You played golf with two old men named Lefty and Righty who kept stealing from each other? They sound like two old scoundrels to me. Did you check your bag to make certain they stole nothing from you?"

"Nothing got stolen, Mom," I insisted, finishing the last three chocolate cookies I'd found in the cookie jar. "Anna Lee is coming over tomorrow night. We are going to look at some colleges."

"Thank you!" my mother exclaimed. "Do you want me to cook something for you and her?"

"No thank you. We're going out for a pizza."

"Did she like your jacket?"

"Yeah," I said quickly, heading upstairs to my room.

On Sunday afternoon, I decided to go to Kasch's basketball game with my parents to kill some time until Anna Lee came over that evening. Usually, some of my friends were there, and I hoped Elbie and Colby would show up as well, but if not, at least Anna Lee would be working in the concession stand. I planned on wearing my jacket to the game, but with the warm temperatures again today, I decided not to. It was fifty-five degrees outside and would be much warmer than that in the gym. Mom had left the house an hour before with Kasch for the pregame meeting at the gym. I put on a short-sleeve shirt and some shorts and headed to the game with Dad in my car.

The crowd seemed much smaller than usual, and none of my friends were there, so I ended up sitting with Mom and Dad briefly and then spent the rest of the time at the concession stand. It was an exciting game, but I was more interested in talking to Anna Lee. I worried, though, that Kasch's game might go into overtime and cut into my time researching colleges with Anna Lee. Fortunately, the game ended in regulation.

"See you in a little bit," I said to Anna Lee.

"Okay. Have everything ready for us," she replied.

My dad decided to go home with Mom and Kasch, so I left alone. I arrived at the house at four thirty, and with Anna Lee coming at five, I hurried up to my room. I began to straighten it a little and then reached into the trash can to retrieve some of the unopened collegiate pamphlets I'd received in the mail this past year.

***

"Hi, Mom!" Anna Lee yelled to my mother as she walked through the garage door and into the kitchen. She gave her a big hug. "How is everybody?"

"Everyone is fine," Mom replied. "Razz is a little stressed. There are too many schools that would be a good fit for him, and he can't decide on which one. Thank you for coming to help him with that."

"Is he upstairs?"

"Yes, waiting for you. Oh, how is the part-time work at school going?"

"Good, but I wouldn't want to make a career of it. Well, it's decision time." Anna Lee winked as she grabbed a cookie from the recently replenished cookie jar. "Yum," she said as she headed upstairs.

***

As Anna Lee walked into my room, I asked a question that had been heavy on my mind.

"Anna Lee, who do you think is better, the Beatles or Elvis?"

"That's like asking me if I like the sunrise better than the sunset, Razz," she replied. "But it won't work. Get the college info out, and let's get started."

After an hour of Anna Lee urging me to stay focused, we eliminated a few of the schools and then narrowed the remaining choices to three. The University of Kentucky was a great school and high on my list. It had everything I wanted, plus that was the school Anna Lee had received a golf scholarship to and planned to attend. It had a beautiful campus with many great amenities. The negatives were the uncertainty of any financial aid or golf scholarship for me and that the campus was enormous, much larger than I expected. Another was the University of Evansville, a nearby mid-sized university. We counted the many advantages of going to a closer school, and I had already met the UE golf coach, so I felt I had a chance to receive a golf scholarship. Our main concern was that I wanted to get further away from home, but under the circumstances, that wouldn't be a deal-breaker.

The third school was Brescia University, a smaller school located in Owensboro, a twenty-five-minute drive from my house.

I felt confident I could get a golf scholarship there. The idea of a private, more intimate school was appealing to me, but its athletics program competed at the NAIA level, and I wasn't sure about staying that close to home, or worse, living at home while attending college. I had hoped to get further away to broaden my experiences.

I had seen all three schools and was familiar with each of them, and we both felt any of them would work. Anna Lee and I filled out the letters of interest to the financial aid offices, addressed them, and gave them to my dad to mail in the morning.

A cold front moved in that night, sending the temperatures into the low thirties by morning. I went to the closet to get my jacket to wear to school, but it wasn't there. I searched my room, but still no jacket. Grabbing my books, I ran downstairs and began a frenzied search, checking every room. I then checked my car, golf bag, and the garage. Now frantic, I burst into the kitchen.

"Dad, have you seen my jacket?"

"Your varsity jacket?"

"Yes. I can't find it."

"Where did you wear it last?" he asked, getting up to help search.

"I don't know."

"Alright, just think back. Where do you remember wearing it last?"

"I know I wore it to the golf course, but that is the last time I remember wearing it."

"Those scoundrels probably stole it," my mom insisted from the laundry room.

"What?" my dad asked, stunned at the accusation, and he looked at me in disbelief.

"They're not scoundrels, Mom. Just two old men I played golf with Saturday. They didn't steal it."

"Did you go anywhere afterward?"

"Elbie's."

"Call him. I'll start looking."

I called Elbie, but he said he hadn't seen my jacket and didn't remember me wearing it when I stopped by Saturday.

Despite searching the house, calling Anna Lee, checking with the janitor at the school gym where Kasch played, and calling the golf course, the jacket was still AWOL. The next few days, I continued searching for my varsity jacket, but eventually I gave up, assuming I'd dropped it on the course last Saturday. Hopefully, someone had found it and would recognize my name on the jacket.

The next Saturday, I hurried to play golf at noon, hoping to find my jacket in the clubhouse or find Lefty and Righty. Maybe they had seen it and were holding it for me.

I pulled into the parking lot and searched for the rusty old Ford Galaxy. Seeing it over in the far corner of the parking lot, I pulled up and parked next to it. After opening the door and stepping out of the car, I peered curiously into the Galaxy. The back seat and floor appeared as a collection point, filled with old clothes, crumpled boxes, an assortment of miscellaneous junk, and a few stray rusted golf clubs sticking out like random twigs in a brush. *That's got to be their car*, I thought.

The golf pro in the clubhouse had not seen my jacket, nor had anyone mentioned it, so I disappointedly headed to the first tee, hoping to see my "scoundrel" friends. To my further disappointment, they were not there.

After making par on the first hole, I felt I needed to focus more on my game today and committed to shooting in the mid-seventies. *That would be great*, I thought while walking up to the second tee box. I looked up, and there was Righty, waving his club at me, with Lefty by his side.

"Well, look who's here," Lefty said.

"Right on time. We were just getting ready to hit. Let's get started while the sun is still up," Righty said, motioning me to hit first.

"Hey, guys," I greeted. I hit my drive flawlessly down the middle.

"Wow wee!" Lefty exclaimed. "Nice swing."

"What about the drive?" I asked.

"We don't need to watch the drive," Righty said. "If the swing is good, the drive is good."

"I lost my jacket here last week. Did you guys see it by any chance?"

"What jacket was that?" Lefty asked, looking around.

"My varsity jacket."

"The one with your name on it?" Righty asked, surprised, as he began to search the area for the jacket.

"Yeah."

"Oh, wow, that's a shame," Lefty said, shaking his head.

"Oh, man, that's a bummer," Righty added, turning to Lefty.

"Well, who would want a jacket with your name on it?" Lefty asked. "Surely, if they found it, they would turn it in."

"Don't worry, kid," Righty said calmly. "It'll show up."

I put my mind on improving my game and quit worrying about the jacket for the time being. However, I was a little tense today, realizing I was not where I needed to be and would have to be more consistent with my game for the spring tournaments or there would be no golf scholarships. After seven holes, despite the par on number one and three others, I was four over.

On the eighth hole, while Lefty was getting ready to hit, Righty pulled the golf towel that he'd stole from Lefty last week from out of his bag. He dropped it onto the ground, but curiously, he appeared to do so purposely. He quickly picked it up and fastened it to his golf bag before Lefty finished hitting his ball.

239

Then Righty addressed his ball, preparing to hit his drive. With his normal awkward swing, the ball took off like a guided missile, straight to the lake along the left side of the fairway.

"Hallelujah!" he shouted, dropping his club and placing his hands on his hips.

"Why do you always say that every time you hit your ball into the water?" I laughed.

"That's the name of his angel," Lefty said matter-of-factly.

"What?" I asked, my voice slightly rising and snickering a bit.

"His angel. That's her name. He thinks his angel should help him keep his ball out of the water."

"You are kidding, right?" I said, staring at the two of them.

"How do you know my angel is a girl?" Righty interrupted indignantly.

"Don't you believe in angels?" Lefty asked, continuing to look at me, ignoring Righty's question.

"I guess. I don't know," I answered, a little surprised.

"Humph!" Lefty retorted grumpily with a rare frown on his face. "Everybody has an angel. They kind of watch over you and help you make the right decisions on the really important stuff, and they also try to keep at least one wary eye on you. I don't think they are supposed to change things to help you out, though, but sometimes they'll nudge you a little bit if it's necessary. Of course, they don't care about itsy-bitsy spider stuff like jackets or where a golf ball goes. They might help you find someone else's ball just for fun, but I don't think it would be legal for them to help you find your ball; that's Saint Anthony's department. Of course, everybody knows that left-handed guys have man angels and right-handed guys have girl angels. And you know what they say about right-handed guys."

"What's that?" I asked, even though I was sure I shouldn't have.

"That right-handed guys don't know they have girl angels."

"I never heard anybody say that," Righty argued.

"You just heard me say it!"

Righty looked at me, rolled his eyes, and dropped another yellow ball to hit. Before he could swing, Lefty stopped him.

"Wait a minute! Is that my golf towel on your bag?" he suspiciously asked as he stepped over to Righty's bag to inspect the towel.

"No, that is mine," Righty replied defensively. Then he snatched the towel on his bag out of Lefty's hand.

"No, it isn't. That's the towel I bought in Egypt a few years ago; cost me a hundred dollars," Lefty said defiantly with his hands on his hips.

"Now, you didn't buy this in Egypt, you didn't pay a hundred dollars for it, and I saw it on the ground and picked it up just a few minutes ago. Those are all facts, so unless you can prove any of those wrong, the towel is mine," Righty said smugly as if he had just beaten Lefty's four kings with four aces in a poker game.

"Hmph," Lefty said, hiding a sly grin on his face as he turned to me, and then he took off down the fairway alongside Righty, the two of them arguing all the way.

At the seventeenth green, Righty came over to shake my hand, followed by Lefty.

"Are you guys leaving?" I asked curiously.

"Yeah, we have to be somewhere in a few minutes," Righty answered. "Lefty took up too much time talking about angels."

"Maybe we will see you next week, kid," Lefty said as he turned to walk back to the tee box on seventeen.

That's weird, I thought as I turned to the eighteenth tee box.

Starting my last hole, I hooked my drive into the weeds. While hunting for it, I found a pink golf ball and a yellow one. I laughed for a minute, thinking the yellow one probably was one of Righty's lost balls. I put them into my pocket, thinking I would give them to my two cousins, Leta and Teen.

On my way home, at a stoplight, I decided to turn right instead of going straight home. I had time to stop and see my cousins. It would only take a few minutes. I pulled into their drive, grabbed the two golf balls from my pocket, and knocked on the door. I heard the running footsteps of my cousins, and then the door burst open, and two small smiling, excited faces peered from behind it.

"Mom! It's Razz!" they both yelled enthusiastically.

I patted Teen playfully on her head and gave her the pink golf ball. I picked up Leta, tickled her for a minute, and gave her the yellow one.

"Hi, Razz," Aunt Mae greeted. "Heard you played golf today."

"Who told you?"

"Oh, just a little birdie." She laughed. "Speaking of birdies, did you get any?"

"I had one," I answered, putting Leta down so she could go off to play. "It's always tougher in this cold weather."

"I also heard you lost your jacket."

"It will show up. Who would want a jacket with my name on it, anyway?"

"Not me," Aunt Mae said with a laugh.

From behind me, I heard Leta singing "The Itsy-Bitsy Spider." I turned to see her rolling her yellow golf ball up the wall while singing. I laughed and turned to Aunt Mae.

"Welcome to my world," she said.

"I better get back home," I said, still laughing. "Don't want to miss dinner."

When I arrived home and walked into the kitchen from the garage, I noticed several envelopes stacked on the counter as I passed by on the way to the stove.

"They're yours," my mom said excitedly. "Open them!"

I first tasted a couple of bites of the meatloaf on the stove and then turned indifferently to the envelopes on the counter. There were three, one from each of the three schools I'd sent a letter of interest.

"Wow, that was quick," I casually said, grabbing them on my way to my room.

"You can open them right here, you know," my mom said.

I'm sure she held little hope that would happen. I hurried up the stairs to my room to avoid hearing any more pleas from her.

After reading all three responses, I still could not reach a decision. The University of Kentucky had sent the forms to request acceptance and an application for applying for a grant, but there was no mention of a golf scholarship. UE had no golf scholarships left to offer, but they'd included a letter of acceptance and the telephone number of the financial aid department to see if I could qualify for any grants. With Brescia's letter of acceptance, they apologized that all this year's golf scholarships had been offered and accepted. However, they explained that the financial aid administrator would be calling me to discuss the scholarships and grants I might qualify for if my GPA was 3.7 or higher. Unfortunately, those scholarships would only cover tuition and none of the room and board. The financial aid administrator wrote he was looking forward to personally helping me through the process and would explain all options available to me. He could call me on Wednesday evening if that were convenient for me.

At dinner, I discussed the letters with my mom and dad and reiterated my exasperation with this vetting process.

"I think I'm closer now, but I still can't make a decision," I said, showing my frustration.

"I know it's difficult, Razz," my dad agreed, "but it would be best to make your decision by next week so that we can focus on that school and what we need to do from there. Don't worry so much; things have a way of working out."

"Get the acceptance forms from UK and call UE and Brescia. Let us know what the financial aid administrators say, and we will talk more about it then," my mom suggested.

The call with UE went well, and with the possibility of some grants, it was a school I still considered. The call from Brescia also went well. The FAA seemed genuinely concerned for me and my decision process. I also liked the more intimate, family atmosphere of the smaller school. He explained that although there were no golf scholarships left, they did have other scholarships available if my GPA was 3.7 or higher. However, he candidly explained that if it wasn't, the cost of an education at Brescia would be higher. He also told me that he could not guarantee I could walk on for golf. Their budget was limited, but if an opening developed, they would let me know. I also received the acceptance forms from UK, leaving all three for consideration

Although the calls were helpful, I still was no closer to a decision than before.

The next Saturday, the unusual moderate temperature returned, and it continued into the first week of March. I headed to the golf course with the looming decision weighing on me. I hadn't even thought of Lefty and Righty until I saw the dilapidated old Ford Galaxy in the parking lot.

Teeing off alone on the first tee, I hoped to catch up with them. Walking up onto the first green, I peered over to the second tee box but saw no one there. More concerned with the three schools, I three-putted to a double bogey. Disgusted, I threw my bag over my shoulder, hung my head, and slowly walked to the second tee box when I heard the cheerful voice of Righty.

"Well, look who's here!"

244

"Hey, guys," I said, surprised.

"Let's get going," Lefty said, motioning for me to tee off. "We have work to do today."

The game today seemed a little more subdued. Righty kept hitting his ball into any body of water that was within reach, followed by a "Hallelujah," and Lefty narrowly missed any window within eyesight. But the usual bantering and chatter were missing.

On the fourteenth green, Lefty dropped his ball and then laid his putter down on the Bermuda grass. Righty placed his yellow ball into his bulging pants pocket, where a half-dozen others rested, and leaned off to one side, supporting his weight on his putter.

"Alright, kid," Lefty said. "Give it up."

Not sure what he meant, I looked at him quizzically.

"What is bothering you, boy," Righty asked. "Your body may be here on the course, but your mind is having an out-of-body experience. I'm sure it is somewhere having a lot more fun than you are."

"Well, there are several colleges I'm interested in, but there are too many..." I hesitated for a minute and then decided to confide in them what really bothered me.

"My three friends and I have been close for most of our lives. We were, and still are, always together. Now we are all going separate ways to college, and I will miss them. It is bothering me so much that I don't even want to go to college."

"They must be amazingly good friends," Righty said.

"They are."

"Razz," Lefty said, "you know, when I hit my ball, I slice it to the left. Righty slices his to the right. He goes to get his ball in the weeds, and I go to the other side to get my ball in the woods. Our next shot, I end up in the bunker, and Righty hits his ball over the green, onto the backside. But finally we end up together on the green, and both balls eventually end up in the same hole. Friends are like that; each one has to travel the road that is best for them. But if you are true friends, it doesn't matter which road you each travel; it's what you do when you end up on the green together again."

"Maybe, but it's difficult knowing they won't be there to help me along the way," I replied. "We've always been there for each other."

"Razz," Righty said, "everyone and every relationship is always evolving, always changing. If you don't change, you will find yourself left behind. Don't be afraid of change."

"One can be separated but still stay together," Lefty continued. "Stay in contact, focus on your schoolwork, and look forward to the times when you will be together."

"Hey, maybe his angel can pull a few strings to make it all work out for him," Righty added hopefully.

"Maybe. You never know what your angel will do," Lefty said with a nod.

"Razz, just narrow the schools down to two or three and then decide," Righty added. "If you can't decide, then pick the one with the prettiest girls."

"Don't listen to that part," Lefty said with a reproving stare at Righty.

"Do your research, decide, and then just trust your decision," Righty said, putting his putter in his bag and heading off the green.

"Gotta trust yourself, Razz, and your friends have to do the same. If your friends are as good as you say they are, they will always be there to help you." Lefty picked up his ball and putter and headed to his cart.

"Aren't you guys going to finish?" I asked, slightly confused.

"We have an appointment we need to keep," Righty added. "See you another time."

"We're out of time," Lefty said. "Just remember, don't ever give up. You never know when a small box full of answers will fall into your lap."

I stood there for a minute as I watched them head down the fourteenth fairway and then disappear as they rounded the turn in the tree-lined dogleg.

After finishing my round, I went home and decided it was time to grow up. I sat in my room and made a list for each school, and then I reached a decision. It was difficult, but even though Anna Lee was going to UK, and though I'd hoped to play golf at UE, I decided on Brescia because I felt more comfortable with a smaller school. They were well known for their accounting and business administration programs. I could minor in business as a plan B. Hopefully, something would change so I could play golf, but that wasn't as imperative as getting a degree. Every time I'd visited there, it had felt like home to me, and I felt I could trust myself with this decision. Mom and Dad, though surprised, supported my choice even before I said I intended to work part time to help pay the additional costs.

Anna Lee, though disappointed we would not be at the same school, agreed it was the right decision for me. The next few times I played golf on Saturday, I did not see Lefty or Righty on the course. I hoped to see them so I could tell them about my decision, but I never saw them again.

I began the fall semester at Brescia in early September 1969. My parents agreed to help pay the costs for me to stay at the dorm for the first year, so that helped. I had already made a few friends from classes, but it was a little lonely the first couple of days; I missed Colby, Elbie, and Anna Lee. On the third day of school, I began to feel even more depressed. Not only did I miss my friends, but this year was the first time since seventh grade that

I'd attended a school without being involved in some sport, and I missed the competitive atmosphere. After my English lit class, I was shuffling slowly across campus toward my dorm, reconsidering my decision, when I heard someone shouting.

"Razz!"

I turned to see Anna Lee, her arms full of boxes and books, running toward me with a huge smile.

"Anna Lee, what are you doing here?" I asked, shocked at the sight of her.

"I just enrolled."

"What!"

"Can you believe it?" she asked excitedly.

"Here?" I asked in disbelief.

"Yes! On enrollment day at UK, they had no record of me. Nothing! No golf scholarship, no record of my application or acceptance, nothing. I felt like a beggar trying to get in for free."

"You are kidding, right?"

"No, I am not. The registrar apologized and said this was the strangest thing he had ever seen in all his years. A situation like this had never happened before. They couldn't understand why or how my information was missing. He said it was a freakish dilemma, as if someone had intentionally removed all my information, but he could not understand how that could ever happen. He told me I could start in the spring semester, but not now, since most of my classes were already full. I lost it! I was so upset that I went back to my car to go home."

"But what are you doing here?"

"Well, I was so depressed and upset that I ran back to my car and just sat there, trying to figure out what I was going to do. Then I remembered this package."

She put her books down on the sidewalk and showed me a box she held in her arms.

248

"It has your name on it but my home address. The postman brought it to my house just before I left for school. I didn't have time to open it and just threw it in the back seat, not knowing if it was for you or me. Anyway, I picked it up and opened it, and this is what was in it."

She opened the box to reveal a varsity jacket. Then she turned it over to show me my name embroidered on the back.

"That's mine!" I exclaimed.

"Yes, and this is what was in the pocket." She reached into the front pocket and pulled out a ball marker. It was the one that I had used before I'd lost the jacket.

"That's mine, too. But where did it come from?"

"I don't know; there's no return address."

"You're kidding me, right?"

"No. Anyway, right then and there, I decided to call Brescia. I explained everything to them and that I needed to start school somewhere right away. They said this was perfect timing as one of the freshman girls who had received a golf scholarship had just withdrawn and forfeited hers. They sped up my application, and here I am, on a full scholarship."

"That's awesome, Anna Lee!" I said excitedly.

"Yeah, but that is not the best part, Razz. They connected me to the girl's golf coach, and she confirmed everything. We spoke for quite some time; then the coach mentioned that the girl had withdrawn because her boyfriend had decided not to go there at the last minute. He also forfeited his golf scholarship. I asked if it was still available. She said she thought it was but would have to check with the boy's golf coach to be certain. I told her about you, and she put me on hold and called the boy's golf coach right then and there. The boy's golf coach said that, ironically, he had been trying to contact you, and even had called your high school coach. He remembered you and wanted to talk to you right away. It's a full scholarship, Razz!"

"Oh my gosh! Do you have his number?"

"Yes, call him now. Hurry!" Anna Lee urged as she pulled a small piece of paper with the coach's number on it from her pocket.

I hurried to my dorm and nervously tried to dial his number on the phone in the hall but kept getting it mixed up. I fumbled so much I had to re-dial the numbers three times before reaching the golf coach.

The coach seemed excited to hear from me and wanted to meet with me the next day. Although he couldn't promise the scholarship over the phone, he said it was his to give and, right now, I was the only available candidate. He said that he remembered watching me play well in a tournament in Henderson last year. So, with fall practice starting next week and me already being enrolled, the meeting was just a formality.

I put my books down and tried on my jacket, making sure it still fit. I pulled out the ball marker from my pocket, flipped it over, and noticed something on the underside of the round marker. Someone had written with a Sharpie a small L on the left side and a small R on the right.

"Are you kidding me?" I laughed.

The first weekend in October, I had errands to take care of in town. As I passed the city course, I glanced at the parking lot and found myself making a U-turn at the next light. I hoped I could find Lefty and Righty to figure out where, or who, had found my jacket and to thank them for sending it.

I pulled into the parking lot, looking for the antiquated Ford Galaxy. It was not there, so I parked the car close to the pro shop and walked in, greeting the golf pro behind the counter.

"Hi, I'm trying to find out the names of the two old men I played with several times last February and March. Would they be in your tee time register?" I asked.

"Well, if they played here, they would be. You're Razz, right?"

"Yes."

"February, February," he said, thumbing through the register. "Here you are. Twelve o'clock tee time. But you were by yourself."

"I caught up with them on the second tee box each time."

"I see you here three weekends in a row, but the last tee time before yours was eleven ten. The previous week was ten fifty, and the first week was ten thirty. But I know all those groups. They all were foursomes, and they weren't old men."

"They drove a beat-up old Ford Galaxy," I added, hoping that would help.

"Can't say I remember seeing that. My dad had a Ford Galaxy when I was a kid. Huge cars, those Galaxies. I would have noticed if there was one on the lot. You say it was two old men and you met up with them on the second tee, right?"

"Yes."

"Did they finish with you?"

"No. Both of them always had to leave before teeing off on eighteen."

"Figures. It looks like they were jumping on the course without paying. Sounds like two old scoundrels to me."

Chapter XXI

1969

Colby's Decision

The fall of 1969 was exciting but very bittersweet for us; we no longer were together. There were no cell phones then, but we burned a lot of dimes calling each other from the dorm hall phones. Elbie studied accounting at Western Kentucky University in Bowling Green and then studied for his CPA and masters at Vanderbilt in Nashville. Though Anna Lee wanted to attend the University of Kentucky, a "mysterious intervention" prevented that and steered her to attend Brescia with me for two years. She received her associate degree there and originally planned to attend an arts and design school in New York after that. However, she began to have doubts about leaving and vacillated between remaining at Brescia or going to New York.

Elbie, in a rare deviation from his conservative nature, jumped in and vehemently insisted she go to New York.

"You will never be happy here!" he strongly chastised her in a brash reproach. "You will go to New York, or we will carry you there!"

At first, Anna Lee was taken aback by Elbie's reprimand, but then she realized he was right. She would regret it for the rest of her life if she did not venture out in search of her identity. In the fall of 1971, she packed her bags and was off to New York City to attend Parsons College in Greenwich Village.

Colby, however, chose a different path, shocking us completely and thrusting us into the reality of our time. It was a troubled year; in 1969, the Viet Nam war, politics, and intense activism all arrived, trying to squeeze through the same, tiniest of pinholes in time. There just wasn't room for everybody to get through, with feelings of animosity coming at you from nearly every direction.

Most everyone had a friend or family member, or at least knew of one, who did not come back from that war. Colby, Elbie, and I all had high draft numbers, so at least for the time being, we could attend college. Colby was likely to receive a scholarship wherever he wanted due to his exceptional grades and family income. However, Colby was intent on becoming an aeronautical engineer and specifically wanted to attend Washington University in Seattle, a very long way from Kentucky. He had not received a reply about his scholarship from them yet, but we were positive it would come.

Colby decided to take matters into his own hands. He chose to join the Marines and would attend school when he returned. The money he would receive from the GI bill would help offset the costs of tuition above any partial scholarships. We were both shocked and disappointed at his decision, and especially his lack of discussion about it with us beforehand. There was no doubt, at least among the rest of us, that he would receive a full scholarship.

"You what!!!" Anna Lee screamed upon being informed.

"It's something I had to do, Anna Lee," he replied. "I need to be sure that I can go to school in Seattle. Doing this will help make it certain."

Anna Lee angrily charged toward him, pushing him back stiffly with her hands.

"Colby, you big dummy, the odds of you not coming back from that war are a lot higher than you not getting that scholarship! What is wrong with you!"

"I can't take the chance, Anna Lee. I will be okay."

Anna Lee jumped into his face, thrusting her finger into his chest.

"You better come back to us! Do you hear me?!! You better come back to us, or I'll come after you!" I don't know if Elbie or Colby could see the fear and hurt in her eyes, but I did.

Elbie and I remained silent. Both of us shared Anna Lee's feelings, but we also understood Colby's caution. She quickly turned and marched back to my car.

The four of us had been inseparable for over ten years now. Colby's leaving tore at our hearts, especially Anna Lee's. He was as much a part of her as Elbie and I, but Colby was her equal. I'm sure she felt a part of herself was leaving, and she could not cope with that.

Elbie and I stayed with Colby for a few minutes while Anna Lee stubbornly remained in the car. We assured him he had all our support in his decision and wished him well. I tried to explain to him that Anna Lee was merely afraid of losing her friend and did not know how to deal with that.

Elbie and I returned to the car, where Anna Lee waited with a determined frown of despair. I sat down, started the engine, and looked back at Colby as we pulled away from his home. From the look on his face, I think he, too, now realized he was leaving his friends. He usually analyzed every decision impeccably, but in his concern for certainty, I don't think he considered all the ramifications, nor did he anticipate how it would affect his friends.

"He won't make it back," Anna Lee said to no one in particular. "He's too kindhearted. He will get killed trying to help someone else."

Neither Elbie nor I answered. We both worried that Anna Lee was right.

The day Colby departed for duty, we met the Harris family at the bus station to see him off.

Mrs. Harris was distraught, as only a mother could be when saying goodbye to a son, knowing she may never see him alive again. The tissue in her trembling hands shook visibly and could no longer hold the moisture from her free-flowing tears. Mr. Harris tried valiantly to keep his composure, but he could not contain it when the time came to hug his son for the last farewell.

After all the Harrises, including Colby's brother and sister, said their goodbyes, Elbie and I gave our friend a warm farewell embrace. Anna Lee remained stoic, standing motionless off to the side and in silence. I could tell her emotions tore deeply into her heart, leaving her unable to move. Finally, Colby realized that as well and began to step toward her. As he did, she jumped into his arms and hugged him tightly. Both were unable to speak, but there was no need for that anyway.

As she let go of him, she rubbed his shoulder and took a deep breath.

"Be careful, Colby," she pleaded. "Don't do anything stupid. You have to come back to us, you hear me?"

He nodded, still unable to speak. Then he gave his mother one last hug, grabbed his bags, and walked to the bus. When he reached the steps, he turned to his dad and saluted him. With that, he boarded the bus and was on his way to Fort Campbell, Kentucky, for basic training.

It turned out that Colby's decision was opportune. Two weeks after he left for basic training, he received a reply from Washington University offering a partial scholarship. Just as Colby had assumed, his parents would not have been able to afford to make up the difference. Now, if he could only survive the atrocities and the extreme dangers of war, his tuition was assured.

We heard nothing for the next six weeks until he was finally allowed a weekend furlough. It nearly killed us, but we didn't bother him, as we felt his family needed the time together. The three of us did call him Sunday before he left again to wish him well. Anna Lee and I met at Elbie's house to call him. We huddled close to the ear of the phone and often fought to speak.

Colby was glad to hear from us, and we could tell he was excited to be a Marine.

A few months later, we heard he had been assigned to train as a helicopter pilot at the Primary Helicopter Center at Fort Wolters, Texas. We should have known Colby would somehow fly something before he got out of the service. Only Colby could have advanced to that opportunity so soon, although we wondered if it might make it even more dangerous for him. Letters were few and far in between, so we kept informed through Mrs. Harris, although even she didn't get as much information as she wanted.

Less than a year later, Colby was on his way to Viet Nam as a Huey pilot. Most of us quit watching the nightly news as it was too painful knowing Colby was in the midst of that. We missed our friend, and each day, we expected to receive the news that we all dreaded.

Occasionally over the next two years, we often heard that Colby had received another decoration for bravery in rescuing troops or the wounded from battlefields when under intense fire. Anna Lee had been right in that respect; he was too kindhearted, but so far, he was still alive.

In March of 1973, Elbie was close to finishing his degree at Bowling Green, and he began planning to study for his CPA and masters at Vanderbilt. I was finishing my accounting degree at Brescia, and Anna Lee had found her place in New York. I don't know how she'd managed to do it, but she, too, was close to receiving her design and fashion degree at Parsons College in NYC. Of course, Anna Lee could accomplish anything when she put her mind to it, but how a girl from Kentucky, one who wore mostly blue jeans, a t-shirt, and a ball cap, had decided on a fashion degree in New York and been accepted was beyond us.

Then, in late March of 1973, two months after the signing of the Viet Nam peace treaty, the news of the war finally ending permeated every corner in our country. Colby was one of the last pilots to remain, flying US troops and prisoners of war from Hanoi. At long last, we could breathe a sigh of relief when, less than three months later, he finished his four-year tour and headed home.

He went off to college in Seattle and eventually made his home there. As his career progressed, he became a prominent engineer at an airplane complex near the city. His dad had always insisted that Colby get good grades. He explained that he would have enough difficulties in life, some through no fault of his, but a good education would be an asset no one could take away. An education, Mister Harris always said, would open doors you didn't even know existed. As usual, his dad was right.

A few years back, I was traveling out west and decided to take a side trip to visit Colby. Although we talked almost weekly on the telephone, it had been a while since I had seen him. I could not get over how much he looked like his dad when he opened the door.

We reminisced about our lives, our families, and even our time growing up. I asked him if he had any memories of the day we'd eaten the watermelon. He bellowed a hearty laugh, sounding much like his dad did when he was alive. Oh, yes, he remembered that day well, especially the chicken coop.

"I never took anything after that if it wasn't mine to take," he said.

I nodded.

"I will always remember your dad," I told him in a respectful tone. "He was a good man, a venerable man."

He thanked me for the kind words about his departed dad.

We talked some more, and before I left, we planned on making a trip back there one day. It was likely that the barn would no longer be there, but we wanted to visit the place where we'd learned a lesson that we would carry with us for the rest of our lives. As I got up to leave, Colby told me he had done some research once. It turned out that Daniel Boone had stopped by that part of Kentucky at different times. Although it was unlikely that he'd built that barn, he might have slept there a night or two while passing through.

I smiled and nodded, and with a wink, I said, "I bet he even ate a watermelon there, too,"

"Probably did." Colby laughed. "Probably did. But I bet he asked first."

Chapter XXII

1979

The Yellow Rose Group

After graduating, our careers separated us by distance, but we remained close, visiting each other whenever possible or staying in touch by telephone. Colby now lived near Seattle and was rapidly making a name for himself as an engineer in aviation.

Elbie left a successful career with a large CPA firm in Nashville to start his own firm in Bowling Green. Anna Lee was finally at peace, with a burgeoning career in New York City designing façades and lobbies for office buildings. I stayed in Daviess County, Kentucky, and began buying properties, primarily farmland. I rented out the land to local farmers to raise the crops for income.

In the summer of 1979, Elbie, Colby, Anna Lee, and I met at my place. We usually got together at least once a year and coincided that with an opportunity to visit family back home. I shared with them my new business of purchasing properties. Colby became very excited about that, and from there, we decided to start an investment company with the four of us as equal shareholders. We pooled our money to buy income-producing farmland and other rural properties.

I think, at first, it was more of an opportunity for us to stay connected than a money-making venture, but soon we found the business was becoming very profitable. When deciding a name for the company, Anna Lee and Colby said they didn't care what we named it, so Elbie and I decided on "The Yellow Rose Group." Each of us used our various individual talents and shared equally in the affairs of the business.

We decided to always keep at least twenty-five percent of the land we purchased in woodlands. If there wasn't enough

259

existing timber to meet the twenty-five percent, we planted oaks, walnut, ash, and other species of trees to fulfill our twenty-five percent goal. We felt the forests were disappearing, and since they were such large a part of our beginnings, we wanted to keep some of the land for timber; the rest was rented for crops.

We first purchased some property in the Tywhoppity Bottoms area, and we kept on buying until we owned over six thousand acres in western Kentucky and southern Indiana, just across the river. The income from the farmland eventually paid off the mortgages, allowing us to continue buying additional properties.

We discovered oil on some of the land, which produced a nice profit, and coal on some others, but it was mostly farmland. We always put in our lease agreements that the coal companies had to return the land to its original state, or better, after mining.

The Yellow Rose Group turned out to be very serendipitous as it gave us a reason to keep in touch with each other. It was fun, profitable, and entertaining. It also gave us a purpose, creating more woodlands, and allowed us to set up a charitable foundation to benefit those less fortunate.

Since I was the only one living in the area, I was involved more than the others, but they insisted I accept a salary for doing so. We never argued about anything related to The Yellow Rose Group, and it held us together, the same as we were when younger. Most of our purchases turned out to be very profitable, both as a source of joy and of fortune that we never anticipated.

However, one did not.

Chapter XXIII

1990

The Schoolhouse

After eleven years, The Yellow Rose Group operated almost on auto-drive. Employees handled most of the day-to-day business, and I hired a realtor to help find us potential properties. Hiring her turned out to be a wise business decision. Our assets grew exponentially and allowed me more time to work on my farm and even play some golf. Occasionally I took up other endeavors, not so much for the money, but often only to entertain a passing whim.

I also had more time to spend with my two children, who were now in their early teens. Like most kids that age, they mysteriously had been given all the knowledge of the world in one night.

Surprisingly, they got along with each other most of the time, but they had their moments when sibling rivalries broke all peace accords. I have now concluded that sibling rivalry transcends all others and, in comparison, makes the wars between ancient Greece and the Persian Empire seem like a kindergarten tee ball game.

When we attended grade school many years ago, our school had six classrooms, a lunchroom in the basement, and, of course, the principal's office. The principal doubled as the seventh- and eighth-grade teacher, and with only six classrooms for all eight grades, several of the classrooms simultaneously held two grades. With barely a hundred kids in the entire school, most of the classes comprised less than twenty students. We thought the school was modern; at least, it was compared to the old, wood-framed, one-room schoolhouses many of our grandparents had attended.

There is a one-room schoolhouse that still stands on my farm. It rests on a small plot of forty acres that was adjacent to my land. I purchased that forty acres shortly after buying our home and farm. The abandoned schoolhouse is nestled on the fringe of the woods, up on the hill, overlooking the cow pasture. At one time, there was a dirt road leading to the schoolhouse, but it was sown long ago with tall fescue grass for the cattle to graze. That left the structure isolated on the top of the hillside like a cloistered abbey.

The many years of neglect left it in poor condition. It is of no use to anyone except as a refuge for a few small calves trying to slip in out of the rain. Glass no longer remains in either of the two windows, giving easy access to any vagrant insects, especially wasps. The wooden door precariously hangs by one determined rusty hinge, fastened with a couple of old, rusty penny nails. The dirty wooden floors, worn from the many leather shoes pounding their way outside for recess over the years, is mostly concealed with loose straw and dirt unwittingly ferried in by the playful calves. It seems small for a classroom, no bigger than most people's living rooms today, and I cannot picture more than twelve to fifteen kids and a teacher fitting in there for a school session.

I will never forget the day an older lady, driving a small gray Pontiac, came up the road and stopped in front of our house. I curiously watched as she struggled in pain, trying to climb from her seat, proof that time eventually pilfers the fleeting youth that most of us are oblivious to until far too late. Her plain clean dress, wrinkled from sitting too long in the driver's seat, befitted her frail body, but her gray hair, still set as if she'd just left the beauty parlor, showed no signs of stress. I saw her struggle a few steps with her cane, but she suddenly stopped, surveyed the house and barns, and then glanced up the hill and spotted the old schoolhouse. As if a fresh, cool breeze had whisked by, reviving her spirit, she picked up her cane and tucked it quickly under her arm.

Appearing twenty years younger, she walked briskly toward the barn. I watched, puzzled by all this, as she approached the gate to the cow pasture, never taking her eyes off that old schoolhouse. She stopped at the wooden gate for a moment and then tried furiously, at least, with as much fury a woman of her age could muster, to unfasten the lock. Unable to open it, she settled for climbing onto the gate and leaning over to stare at that old schoolhouse. With both feet firmly planted on the first plank for a better view, she remained there quietly.

I thought all this a little peculiar, so I opened the door and walked curiously past the barn and on to the pasture gate.

"Afternoon, ma'am," I politely said when I reached her.

She turned, seemingly upset at the interruption, and glared at me as if I were a trespasser, even though it was my farm. I took no offense, though.

"Afternoon," she finally answered, her face changing to a smile as she turned back to the schoolhouse again.

"We used to play up there when we were little girls," she said sentimentally, pointing her delicate finger at the schoolhouse. "Still looks the same."

I couldn't understand her emotional attachment to an old one-room schoolhouse, but I found myself asking, "Ma'am, would you like me to take you up there on the tractor?"

She turned to me, nodded, and replied, "Yes, I would."

I went to the barn, started the tractor, drove it over to the fastened gate, and then stepped down to open it.

"Let me help you, ma'am," I said as I helped the petite lady up on my old green tractor.

"Now, you hang on tight to that fender," I told her. "I don't want you falling off."

She nodded and grabbed the fender tightly with her thin, frail fingers. I put the tractor in low gear, knowing that if I went too fast, those small, delicate fingers would not be able to hold on.

As the noisy tractor passed the pond, it startled a dozen or more frogs from their afternoon nap. The water rippled from the frightened frogs seeking safety. As we continued up the hill, I checked to see if her grip remained firm enough to keep her from falling and tumbling back down the hillside.

As we approached the schoolhouse, I noticed from the corner of my eye that she had begun to fidget excitedly, much like a six-year-old waiting for recess. I'm sure that if her aging body had let her, she would have jumped eagerly from the tractor, hitting the ground in a dead run toward the dilapidated old building. I still could not figure out why she was so excited about an unsightly old schoolhouse. Lately, I'd had a growing notion of putting a match to it so that I could sow a little grass seed there. Knowing how those calves loved fresh green grass, they would not miss the old structure, either.

When we reached the schoolhouse, I stopped the tractor. But before I could engage the brake and turn off the diesel engine, the lady was already off and peering inside the door. I turned off the diesel engine, and as it idled down, I sat for a moment to let her have a look.

"Were you a teacher, ma'am?" I asked from my seat.

She continued to look from top to bottom, front to back. Finally, she turned her head to me briefly. "Yes and no." She smiled at me and stepped inside.

Okay. I laughed to myself, not knowing what that meant. I stepped down from the tractor and slowly walked over to the door. I sensed this old shack had a special meaning to her and didn't think it right for me to step inside, so I peered inside from the front door, noticing her standing in the back with both hands on her cane.

"Ma'am, are you okay?"

"Yes. Yes, I am," she replied contentedly.

Ignoring me, she continued to look around as if she could see things I couldn't.

"There were five of us," she said softly, "five sisters. When we were little girls, we came up here to play school. Sometimes I was the teacher. Sometimes one of my sisters played that role. When we finished our chores, we would come up here and play for hours. We would make-believe, tell stories, and sometimes just sit and talk. We were all very close, and this little schoolhouse was a big part of our lives."

She stopped for a minute, and then a big grin spread across her face like sunshine bursting from behind a dark November cloud.

"And oh, did we laugh."

"Did you used to live on this farm?" I asked.

"Yes. Everyone called this the Benny Farm back then. It used to belong to my dad's old uncle Benny." Her voice drifted off as she finished.

"I heard something about this being called the Benny Farm when I bought this place," I said.

She was quiet for a moment. There was a poignant reverence in all this that moved me. I almost felt as if I should bow my head.

"I'm the only one of us left now," she said sadly, surveying each wall of the room. Then she stopped as she looked upon the opposite wall, about six feet high.

"There it is. See those four names there?" she asked, pointing to four faded names penciled high on the wall.

I had never noticed them before and said nothing.

"My two older sisters wrote their names there one summer day. The rest of us were too small to reach that high. They said we had to write our names there when we were old enough to reach.

They said we could never be big girls unless we could sign our names that high on the wall. But we had to sell the farm soon after that. I was nine years old then, and I never did get to sign my name.

"My two younger sisters bragged to me that they snuck back up here some years back and wrote their names up there, too. I never really believed they did that, but I guess it was true."

She hesitated for a moment. "They are all gone now. I'm the only one left," she repeated, lowering her head and becoming quiet as I stared at the four elusive names that had escaped my attention for the ten years that I had owned the place.

I stepped back and walked to my tractor. Then I climbed up and opened the toolbox. I searched briefly, rustling among the tools, spare nuts, and bolts, and then deep down at the bottom, I found what I needed. I stepped down and walked softly back to the schoolhouse, but this time, I walked inside.

Approaching the elderly lady, I held out my hand and offered her a dirty old number two yellow pencil without even a nub left of the eraser. She looked at me and smiled behind the tears moistening her eyes. Taking the pencil from my hand, she stepped over to the wall. She looked at the four names for a minute and then slowly raised her trembling hand to sign her name. Wiping the tears from her eyes, she turned and offered the old yellow number two to me with a gentle, satisfied smile on her face.

"You keep it," I said, and her smile widened, though I could tell she was too choked up to say anything right then.

I led her from the schoolhouse and helped her back onto the tractor again. As I slowly drove her back to her car, she watched the schoolhouse fade away from behind. Reaching the grey Pontiac, I turned off the tractor engine. Nary a word had been spoken by either of us the entire way back. I opened the car door and gently helped her get in.

"I'm glad you came," I told her.

She looked up at me with a smile and said, "I am, too. Thank you."

She put the pencil gently but ceremoniously into her purse as if it were a trophy and then looked back up at me.

"Well, they have nothing on me now, do they?" she proclaimed, bursting into a big smile.

"No, ma'am, they don't."

She nodded, put the car in gear, and drove off with a renewed smile on her face. As she drove down the road and topped the hill, I noticed that small, frail hand of hers waving outside the window. I couldn't tell if she were waving goodbye to me or the schoolhouse as she drove by. It didn't matter, though, because I never again thought of putting a match to that old schoolhouse, and as far as I know, those five names are still high on the wall.

Chapter XXIV

1996

Mud Mountain

Few people know this, but I taught math at one of the local high schools for one year. I really didn't want to and didn't need the money, but they were short a teacher, they said I qualified, and it seemed an opportunity for a different experience. With both my children off to college, I also found myself needing something to give me a sense of worth in this transitional period. So, I put on my teaching hat, but I soon learned more than I taught.

Tish was one of my students in geometry class. She also happened to be Anna Lee's only niece. The truth is, she was Anna Lee's cousin's daughter, but Anna Lee had "adopted" her as her niece.

I tried not to be partial in any way, and I think I succeeded to some degree in that area. However, I still thought I retained the right to privately believe Tish was one of the prettiest girls in the school. She also was one of the most popular, not because of her looks, but because she possessed a genuine kindness toward everyone, a trait undoubtedly inherited from her "aunt."

Most everyone got along with Tish, both the boys and the girls. Her word was good, and that earned her a lot of respect. Chad, the muscular, athletic quarterback on the football team, was her steady at the time, and they made a handsome couple.

Elise, a quiet, slightly shy young lady, moved in from out of town shortly after school started. That made it difficult for her to get to know anyone, as most friendships were already established and set. She wasn't unfriendly, just a little reserved; still, most kids seemed to ignore her. It wasn't necessarily an intentional slight, but a simple matter of convenience, or at least, that is what I hoped.

Eventually Elise began to sit alone each day, keeping to herself as much as she could, and that bothered me as I had once experienced that loneliness myself. I spoke to her a couple of times in the lunchroom and enjoyed talking to her as she seemed very witty, but a teacher can't be a friend like someone her age. I inconspicuously tried to maneuver a few students toward her, hoping to spark a friendship or at least an acceptance of her, but despite my best intentions, there are some things a person must do themselves.

A few weeks later, Tish noticed Elise sitting alone in the corner of the lunchroom. She kept glancing over at Elise for a few minutes. Then she gathered up her food tray, left her friends' table, walked over to Elise, and sat down beside her. I was so excited for Elise. It wasn't long before they both were laughing and enjoying each other's company, oblivious to the other students' reproving stares and frowns. Although I never heard it, I know Tish was at first politely chastised by some for befriending Elise. Even Chad questioned her choices, but it didn't matter; Tish had found a new friend.

There was a social one Friday night, and most of Tish's friends were attending. Tish, of course, was invited, but when she showed up with Elise, she caused quite a stir. Amy, one of her best friends, pulled her aside.

"Why did you bring her here?" Amy said in a demanding tone.

"What do you mean?" Tish returned.

"You know what I mean," Amy snarled as she glared over Tish's shoulder at Elise. "She's not like us."

"Not like us?!" Tish repeated incredulously

"You know what I mean, Tish."

"She's my friend, Amy, just as you are."

"Well, I hope you enjoy your new friend because, if you keep it up, she is going to be the only one you have," Amy barked, and then she stormed off.

Chad stood nearby, overhearing the entire conversation. Tish noticed him as Amy walked away. He looked at Tish without emotion and turned to talk to his friends beside him.

That hurt Tish more than Amy's words. She and Elise didn't stay long as it became increasingly apparent that they weren't welcome. On their way home, Elise turned to Tish.

"Tish, you shouldn't be with me anymore. You're going to lose Chad and all your other friends if you do. I won't let that happen. I'll be okay."

"Elise, maybe they never were my friends," Tish replied.

The next day at school was different, very different. The friendly chatter and boisterous laughter had disappeared, replaced with a muffled silence broken only by the shuffling of feet down the halls. In each corner, a group of students quietly whispered with an occasional furtive turn of the head to make certain no one else was listening. When Tish and Elise walked by, the whispers stopped, and heads turned to watch them with scornful eyes as they continued down the hall. Then the whispering re-emerged. Even the lunchroom banter was at a lower key. Tish and Elise sat alone, ignoring the disdainful glances cast their way. Tish didn't mind her friends shunning her—she had too much self-confidence for that—but the snub from Chad hurt her.

Eventually the two girls became friends with students from the school across town. There were rumors, too, that both Tish and Elise had new boyfriends from that school as well.

The derision eventually faded, and the boisterous chatter returned when the annual fall Mud Mountain Run neared. Mud Mountain was relatively small in height, only a little over six hundred feet high, but it had a challenging and very steep trail that led to the top. Every year, boys from the baseball, football, and basketball teams raced up the mountain to determine a champion. To make it even more interesting, the night before the race, the volunteer fire department drove up the other side to the top of the mountain and turned on the water hoses. The water from the hoses trickled down, saturating the slope, with the runoff settling at the bottom, creating a giant mud pit almost as big as the infield of a baseball diamond. The boys would have to first navigate through the mud pit and then up the long, slippery slope of the mountain. Only the strongest of boys could endure the treacherous and enduring race. It was the most prestigious and popular of all community events, with most folks able to recite the litany of champions for the last twenty years.

As the excitement of the upcoming race grew, the anticipation reached new levels, and the buzz in the halls at school returned once again. However, the buzz was for a different reason this year. Tish and Elise had both decided to enter the race, causing quite a stir as, in past years, only boys had competed. No girl had ever considered racing, much less put their name on the sign-up sheet. There followed many arguments about whether Tish and Elise should be allowed. Finally, despite the indignant grumblings of many and the outright howls of others, a committee of teachers permitted the girls to enter. The decision was grudgingly accepted. After all, some said, a girl could never make it to the top of Mud Mountain anyway.

Tish and Elise immediately began training for the race, knowing that they had to finish to avoid the harsh humility that would inevitably follow if they didn't. They jostled among the contentious boys on the track for practice, ignoring their catcalls and ugly derision. Better get used to this, they thought; it was going to be a lot worse on the mountain. Winning the race would quiet the contemptuousness once and for all. But even if they didn't win, a good finish would make a statement.

The news of Tish and Elise entering the race did not bother Chad, but the idea of Tish having a new boyfriend did. He became very subdued, and his performance in the Friday night football games began to suffer.

I saw him stop Tish one day as she walked down the hall. Pointing his finger at her, he sounded caustic and said some very unpleasant things to her. Shaking his head angrily, he turned and walked away. To Tish's credit, she maintained her dignity and said nothing, but I could see the hurt in her eyes. Chad became even more sullen after that, pretending to be more interested in his studies to avoid conversations with friends.

I had been watching all of this without comment, but the Friday morning before the Mud Mountain race, I asked Chad to see me after class. As the other students left the room for their next courses, Chad sat sulking with his long legs sprawled out from beneath the desk, glaring at the floor. Once the last student had walked out, he rose, obviously annoyed, and lumbered toward me.

"Chad," I asked, "what does an apology cost you?"

He stared at me, puzzled, and then replied with a simple, "What?"

"If you apologize to someone, what does it cost you?"

He stared at me again, unsure of how to answer.

"I don't know… It doesn't cost me anything, I guess."

"Then why do you treat an apology as if it were a piece of gold?"

"What do you mean?" he asked, lowering his brows, bringing back his recently familiar frown.

"You hold on to an apology as if it were a newly found golden nugget, clutching it tightly in your fist, shoving it deep down into your pocket, hiding it from even the faintest light of day. Someday you will realize that an apology is just like a golden nugget; one can only realize its worth when you give it away."

He stepped back with a blank stare on his face.

"Chad, you are carrying a toxic preoccupation with what others think of you. You have less control over what others think than a cow does over the flies that will be biting at her all day. The more important question is, how do you feel about yourself? Once you put that into the proper perspective, what others may or may not think won't matter much to you."

He stood before me, motionless, still not speaking.

"Go on, Chad, or you will miss your next class," I instructed, a little perturbed with him, and I turned to my desk.

As he entered the hall, I watched him from the corner of my eye. When he turned his head back toward me, I could tell he was trying to grasp the intent of our conversation but was too proud to ask.

The next morning, the wet Mud Mountain trail glistened in the glow of the early morning sun. The crowd, holding their biscuit and ham sandwiches and juice, purchased from the vendors down by the mud bog, began lining the slope along the ropes that stretched up both sides of the trail. Proud mothers and other supporters waved signs encouraging each person's favorite to win the race. It was the most festive event yet, and inarguably the biggest crowd ever, with packed crowds lining both sides up the mountain.

They'd asked me to be the marshal to start the race. I'm not sure why they did that; there were many others more qualified than I, but I reluctantly agreed.

The jocular boys each described with great fanfare and animation how he was going to win. Chad was a bit more subdued, but he forced a smile upon his face when any friend spoke to him. Only a very few of us could tell his heart was not in the race this year.

When Tish and Elise arrived in t-shirts and running gear, the murmurs of the crowd increased. I could hear familiar voices heckling the two young ladies, who, at least to my mind, deserved robust applause for their courage. A few faint voices could be heard calling out some encouragement to the two girls, but those folks were usually met with a stiff elbow admonishing them to be quiet.

The boys gathered in a boisterous circle, most with their backs to Tish and Elise. The two girls stood alone, focused like hawks staring down a foraging field mouse. I could feel their determination, but also the enormity of the pressure they had placed upon themselves. I feared an imminent heartbreak, for both the girls and me. The boys, all well-trained athletes and in great shape, would have difficulty making it up to the top of the mountain. Tish and Elise, with only two weeks of training, lacked the time to build the strength and stamina it would require.

I picked up the microphone and instructed the contestants to position themselves at the starting line. The boys immediately lined up tightly, leaving no room for Tish and Elise to position themselves. I asked the boys to make room, but they would not budge and continued to taunt the girls. Finally, subduing the urge to chastise the boys publicly, I instructed the two boys at the end of the starting line to make room for the girls, and I explained that the race would not start until they obliged.

One of the other teachers was the gunner. He held a pop gun that would signal the start. I made sure everyone was ready and picked up the microphone again.

"Mister gunner, the contestants are ready," I shouted and nodded at him as the roar of the crowd grew.

With that, the gun went off, and the race began, followed by the thundering cheers of the fans. To most everyone's surprise, Tish and Elise somehow made it through the mud pit and started up the slippery slope of the mountain, with Elise leading the race and Tish a close second. One of the boys was a half-step behind Tish, and Chad was slightly behind him, in fourth place. Each one picked up speed as they went up the mountain, but footing was essential as a single slip would certainly end any chance of winning.

Tish and Elise held their lead as more moms, and even some dads, began encouraging them. A few boys had already lost their footing on the slope; humbled and embarrassed, they'd tumbled halfway down the mountain to the bottom of the hill.

Now, what happened next was debated for years to come. I will just give you the facts as I saw them, without judgment. Chad passed the boy in front of him and then Tish. Then the boy caught up to Tish, with both running side by side. Although his feet never gave way, his upper body moved as if he had slipped. His shoulder bumped into Tish, causing her to lose balance and forcing her into an awkward tumble into the mud. She began an uncontrollable slide partway down the hill, and when she finally stopped, everyone had passed her. Tish tried to get up, but she heard something pop in her knee and immediately fell into the mud. Her leg could not support the slightest weight, and any effort to do so resulted in agonizing pain. Again, and again, she made a heroic effort to get up and take a few one-legged hops up the hill, but each time, she ended up painfully slipping back onto the muddy ground.

Elise sensed something was wrong with Tish and glanced over her shoulder to see her struggling in the mud, unable to stand. When Elise paused to glance backward, that fraction of a second was enough for the remaining boys to pass her. Several of them brushed against her, causing her to lose balance as well and begin a tumbling descent. She stopped her fall by forcing her heels deep into the mud, and then she slowly slid down to Tish, reaching her just as Chad crossed the finish line, followed closely by the other boys, who began their celebration.

Elise helped Tish to her feet, and they continued up the hill together. A few scattered spectators jeered them, but now they were the ones who felt a stiff elbow in the ribs. An increasing

275

number of spectators began vigorously encouraging the two girls, who valiantly strained to make it to the top. But with Tish's bad leg and the increasingly slippery slope, they continued to fall face first into the mud more times than not.

Each time they got up, their hair and faces were so thickly caked with mud that you could not tell them apart. They were now simply two exhausted girls desperately struggling alone to finish what they had started. But with the pain in Tish's leg and the exhaustion bearing down on Elise, it was evident to all they would not make it.

At that moment, Amy grabbed the rope and ducked under it, running up the slope to Tish's side. She picked her up, and with Elise on the other arm, they inched upwards. By now, the muddy hill was as slick as melted butter on glass. Despite the increasing encouragement of the crowd, they continued slipping and tumbling into the mud.

Two more girls crossed the ropes to join and help. They all slipped, but with each fall, they rose again, continuing their arduous march to the finish line. More girls continued to join them until nearly every girl, and even every mother, was helping Tish and Elise to the finish line. By now, every spectator, sensing something special, continued to shout encouragement, cheering even louder than when Chad had crossed the finish line.

Chad kept glancing down the slope at Tish's epic struggle. I could see he was genuinely worried for her, and he started to go down to help. But when he noticed all the girls rushing to her side, he knew this was something they needed to do themselves.

By the time the exhausted girls crossed the finish line, their fashionable clothes were soaked and ruined. Their hair and faces, caked with mud, could be restored, but not their clothing. However, their beaming pride transcended any soiled appearance, and their infectious sense of unity remains embedded in my memory to this day. The boys, still celebrating their win with ever-higher high fives, were oblivious to what the girls had accomplished—except for Chad, who continually kept at least one eye on Tish.

I picked up the trophy as the crowd quieted. I looked at Chad, then Tish, and then back at Chad. He looked at me and nodded. I had never been so proud of him; he finally understood. He knew what I was thinking and tacitly gave me his unselfish approval. I walked over to a surprised Tish and Elise and handed them the trophy. I simply said, "You earned it,"

As the surprised but elated girls held the shiny trophy with their muddied hands, some of the boys were aghast, but the roar of the crowd let them know it was time to let it go.

Tish looked over at Chad, and I saw him silently mouth the words to her, "I'm sorry."

Tish smiled, her bright white teeth contrasting with her muddied face. I think I was the only person there who noticed the tear streaking down her cheek.

Each of the girls took turns holding the trophy before I carried it to the school and displayed it in the trophy case. It rests there today, muddy handprints and all, with a simple plaque beneath that reads:

Mud Mountain Champions; The Girl's Class of 1996

That was the only year I taught school. They asked me to come back, but I could not do it. I knew that, at least for me, there could be no other class like that one. I could never get past the fact that they'd taught me more than I had them.

Many years later, while traveling, I saw Elise in an airport. She was a lovely woman then, happily married, successful, and with two beautiful, almost-grown daughters. I asked if she'd ever told them the story of the Mud Mountain champions. Many times, she said, and yes, she and Tish remained friends, with both their families taking at least one vacation together each year.

I smiled softly and said that she could never know how proud I was of her. Tears quickly filled her eyes, and then she told me that meant more to her than I would ever know. She hugged me tightly and wiped her eyes. I told her I could take no credit for what she had accomplished, and I wished her well.

Though I have often heard bits of information about both Tish and Elise from others, I've never really understood why my being proud of Elise moved her so that day in the airport. I only taught her in one class that year and couldn't remember anything I had done or said to warrant her respect. My mother once told me, "You never know who is watching you, so always, always be your best." I suppose that is true. It is a shame, though, that many of us don't appreciate the things our mothers tell us until it is far too late.

Chapter XXV

1997

The Arrowhead

I usually walked every property before we purchased it. I felt I needed to get the feel of the land to know if it was a good fit for us. One day, while walking a prospective piece of property, about two hundred acres of mostly timberland, I noticed a small pebble half-submerged in the ground. I quickly recognized it and picked up a perfect arrowhead, something I hadn't found in many years. As I held it in my hand, it reminded me of when I was young. Colby, Elbie, Anna Lee, and I had often walked the hills, woods, and freshly plowed fields, searching for Native American arrowheads and spear tips. We always found at least a few that were still intact and in good condition. With each find, we conjured fascinating stories of how that arrowhead had become lost and of the Yuchi Indians who'd lived in that area a long time ago.

I was blessed during the first ten years of my life to have my great-grandfather still alive. He told me a story that his father, Ivo, had told him many years ago. He said his father had become very emotional when he'd shared this story with him. Below is how my great grandfather relayed the story to me.

***

My father said he remembered vividly the few Indians who still lived in the area when he was a child in the 1830s. He told us that most of the stories we heard about Indians were not true. Many tribes, he said, like the Yuchi, were kind people who loved to laugh and enjoyed their rustic life in the hinterlands. One did not have to be afraid of them if you treated them right. He told me that he'd made friends with one little Indian boy when he was seven years old. His name was Coweta, meaning hawk man. He had dark skin, black hair, and was about the same age and size as my father. They pretended to be fearless hunters and sometimes played chase or hide and seek.

The Yuchi lived in a small, intimate village sitting on the banks of a crystal clear, picturesque lake that they used for washing and swimming on sultry Kentucky days. The spring that fed the lake provided fresh drinking water, and the abundance of fish in the lake provided food most of the year.

He explained that he and Coweta often caught turtles and snakes in the lake, and sometimes Coweta's father would let them fish. The two young boys were too small and inexperienced in catching fish with spears, but they still liked to try. The spears the Yuchi made were from the plentiful ash or birch wood and had a stone-sharpened flint spearhead attached. It took much skill to shape the flint into a sharpened, evenly weighted spear or arrowhead, and only those who tried to do that could appreciate the quality of one.

The thick forest covered the entire valley, and at one time, it had been the home of many deer and other animals. As more farmers had moved in, they'd cleared the forest acre by acre, reducing its size.

One day, Coweta came to their meeting place in the woods with his head hanging and with a slow, listless pace in his step. That was unlike him, as his usual pleasant demeanor and the smile that he always carried cheered anyone he happened to encounter. His greetings with my father always included a warm embrace and an excited eagerness to start a game or begin an adventure.

"What is wrong, Coweta?" my father asked him curiously.

"We will be leaving soon," he said as he raised his head. "The Indians and the government reached an agreement, and we will have to go to a new place to live."

"Where will you go?" my father asked, surprised but not yet grasping what Coweta was saying.

"I heard them say the name of the place, but I can't remember. My father said it is very far and we will be joining many other tribes, including the Cherokee, Creek, and Seminoles, along the way. He said it would be a difficult journey of over one thousand miles for some. We must travel on foot, and my father is very fearful that many will not survive it."

"Can't you just stay here?"

"No. No one wants to leave, but he said we must follow the agreement that orders all us to move to another territory."

They sat quietly on a large limestone boulder overlooking the beautiful lake. For a long time, the two friends did not speak. Finally, Coweta reached into his pouch and pulled out an arrowhead made from animal bone.

"I made this for you," he said as he extended it to my father. "I put my mark on it. It is yours now."

My father looked at the arrowhead with a sense of reverence. Coweta had etched a flying hawk on one side of it, and my father said he knew it took Coweta a long time to make this. Carving any bird on the small arrowhead would be very tedious, and certainly took a lot of patience.

"Thank you, Coweta," my father said quietly, his eyes still on the arrowhead. He turned it over gingerly with his fingers, inspecting both sides, appreciating the craftsmanship of his friend.

Then Coweta pulled out another arrowhead just like the one he had given my father. It, too, had a flying hawk etched on one side.

"I will keep this one to remember you by," he told my father, looking at him with his dark eyes and sullen face. He seemed to be trying to force a smile, but a lonesome softness in his eyes was the best he could compose.

They sat a long time on the rock in silence. Finally, Coweta rose and said a final goodbye to his friend. They never saw each other again.

I was ten years old when my great-grandfather passed away, but he was very special to me. I will always remember the day he told me this story and gave me that arrowhead. I could see that the story and the arrowhead meant very much to him and that he, too, held an emotional attachment to both.

Sometimes, when I am lonely and thinking of him, I will walk the hills and woods, looking for arrowheads, but there are few of them left now. Most have already been picked up or have slowly sunk in the soft soil over the years. There are no signs that the Indians ever lived there now. The lake is still there, but it is dirty and muddied by the farmer's cattle. The rock where Coweta and my great-great-grandfather probably sat seems oddly out of place now. The woods are gone, too, routinely cut down to open the land for more pastures without any other considerations. Sometimes I stop on top of the hill and look at the valley below. I try to envision the woods covering the vast land and the Indians who peacefully lived there.

I have my collection of arrowheads I found when I was a young boy. I keep them at home for safekeeping. However, I always carry my great-great-grandfather's flying hawk arrowhead with me. Sometimes when I go to a craft show or flea market, there might be someone who has a collection of arrowheads for sale. I usually stop and talk, sharing stories of how we found them when we were kids. I never buy any, though; those would have no meaning to me.

Last year, while passing through Oklahoma, I stopped at a large flea market with hundreds of vendors. With little else to do, I browsed the aisles of booths to pass the time. As I turned to walk down the last aisle, I noticed a young boy alone at a booth a few steps away on my left. He appeared to be ten or eleven years old and had many arrowheads and other artifacts spread across his table for sale. I looked over his collection and became puzzled about how this young boy had so many excellent arrowheads. I had seen many collections of Indian artifacts over the years, but this was the best I had ever seen. Everything for sale was genuine, and not a single tourist trinket polluted his table. Impressed with the quality of the pure flint arrowheads and the craftsmanship of all the Indian artifacts, I stayed much longer than I normally would.

After carefully inspecting a few of the items for sale, I asked the patient boy if he had found all these himself. He explained that his family had passed them down from one generation to the next. We talked for a few minutes, and he seemed to be an intelligent young man. He was handsome and polite, and I could tell his parents had taught him suitable manners. To this day, I still do not know what prompted me to do so, but I reached into my pocket and pulled out my flying hawk arrowhead. I had never shown it to anyone else before. The young boy looked at the rare bone arrowhead for a minute, turning it over several times, and then looked up at me. He stared curiously at me with his dark eyes and then turned his head over his shoulder and politely said, "Grandfather."

Turning his head back toward me, he handed me my arrowhead.

I heard a shuffling and then a muffled grunt from the back of the tent and noticed an older man, close to my age, rising slowly from a worn wooden chair, struggling to hide the pain in his legs and back. Most likely, the summons was an ill-timed interruption of a good nap. He moved stiffly at first, but once he'd worked out the kinks, his walk and mannerisms gave the appearance of a refined gentleman. Despite his stubbornly aging body, which surely ached inexorably, he never uttered the slightest of complaints.

He looked kindly at the boy, who nodded at me without a word. His straight, dark hair softened with an equal amount of gray, was shoulder length. He turned his head and stared silently at me, his dark eyes studying mine. Without thinking, and for no reason other than that words evaded me at that moment, I held my hand out and opened my fist, revealing my flying hawk arrowhead.

He stared at it without speaking for a moment. Then he looked back at me.

"Where did you get that?" he asked slowly in a low, soft, monotone voice.

"My great-grandfather gave it to me," I answered. "He said his father, Ivo, received it as a gift from a young Indian friend when he was a child."

With squinted eyes, he studied me as if he were reaching deep into my soul to determine my integrity.

"Where did your great-great-grandfather Ivo live?"

"In Kentucky," I replied, lowering my head to look at my flying hawk arrowhead, remembering the day my great-grandfather had given it to me.

The gentleman never took his eyes off me. Then he silently reached into his pocket and pulled out an object concealed by three of his four fingers. When he opened his fist, resting in his palm was a flying hawk arrowhead made from bone and identical to mine.

"I have heard the name Ivo before. My father gave this to me," he revealed in his slow, soft voice. "He said his great-grandfather Coweta made two of these and gave the other to a special friend named Ivo when he was a young boy living in Kentucky. This arrowhead has passed to each generation since and has been treasured immensely by all those who carried it. We have often wondered what became of the other one and worried it was long lost. I, like my fathers before me, have always held this as something special. Other than my family, you are the first person I have shown it. My name is Calian. What is yours?"

"Friends just call me Razz," I said with a smile. "I'm glad to meet you."

Calian and I talked for hours and developed a friendship that lasted the rest of our lives. The boy, his grandson, listened intently to our stories, becoming enthralled with the histories of our families.

In the past, I had read with great interest the many stories of the Trail of Tears, yet I could never bring myself to ask Calian about his great-great-grandfather's part in that, or those in his village who did not survive it.

When I started to leave that day, I offered Calian my flying hawk arrowhead. He took it and smiled. Then he, too, reached out to give me his flying hawk arrowhead. I think we both felt our great-great-grandfathers were smiling down upon us. When the time comes, I will give my grandson my flying hawk arrowhead and tell him the story of my great-great-grandfather, his friend Coweta, and my special friend Calian as well.

Chapter XXVI

2006

The Purchase

By the late 1990s, The Yellow Rose Group had become a very profitable enterprise, allowing us to help many charities. In 1996, to help improve the employment in that area, Colby suggested we donate over six hundred acres of our land to the state to help entice an airline industry to build a training facility and parts warehouse employing more than a thousand workers. With Colby's help, we made that happen. Colby did all the legwork, meeting with the politicians and the county's economic development department. Of course, the locals and the politicians were ecstatic, elevating us to instant celebrities in our state.

Most of the time, the four of us were in agreement with a purchase. However, there was one farm that caused some concerns, eventually leading to a substantial expense and tremendous anguish for us. It was a small piece of property, less than four acres, in Southern Indiana consisting almost entirely of scraggly woods, with none of the acreage tillable. An elderly lady lived on a sixty-by-eighty-foot lot at the front of the property. That lot and a small strip on the west side were the reasons we bought it; having that piece of land enabled us quicker access to the farmland we already owned behind it.

Elbie, our accountant and legal authority for all our properties, hesitated on purchasing this property, voicing his concerns at every opportunity. A title search revealed that a quitclaim deed had been used to buy the property. Ordinarily, that wouldn't cause concerns, but Elbie kept insisting he had a bad feeling about this one.

A further search revealed that Niner Peak had purchased the property from the elderly lady, but for some strange reason, he'd allowed her to retain the right to live there for the duration of her life. That purchase had been recorded three months ago, on March 15, 2006, for twenty-nine thousand dollars, an unusually low sum. Niner offered it to our group for one hundred and ninety thousand dollars. Elbie smelled something suspicious, especially since Niner Peak was involved.

We argued that although Niner most likely was unethical in some way with the elderly lady, we were not a party to that. We assumed he purchased it upon suspicions that The Yellow Rose Group needed it for access to the adjacent property and hoped to make a quick profit.

Elbie would not relent and continued to advise caution.

"He knows we are the owners of The Yellow Rose Group!" he insisted.

"How would he know that, Elbie?" Anna Lee asked.

"It's a matter of public record. All he needed to do is check at the courthouse. Anyone can get that information."

Despite Elbie's concerns, we finally agreed to purchase the property at half of what Niner was asking.

Two weeks later, we found out from a neighbor that yes, indeed, Niner had been less than ethical in his purchase. He had convinced the elderly lady that her property was going to lose value quickly because The Yellow Rose Group intended to build ten chicken houses right behind her home. Niner had told her he would take the property off her hands and signed an agreement to let her live there as long as she wished—if she could stand the stench of thousands of chickens.

We felt terrible about the situation, and it bothered us to be a beneficiary of that even though the offense was not ours. Of course, when we completed the transaction, the clause allowing the lady to live in her home remained and building chicken houses was never a consideration for any of our properties. A few weeks later, Colby suggested we test the land for oil before we started with the construction of the access to our other farmland behind the house.

"Colby, there is nothing that suggests there is any oil on that property," I said. "Why would we go to the expense of doing that?"

"I think we should do it, Razz," he replied.

The one thing Elbie, Anna Lee, and I had learned over the years was that when Colby had a feeling, we should listen. We began test drilling a few weeks later with no expectations. However, as usual, Colby was right. They found a large reserve of oil that extended onto our adjacent property, but the most efficient place to set the wells were on the newly purchased property, only several hundred feet from the elderly lady's home.

I asked to set up a conference call with the four of us to discuss this development and the best way to proceed.

Once everyone had joined in, Elbie asked why we needed a conference call.

"What is going on, Razz? Why can't we move on with this? It's a very opportunistic find?"

"I don't feel right about this, Elbie."

"I don't either," Anna Lee added. "Talk to us, Razz."

"Wait a minute," said Elbie. "I was the one who was worried before we purchased it. I capitulated, and now you guys are concerned. What's not to feel right about finding a vast reserve of oil?"

"The elderly lady," I answered. "You were right to begin with, Elbie. This whole thing makes me feel complicit."

"I agree," Anna Lee jumped in. "This is wrong."

"We did nothing wrong," Elbie insisted. "Everything we did was legal. We can't go around and correct all of Niner's wrongdoings."

"You were right to caution us in the beginning, Elbie. We should have listened to you," Colby said. "But now we have an opportunity to make this right. What are you suggesting, Razz?"

"Now, just wait a minute," Elbie protested. "There is a lot of money involved here. I feel bad for the elderly lady, too, but we are not culpable in any way."

"Elbie, that is not us. We have never done anything that would taint our conscience," Colby argued. "I know no one else would ever blame us in any way or would ever feel we were a party in deception, and I know we did not violate any ethics. But when the money starts coming in, are you going to be able to go to bed at night without thinking this wasn't ours to take?"

There was a long silence, and then Elbie spoke up. "I knew Niner was going to cause us a problem with this."

"Elbie, this is a chance to redeem Niner's wrong. I understand we are not legally or morally obligated to do anything," Anna Lee said, "but we can. We can make it right, Elbie."

"I'm not convinced, guys. We are under no obligation of any kind," Elbie argued. "But I will listen to what are you suggesting, Razz."

"The lady was duped," I explained. "She would have never sold the land otherwise. She is in her late seventies. I don't know how long she will live, but I say we give her the royalties from the oil for as long as she is alive. We retain ownership, and when she passes, then we begin to collect the royalties."

"You are kidding, right?" said Elbie. "I want all of you to understand we are talking about a huge sum of money, possibly as much as two hundred thousand dollars a year."

"I'm in," Anna Lee said without hesitation.

"I'm in," Colby agreed.

"Guys, she might live another fifteen years!" Elbie protested. "We could be talking about millions of dollars."

"Elbie," I said without emotion. Then I paused. "Do you remember the name Bobby Day?"

Elbie was silent for a moment. Then he said, "Razz, you go talk to the lady and explain why we are doing this. I think her name is Ms. Sanderson. I will do everything else to make this happen, and you let her know she will never have to worry again."

"I will take care of it, my friend," I replied.

The next morning, I drove across the bridge at Owensboro to the farm just north of Rockport, Indiana, to visit with Ms. Sanderson. I walked up to the door of the small home, which was noticeably in dire need of a paint job. The yard, clean and freshly mowed, was adorned with numerous flower beds. There were seven or eight of them, with the soil recently turned and ready for planting. The one in the front of the house was full of freshly planted petunias surrounded by three shrubs of blooming peonies.

I knocked lightly, and after a short wait, an elderly lady opened the door with a gentle smile.

"Good morning, ma'am. Are you Ms. Sanderson?" I greeted.

"Yes, I am," she answered pleasantly.

She invited me in, and we sat in her front room to talk. The aged furniture, worn from wear, rested on a small oval rug that covered little of the stained, wooden floor. The walls, sparsely decorated with only a few simple family photos, begged for a fresh coat of paint. But the tidy, clean house smelled of fresh peonies and offered a pleasant, warm welcome to any guest.

"I love the scent of fresh peonies in the house," I remarked. "My mother always filled the house with them to mask the odor when she fried fish in the kitchen."

"Your mother must have been a smart lady, but I don't need to cover the smell of fish. I am allergic to seafood. I just like the fresh aroma of peonies, and you never know when a handsome young man will come to visit," she replied with a playful wink of her eye.

I laughed and nodded. Her friendly and pleasant demeanor put me at ease immediately. She was a delightful lady, and I wished I knew her better.

I explained the reason for my visit and our concerns about Niner's purchase. She replied that only recently had she discovered his duplicity but that it was her mistake in trusting him. I then explained our discovery of oil on the property. She said she had wondered if we'd found anything, and then she lowered her head and shook it slowly.

I told her of our desire to let her continue to live there and that we wanted to give her all the royalties from the oil while she was alive.

"My lord, son. Why on earth would you do that?" she replied incredulously. "You weren't involved at all."

"No, ma'am, we weren't, but this is just how we do business. The four of us agreed we could not accept that money in good conscience while you were alive."

"Have you all ever made any money in your business?" she asked skeptically. I suppose, to her, we appeared either incompetent, foolish, or both.

"Yes, ma'am. We have been very fortunate."

She thought for a moment and then reached for a Kleenex on the coffee table. She clutched it in her fist and looked at me with genuine kindness in her eyes. She reminded me of others in my life who shared that kindness, and I felt completely comfortable with her.

"See those pictures on that wall?" she asked, pointing to the few photos of a couple of families. "That is my daughter's and my son's families. We've all had Niner Peaks in our lives at one time or another, but we've persevered. Our lives are simple, but we are happy. We have learned to make lemonade, so to speak. I

291

do not want you to feel compelled to give me that money. I do not have much longer on this earth, and I will survive without it."

"Ms. Sanderson, we do not feel compelled to do this. We want to do this. Please," I begged.

She looked at me for a moment and then at the pictures of her son, daughter, and grandchildren.

"Okay, if you insist, I will allow you to do this under two conditions," she finally acceded.

"Good. What are they?" I eagerly asked, moving to the edge of my chair.

"First, from the money you were going to give me, I want you to take ten percent of that and give it to the Haven House in Owensboro. It is a place of refuge for women who are being abused by their spouses. Second, the rest of it, I request you place in some kind of trust for my daughter and son so they can have it when I pass. I don't need it. I can get by just fine without it, but my children and grandchildren could use it."

"Consider it done, Ms. Sanderson," I replied with a smile. "I will have our accountant get the papers drawn up for you to sign and set up the trust for your children. He will handle it all, so you will have to do nothing. However, you will receive statements on the trust so you can keep track of how much is in it. You will also receive statements reflecting the gifting of ten percent from the trust to the Haven House."

"Well, that will give me something to read, then, won't it?" she answered with a cheerful smile.

"Yes, ma'am, it will," I agreed, knowing how much mail she would now be receiving. "By the way, since The Yellow Rose Group is the legal owner of this house, would you mind if we put a little paint on the outside?"

"Oh, my. Not at all. That has been worrying me for some years now. Thank you so much," she replied, her smile widening.

We hired a painter to put a fresh coat of white paint on the house, improving the appearance considerably. We also paid him to paint the inside rooms of the home and let Ms. Sanderson choose the colors. The painting brightened the home and pleased my new friend. However, since Elbie took care of everything for her, I never saw her alive again.

Ms. Sanderson lived almost ten more years after I met with her. The money from the royalties and the growth of the investments Colby had put it into amounted to nearly two million dollars at the time of her death. Although that was a lot of money, none of us regretted our decision. Elbie never remarked about the costs again and did everything possible to please Ms. Sanderson.

When she passed, I felt the need to visit her at the funeral home. Elbie had already informed her daughter and son of the trust, so I went simply to find closure for one who had touched my life, if even briefly.

I knew no one there, so I sat quietly in the back until I saw an opportunity to view her in the casket and say a quick goodbye to a wonderful, sweet lady. After doing so, I quietly slipped out the door and headed down the hall to the exit.

"Sir! Sir!" I heard someone call from behind me. I stopped and turned to see a man and a lady in their mid to late fifties approaching me with curious looks on their faces.

"Sir are you from The Yellow Group?" the gentleman asked.

"The Yellow Rose Group, yes. Can I help you?" I asked politely.

"We wanted to thank you; about the oil trust, I mean," he replied. "I'm Danny Dale, and this is my sister, Lena Frances." He reached out to shake my hand.

"You are welcome," I said. "But there are four of us, and we all agreed it was the right thing to do."

"My mother never told us about the trust until just before she passed. She said a miracle fox had set that up for us," Lena Frances said.

"A miracle fox?" I laughed.

"Yes." She smiled. "That is the term my mother always used when someone did a good deed. It was a reference to someone who saved her many years ago when she was in need. She always called him the Silver Fox in the night."

Tears quickly moistened my eyes, and I could not speak. I became consumed with an immense joy so intense that I felt faint.

"Are you okay, mister?" Danny Dale asked as they both became concerned at my pale condition.

I held up a finger, suggesting they give me a moment, and then asked, "What was your mother's first name?"

"Silvie," Lena Frances replied, puzzled.

I put my hand over my mouth as I could not determine if I would shout for joy or cry. It took me a few seconds to regain my composure.

"When I was a small boy, there was one night when I met a woman in trouble carrying her two babies on a dusty gravel road. She was badly injured but would not give up. I helped them back to my house, and they stayed with us for three weeks until she was healthy enough to leave on her own. Her name was Silvie."

Lena Frances put both hands over her mouth and began crying, and Danny Dale was also visibly moved, his eyes moistening.

"I came to love her just as I did my mom, and I cried when she and her babies left. For many years, I searched crowds, hoping to see her face, hoping I could recognize her, but finally I gave up as the years went by. I never forgot her, though, and often spent time wondering how her life, and her children's lives, turned out and where they were. All this time, she was so close. I even spoke to her in her home, though I didn't know who she was."

I began to break down, my voice cracking as I tried to finish. "I should have known. I could have hugged her and talked to her, but..." I hesitated, gathering my voice. "I'm happy."

I could say no more, barely able to get the word "happy" out.

Lena Frances hugged me as we both shared tears, while Danny Dale put his arm around my shoulders and hung his head.

I asked if I could go back in to say goodbye to Silvie. They each held one of my arms gently and walked me back into the room. The three of us talked to each other, and about Silvie, for a long time. We laughed and shared memories, and then we said our last goodbye. This time, it was not filled with grief, but with joy, gratitude, and friendship. Maybe that is the way it should be.

Since that day, we have kept in touch, talking about their families and sharing stories of their mom. Sometimes I lament being so close yet never knowing it; I could have been her friend if only I had known. However, I quickly put those feelings aside, and I am thankful for the moments we shared in her home. I will never regret that we, for no logical reason on earth, helped Silvie and her family by setting up the trust.

Silvie called me a miracle fox. A fox is a creature of stealth who slips away, never to be seen again. I guess, to Silvie, I was a miracle fox, but I will always remember her as my second mom.

Chapter XXVII

2016

The Suit

About three weeks after Silvie passed, I spent a long day with the attorneys, dissolving Silvie's trust and distributing the money to the beneficiaries, Danny Dale and Lena Frances. Exhausted, I looked forward to a relaxing evening. However, immediately upon entering the house, I noticed my voice mail light blinking feverishly with several messages from Elbie to call him ASAP.

"What is going on, Elbie?"

"Razz, we have a problem!" Elbie said breathlessly.

"What's up?"

"We are being sued!"

"Sued!?"

"Niner is back! He is suing us for five million dollars."

"What!?"

"He is suing us for five million dollars, with damages for even more."

"No way!"

"Yes. Niner has a contract proving that we do not own the mineral rights for the oil and gas on the Sanderson property, and he has the deed to confirm that."

"No way! Didn't you have the legal firm run a clear title on that?'

"Yes, I did. We even received a warranty deed to show that. But he has a legal contract, dated before ours, proving that Mrs. Sanderson deeded him all the oil and gas rights to that property. Somehow the attorneys missed that in the title check. We owe him for all the oil royalties we paid to the Sanderson Trust and all future oil royalties on that property, plus damages for fraud. Razz, I did everything right!"

"But we purchased the property and the mineral rights from Niner," I asserted. "He can't sue us for something he sold us."

"He sold us the mineral rights, alright, but the oil and gas rights were separated when he bought the property from Ms. Sanderson; Niner still owns them."

"This doesn't sound possible, Elbie."

"I know it doesn't, but it is. I will know more tomorrow after meeting with our attorney. Would you mind calling Colby and Anna Lee to set up a conference call at five o'clock tomorrow night? I will be up all night trying to find all the paperwork. Razz, will this never end? Will we never be rid of this monster!?"

"I don't know, Elbie. I don't know."

Elbie was right. I, too, wondered if we could ever be rid of that horrid creature.

When the four of us joined the conference call the next night, Elbie shared the bad news. Niner's documents all appeared legal. His corrective quitclaim deed separating the oil and gas rights had, indeed, been signed and notarized the day following the sale of the land from Silvie to Niner, but it had mistakenly not been recorded at the circuit clerk's office. That explained why our attorneys had found no trace of it when they'd performed the title search. Silvie also had signed and notarized a letter explaining that she intended to separate the oil rights from the original deed.

Niner claimed that he thought his notary had filed it in a timely manner and that he only discovered the filing error after he began a search for it upon Silvie's passing. He quickly filed it the next day when he found out we had started drilling ten years ago.

Charlie LaDucia, our attorney, said Niner appeared to have a good case, but he would ready our defense to present before the judge. Once again, our nemesis had thrust himself into our lives; this time, though, he could break us.

"This doesn't sound right, Elbie," I remarked. "Why would she do that?"

"I don't know, Razz, but she did. It is all legal."

"Elbie, if it wasn't filed with the court, wouldn't that void the deed?" Colby asked.

"No. A corrective quitclaim deed does not have to be filed with the court to be legal," Elbie answered. "His deed is legal, and we are screwed."

"I cannot believe that man is destroying us once again," an incensed Anna Lee bemoaned. "Why can't we be rid of him?"

The trial started August 24, on a Wednesday. The four of us sat next to Charlie, waiting for Niner and his attorney to enter the courtroom. It had been nearly five decades since we'd last seen him, and each of us wondered if he was still the massive brute who had tortured us in school. When he arrived, Elbie and I turned to see him. He was no longer the muscular monster we remembered, but a skinny, weak, gray-haired older man with a gray goatee. However, none of those changes could mask the revolting, familiar sneer on his face. He glanced at us, briefly flashing his familiar devilish grin.

Colby and Anna Lee stared at the judge's bench, never once glancing at Niner.

After Judge Thomas entered, the formalities were completed, and the jury was selected, the trial began with Niner taking the stand. He explained how he'd had to leave town shortly after Silvie deeded the property to him. His secretary, Janita Eldridge, called him the next day to inform him that Silvie had mistakenly not signed the deed giving Niner the oil and gas rights to the property. He instructed Janita to take Silvie to lunch at a nice restaurant in Evansville and have her sign a corrective quitclaim deed. He requested she also sign a notarized note explaining she intended that the oil and gas rights be separated from the other mineral rights and sold separately to Niner.

The documents were reviewed by both Judge Thomas and attorneys and were then recorded.

Then Niner's attorney asked why the documents had not been filed in a timely manner with the circuit clerk's office. Niner explained that he'd instructed Janita to file them and thought she had done so.

Upon cross-examination, Charlie asked Niner where Janita Eldridge was.

Niner explained that Janita, unfortunately, had an abusive husband. For many years, he'd tried to protect her as much as possible and also helped her with some debts she had. However, the day that Janita was supposed to file the deed, her husband began to cause her considerable trouble, and she fled the state to avoid him. Niner had not heard from her since, and he had no idea where she'd gone.

Charlie returned to our table to get a document, muttering under his breath, "Convenient."

Charlie then asked Niner if he had any other proof that Silvie had signed the documents in Evansville since he had been out of town.

"Well, sir," Niner answered politely, "of course, we have the notarized documents presented to the court, and additionally, Janita called me after her lunch with Silvie. She said they ate at Bonefish and that Silvie loved the Bang Bang Shrimp; Silvie explained she had never eaten there before and hoped to do so again."

The day continued with Niner making a solid case for himself, and it appeared our fate rested with the jury. Charlie said it did not look good but that if we had anything else that might help, we should call him that night.

The four of us went out to eat to discuss our demise and Niner's hold on our lives.

"It looks like we are going to be out millions of dollars," Elbie said, resigning to the evidence.

Anna Lee shook her head in exasperation and simply replied, "Anybody but Niner!"

Colby was more pragmatic and wanted to know what it meant for The Yellow Rose Group.

"We may be ruined, Colby," Elbie replied. "I don't know yet, but I do know we will have to start selling a lot of properties to raise the cash. A verdict against us will cost us multiple millions.

"I don't think I will ever eat Bang Bang Shrimp again," Anna Lee muttered, shaking her head.

I rose and shouted, startling my three friends, "Shrimp! It's the shrimp!" A smile broadened across my face.

"What are you talking about, Razz?" Elbie asked, confused at my sudden change of attitude. "I don't see any reason to celebrate. We are going to lose everything."

"No, we aren't, Elbie. He is in my court now."

Chapter XXVIII

2016

The Verdict

I sped home as fast as I could without getting a speeding ticket. I parked the car in the drive and hurried into the house. Picking up the telephone, I dialed a now-familiar number.

"Hello, Lena Frances. How are you?" I greeted as she answered the telephone.

"I'm fine, Razz. How are you?"

"Well, I have been better."

"What's wrong, Razz?"

"Lena Frances, you once told me if I ever needed anything, to let you know."

"Absolutely, Razz. I meant that when I said it."

"Lena Frances, I need your help."

The next morning, Niner and his attorney were sitting comfortably at their table. Colby, Elbie, and Anna Lee sat next to Charlie, waiting for me to arrive. I rushed into the courtroom about two minutes before the judge made his entrance. Lena Frances and Danny Dale followed me and took a seat behind our table.

"What is going on, Razz?" Anna Lee asked, leaning over the table and trying to see me on the other side of Charlie.

"Just give me a couple of minutes, guys," I hurriedly answered. "I need to go over this with Charlie."

I had called Charlie early that morning and explained that I had some documents he needed to see, and I requested that he call Lena Frances Hancock to the stand. As I sat at the table, I hurriedly finished explaining everything to Charlie, who, by now, was grinning from ear to ear. Before I had a chance to explain to the others, the judge entered, and the courtroom became silent.

When Charlie called Lena Frances to the stand, I noticed Niner's attorney whisper something to him, followed by Niner shaking his head smugly, indicating a "no" answer.

The judge asked if the plaintiff objected to this witness, and Niner's attorney replied, "No."

Charlie formally greeted Lena Frances and asked if she was comfortable. Then he proceeded.

"Mrs. Hancock, may I call you Lena Frances?"

"By all means, please do," she replied.

Charlie briefly explained what the charges were and began his questioning.

"Lena Frances, are you aware that your mother, Silvie Sanderson, signed a corrective quitclaim deed assigning the oil and gas rights on her property to Mr. Niner Peak?"

"No, I am certain she didn't," she answered, slightly peeved.

"Were you present when your mother signed the deed?"

"No, sir, I wasn't."

"Then how could you say you are certain she did not sign away the oil and gas rights?"

"Because we both reviewed all the documents the night before Mr. Peak came for her signatures. There was no deed to separate the oil and gas rights from the property, nor was there any discussion to do so. My mother would never sign anything that I had not reviewed with her and given my approval."

"So, you were not present the following day, the fifteenth, when she signed the documents in front of Mr. Peak?"

"No, I was not."

Elbie and Anna Lee both looked over at me as if I had made Niner's case for him and sealed our fate. I noticed most of the jury either making notes or nodding their heads upon hearing Lena Frances admitting she had not been present.

"Now, Mr. Peak has testified and introduced notarized documents that your mother signed on March sixteenth, 2006, at a restaurant in Evansville, Indiana, with his assistant, Janita Eldridge. Were you present for that?"

"No, I was not," Lena Frances replied tersely.

Niner leaned back in his chair, grinning like a Cheshire cat. Elbie and Anna Lee lowered their heads, and several jurists put away their pencils.

"Then, Mrs. Hancock, how can you say your mother did not sign the deed giving Mr. Peak the oil and gas rights when we have documented proof that it was signed by her and notarized on March the sixteenth?" Charlie asked, feigning disbelief. "This happened ten years ago. Maybe you forgot or got it mixed up."

"No, sir, Mr. LaDucia, I did not forget, and I did not get it mixed up. I am one hundred percent certain my mother did not sign that document, especially on that date."

"Lena Francis, please forgive me, but the facts entered into this court prove otherwise. If you were not with your mother, you have no proof that she did not sign that deed."

"Mr. LaDucia, I did not say that I was not with my mother. I only said I was not with my mother in a restaurant. I was with my mother the entire day, but she wasn't in a restaurant. She was in the intensive care unit at Saint Mary's Hospital the entire day, and I was by her side the entire day."

"Oh, I am so sorry. But why was she in the hospital?"

"After she signed the deed with Mr. Peak on March the fifteenth, the original deed selling the property and all mineral rights, she called me at work and asked if my brother and I would take her out to eat that night. Danny Dale, my brother, picked her and me up to take her to a restaurant in Newburgh, Indiana.

"Unfortunately, she had a severe reaction to something she ate at the restaurant, and we had to rush her to the hospital. She was barely able to breath when we got her there."

"But Mr. Peak has testified, in vivid detail, that she was at Bonefish the next day and she loved their Bang Bang Shrimp."

"Well, Mr. Laducia, that would be a lie if he testified that. My mother was highly allergic to seafood. As a matter of fact, that is why we had to take her to Saint Mary's. She ordered a chicken pasta dish, but they accidentally put some shrimp in it. Had we not gotten her to the hospital when we did, she would have died.

"We arrived at the emergency room about seven thirty the night of March the fifteenth. They rushed her to the ICU. A little after four o'clock the next day, March the sixteenth, they let her out of the ICU, but they refused to release her from the hospital until the next morning, the seventeenth. I was with her the entire time, and I can assure you that neither Mr. Peak nor his assistant was there. I can also assure you that my mother was not at a restaurant."

The four of us noticed Niner squirming in his seat but glaring at Lena Frances.

"Lena Frances, that is certainly contrary to what Mr. Peak has testified under oath. Now, I believe every word you said, but this is a court of law. Words are taken with a grain of salt unless they can be verified. Would you have any proof at all to substantiate what you are testifying?" Charlie asked in his most pleasant voice.

I knew that Charlie already knew the answer to his question, but Colby, Anna Lee, and Elbie did not. I enjoyed watching them as they darted nervously to the edge of their seats, hoping for a favorable answer.

"I have all her medical records right here, Mr. Laducia." Lena Frances beamed as if she had just won a prize. She opened the folder she had brought with her to the witness stand.

"Here is the bill from St. Mary's. See right there?" She pointed to the bill. "The date of admittance was March the fifteenth, seven twenty-six p.m. And here it shows her release at nine twelve on the seventeenth. And here is the bill; twelve hundred and forty-two dollars. That is just for one day and two nights. Isn't that awful, Mr. Laducia? We could have stayed in a fancy hotel for a week for less than that."

Charlie took the bill from Lena Frances and presented it to the judge. Niner's attorney rushed to Charlie's side to review it as well. Judge Thomas lowered the hospital bill just below his raised eyebrows and stared at Niner. Even though I could only see the top half of Judge Thomas's face, I could tell he was not a happy camper.

"Are you finished with this witness, Mr. Laducia?" Judge Thomas finally asked Charlie.

"No, Your Honor, just a few brief questions."

Charlie walked back over to Lena Frances as Niner's attorney returned to their table. He did not look at or say anything to Niner.

"Lena Francis," Charlie continued, "I am troubled about one thing. I have in my hand the notarized signature of your mother on this deed separating the oil and gas rights from the sale of the property. If your mother did not sign this on March the sixteenth, when did she sign it?"

"May I see that?" Lena Frances asked.

She glanced at the deed and immediately said, "This is not my mother's signature."

"What?" Charlie asked, surprised. I had not discussed the signature with him.

"It is not my mother's signature."

"But it looks identical to the other signatures we have of your mother."

"No, it does not," Lena Frances replied calmly. "There are no dots over the S's of her name. If you look at the other signatures, there will be dots above the two initial S's of her name."

"Why would there be dots over the S's of her signature," Charlie asked incredulously.

"My mother always put a dot over the first S's in her first and last name. She was very proud and steadfast in doing that. She said the dots represented her guardian angel watching over her. It was her way of making sure her guardian angel didn't forget her."

Charlie took the deed from Lena Frances and walked over to the judge's bench. They, with Niner's attorney, inspected every document that Silvie had signed. The deed and note that had been notarized on March the sixteenth, giving Niner the oil and gas rights, were the only ones that did not have a dot over those two S's.

After they finished reviewing every signature, Lena Frances continued.

"You will not find a signature anywhere where my mother did not dot her S's."

I noticed Colby, Anna Lee, and Elbie staring at me, their mouths gaping in disbelief. I intentionally ignored them but flashed a broad smile they could not miss.

"Thank you, Lena Frances," Charlie said a bit more professionally. "Now, it is imperative that we reveal everything that Judge Thomas and the jury needs to hear, so I must ask you, have you ever met with Mr. Peak before?"

"Yes, once. I was with my mother when he came to her house around March the first to see if she was interested in selling her home and property."

"Did you have a favorable impression of Mr. Peak at that time?"

"Yes, I did…at that time."

Charlie had begun to walk toward our table, but he quickly spun around. "Did your opinion of him change, Lena Frances?"

"Mr. Peak was very pleasant that day, almost too friendly. He was persuasive but appeared concerned for my mother. He explained that The Yellow Rose Group owned the land behind my mother's property and that they were going to build ten chicken houses right next to her house. He said his offer was more than fair considering that, but he urged my mother not to sell if she did not want to. 'Just remember,' he warned, 'ten chicken houses could hold up to thirty thousand chickens.' Then he leaned forward toward my mother and asked if she could imagine the stench from thirty thousand chickens and their daily droppings.

"Why, that scared us to death, and we both agreed that selling the property was the best thing to do. We were poor folks, Mr. Laducia. We couldn't afford an attorney at that time. We trusted Mr. Peak and told him to get the paperwork ready for me to review before my mother signed the deed.

"Then, a few months after we sold to Mr. Peak, we found out he'd sold it to The Yellow Rose Group for three times what he paid us. We also found out The Yellow Rose Group never had any intentions of putting chicken houses behind my mother's home. Mr. Ross, from the Yellow Rose Group, told me they would never build a chicken house there, and they haven't."

"So, that is why your opinion changed about Mr. Peak?" Charlie asked.

Lena Frances's face suddenly filled with anger, and she sat stiffly in her chair. Looking directly at Charlie, she said in a very stern voice, "Mr. Laducia, my mother loved that house. She loved her yard, her flowers, and the big farm behind her that The Yellow Rose Group owned. My mother raised my brother and me in that house. She was in her late seventies when she sold the home to Mr. Peak. When she sold it, she felt she had betrayed some people who had helped her one time in her life.

"You see, a long time ago, my father was an alcoholic and an abusive man. My mother finally had to leave my father with nothing but my brother and me in her arms. When she left him, a young boy found my mother and took her to his home. His parents called a doctor to mend her injuries, and his mother cared for her until she was well enough to leave. The boy's father and the doctor scraped up enough money to buy that home for my mother so she would have a safe place to raise her two children. They helped her in a time of need, and it ripped out her heart to sell it.

"My mother insisted that Niner allow her to stay in the home as long as she lived, but she always felt she had betrayed those special people, who carried a kindness in their hearts."

Lena Frances lowered her head and paused briefly. Then she continued.

"My mother initially planned to stay in the house until they built the chicken houses. But when she found out Niner had tricked her, she regretted selling the house until the day she died. So, yes, Mr. Laducia," Lena, Frances almost shouted, "my opinion of Niner Peak has changed!"

Niner lowered his head and leaned over the table. His attorney said something to him, and Niner shook his head.

"Does the plaintiff's attorney wish to cross-examine the witness?" Judge Thomas asked.

"No, Your Honor," answered Niner's attorney. Then he gathered his papers and put them in his briefcase.

"We will review the evidence of this last witness and recess until nine o'clock tomorrow morning, when the jury will be sent to reach a verdict."

We returned to the courtroom the next morning, anxious for a favorable decision. Charlie said we had a good case and hoped the jury would side with us based on the evidence, but he could not guarantee anything. "Court cases are about as predictable as the weather," he said.

Niner and his attorney entered the courtroom and sat with little emotion. Niner looked like a beaten old man and wore a look of complete resignation on his face. As the judge entered, the

308

courtroom grew silent. He sent the jury to the jury room, and we began our nervous wait.

The jury returned in less than an hour and presented the verdict. They dismissed all claims against us, and Niner was to receive no restitution of any kind. The courtroom erupted in joyous relief, and Judge Thomas quickly hammered his gavel on his desk for order.

He glanced silently over the jury's signatures and addressed the court.

"The jury has found for the defendants. I, however, have additional comments. Mister Niner Peak, please stand."

Niner rose reluctantly and stared blankly at the judge.

"In light of the new and credible evidence submitted yesterday, and after receiving verification from both the hospital and a qualified, experienced handwriting expert, there is credible evidence to proceed with charges against you. I am ordering the deputies in this courtroom to arrest you on charges of alleged fraud, filing falsified documents with the circuit clerk's office, falsifying a legal document in an attempt to defraud, falsely notarizing legal documents, and perjury. There may be other charges as this investigation proceeds."

We could see Niner's expression change. The anger we remembered was gone, replaced by a strange look we did not recognize. I could not discern what type of expression it represented, but he suddenly became unrecognizable to me.

"Niner Peak," the judge continued, "as you have a documented history of this kind of behavior, I want you to understand that if found guilty of these charges, you may be sentenced to prison for a period of six months to thirty years. I want you to also understand that as part of my decision on this case, I am also issuing a restraining order. From this day forward, you are never to initiate contact of any kind with anyone from The Yellow Rose Group or the Sanderson family. If you do, you will suffer the consequences as ordered by this court; that means that if you come within one hundred feet of these individuals, I will send you to jail per my discretion. The court is adjourned!"

With that, he hit the desk with his gavel and quickly left the courtroom. This time, the cheers that erupted were significantly louder than the bailiff's "All rise" order. During the subsequent celebration, I glanced at Elbie as he thrust his fist in the air, closed his eyes, and shouted, "Yes!!!"

Colby remained seated, emotionless, and gathered his papers. I thought that unusual for him, but I paid little attention. Anna Lee rose quietly from her seat and walked over to Niner and his attorney while the deputies handcuffed him. She held a friendly smile on her face as if meeting a good friend.

"Mister Peak," she said, in a pleasant, compassionate voice, "for a long time, I carried a hatred for you. But one day, I realized I was only hurting myself; I found that I kept you in my life with the hate I held. So, many years ago, I forgave you. In my heart, I forgave you for the cruel things you did to me.

"I am sorry for the life you had as a child and the pain you suffered from your father. I hope you believe me when I tell you I hope the rest of your life will be better than your past. I truly wish for you to find peace and happiness in your life. But," she finished, her tone changing to a very detectible firmness, though she still held a pleasant smile on her face, "don't ever enter my life again. Do you hear me? Do not ever enter my life again!"

With that, she turned and casually walked back to our table to pick up her belongings, and then she left with us.

The four of us celebrated that evening at my house. The stench of Niner had at last lifted from our lives, and we laughed and talked into the night. I noticed Colby seemed distracted at times, but I thought the trial might have weighed more heavily on him than I'd realized. I knew Niner had never bothered Colby as much as he had Elbie, Anna Lee, and myself, but Colby always excessively worried about his friends.

Without the weight of Niner pressing on his chest, Elbie could finally breathe, but he also had something on his mind.

"Hey, guys, can I make a suggestion?" he asked during a brief break in our celebration.

"Sure, Elbie," I replied. "What do you have in mind?"

"Well, since we will be collecting the oil royalties now, what would you think about us continuing to donate ten percent to the Haven House in Silvie's honor?"

"I love it!" Anna Lee quickly answered.

"Awesome idea, Elbie," Colby joined in.

"Make it happen, Elbie," I added.

I often found myself thinking about Niner and his term in prison. He received five years for fraud and perjury. I felt he deserved more for the many others he'd hurt, including Silvie, but I always wondered why he'd chosen Elbie and me to suffer his torments. I remained curious if he felt remorse for his conduct and whether he could change.

I could not yet forgive him as Anna Lee had, and that prevented me from finding peace with that chapter of my life.

A year later, I decided to lay this to rest, as Anna Lee had, and the only way to do it was to go and talk to him.

I scheduled a visit to the prison without Niner's knowledge. I waited in the visiting area, seated in a simple chair behind a window with thick glass. I don't think Niner had many, if any, visitors, as I noticed him straining around the officer to see who would want to see him. When the officer led him to the glass on the other side of me, his entire body drooped, and he hung his head. The officer seated him, and Niner did not look at me for several seconds.

"How are you, Niner?" I finally asked.

He seemed surprised by my concern but remained silent.

"Niner, why us?" I asked. "Why Elbie and me?"

He took a deep breath and answered in a soft voice filled with hopeless resignation, "I did it because, at the time, I envied you. You had a happy life, and I hated you for that. There was no happiness in my life, so I tried to take it away from you. It helped me feel that I wasn't alone. I am sorry for the things I did to you and your friends. I was an angry person, and I wish I could go back and change things, but I can't."

"Why didn't you try to change, Niner?"

"I did try, many times, but nothing good ever came of it. I didn't know how to live any other way."

"Do you regret it?"

"Yes. I've grown more here in the last year than I did in the other sixty-seven years of my life. It eats at me that I can't go back and change what I did."

"Niner, we all have done things that we wish we could go back and change. But we can't. The only thing that matters is what we do now, and tomorrow, and the next day," I paused and took a breath before continuing. "Niner, I have to put this down to have peace in my heart. I forgive you. I wish you well."

I scooted my chair back and began to leave, but he stopped me.

"Razz, the girl. Every night, when it's dark and I'm lying on my bed, completely alone in this world, I see myself hurting her. I see myself ripping the happiness off her face. I see me tearing up her dress. Every night, I see that, and I want to hurt the kid who did that to her. I want to throw him on the ground instead of her. Would you tell her I am sorry I hurt her? Would you tell her that I'm sorry I tore up her pretty dress? Would you tell her for me, please?"

I will never forget his face. The angry boy was gone, replaced by a man filled with immense loss and loneliness.

"I will, Niner," I answered. "I will tell her. I know that will please her."

I could see tears forming in his eyes. I nodded, turned, and left. I don't know if my words comforted him or not. If they did, that is good, but that was not my priority. I needed to lay that resentment and anger down and cast it away; otherwise, I would never be able to gain true peace in my heart.

Chapter XXIX

2016

The Question

The night after the trial was over, as we celebrated at my house. I paid more attention to Colby. His curious silence and subdued demeanor were an aberration for him and his usual cheerful attitude. I could not quite put my finger on it, but I sensed something was wrong. Whether he had problems at home or elsewhere, it was time for me to sit with my friend.

As Elbie and Anna Lee were leaving, I stopped Colby and told him I had something I wanted to show him. We waved goodbye to our two friends as they drove away to visit with their families who still lived in the area.

I led Colby to my den, asked him to sit on the couch, and then sat in a chair across from him.

"Colby," I asked, "what is wrong."

"Nothing, Razz. I'm excited that we finally won and distanced ourselves from Niner once and for all," he replied with a smile.

"Colby," I asked again, but a little more firmly, "what is wrong?"

He hesitated, and I made sure our eyes met. He knew it was time to share.

"Razz, I have cancer."

Chapter XXX

2019

The Departure

"Can you believe the governor, the two senators, and three congressmen of the state of Kentucky, along with numerous celebrities, are in the other room partying with our friends and we are in here sitting by ourselves by choice?" Elbie asked as the noise of the boisterous party escalated in Colby's large family and entertainment rooms. Colby's elegant home and beautiful grounds, situated just outside Seattle in the Sammamish area, was a far cry from the simple homestead where he'd grown up in East Daviess County, Kentucky.

Elbie, Anna Lee, and I quietly escaped for a few moments of respite to reflect on how we had arrived at this moment. We sat alone in the ornate sitting room, next to the oversized windows overlooking the captivating views of a large lake. A lone goose entertained us as he floated silently on the water, gliding aimlessly in the middle of the lake, surrounded by trees on three sides. He had been there since we had arrived.

***

Elbie married Mary Jane Toler in June of 1974. Mary Jane asked Anna Lee to be a bridesmaid, and I know that pleased Elbie. Colby married El, a beautiful young lady, in 1977. El, in many ways, was a mirror to Anna Lee: strikingly attractive, tall, free-spirited, and intelligent. Her humor charmed all of us, and she became as dear to us as the rest.

After Anna Lee left Brescia for New York to further her career, I finally accepted that Anna Lee and I would never be more than what we were: two peas in a pod and the dearest of friends, but no more than that. My VW Bug and I wore out the road from Owensboro to Evansville to see Angie, the prettiest girl I'd ever

315

seen. Yes, that is the same Angie I met twice, once crying on a sidewalk in New York and then again in a diner in Evansville when I was with Elbie and Antz. She and her father lived in Evansville, twenty-two miles down the river on the Indiana side of the Ohio. She lived at home while attending the University of Evansville. I married Angie in 1975 after she graduated, and I have never regretted it.

Our group quickly accepted Angie, and she became a confidant, a nurse, a friend, and a Samaritan to all of us. She also, at one time or another, was a pillar that we each leaned upon.

Angie asked Anna Lee to be her maid of honor. That did not surprise any of us, and it filled Elbie, Colby, and me with tremendous joy. However, it shocked Anna Lee, and she incredulously asked Angie if she did not have other lifetime friends she could ask. "Oh, yes," Angie replied, "I have many who have been the dearest of friends for all my life, but you are the one I want to be beside me on my wedding day."

I was standing behind Anna Lee when Angie told her that, so I don't know if Anna Lee shed a tear or not, but I could clearly see it overwhelmed her and moved her in a way I had never seen her moved before. Anna Lee hugged Angie tightly for a long time, and I think Anna Lee finally found the sister she'd always wanted.

Anna Lee never did get married. She met Paula in New York in 1976, and they remained friends for the rest of their lives. Paula was the perfect complement to Anna Lee; she encouraged her free spirit and gave her the confidence to excel in ways she could never have, but also reigned her in when necessary, something none of us was ever able to do.

We tried our best to make Paula welcome to our group, and we treated her with the same love, kindness, and respect we did the others. We enjoyed many wonderful times with her, but I always sensed she felt like an outsider, especially with me. I tried my best to make her feel more a part of our group, but I detected hesitancy in her. However, she never displayed that with any of the others. I couldn't understand that, but I often suspected Angie knew what was bothering her. However, she never shared that with me.

***

"Angie, Mary Jane, El, and Paula are the life of the party in there," Anna Lee remarked, nodding her head toward Colby's entertainment room. "The four of them are congenial enough that they can socialize in any circle."

"They have been like that for over forty years," I added. "We are fortunate to have them in our lives. We may never have been as successful without them."

"Hey! Hey!" Elbie interrupted. "I deserve some credit here. Anna Lee, you were backing out of going to school in New York, and I convinced you to go. So, if it weren't for me, you would have never met Paula. And Razz, I missed seeing Roger Maris hit his sixty-first home run just so you could meet the girl you were going to marry, so, give me some credit here." He feigned that he'd suffered a slight.

"Elbie, the four of us were like a wheel; Colby was the hub that held the spokes in place, Anna Lee was the axle, and you were the rubber tires that got us where we needed to go," I replied with a smile, attempting to appease his false umbrage.

"Yep. But that tire went flat some time ago," Anna Lee said smugly, not missing a chance to tease Elbie.

"Alright, then," Elbie said defiantly, "if that is the way you two want it, I'm going in there to party. Maybe I can find some respect in there with the politicians."

"Good luck with that." Anna Lee laughed, as did I.

I turned curiously to check on the goose in the lake when I noticed thirty or more geese flying above.

"There's a large flock of geese circling above," I said as I glanced out the large window overlooking the otherwise tranquil lake.

The three of us rose from our seats and stepped over to the window. We gazed silently, intrigued, as the flock of geese descended upon the lake, landing in unison and creating a scene of theatrical flair, and began a seamless, facile glide across it toward the lone goose.

They circled him quietly several times, and then each of them took turns approaching him as if comforting an old, forlorn friend. Once each had shared their brief, private moment of solace with the lone goose, the entire flock began honking loudly. Then they rose in unison, taking flight in a spectacular, breathtaking display, and resumed their journey, leaving the lone goose abandoned and alone again.

"Are you kidding me?! Are you really kidding me?!" Anna Lee cried. "No frigging way!"

"Colby got you, Anna Lee!" Elbie exclaimed, bursting into laughter.

"He can't do that to me! It's not right."

"The worst part of it is, Anna Lee, you have no way to rebut Colby now," Elbie needled.

"I hate to tell you this, Anna Lee," I said sympathetically, "but he told you he would do this to you that day in Hancock County on our way to the Marshal Mansion."

"I know! I know!" Anna Lee screamed, shaking her fist in the air. "Colby, I'm coming after you one day, so you better start running."

She looked at me, exasperated, as if to say, "What am I going to do now?" I laughed and put my arm playfully around her shoulder.

"Anna Lee, you can't win them all, but if you have to lose, there is no shame in losing to Colby."

318

She looked me in the eye for a moment with tears swelling in hers. I then realized she wasn't teasing; she truly missed our dear friend, just as Elbie and I did. Colby was undoubtedly the hub in our lives, an amazing, erudite, talented, kind man filled with an unbounded empathy for others.

The three of us hugged each other for the first time without Colby. Our lives would be different without him, but we would go on.

"Guys, would you like to come with me to the woods by my papaw's old homeplace sometime? I need a visit."

"Sure, that would be nice. We all need to share some memories," Elbie answered as I nodded.

I immediately thought of the chicken coop, Shae, the Marshal Mansion, and all the other adventures where Colby and I learned the lessons of life. I knew Elbie and Anna Lee both held many cherished memories of him as well.

"I keep expecting to see a yellow rose appear somewhere," Elbie finally said.

"Or an albino deer," I added with a soft smile.

"Or a chestnut horse with a diamond spot on his forehead," Anna Lee said.

"What? How did you know about Regal?" I asked her.

"What do you mean, what? I was there when they built Mr. Harris's barn," she answered, a little perturbed.

"You were not," I insisted.

"Razz, I was a girl. You didn't even know what a girl was at that age. Girls were invisible to you boys back then, but that suited us just fine. My mom made me take you a glass of lemonade after the Harrises' barn was finished; she thought you were cute. But I thought you were just another grotesque boy and resented her for making me serve you."

"I didn't know that," Elbie said, just as surprised as I.

"Girls don't tell all their secrets," she replied in a supercilious way that only a woman could do while simultaneously making a gentleman feel complimented.

"Well, if Colby wanted us to party today, I think we shouldn't let him down," I said. "Let's go in there and celebrate for our friend."

We joined the party, mingling with Colby's many friends. After a few minutes, I found myself alone, looking at some pictures of Colby's family.

"He was truly a good man, wasn't he?"

It was Paula, standing behind me and looking over my shoulder.

"Yes, he was," I replied softly.

We were silent for a brief moment.

"You know, Razz, for a lot of years, I resented you and your relationship with Anna Lee. I felt you were the competition. But today I finally realized you were never competing; you simply were part of her. Without you, she would not be the same person I cared for so dearly."

I smiled and started to say something, but she continued.

"I want to share something with you, Razz," she said, her eyes expressing a sincerity I had rarely seen in her before.

"One evening, many years ago, Anna Lee seemed unusually quiet, carrying a subdued sadness, which caused me some concern. It was a night of the summer solstice, and we had spent the evening sitting alone, reminiscing. After a while, I finally asked her what was bothering her. She told me the story about how the four of you spent the night in a haunted house or something like that."

"The Marshal Mansion," I explained.

"Yes, that was it. She said she was lying on the floor next to you in the darkness when she reached out to hold your hand, but then she pulled it back. She said that at that moment, she loved you more than any man in her life, before or since. She also said that when she began to reach for your hand a second time, there was a loud crash that scared all of you."

"I remember that," I said, the memories of that night flooding my senses.

"Anna Lee said there were times that she wished she had grabbed your hand, but finally she realized that she could have never made you happy. She said that if she had held your hand, your friendship would have eventually ended, and your lives would have separated." Paula paused for a moment. "I don't know why, but I just felt I needed to share that with you."

"Thank you, Paula. That means a lot to me," I answered as I tried to harness my emotions. "It is funny, though, as I have often thought I could have never made Anna Lee happy as well. I guess we were like two athletes in a marathon; running side by side, we fed off each other's energy and strengths. But if we got too close, we would bump into each other, causing both of us to stumble and fall. Our friendship, in the form that it was, and is, is the only way it could be. If she had held my hand that night, we would have lost each other completely in a few years, and I might have never married Angie. You will never know how much I appreciate knowing Anna Lee felt the same."

I reached over and hugged Paula tightly, and she reciprocated with the same intensity, both of us in a warm embrace that only true friends could share. Each of us always held Paula as a dear friend and loved her as an equal part of our family, but I think she and I developed a special bond that day. We both shed a few tears, not in sadness, nor joy, but from the realization of our complete mutual acceptance and a shared peace.

I raised my head and noticed Angie and Anna Lee smiling at the two of us, much the same as one would give an approving smile to a precocious child who has finally reached a coveted milestone. I motioned Paula toward Angie and Anna Lee, who both proudly flashed their tacit approval. She covered her face with her hands in a demurred effort to hide her embarrassment. We gathered our composure and joined Angie and Anna Lee in celebrating as Colby had asked. Although I'd lost one friend, I'd gained another, and I had never experienced so much love for my remaining family and friends as I did on that day.

I could not help but think of the lone goose circling on the lake and those who had offered their tender solace to it. I felt that Elbie, Anna Lee, and I were just like the lone goose, waiting in silent grief for Colby to send his friends, and their love, to replace our pain with joy.

I often think back to the Alder Ridge Cemetery and the folks who lived there in the 1800s. I'm certain many of them held deep friendships just as Colby, Elbie, Anna Lee, and I did. One by one, time took them all away until there was only one left to hold their memories, memories so dear that emotions were laid bare and left completely untethered. Although life marches on unimpeded, as it has been since the beginning of time, I sometimes wonder if they ever really left at all.

When I think of Colby, he is still at my side, just as Elbie and Anna Lee are. His imprints are everywhere I look, and his touch has spread far and wide. I can still hear his laugh, and the lessons he taught me, I firmly hold dear. He is still here with us; he just figured out the ultimate way to get one over on Anna Lee. But in doing so, he also brought those of us remaining closer together.

Shae was right; Colby carried a kindness in his heart and didn't even know it. But I think that can be said about the four of us. Both Elbie and Anna Lee also carried that kindness in their hearts for most of their lives. It wasn't something that they were born with, it was incrementally earned with each experience, and learned with each lesson. Yet, to talk to them, one can plainly see that they, too, don't know it. I hope, that one day, someone can say the same about me.

322

"A Kindness in Their Hearts" was over five years in the making. It is a fiction novel that is "loosely", or should I say, "very loosely" based on actual experiences of mine, or friends of mine, while growing up in a small town and the summers helping my grandparents on their farm. But, the core of most of those experiences were no different than those of anyone else in any other setting or any other land.

Visit https://jimweafer.com

Made in the USA
Columbia, SC
03 February 2020